W9-ADX-034

PRAISE FOR THE AUTHOR

"He has a gift for dialogue." —*The New York Times*

"Really special." —*Denver Post*

"A crime fiction rara avis." —*Los Angeles Times*

"One of the best writers in the mystery field today."
—*Publishers Weekly* (starred)

"Ebullient and irresistible." —*Kirkus Reviews* (starred)

"Complex and genuinely suspenseful." —*Boston Globe*

"Credible and deeply touching. Russell has us in the palm
of his hands." —*Chicago Tribune*

"He is enlightening as well as entertaining." —*St. Petersburg Times*

"Enormously enjoyable." —*Ellery Queen Mystery Magazine*

"Russell is spectacular." —*San Diego Union-Tribune*

"This work by Russell has it all." —*Library Journal*

"Grade: A. Russell has written a story to satisfy even the most
hard-core thrill junkie." —*The Rocky Mountain News*

A
COLD
WAR

Other Titles by Alan Russell

THE GIDEON AND SIRIUS NOVELS

Burning Man

Guardians of the Night

STAND-ALONE TITLES

No Sign of Murder

The Forest Prime Evil

The Hotel Detective

The Fat Innkeeper

Multiple Wounds

Shame

Exposure

Political Suicide

St. Nick

A
COLD
WAR

ALAN RUSSELL

Russell

This is a work of fiction. Names, characters, organizations, places, events, and incidents are either products of the author's imagination or are used fictitiously.

Text copyright © 2015 Alan Russell

All rights reserved.

No part of this book may be reproduced, or stored in a retrieval system, or transmitted in any form or by any means, electronic, mechanical, photocopying, recording, or otherwise, without express written permission of the publisher.

Published by Thomas & Mercer, Seattle

www.apub.com

Amazon, the Amazon logo, and Thomas & Mercer are trademarks of Amazon.com, Inc., or its affiliates.

ISBN-13: 9781503945807
ISBN-10: 1503945804

Cover design by Mark Ecob

Printed in the United States of America

To those who worked on the
Underground Railroad
in the 19th century,
and to those who are working
on it today.

THE CREMATION OF SAM MCGEE

BY ROBERT W. SERVICE

There are strange things done in the midnight sun
By the men who moil for gold;
The Arctic trails have their secret tales
That would make your blood run cold;
The Northern Lights have seen queer sights,
But the queerest they ever did see
Was that night on the marge of Lake Lebarge
I cremated Sam McGee.

Now Sam McGee was from Tennessee, where the cotton blooms and blows.
Why he left his home in the South to roam 'round the Pole, God only knows.
He was always cold, but the land of gold seemed to hold him like a spell;
Though he'd often say in his homely way that "he'd sooner live in hell."

On a Christmas Day we were mushing our way over the Dawson trail.
Talk of your cold! through the parka's fold it stabbed like a driven nail.
If our eyes we'd close, then the lashes froze till sometimes we couldn't see;
It wasn't much fun, but the only one to whimper was Sam McGee.

And that very night, as we lay packed tight in our robes beneath the snow,
And the dogs were fed, and the stars o'erhead were dancing heel and toe,
He turned to me, and "Cap," says he, "I'll cash in this trip, I guess;
And if I do, I'm asking that you won't refuse my last request."

Well, he seemed so low that I couldn't say no; then he says with a sort of moan:
"It's the cursèd cold, and it's got right hold till I'm chilled clean through
    to the bone.
Yet 'tain't being dead—it's my awful dread of the icy grave that pains;
So I want you to swear that, foul or fair, you'll cremate my last remains."

A pal's last need is a thing to heed, so I swore I would not fail;
And we started on at the streak of dawn; but God! he looked ghastly pale.
He crouched on the sleigh, and he raved all day of his home in Tennessee;
And before nightfall a corpse was all that was left of Sam McGee.

There wasn't a breath in that land of death, and I hurried, horror-driven,
With a corpse half hid that I couldn't get rid, because of a promise given;
It was lashed to the sleigh, and it seemed to say: "You may tax your brawn
    and brains,
But you promised true, and it's up to you to cremate those last remains."

Now a promise made is a debt unpaid, and the trail has its own stern code.
In the days to come, though my lips were dumb, in my heart how I cursed
    that load.
In the long, long night, by the lone firelight, while the huskies, round in a ring,
Howled out their woes to the homeless snows—O God! how I loathed the thing.

And every day that quiet clay seemed to heavy and heavier grow;
And on I went, though the dogs were spent and the grub was getting low;
The trail was bad, and I felt half mad, but I swore I would not give in;
And I'd often sing to the hateful thing, and it hearkened with a grin.

Till I came to the marge of Lake Lebarge, and a derelict there lay;
It was jammed in the ice, but I saw in a trice it was called the Alice May.
And I looked at it, and I thought a bit, and I looked at my frozen chum;
Then "Here," said I, with a sudden cry, "is my cre-ma-tor-eum."

Some planks I tore from the cabin floor, and I lit the boiler fire;
Some coal I found that was lying around, and I heaped the fuel higher;
The flames just soared, and the furnace roared—such a blaze you seldom see;
And I burrowed a hole in the glowing coal, and I stuffed in Sam McGee.

Then I made a hike, for I didn't like to hear him sizzle so;
And the heavens scowled, and the huskies howled, and the wind began to blow.

It was icy cold, but the hot sweat rolled down my cheeks, and I don't know why;
And the greasy smoke in an inky cloak went streaking down the sky.

I do not know how long in the snow I wrestled with grisly fear;
But the stars came out and they danced about ere again I ventured near;
I was sick with dread, but I bravely said: "I'll just take a peep inside.
I guess he's cooked, and it's time I looked"; . . . then the door I opened wide.

And there sat Sam, looking cool and calm, in the heart of the furnace roar;
And he wore a smile you could see a mile, and he said: "Please close that door.
It's fine in here, but I greatly fear you'll let in the cold and storm—
Since I left Plumtree, down in Tennessee, it's the first time I've been warm."

There are strange things done in the midnight sun
By the men who moil for gold;
The Arctic trails have their secret tales
That would make your blood run cold;
The Northern Lights have seen queer sights,
But the queerest they ever did see
Was that night on the marge of Lake Lebarge
I cremated Sam McGee.

PROLOGUE

Greg Martin avoided his wife's eyes. He didn't want to give Elese any hope that she might persuade him into accompanying her on another shopping expedition.

"If I have to look at another display of bronzed moose nuggets, I swear I'll lose it," he said. "Selling crap is one thing, but actually selling bronzed moose shit . . ."

"You don't like those moose droppings? I thought they'd make a great memento. We could put them next to some of your rock finds on our mantel and shine a spotlight down on them. Wouldn't that look nice?"

Elese pantomimed situating the droppings in a place of honor. She added a little wiggle of her backside to her imaginary positioning.

"If you weren't so cute," he said, "I think I'd spank you."

"If you weren't so stubborn about not going out with me," she said, "I might let you."

They came together in the middle of their stateroom and kissed. Their honeymoon had been spent on the Northbound Glacier Route traveling up the Alaska coast and making stops in Ketchikan, Juneau,

Skagway, and Sitka. Now they were in Seward, their last port of call on the final cruise of the season. Although it was only September, winter was already showing itself in Alaska. The nights on ship had been cold and bracing, but their stateroom had stayed very, very warm.

"Now don't you go romancing any floozies while I'm gone," Elese said.

"I was thinking about calling on Mrs. Carpenter."

Mrs. Carpenter was ninety-seven years old. That hadn't stopped her from flirting with Greg whenever she got the chance.

"Two-timer," laughed Elese.

The cruise had been all they had hoped it would be. They had seen pods of humpback whales, monumental icebergs, panoramic glaciers, soaring bald eagles, and breathtaking fjords. Elese seemed glad Greg had talked her into honeymooning in Alaska. Neither one of them had ever been to the state; everything had been new to them. There was still more sightseeing in store, but they would do it from land, taking a motor coach to Denali and a train to Anchorage. They would finish up their honeymoon in Anchorage, where almost half of Alaska's seven hundred thousand residents lived. Some Alaskans didn't think much of their big city, though. On the cruise Elese had heard one native say, "Anchorage is a wonderful place. It's only twenty minutes from Alaska."

Greg watched his wife primping her long, dark hair in front of the small mirror. Elese could have gone out in a shower cap and still turned heads.

It was his puppy-dog eyes, she had confessed, that had made her fall for him. *Thank God for my big, brown, woeful eyes*, Greg thought. Without them he wouldn't have landed his wife.

She tilted her chin up for a good-bye kiss. He accepted her invitation, planting a long kiss that almost caused a change in her plans.

Greg came up for air first and said, "I want a rain check for later."

"If you're lucky," said Elese.

She picked up her purse and walked out of their cabin. From the door she blew him a kiss.

A kiss, and then she was gone.

* * *

The Seward Police Department shared city hall with other city and state employees, Alaska State Troopers (AST), and Alaska Department of Fish and Game. By night the police generally had the building to themselves. Because Sergeant Evan Hamilton was working late, he caught the Martin case.

Hamilton was a deliberate cop. He liked to cover all his bases. Those who didn't know him often mistook his deliberate style as being plodding and slow, even dull. His appearance seemed to corroborate that. He was a big, middle-aged man who bordered on being doughy.

The cop looked at the man sitting across the desk from him. He was half an hour into his interview with Greg Martin and still not sure what he thought about the man. Martin's every expression and gesture was the epitome of the frantic husband. But there was something about him that Hamilton couldn't put his finger on yet.

"So you took a nap when your wife went shopping?" he asked.

"The answer is 'yes,' just as it was the last three times you asked."

He ignored the man's impatience. Slow and steady wins the race. Hamilton lived by that motto, and it hadn't let him down yet. Seward was a quiet town—no Anchorage, that was for sure—but they'd had their share of crimes, petty and otherwise, to investigate over the years.

"And how long did you nap?"

"Like I already told you, it was about four hours. That's why I was so surprised when I saw that it was seven o'clock."

Hamilton underlined the time in his notes. "And that's when you say you went looking for your wife?"

"At first I assumed she came back from shopping, found me asleep, and didn't want to disturb me. So I went looking for her."

Martin was tapping his fingers restlessly against the top of the desk. Hamilton watched him until he stopped and rested his hands in his lap. "You say you went to some of the lounges and eating areas?"

Martin sighed. "And to the ship's library, and a few of the viewing areas. There are a lot of places to look on a big ship."

"You enlisted the help of several stewards and passengers, and ultimately brought in security, which took another hour and a half."

"Yes, yes, and yes."

"And then you spent half an hour in downtown Seward searching for your wife before coming here."

Martin sighed and nodded, his fingers tap-tap-tapping again. Hamilton made another entry in his notes. His wife's going missing could account for the man's jumpiness. Or it was possible something else was making him nervous.

The desk phone rang. Hamilton glanced at the caller ID and picked up. He kept the call brief, then turned his attention back to Martin.

"The crew finished its preliminary search of the ship. I'm afraid they didn't find your wife. They are now in the process of looking in every stateroom and berth."

"What about the security tapes?"

"The security director is examining the footage right now."

"Something's wrong."

Hamilton studied him before asking, "Why do you think that, Mr. Martin?"

"My wife's been gone almost six hours now. Since our wedding she hasn't been away from my side for more than an hour or two."

"When were you married?"

"September fourteenth."

Real newlyweds, Hamilton thought. He wondered if the bloom could have come off the rose and whether Mrs. Martin had reconsidered having gotten married.

"Where did you get hitched?"

"San Francisco."

"Big wedding?"

Martin exhaled in annoyance. "It was more of an intimate gathering."

"And before the wedding, you knew your wife for how long?"

"Not quite six months."

"Fast courtship."

Martin rolled his eyes and stood. "I am *going* to look for my wife."

"I would suggest you stay here, Mr. Martin."

"What if she somehow fell off the dock into the bay?"

"I already put a call in to the harbormaster. He said he would personally inspect the ferry dock, boat ramps, and harbor area."

Martin sat again, this time leaning forward, elbows on knees. He rubbed the sweat off his palms. "I've never been so afraid in my life."

"What kind of work do you do, Mr. Martin?"

"I'm a geologist."

"What about your wife?"

"She works in advertising doing ad designs. But she's really an artist."

"How did you meet?"

"Through mutual friends."

"You're quite a bit older than her, aren't you?"

Martin sighed. "I wouldn't call seven years 'quite a bit.' She's twenty-two, and I'm twenty-nine."

"You two have any problems during your honeymoon?"

Martin shook his head, straightening. "This is un-fucking-believable. You're questioning me, aren't you?"

Hamilton didn't say anything.

"My wife is out there missing, and you're playing mind games with me. You're wasting time while she could be hurt somewhere. God. Maybe I should be talking to someone who's a real cop."

Hamilton merely shrugged. "Is there any reason your wife might have chosen to leave you, Mr. Martin? A lovers' quarrel, perhaps?"

"We didn't fight," Martin said, his voice barely under control. "She wouldn't be away from me unless something was wrong. Now do your goddamn job. Put out one of those alerts. Get on the horn. Do something."

Hamilton nodded. "I've already done that, Mr. Martin. Now, you said you didn't leave your room until around seven, is that correct?"

* * *

Hamilton hung up the phone. They'd been going at this for three hours now, and he had a feeling the interview was about to get interesting. "Are you certain you didn't leave your cabin at any time from approximately three to seven?"

Greg Martin offered a weary nod. "I read for an hour and then fell asleep."

"We now have statements from two passengers who saw you leaving the ship in the late afternoon."

"They're wrong."

"That's all you have to say about it?"

"That's all there is to say about it. Maybe they got the day wrong. Maybe they mistook me for someone else. What the hell should I say about it?"

"You're a smart man, Mr. Martin. You're a scientist. I'm sure a smart guy like you hates to make a mistake. So when you woke up and realized your marriage was a huge mistake, you decided to do something about it. Does your wife have an insurance policy, Mr. Martin?"

Martin nodded.

"How much?"

"Half a million. I bought policies for both of us. We weren't going to wait to have children. It made sense for each of us to have insurance."

"Did it?"

"I know you're trying to catch me in some kind of lie. But I haven't lawyered up, have I, Sergeant? The only thing that's kept me sitting here is concern for my wife and the hope that I can prod you into doing everything possible to find her. I only pray that all the time you've wasted hasn't put Elese in jeopardy."

Hamilton deliberated for a moment, then said, "We've had a chance to circulate your wife's photo and talk to some of the clerks and store owners in town. Mrs. Martin was apparently looking at jewelry and art all over Third and Fourth Avenues. Employees place her at The Alaska Shop, Starbird Studios, and the Resurrection Bay Gallery. From what we can determine, she was in those stores between three and four."

"And no one's seen her since then? What about security footage?"

"There are very few security cameras in Seward. My AST colleagues have looked through what footage there is. She seems to have dropped out of sight around four o'clock."

"And what does the ship's security show?"

"They're still looking through footage, but from what they've been able to determine thus far, your wife never returned to the ship."

Hamilton's phone rang again. He watched Martin jump a little. He'd grown tenser with every ring. Maybe he was afraid of the news; maybe he was just a good actor.

This time, when Hamilton heard what one of the deputies had uncovered, he got to his feet and carried the phone out of the small office. He spoke softly, keeping his voice low so as to not be overheard. When he returned, he studied the seated man.

"What is it?" Martin demanded. Hamilton wasn't sure if he sounded defensive or nervous.

"I thought you told me that you'd never been arrested?"

"What I said was that I had never been convicted of a crime."

"But you were arrested?"

"Those charges were dropped."

Hamilton gave Martin his unblinking stare. "Tell me about your arrest."

"I was falsely accused of a number of things. My accuser recanted when she became entangled in her own web of lies."

"Accuser," said Hamilton, deliberately drawing out the word. "That accuser was your first wife."

"Our marriage was annulled."

"You told me that your marriage to Elese was your first."

"That's how I think of it."

"You know what I think of that? It strikes me as being deceptive."

Martin's neck flushed red. "I was afraid you would make a mountain out of a molehill. You should be concentrating on my wife's disappearance instead of—"

"Lies tend to muddy an investigation."

"I wasn't lying."

Hamilton kept his expression neutral. "Did Elese know that your first wife accused you of assault and battery, domestic violence, and a host of other charges?"

"Those were all proven false!"

"Your first wife said the reason she reluctantly withdrew those charges was that your legal team scared her, but that you scared her even more."

"The truth scared her."

"Your wife—"

"Do not call her that. My first marriage was a sham. I was young and dumb. I had no idea she had a borderline personality disorder and liked taking OxyContin too much. I married in haste and did all my regretting in leisure."

"The time frame suggests you also married Elese in haste."

"I fell in love. Do you understand that? Everything was right. I wanted to be with Elese for the rest of my life."

"Did you tell her about your first marriage and its subsequent troubles?"

Martin looked away, shook his head, and sighed. "Things were perfect between us. Can you understand that I didn't want to jinx that?"

"So what happened when she found out?"

"Elese didn't find out."

"I imagine she felt betrayed. She couldn't have liked it that you deceived her. Your wife had to have experienced some grave doubts about the man she married."

"That never occurred!"

Hamilton tilted his chin and watched as Martin followed the direction of his nod. Martin's right index finger was pointed like a gun, and his left hand was clenched in a fist. Hamilton watched Martin reclaim control and relax his hands.

Elese's husband had a temper, even though he did his best to keep it in check. And he also had a guilty conscience, thought Hamilton. He wasn't going to be an easy nut to crack, but time was on the cop's side.

CHAPTER ONE

THREE YEARS AFTER ELESE MARTIN'S DISAPPEARANCE

"Yes, another mimosa would be nice," said a giggling Dana Belzer to the flight attendant.

She turned to her seatmate. "Do you know that I've never flown first class before? I love it that your fiancé upgraded my ticket. I love being part of your fairy tale."

It wasn't only the world at large that thought Nina Granville had won the SuperLotto. Even her friends thought it. One month ago Nina's engagement to Terrence Donnelly, of *the* Donnelly family, had become official. The Donnelly family was the closest thing to being "America's royals." They were also a political dynasty, with Terrence their heir apparent to the Oval Office.

Nina had never lacked for attention in her twenty-eight years, but since becoming Terrence's fiancée, her life had become a three-ring circus. She'd grown up in a well-off family, but not Donnelly well-off.

After graduating from college, she had worked as a publicist and then in corporate relations, before landing her current position as senior associate of philanthropic endeavors for the Cambridge Foundation, one of the largest private charitable trusts in the country. Her title was a mouthful; on the job she did a lot of networking with the rich, or what she called "trolling for dollars." She had met Terrence Donnelly while working a fund-raiser.

At their first meeting, he'd had a beautiful woman on his arm. The next day Terrence had called her under the pretense of philanthropic giving. They set up a business lunch, which was where his ulterior motives became apparent. Because Nina proved immune to his bedroom eyes and high-wattage teeth, for perhaps the first time in his life Donnelly was forced to pursue a woman. But what Nina remembered most about that first lunch was that Terrence, a la the Donnelly Family Endowment, had agreed to collaborate with the Cambridge Foundation in several philanthropic endeavors. Despite Terrence's attentions, Nina hadn't lost her head; she'd remembered her job. That memory made her smile.

"Thank you," said Dana, taking the mimosa from the flight attendant. To Nina she said, "This really is a great way to start the day."

"I'm surprised that this time you passed on the warm nuts and chocolate chip cookie."

"I don't want to be full when they serve the mac-and-cheese and lobster. Or maybe I'll have the petite filet. I suppose you'll be having a salad."

"I like salads."

"I hope it comes with gold leaf or truffles."

"Don't start believing those Cinderella stories."

Dana laughed. "Which one? In the past month I've read about you in *Vanity Fair, People, Entertainment Weekly*, and *Time*."

"Yes, and all I was missing was my picture with a sooty face."

"They loved you, Cindy!"

Inwardly Nina groaned. "They loved the fantasy. I was having a lot more fun when I was flying under the radar and no one was watching what I was wearing or taking note of what I was saying or doing."

"Or eating," Dana added.

In an older and more proper voice, Nina mimicked, "When you become a Donnelly, you must be mindful of noblesse oblige."

Dana gave her a quizzical look.

"That's what Marilyn Grant told me. She's Terrence's media relations director. I sort of felt like Eliza Doolittle all the while she explained to me how as Terrence's wife I'll need to demonstrate the obligations of a 'generous spirit.' Everyone in Terrence's inner circle has been offering me pointers on how I need to appear when out in public."

"I suppose that means not drinking multiple mimosas early in the morning."

"I'm sure Sarge—Sergeant Wood is Terrence's deputy chief of staff—would have frowned at my having cream and sugar with my coffee."

The nickname "Sarge" brought up the image of some gruff but avuncular military man, but Nina found Wood to be stiff and, well, wooden. He was probably only in his mid- to late thirties, but his manner made him seem older. Sarge was certainly loyal to Terrence, perhaps to a fault.

"Terrence's inner circle looks out for him, which is a good thing. They have to deal with his image and with his political enemies. They don't want me to give those enemies any ammunition."

In fact, Sarge didn't seem convinced that she wasn't one of those enemies. He was Mars and she was Eros, and their uncommon denominator was Terrence.

"I think Henry Higgins Donnelly is lucky to have you, Eliza," said Dana.

Nina wasn't sure which was worse, being likened to Cinderella or to Eliza Doolittle. But that didn't stop her from having fun with her friend and workmate.

"'The rain in Spain stays mainly on the plain,'" she said in her best Audrey Hepburn imitation.

"'By George, she's got it! Now once again, where does it rain?'"

Nina sang, but not loud enough to be heard by anyone except Dana. "'On the plain, on the plain!'"

And then both women started laughing in a way Nina was sure was not in keeping with the Donnelly image.

*　*　*

Nina used her phone to take a short video of Dana snoring. The mimosas had done her friend in. She'd show her the video later and threaten to blackmail her.

They were now making their way over so-called flyover country. Nina stretched out in her seat and wondered about the lives of those living on the prairie. Thirty thousand feet below her was a mostly open landscape. She'd read an article in *Forbes* profiling the ten states where people were happiest. North Dakota and South Dakota had topped the list, and not far behind were Minnesota, Montana, Iowa, and Nebraska. She'd never visited any of those states. She'd never been to Alaska, either, until now. Fairbanks, the state's third largest city, only had about thirty thousand residents. On the East Coast that would have been considered a midsize town.

It was only because of her engagement to Terrence that the Cambridge Foundation had invited her to join Dana in representing them in Alaska. The director of the foundation was more delighted with her celebrity than she was. Nina still wasn't sure how she felt about her notoriety. For years she'd worked hard and advanced all on her own. Now doors everywhere seemed to be opening magically for her.

The Cambridge Foundation, in collaboration with the Donnelly Family Endowment, had provided funding to the American Museum of Natural History in New York for its purchase of several important native artifacts. The pieces that were going back to New York predated the arrival of western traders: a raven mask, elaborately carved from a mammoth tusk; a scrimshaw hunting charm with drawings of fishermen chasing a walrus; an Inuit basket made from wild rye beach grass; an extremely rare wooden Indian hunting helmet; and a detailed sculpture of a pregnant woman carved out of walrus ivory. All of the artifacts would be placed in the museum's Northwest Coast Indian permanent exhibit.

When she'd been offered the opportunity to travel to Alaska, Nina had been betwixt and between about the long business trip—but that was before Sergeant Wood had lobbied against her going. Sarge thought she needed more "seasoning" when it came to public appearances. But Nina wasn't going to let her fiancé, or especially one of his underlings, dictate what she could or couldn't do. In the end she'd agreed to make her trip without any fanfare or alerting of the media. Nina had pretended to compromise, but the truth was she hadn't minded the idea of traveling as herself, and not as the future Mrs. Donnelly.

Because Sarge took care of Terrence's security arrangements, he had reason to be watching out for her as well. Still, before their engagement announcement, Nina had felt much like a potential vice-presidential candidate being vetted for the ticket. Sarge had been open about his reservations as to whether she was the right wife for Terrence. Nina didn't like to admit it, but there was a part of her that thought the same thing. But was it wrong that she had dreams and ambitions that didn't start and end with Terrence Donnelly?

While Dana continued snoring, Nina pulled out her tablet. She had a June wedding with the world's most eligible bachelor to look forward to. But instead of making wedding plans, she found herself compiling a very different to-do list. There was no particular order to her entries, but even without a designation or heading, it was clear Nina was making a bucket list. She used her stylus to write, and in some cases draw, on the screen.

Learn to surf.

Go on one of those cross-country skiing excursions where you ski from lodge to lodge, stopping for a getaway in each.

Take scuba diving lessons. Get good enough to look for hidden treasure.

Work to save an endangered species (preferably something cute— is that silly?—yes, but still find something that's cute).

Have kids? I think so, but have only two, and don't start popping them out until I'm thirty-five.

Tango in Argentina.

Participate in an archaeological dig.

Do something that matters.

She underlined the last entry. And then underlined it again.

Nina looked at what she'd written and was surprised by a few obvious omissions. She hadn't written *Marry Terrence* or *First Lady*. She raised her stylus to make those entries, but stopped short of writing them down. She didn't want her bucket list to read like a curriculum vitae. And maybe deep down, she still had reservations about committing to those words.

Thoreau had written: "The price of anything is the amount of life you exchange for it." Nina had discovered that saying as an undergrad, and it had resonated with her. It was an economics lesson and a life lesson, and she tended to weigh big decisions by those words. She knew she was far luckier than most, with many more first-world options, but like everyone else, she still had to ante up that price of a piece of her life, be it big or small. Because she was a long-distance runner, that kind of measurement appealed to her mentality. She liked the idea of plotting out her life as she might a race.

Unbidden, Nina remembered one of her grandmother's favorite quotes: "God laughs when we make plans."

* * *

There was a short layover in Seattle, but it was long enough for Nina and Dana to sit down over an obligatory cup of Seattle's Best Coffee.

For the third time Nina played the tape of Dana's snoring, and for the third time they laughed.

"Those mimosas knocked me out," said Dana. "I'm a cheap date."

"That's what I heard."

"Biatch," said Dana, making them laugh some more. "I blame you and the congressman. Now that I'm used to first class, maybe I'll try and crash it like Kristen Wiig did in *Bridesmaids*."

Terrence had been able to upgrade Nina to first class for the last leg of their flight to Fairbanks, but not Dana.

"You're making me feel guilty," said Nina.

"That's the point," said Dana. "So, did your fiancé also get you the presidential suite at our hotel?"

"Am I going to be hearing your version of Oliver Twist for the rest of this trip?"

Dana contorted her face, and in her best cockney accent said, "Please, sir, I want some more."

"Are there no prisons or workhouses?"

Nina knew she was mixing up her Dickens novels, but that didn't matter. The two of them were too busy laughing.

"Listen," said Dana, "I'm happy living vicariously through you, Cinderella."

* * *

On the last leg of the flight, Nina found herself sitting next to an oil-company executive. Early on in the three-and-a-half-hour flight, the man began drinking. "This is how I prepare for business trips to Alaska," he joked, swirling a few ice cubes.

"It's not your cup of . . . tea?" asked Nina.

"You've never been?" he asked.

"This is my first trip," Nina said.

"Business or pleasure?"

Nina decided to tell a white lie. It was easier remaining anonymous, and she didn't want to explain her business to a stranger.

"I'm meeting up with an old college friend," she said. "We'll be doing a lot of sightseeing together."

"Well, there's not much to see in Fairbanks, but the rest of Alaska is a different story. There are parts of the state that are jaw-dropping gorgeous."

With a conspiratorial swivel of his head, he leaned over to her and whispered, "It's almost pretty enough that you can overlook the locals."

At Nina's perplexed look, he elaborated. "Business brings me to Alaska half a dozen times a year. I fly in, and I fly out. It takes a certain kind of person to live in Alaska year-round. You'll find that most of the locals couldn't fit in down in the Lower Forty-Eight. That's why they ended up in The Last Frontier. That's the state nickname. Misfits feel right at home. There are a lot of colorful characters in Alaska, that's for sure."

"I'm sure I'll meet a few of them."

"That's guaranteed."

* * *

Nina and Dana arrived at their hotel at 9:30 at night, which was 1:30 a.m. East Coast time. The front desk clerk warned them that the hotel restaurant closed at ten, and if they wanted to get dinner, they'd better hurry.

"Do you have twenty-four-hour room service?" asked Dana.

The clerk hid a smile and said, "We don't have any room service."

"Tell me my room has a bathtub," said Dana.

The clerk's mouth contorted in a grimace. "I'm afraid we only have showers in the rooms."

"What about a minibar?" asked Dana.

With a shake of his head, the clerk said, "I'm sorry," but then added, "We do have snack machines on each floor, and down this hallway you'll find an indoor pool and spa."

As they started their ascent to their adjoining rooms on the third floor, Nina said, "I'm not hungry, but if you want company I'll go with you to the restaurant."

"Let me guess: you're not hungry because while I was getting a bag of peanuts, they served you a meal on the flight to Fairbanks."

"They did," Nina admitted. "But I only ate half of it. The doggie bag is yours if you want it."

"Woof," said Dana. "I knew my Oliver Twist imitation would work on you. But I suppose you ordered rabbit food?"

Dana liked to complain that Nina's vegetarian diet cramped their restaurant choices. "Pasta primavera."

"At least that's better than tofu," said Dana. "Hand it over."

They made a quick stop at the vending machines near the elevator, and Dana took stock of their selection. "This is beginning to look like a better dinner than I usually have. In fact, I'm going to splurge and make it a three-course meal. I'll have an appetizer of M&M's, then your pasta entrée, and a Reese's Peanut Butter Cup dessert."

When they got to their room, Dana was delighted to find out that Nina's room was the same size as hers. "They must not have gotten the memo about constructing a presidential suite for your stay."

"Whatever you say, Oliver."

"Should we plan on breakfast at seven?"

"That sounds good."

"I'm glad you think so. I'm going to be jet-lagged and out of sorts. Of course, that's dependent on my not being in a diabetic coma. The nearness of those vending machines isn't a good thing."

Nina inserted her key card into the door. "Does a coma mean you won't be snoring so loudly tonight?"

As Nina opened her door, Dana began to loudly hum "Hail to the Chief."

Nina pretended to ignore the musical salutation, but a minute later, she crept out of her room and affixed a paper sign to Dana's door: PRESIDENT BELZER STAYED HERE.

* * *

Their full agenda kept the two women running for all of the next day. When they returned to their hotel in the late afternoon, Dana said she had to take a nap before she fell over.

"Why don't you knock on my door around seven?" she said. "We'll figure out our dinner plans then."

Nina said that sounded good, and then she did her usual—took a brisk walk interspersed with making calls. She never liked being cooped up for extended periods. However, making calls in Fairbanks didn't prove as easy as in New York City. Her eyes stayed more focused on her cell phone's signal than where she was going. Her phone was playing hide-and-seek: the bars kept teasing her, one moment indicating she could make a call, the next moment showing no service.

She considered starting back to the hotel to call Terrence, but resisted the idea, knowing she'd feel stir-crazy without getting her full walk in. The day had grown progressively colder and windier, and she bundled her windbreaker closer to her. She'd been warned that in Alaska the September temperature could range from twenty-five degrees to seventy-five. At the moment it was closer to the former, but despite the cold, it felt good to be out in the open.

The weather seemed to have discouraged all pedestrians save for a homeless man camped on the corner. He was a block over, but she could hear him mumbling to himself, and she tried to make sense of his singsong words:

"The Northern Lights have seen queer sights,
But the queerest they ever did see
Was that night on the marge of Lake Lebarge
I cremated Sam McGee."

Another harmless crank, Nina thought. Once more she jabbed at the redial icon, and this time heard her call going through. At last, some good luck. She tapped the phone with her engagement ring. The diamond was overly large, almost embarrassingly so; its seven flawless carats glittered.

Nina was calling Terrence's private line. It was almost eight o'clock in Washington DC, but Terrence was a workaholic. He rarely left his office before nine o'clock. His staff also put in long hours.

She waited for five rings, worried she might lose the connection before someone answered. Her patience was finally rewarded.

"Thank you for calling Congressman Donnelly's office. This is Brenda. May I help you?"

"Hi, Brenda, it's Nina. Does he have thirty seconds?"

"For you, Nina, he might even have a minute."

"Be still, my heart."

Brenda laughed before putting her on hold.

The homeless man was still doing his mumbling, and while waiting for her fiancé to get on the line, Nina was forced to listen to his ramblings. The man's volume had ballooned:

"He turned to me and 'Cap,' says he, 'I'll cash in this trip, I guess;
And if I do, I'm asking that you won't refuse my last request.'"

A familiar voice came on the line: "Nanook of the North?"

She could picture Terrence with his big Irish smile that so many people found irresistible. "Ah, the Donnelly wit," she said.

"Do I detect a cold wind from the north?"

"I could understand how that might scare a politician full of hot air. You know how it is when cold air meets hot; there's always a storm."

Terrence laughed. "You can take the girl out of Smith, but not the Smith out of the girl."

"You have that right."

"How was your luncheon?" he asked. "Did they serve caribou steaks or filet of moose?"

"Judging by the comments around me, I believe either would have been preferable to the chicken."

"The fried-chicken circuit is good training for you." Behind his laughter was political truth.

"As long as they bring me a fruit plate or dinner salad, I suppose I'll survive."

"And I looked at it, and I thought a bit, and I looked at my frozen chum; Then 'Here,' said I, with a sudden cry, 'is my cre-ma-tor-eum.'"

She covered one ear in the hopes of drowning out the homeless man's gibberish.

Terrence asked, "Have you had a chance to see the sights?"

"I toured the Museum of the North this morning," she said, "and made a few business appearances, but for most of the day I've been stuck in meetings. I was told, though, that Fairbanks has more cracked windshields per capita than anywhere in the US. And I also learned I would have to travel south from here in order to get to the North Pole."

"Will you be visiting there by flying reindeer or by dogsled?"

"Don't laugh," she said. "One of my quick stops today was the Dog Mushing Museum."

"I can see you on the Iditarod Trail."

"I can see you in the doghouse."

The homeless man was still reciting verse as if he were some kind of poet laureate. Nina would have moved away but for fear of losing her signal.

"Some planks I tore from the cabin floor, and I lit the boiler fire;
Some coal I found that was lying around, and I heaped the fuel higher."

"I can't wait to hear about all your adventures," said Terrence. "When you get back tomorrow, I'll have some chilled champagne waiting for you."

"Don't talk to me about anything chilled. It's freezing here."

"Okay, then I'll have a fire waiting for you, and hot chocolate."

"If I didn't know better, Congressman, I might suspect you of ulterior motives."

In and out of her ears, like the buzzing of an annoying mosquito, the words to the poem droned on:

"I was sick with dread, but I bravely said: 'I'll just take a peep inside.
I guess he's cooked, and it's time I looked'; . . . then the door I
    opened wide."

"There's nothing ulterior about my motives. When it comes to you, they're very blatant."

"That's just great!"

"Whoa," Terrence said. "My libidinous thoughts are great?"

"I'm sorry," Nina said, flustered. "I'll have to take a rain check on your thoughts, and I mean that literally. I'm outside, and it's begun to pour, with a little sleet mixed in. And naturally I didn't think to wear a hat."

She raised a hand over her head, but it was an ineffective shield against the sleet.

"And there sat Sam, looking cool and calm, in the heart of the
    furnace roar;
And he wore a smile you could see a mile, and he said: 'Please close
    that door.

It's fine in here, but I greatly fear you'll let in the cold and storm—
Since I left Plumtree, down in Tennessee, it's the first time I've
  been warm.'"

"What did you say? Nina, I think we're breaking up."

The connection went dead.

At least she'd gotten through. Nina slid her phone into her blazer pocket. Maybe it was just as well the call had been interrupted—there never seemed to be a good way to finish their phone conversations. The romantic dance at the end never felt quite right to her. Terrence always professed his love, and then she did the same with a nagging feeling of discomfort. There was a part of her that had always expected she'd be swept off her feet by the man she was going to marry—ridiculous, she knew. Everyone said that she and Terrence were perfect together. It was only in romance novels that fireworks went off, wasn't it? That kind of overblown sentiment just wasn't realistic.

When their engagement was announced, all the female staff on *Entertainment Tonight* had worn black armbands "mourning" that Terrence Donnelly was now off the market. And all of Nina's friends told her how lucky she was. Nina wished she was as excited as other people seemed to be.

The sleet continued to fall. Of course, she wasn't wearing a raincoat. It wasn't easy dressing for this climate.

She looked around. There were no cabs; Fairbanks wasn't New York City. At least her hotel was only a few blocks away. But which way was it? She tried to orient herself by the proximity of the Chena River. From where she was, she could see the Federal Building. *That way.* She'd get back, change, and run on a treadmill—assuming the hotel had a gym.

The sleet began coming down even harder. God, her hair was going to be a mess, and her makeup was probably already running. At least there were no paparazzi in Fairbanks. The bedraggled look was not in keeping with the Donnelly image.

Around her the street was quiet. The natives had probably read the signs of the sky and known it was going to storm. Even that homeless man had found shelter. Nina tucked her chin to her chest and began walking. *Sleet in September*, she thought. That seemed wrong.

Two-by-fours and construction material blocked the right side of the sidewalk. Nina stepped to her left, and her foot caught on something.

She fell, hard, with no chance to cushion the fall with her hands. Her chin slammed into the asphalt, and she cried out. The pain she felt was quickly replaced with anger and embarrassment. How could she have been so clumsy?

She touched her chin; there would be an ugly rash there, no doubt, that makeup wouldn't be able to completely cover. Thank goodness no one had been around to witness her humiliation. As she started to rise, she felt a tug at her ankle and saw that there was some kind of wire entwined around it. That explained why she'd fallen. Somehow her leg had gotten snared. She reached for the wire just as a figure loomed over her. Something hard struck the back of her head.

Dazed, she tried to fight off the hands that reached roughly for her. She tried to scream, but the hands pressed a rag over her nose and mouth. As her lungs breathed in its fumes and consciousness ebbed, Nina heard a familiar voice, but this time the voice was speaking into her ear:

"There are strange things done in the midnight sun
By the men who moil for gold;
The Arctic trails have their secret tales
That would make your blood run cold;
The Northern Lights have seen queer sights,
But the queerest they ever did see
Was that night on the marge of Lake Lebarge
I cremated Sam McGee."

CHAPTER TWO

Nina drifted in and out of consciousness. She didn't really want to awaken. As awful as her dreams had been, she had a sense that the world would look even worse with her eyes open.

Underlying her foreboding was a dull, throbbing pain that seemed to touch every part of her body. She used that pain to try to center her thoughts. Her hand hurt—more than her head, more than anything else. The slightest movement sent pain surging up her arm. Nina struggled to open her eyes. They felt weighted down. Her eyelids trembled, but at last she raised them. Her efforts weren't rewarded. There was a blindfold covering her eyes.

She reached up with her hands to remove it, a motion that caused so much agony that she almost blacked out. Something was terribly wrong with her left hand. Nina shifted around, but there wasn't any position that brought her relief from the pain. Her throat was so dry it hurt to breathe. Even her groaning hurt, but the sounds kept involuntarily escaping her mouth.

She wasn't sure if she heard something or just sensed it, but she was suddenly sure someone was standing over her. She stopped groaning, even stopped breathing, in order to better hear.

"If you need anything," said a man's voice, "I'm right here."

"Wa—wa—"

Her lips were too parched and her mouth too dry to ask more than that, but it was enough. She felt the touch of a water bottle on her lips and raised her head to drink from it, sucking greedily until the bottle was pulled away from her.

"Not too much," he said. "I don't want you throwing up again."

It took Nina several moments to arrange the words in her mind and then say them: "What happened?"

"You've been abducted. A ransom request has been sent to your family."

She tried to digest the information. She was too numb and too disoriented to be shocked. "Why?"

"For money," he said. "If you do everything I say, you'll be released safely."

Focusing, doing her best to concentrate, she said, "My hand." A painful swallow, and then a last push to finish her thought: "It hurts."

"I'll give you some meds."

"Why does—it hurt—so?"

"Because along with the ransom note," he said, "I sent your ring finger. Now your family knows how serious I am."

I sent your ring finger. His words echoed in her head. At first she couldn't make sense of them. When she did, when she realized what he'd done to her, she blacked out.

* * *

Nina had no idea how much time passed before she awakened again. At one point she had found herself being jostled about and realized she was in a moving car, but her consciousness was brief.

When she awakened, the blindfold was no longer covering her eyes, and she struggled to raise her head and look around. She was weak; there wasn't a part of her body that didn't hurt.

She struggled to a sitting position. She was outside, but it was too dark to see much. Beneath her was a tarp, on top of which were several blankets. It was cold enough that her breathing produced a vapor trail.

Her movements brought the man—the butcher who'd cut off her finger—to Nina's side. Her abductor was big and bearded, and Nina realized she'd seen him before. He was the same man who'd been uttering that awful poem on the streets of Fairbanks. At the time she'd thought he was crazy and homeless. Now he didn't look either of those things. He looked dangerous.

"I made you some broth," he said, offering her a steaming cup.

Nina didn't respond. This creature had maimed her. She shifted her gaze from her bandaged hand to him. He didn't turn away in shame, but instead stared at her with his hard, black eyes in a familiar way that made her shudder. She hated his insinuating glance. Who was he to look at her in such a way? Nina tried not to show him how afraid she was. The pain in her hand sparked her anger.

"What kind of animal are you that you could mutilate my finger?"

"I'm the kind of animal that means business."

"Business?" she asked.

"Nothing hurries up a ransom delivery like a finger."

He spoke as if he knew this for a fact. There was no apology, no commiseration, no regret about what he'd done. This wasn't a man, Nina decided. This was a monster.

"You didn't need to hurt me. My family and my fiancé would have paid without your act of brutality."

"Now they'll pay that much quicker. That will be good for me and good for you. If they pay quick enough, they might even be able to reattach that finger of yours."

Nina glommed onto his last words. "What do you mean?"

"It was a clean cut, taken right below the joint. That's the trick. You have to know where and how to cut. I rubbed my hunting knife with alcohol before I did it. A surgeon couldn't have removed it any better."

The calm way in which he described his brutal act sent icy tendrils through her chest. Fear—and a small thread of hope. If she cooperated, her finger could be reattached.

"It was actually a lot more work sending off your finger than taking it off."

"What—what do you mean?"

"I had to get dry ice and then package up your nicely manicured finger just so. It cost a fortune for one-night shipping, but if everything goes right, one of those fancy plastic surgeons will be able to reattach it in a few days. All you'll need is another fat engagement ring to cover up the scar."

"Thank God." Nina's sense of relief was overwhelming.

"The clock's ticking on that hand of yours, though. If the surgery's going to be successful, they'll need to operate soon. So if you want to get reacquainted with your finger, you'll have to do exactly as I say. If you follow my instructions, tomorrow night your boyfriend will be tucking you into your silk sheets. But if you don't do as I say, I'll kill you."

Nina's breath caught. In her entire life, no one had ever raised a hand to her or voiced such savage threats. She had no doubt but that he would kill her. She did her best to keep her terror in check, but she suspected he knew just how scared she was.

"I'll do as you say," Nina said.

He nodded, as if expecting no other answer, and then leaned over the fire and stoked it. Nina looked around and shivered. There was no indication of where they might be. In the darkness she could see little else besides the shrubbery that surrounded them. There was no road, or at least none she could make out.

"Where are we?"

"We're in a spot in the great state of Alaska that probably doesn't even have a name."

"Will the ransom be delivered here?"

"No. We'll pick it up at another site."

The sound of his voice was deep, without any detectable accent. He was looking at her again, and Nina was glad of the darkness, imagining it as a barrier between the two of them.

She tried to speak in a professional and impersonal tone. "Is there any way I can make a call? I want to reassure my family, and my fiancé, that I'm all right."

"No calls."

Okay, then. She considered her situation. She was weak and needed her strength. "Perhaps I could have that cup of broth now?"

He said nothing, merely reached for the cup and placed it in her right hand. His hands were calloused and rough, and she involuntarily pulled away from his touch, spilling some of the broth. He seemed to find that amusing.

From its smell alone, Nina knew she was holding chicken broth. Normally she would have refused it, but she needed her strength. She took a sip. The liquid was warm and welcome, especially on such a cool night. She kept sipping and quickly finished the cup.

"I'd like more," Nina said.

She thought of Dana and her Oliver Twist impression. Dana would have reported her missing by now. The police would be looking for her.

"Later," he said. "First, we'll see if it keeps in your stomach."

If she was that hungry, how long had she been held captive? It might be helpful to know that. She'd been taken in the late afternoon. "What time is it?"

"It's late. If you hope to sleep, you better take a pain pill."

He stretched out his dirty hand, and she took the pill and put it in her mouth. Escape was out of the question, she supposed. She had no idea where she was. Out in this wilderness, it would be easy to get lost. She had to think positively: the ransom would be paid soon, and her finger would be reattached. Others would help her.

Nina swallowed the pill. She wanted the pain to go away. She wanted relief from this terrible experience.

"Sweet dreams," he said.

His amusement made bile rise in her throat. She turned her back and stretched out atop the blankets. Even in the best of conditions, she didn't enjoy camping. It had only taken one back-to-nature outing with a former boyfriend to convince her that she enjoyed room service more than tenting it. This, though—this was much worse than having to deal with an uncomfortable bedroll and the cold.

Imagining her freedom helped distract her from the pain, as did thinking about how her abductor would pay for what he'd done. The medication made her sleepy, but one troubling thought kept surfacing: *He never tried to hide his face.* If he wanted to avoid being identified by her, why hadn't he disguised himself?

Maybe he planned to escape to some foreign country after getting the money. Or it was possible he was just careless. Most criminals weren't very smart, right?

Anyway, it didn't matter. Once the ransom was paid, this nightmare would be over. If all went well, she would soon have her finger reattached. A missing digit wouldn't be in keeping with the Donnelly look.

Things will be better in the morning. Clinging to that thought, Nina finally managed to sleep.

* * *

Nina liked to waken to classical music to start the day. It set the right tone for the morning. But it wasn't classical music that woke her.

"Move!"

His voice screamed into her ear. That would have been bad enough, but when he yanked her arm, the stab of pain from her mutilated hand almost made her physically sick.

"Now!" he screamed. Nina struggled to her feet. It was still dark outside. Their camp was already broken down, nothing left to show they had stayed there for a night.

"Back of the van," he commanded. "Move it."

A pressing need made Nina speak. "I have to go to the bathroom."

"Honey pot's in the back," he said.

She hurried over to the rear of the open van and found a small space that had been cleared for her. The back of the van was filled with large sacks of food, including rice, beans, and flour. She didn't know what a honey pot was, but she looked around for what she assumed was a portable toilet. The van doors closed behind her. Nina heard the click of a padlock.

To her dismay, the *honey pot* wasn't more than an oversize pan. As the bearded man sat down in the driver's seat, Nina said, "Please let me out. I'll be just a minute."

He started the engine. "We have an appointment to make."

"I promise I'll be quick . . ."

He answered by hitting the accelerator. With her good hand, Nina grabbed hold of the seat in front of her. The road was rough, each jolting movement pressing into her bladder. The van's poor suspension added to Nina's agony. After a few miles of torture, the ride improved somewhat and their speed increased, but Nina was still painfully aware of every pothole and dip they encountered. Each minute became more uncomfortable than the last. Nina eyed the so-called honey pot, and then she raised her eyes and found her captor looking at her in the rearview mirror.

"I need you to pull over," she said.

He shook his head. "You can piss in the pot or piss in your pants. It's your choice."

Nina trembled, but not from the cold. She had never felt rage like this, but she wasn't going to give him the enjoyment of watching her yield to the chamber pot. She wasn't going to be a spectacle for his viewing entertainment. Tears started falling. There seemed to be no end of them, and Nina didn't try to stop their flow. She told herself they were relieving the pressure on her bladder, although that was hard to believe. She clenched her hands, wondering at this monster's cruelty. In her entire life, she had never hated anyone, but in the depths of her stomach, she was beginning to know what hate felt like. She wanted to hurt this man, to return his violence and cruelty.

For what seemed like an eternity but was probably less than an hour, the van rattled and rocked before finally coming to a stop.

"Let me out," she said. She felt like a young schoolgirl again, beholden to a sadistic teacher for a potty pass. The plea, the begging, came out in a beseeching whine: "Please."

He didn't answer, didn't even acknowledge her having spoken. Rifle in hand, he got out of the van, and she heard his footsteps walking around the area. After what seemed like an eternity, he removed the padlock and opened the back door of the van. Crablike, Nina crawled over the supplies, moving toward the opening. She tried to ignore the stabbing pain from where he'd cut off her ring finger.

At the door he stopped her with a rough hand. "You'll stay within my sight," he said.

Nina nodded. He held on to her for a moment longer than necessary, then let her go. She ran toward a stand of trees. Any illusions she'd had about maintaining her dignity vanished. At the first tree, she dropped her pants and lowered herself down. When she finished she was weak with relief.

At least it was still dark; the sun was just beginning to show itself. Something rustled in the brush next to her. Wild images flashed through her mind. She tried to hop away to safety, but she fell. Her injured hand struck the ground, and she cried out in pain.

"What happened?" the man yelled.

"Something moved," she said weakly. "I think it was a snake."

"There are no snakes in Alaska, *cheechako*."

She got to her feet. With her right hand, she tried to pull up her garments. Her left hand throbbed. She brushed dirt from the bandage, hoping none had found its way under the dressing. As she did so, she looked around.

They were on a river, or maybe it was a lake. A cold wind was blowing; the air was heavy with moisture, and the ground was wet. A sulfurous smell came from decomposing plant vegetation at the shore of the lake. The body of water appeared to be sizable, but there was no one else in the area to be seen. No telephone wires or power poles or asphalt roads. She wasn't used to seeing a lake without homes lining its shoreline.

It wouldn't even do any good to yell, she realized. No one was around to hear her.

She slowly made her way back. He had put a tarp and blanket on the ground. "Get comfortable," he said. "Last night I fried up some bacon. That will be breakfast."

Nina shook her head while settling atop the blanket. "I don't eat meat."

"Is that a fact?" He sounded amused. "I'll make you some orange juice then, unless you don't drink juice neither."

She didn't answer. He went to the van and mixed up some water and orange powder. A few moments later, he handed her a cup and said, "Tang. My old man used to say it was the drink of astronauts."

Nina took it and drank. He'd used too much powder, making its sweetness cloying, but she was thirsty.

"Is this where the ransom payment's going to be delivered?" she asked.

He nodded.

As Nina finished her drink, she began to feel better. Everything would turn out all right. Once the ransom was paid, she would be set free.

"How will I get back to civilization?"

"You won't. I'll tell the authorities where you are."

"Where am I?"

"You're a hell of a long way from New York City, *cheechako*."

"What does that word mean? And how do you know I'm from New York City?"

"A *cheechako* is a tenderfoot, an outsider who doesn't know the first thing about the great land. That's the Aleut translation of *Alaska*: great land."

He made it sound as if being a tenderfoot was a crime.

"As for your living in New York City," he said, "when you demand ransom for someone, you better know where they live."

Nina suddenly felt light-headed and realized she hadn't eaten in some time. "Do you have some bread or crackers or chips? I think I've got low blood sugar from not having eaten."

"Low blood sugar?" he said. "We can't have that."

While he rustled around in the back of the van, Nina began to hum, then to whistle. She never knew whistling could be so much fun. It wasn't something she ever did, but now she couldn't understand why that was. She was still whistling when he came back with a bag of Doritos. Nina grabbed a handful of chips and started chewing. That made it impossible to whistle, so between mouthfuls she began talking. It occurred to her that she was speaking with her mouth open, but for some reason she wasn't bothered by that.

"You never introduced yourself. What am I supposed to call you?"

"Call me Baer, spelled B-A-E-R."

The name seemed appropriate. The man reminded her of a bear. He was hairy, and dark, and large, and wild. For whatever reason he seemed to be in a good mood now. Nina wasn't feeling bad herself. Her left hand wasn't bothering her as much. She raised it up and stared at the bandaging. There was a space where her ring finger used to be.

"I hope your money arrives soon," she said. "My finger's waiting for me."

That idea struck her as being funny. She knew it shouldn't, but it did. The thought of her disembodied finger tapping impatiently made her laugh.

She kept laughing. There was no reason for her to worry. "I'm going to get some *pain au chocolat* from Claude's when I get home. No one makes pastries like Claude. He learned his skills in France, where he was a pastry chef for a two-star restaurant. We're talking Michelin."

"Better drink some more juice," Baer said, handing her another cup.

"Tang," she corrected. "Do the astronauts really drink it?"

She drank up again. The drink was still too sweet. The sugar wasn't even completely dissolved. The wind was still blowing hard, but she didn't feel cold anymore. She puckered her lips and began to whistle, trying to be a part of the wind's chorus.

"Hot, isn't it?" she said, abandoning her whistling.

Baer said nothing, but Nina didn't notice. She was in her own world now, floating from thought to thought. Her head drooped. *A nap*, she thought, *would be nice*. She drifted away, but didn't quite sleep. She almost felt as if she were sailing. When she opened her eyes, Baer was standing over her.

"Time to get ready for your flight," he said.

His words sounded as if they were being shouted from a distance. He reached inside his jacket pocket and pulled out a roll of duct tape. Nina watched as if she were standing outside her body, a casual observer. A large, very sharp-looking knife suddenly appeared in his hands. She wondered idly whether this was the blade he'd used to take off her finger. He stretched out a length of tape and sliced through it.

Baer reached for her wrists, circling both of them in the hold of his large hand. "Time to buckle up," he said, wrapping her hands together with the tape.

Nina tried to speak, but all she could manage was a gurgle.

CHAPTER THREE

As Tomcat Carter made his pass over Fish Lake, he saw Adams and all his gear waiting for him on the bank.

The two men had met at a bar in Anchorage four years ago. At the time, Tomcat had been running charters and flightseeing excursions in and around Denali National Park. When this man Adams learned that Tomcat was dropping off his charters in the small town of Talkeetna, the two of them had made their own flight arrangements. Adams had put down a sizable deposit, and he and Tomcat had agreed to meet-up at Fish Lake, a spot five miles outside Talkeetna. Their destination, Adams said, would be a lake in the interior that wasn't far from his hunting cabin.

That was enough of a destination for Tomcat's purposes. Alaskan bush pilots were notoriously independent and not keen on Big Brother knowing any more than was necessary. Many of his clients were just as secretive, not wanting others to discover their favorite hunting and fishing spots. Besides, cash talked.

Four years ago, Adams's ultimate destination had proved to be a lake that, like so many others in Alaska, was anonymous. They had set down well east of Manley Hot Springs. It was one of those places in the interior unnamed on any map; its remoteness and the hilly, harsh terrain had discouraged even the native people from settling anywhere nearby.

Although he'd flown Adams to the same destination several times since, Tomcat still knew virtually nothing about the man other than that he was a trapper who lived in the interior. Tomcat had given him the nickname "Grizzly." Grizzly believed it was the "end days," but he wasn't religious about it, not one of those people who thought Jesus was coming back. He thought civilization was on the brink of extinction, and that wars and plague and the like were imminent. The man was probably crazy, but so were lots of his clients. Grizzly paid cash, which was good enough for Tomcat.

The pilot banked his Cessna 185 and came in for his final approach. Flying was about the only viable option for traveling within the state. Tomcat always explained to outsiders that if you put an overlay of Alaska atop a map of the continental United States, it extended from Georgia to California. Despite its size, Alaska had few roads outside of its major cities, and even by the most charitable estimates, there were fewer than twenty highways in the state. Roughly one in sixty Alaskans had a pilot's license. It was because the state had so few major roads that Tomcat had job security for as long as he lived.

The weather had worsened over the course of that morning, growing colder and windier, and the single-engine plane wasn't having an easy time of it. Flying conditions in Alaska were among the most difficult in the world. Staying alive was the challenge every bush pilot faced.

Tomcat kept adjusting his plane during the descent, with the Cessna's wings tilting one way and then the other. The wind buffeted the plane's floats, and Tomcat tried to keep her steady. By next week he'd have to switch out the floats for tundra tires or even skis.

The plane hit the water too hard, bounced up, and then came down again. After settling down for good, Tomcat taxied over to where

Grizzly and his provisions were waiting, angled the craft so that it was facing into the wind, and then turned off the engine.

As he hopped out of his plane, Tomcat shouted, "I give myself a ten for the artistic part of the program. Of course, I always say if you can walk away from the plane, there's no such thing as a bad landing."

Grizzly pulled on the plane's line, bringing its aft up on the shore. "It's about time you showed up."

"Well, good morning to you, too, Mr. Adams. In case you hadn't noticed, this isn't exactly a perfect flying day, and you didn't make things any easier by having me pick you up here instead of just flying you out of Anchorage. Airports from Juneau to Fairbanks got their favorite Jew holiday going on today: Passover. Just about everybody's closed up shop on account of fog and generally shitty conditions. I probably should have stayed in bed, and that's not just my opinion. The woman I was sharing my bed with had some convincing arguments for me to stay put."

"Maybe she's seen your landings," Grizzly said.

"Textbook landings are for pussies. What I do is crash with aplomb."

The pilot wasn't a large man, but he had big hands, a big voice, and a big head. He shook that head as he appraised the waiting bags. "Jesus Christ, Griz. You didn't warn me that you were going to be bringing everything but the kitchen sink. How many pounds you packing?"

"Not much more than the usual. Six hundred pounds tops."

"Shit."

"You've hauled more than that."

"Yeah, and I used to be able to screw all night. In my old age, I'm becoming more and more aware of the forces of gravity, especially on a day like today."

"In your old age, it sounds like you're becoming damn cranky. Let me guess: that slipped disk of yours is hurting like hell."

"You got a future as a carnie, Adams, guessing people's weight."

"And here I was going to volunteer to stow the gear."

Tomcat shrugged and pretended he didn't care. "Let's weigh it first," he said, "and then you can knock yourself out."

The pilot was glad to give his chronically bad back a break. He studied the scale's readouts, writing down figures, while Grizzly did all the lifting. Every box and bag was weighed, and then Tomcat decided how the containers were to be stowed for ideal weight distribution. He supervised Grizzly's tying down of the cargo. The last thing you wanted on a small plane was shifting cargo.

The high-winged plane was officially a six-seater, but the fifth and sixth seats had been removed. Two of the larger bags were strapped into the empty seats. A large duffel bag was stowed in the back. What concerned Tomcat most was the dry dog-food vault designed to hold a sixty-pound bag of kibble. Adams had filled the vault, resulting in what Tomcat called a ballbuster. Finally it got stowed to his satisfaction.

After everything was put away and Adams was strapped into the remaining seat, Tomcat sat at the controls and went through his checklist. The plane wasn't at its weight limit, but he was hauling more than he would have liked, especially with the iffy weather. He took a deep breath and then blew it out. If he was going to do this, he had to get going. Daylight was burning.

He positioned the Cessna into the wind, then opened the throttle. In a pinch the plane could get airborne in 700 feet, but when it was weighed down, you wanted more room to maneuver than that. The Cessna gained speed as it moved down its water runway. More snow was falling now, and Tomcat alternately cursed and exhorted the machine as it rose into the air. Slowly, begrudgingly, it gained altitude.

"Come on," he said over the noise of the straining engine. "Get up, you piece of shit."

He slapped the instrument panel with his hand like a galley master beating a drum. Even as they gained more altitude, gusts of wind buffeted them from side to side. The wind he could deal with. What he didn't like was the way the wet snow was already clinging to the craft.

"These are screwed conditions!" Tomcat shouted.

"You afraid of a little snow?"

"Afraid of this crate goddamn icing up? You got that right. There's a saying, Griz: There are old pilots and there are bold pilots, but there ain't no old, bold pilots."

"What little girl made up that poem?"

He responded to the goad with a disgusted sound, but his attention was on flying. *He shouldn't let Grizzly Fucking Adams get under his skin*, Tomcat thought. Like the real Grizzly Adams, this guy was a mountain man. They were a rare breed—which, he thought, was a good thing.

As the plane climbed, Tomcat craned his neck, trying to see through the snow to the ground below. Already the ground was a carpet of white. They were flying into winter, and it threatened to come sooner rather than later.

"When the firewood bloomed in the middle of July, it didn't lie. Winter's come early this year, and it's going to be long and cold."

The early blooming of the firewood plant was a portent for Alaskans, signaling an early and lengthy winter. Apparently that prospect didn't bother Grizzly Adams. "Good," he said.

"You're the only goddamn person I know who looks forward to eight months of winter. You're the last of the mountain men," said Tomcat. "No one else is trapping or homesteading anymore, but here you are living in the middle of goddamn nowhere. Even the Natives don't live out your way. How far is it to your nearest neighbor, fifty miles?"

"Not far enough."

"So, being such a lover of humanity, what did you do during your big getaway?"

Grizzly shrugged.

"What are you, a goddamn Trappist monk?"

"No, I'm a goddamn trapper."

"Yeah, you're the last of the Mohicans. I'm surprised you're still in business. These days it's getting so that you can't even take a piss out of doors without some Fed writing you up. You better hope those bureaucrats don't start reaching their fingers up your way."

"If they do, those fingers will get frostbit."

"You're right about that. They probably don't want to have anything to do with someone crazy enough to live so far from civilization. How the hell do you keep from going nuts, Adams?"

Instead of answering, his passenger shut his eyes and turned away. His breathing grew heavy. Tomcat wasn't sure if Adams was faking his snoring to avoid conversing or if he really had fallen asleep.

"Ask me," said Tomcat under his breath, "you already are crazy."

* * *

As with so many things, the tipping point seemed to have materialized suddenly, whereas in truth everything had been building up over time.

The Cessna shook violently. Tomcat cursed with equal violence. He looked straight ahead and then right and left. The windows might as well have been painted opaque white. He relied on his training to try to fight off the vertiginous sensation. There was no perspective, nothing by which to gauge the direction they were flying, or even which way was up. With bone-white knuckles, he gripped the throttle as if their lives depended on it. Maybe they did.

The sounds from the engine weren't reassuring. It was straining and sputtering. Tomcat's cursing finally roused his passenger, who stretched, took a few breaths and a look around, and then said, "We're flying around in circles."

"Tell me something I don't already know, Einstein."

"Why?"

"Because we got close to zero visibility, and I'm not real fond of flying in what looks like a bottle of milk. But that's not the worst of it.

We've been icing up. And by the sounds of it, the air inlets and induction filter are in danger of plugging up."

"What does that mean?"

"It means we're up shit creek without a paddle. We got to get higher, or we might come to a *very* abrupt halt."

"So, let's get higher."

"While you've been snoring, I've been doing everything but flapping my arms. The engine's already giving its all. I push any harder and it's likely to cut out on us."

"Can we land?"

"Not without some window of visibility. And if we go looking for that visibility, we might find ourselves poleaxed by some rock or come face-to-face with a mountain. Going higher is our answer."

Everything seemed to be conspiring against that. The wind kept slamming the plane, slapping it downward. A sudden wind shear cuffed the Cessna, and it dropped like a boxer with a glass jaw. The howl of the whipping air drowned out all noise, and both men strained to hear the sound of the engine. For a long moment, there was nothing, as if it was catching its breath, and then its labored roaring resumed.

Tomcat wiped away the sweat running down his face. Grizzly Adams didn't even look concerned. Perhaps he didn't realize the seriousness of their situation, or perhaps he didn't care. His concern didn't seem to be so much about getting down in one piece as it was in getting to his destination.

"How far are we from Last Lake?" he asked.

"At least thirty miles out."

"That's not so far."

"It's far enough that we might never reach there. What we got to do is lighten our load. You need to start tossing everything out, and you need to do it now."

"You serious?"

"I'm as serious as death. Do it!"

Adams unlocked his seat belt and took a few unsteady steps back to the hold.

* * *

The insistent sound of a screaming train whistle kept invading Nina's thoughts. The noise was growing louder, if that was possible. As much as she wanted to ignore it and continue sleeping, she couldn't.

It was dark outside. No, that wasn't it. She moved her head around. Some kind of cover surrounded her. She tried to push the shroud away only to realize that both her hands and feet were tied. A scream rose up from her chest, but her cries were muted by the duct tape running across the center of her mouth.

Baer, she remembered, had trundled her up. He was the one who must have put her in this bag. What if he'd buried her alive? Nina suddenly couldn't breathe. It felt as if a pressing weight was on her chest and everything was closing in on her. Her heart pounded, her pulse raced, and her stomach was doing flip-flops. She fought off nausea, afraid of being asphyxiated by her own vomit.

A sudden jostling threw Nina to one side, and then the other. *Don't panic*, she told herself. *Think.* Baer had probably gotten his ransom money and was now making his getaway. He'd been afraid someone might recognize her, and because of that he'd hidden her away in some kind of bag. That had to be it. She was in the back of his moving van. By the feel of it, the vehicle was being driven hard.

She chewed on the duct tape but was unable to free up her mouth. Still, the chewing helped alleviate the pressure she was feeling in her ears. Maybe they were up on a mountain pass. That might explain the wind as well. A persistent frosty breeze penetrated the bag; at least she didn't have to worry about fresh air. The whistling of the wind was louder now, sounding more like a buzz saw.

And then it felt as if a carpet was being pulled out from under her; a sense of vertigo overwhelmed her and Nina screamed, but she couldn't even hear herself through the duct tape. For a long moment, gravity lost its hold on her, and she had the sensation of her stomach and throat being in free fall. She thought the van was falling off the side of the road until gravity reasserted itself.

She wasn't sure which was churning more, her stomach or her mind. Everything felt in flux. She tried to focus, but her head was swimming in violent waters. She didn't know what was happening, and that made everything worse. Thinking was an effort. Nina tried twisting her wrists and feet, but the duct tape stifled anything but minimal movement. There was no give there.

Then, without warning, she felt herself sliding backward. Nina kicked out with her legs. She had to get out. The bag brought her feet up short, but she kicked again and again.

* * *

On the plane's rearmost seat, the duffel bag shifted and moved as though it were full of snakes. The dipping plane and the frigid air had awakened its occupant.

Baer braced for the onslaught as he opened the aft cargo door. It popped free, wind blasting into the cabin and sucking unsecured papers out of the opening. Nature, abhorring a vacuum, became a vacuum cleaner, putting its grip on everything inside.

He tossed the fifty-pound bags of beans and rice first. Seven-pound containers of tomato sauce went flying out, along with boxes of pasta. He freed the dog-food vault, and then dragged it over to the opening. It was a tight fit, but he was able to squeeze it through, and it dropped into the void.

"Get rid of goddamn everything except the yellow bag in the cargo hold!" yelled Tomcat. "That's the survival kit."

Baer continued tossing until only the survival bag and the duffel were left.

* * *

Huddled inside her bag, Nina willed her body to be heavy. The wind was grabbing at her, screaming for her to come along with it. Whatever was going on outside her shroud terrified her. The noise was overwhelming. It was in her head, had a grip on her mind, and threatened to overwhelm her. Senselessness would be a blessing. Nina wondered if she was going crazy.

Although she couldn't see, she squeezed her eyes shut anyway. Nina was now sure she was no longer in the van but a plane. Baer had said something about a flight. That explained her stomach's feeling like it was on an express elevator. But it didn't explain the noise in the cabin. It sounded as if the Furies had been unleashed. Something was very wrong. Cold wind whipped at her through the cloth, clawing at her, pulling her into the air.

* * *

As the plane bounced, the duffel seemed to levitate for a moment. Baer snatched its grip.

The screaming wind whipped at his hair. He hoisted the duffel over to the aft cargo door. As he prepared to let it go, he noticed the plane's nose was up. The Cessna was angling higher, gaining altitude.

Inside the craft, Tomcat began to raggedly cheer. Outside the craft, the wind seemed to shriek its disappointment.

"Close the goddamn cargo hold!" yelled Tomcat.

Baer did as the pilot asked and then secured the duffel on the floor behind the seats, where Tomcat would be unable to see it flopping like a fish on shore. It wouldn't be long before the woman tired herself out. There were enough drugs in her system to put out an elephant.

Ten minutes later the white curtain seemed to lift long enough for Tomcat to get some idea of the surrounding expanse. He peered at the GPS readout. Below, Baer could see thickets of spruce, birch, larch, and aspen.

"You work this land?" Tomcat asked. "You know it at all?"

Baer shook his head. "I don't run my traplines this way."

They were still at least fifteen miles as the raven flew from what he and Tomcat called Last Lake. Tomcat took the plane lower. The polar winds still raged, but at least they weren't flying blind. Snow was falling, but for the moment at least, the flakes were more nuisance than hazard. Below, a line of blue cut through the landscape. Tomcat shifted course to follow the river.

"What are you doing?"

"What do you think? I'm looking for a good spot to land."

"Why put down here?"

"Why does a dog lick its balls? Because it can."

Tomcat pointed to the dense layer of fog spreading out over the landscape. "I want to get down while we can still see. We got thickening pea soup below, seventy-mile gusts, and an Arctic storm chock-full of snow and blow. I'm ready to find any port in the storm."

"We're not that far from the lake. Why don't we just keep flying?"

"Call me fucking foolish, but I feel like staying alive. We're landing at the first fucking good spot we find."

He took the Cessna still lower. They were far enough north that there were fewer big trees to worry about hitting, but there were plenty of hills. "Rock, snow, and ice," Tomcat said, staring at the forbidding world beneath them. "Must feel like a real homecoming to you, Adams. Ask me, it feels like the end of the world."

"I wouldn't call it the end of the world," said Baer, "but you can almost see it from here."

They followed a stream that was beginning to ice up in spots. It opened up into a body of water. Tomcat dropped his plane lower, scanning what looked like a small lake for any stumps or boulders or snags waiting to snare him. Sometimes Alaskan lakes were illusory, more boreal puddles than not. This one appeared to be plenty long and deep.

"She'll do," he announced.

"Did you call a Mayday back there?" Baer asked.

"No."

"So if we'd crashed, no one would have come to our rescue?"

"You crash, you die. Yelling 'Mayday' doesn't change that. If we'd crashed, the emergency locator transmitter would have flipped on, but we wouldn't have been in any condition to care."

"You didn't log a flight plan?"

Tomcat made a disdainful snort and then turned his head and looked curiously at Baer. "Is that worry I hear in your voice, Adams? Is there actually blood in your veins instead of antifreeze?"

Baer didn't answer.

"If we'd crashed," Tomcat said, "they might not have found our bodies for years."

He turned his attention back toward the lake, and the plane began its descent.

* * *

It was another crash with aplomb, but now they were safely down.

"There's no such thing as a bad landing," the pilot announced, the same thing he'd said that morning.

Tomcat cut off the engine, leaving a sudden silence in the cabin. That made the loud thumping coming from the back of the plane all the more apparent.

"What the hell is that?" he asked.

He removed his seat belt and swiveled his body back to get a better view. When he saw the moving duffel bag, his eyes widened.

"I got a bitch in the sack," Baer said. "I'm going to add her to my sled team."

"You stuffed a poor dog in a bag? What kind of sorry bastard are you?"

"She's a mean one."

"You should have gotten one of those kennels, then."

"Didn't have time."

"Let her out."

"I told you, she bites."

"I'll take my chances," said Tomcat. "The poor thing is probably scared out of her mind."

Baer nodded and then released his safety belt. In the same movement, he released the hasp to his leather sheath and silently pulled out his large hunting knife.

CHAPTER FOUR

When Baer finally unzipped the large duffel bag, the afternoon sun was almost played out. Despite that, Nina had to close her eyes and turn her head from what seemed like burning light. As disoriented as she was, it was still a relief to be able to see something other than the confines of a bag. She'd been afraid she would never be free of that body bag.

Baer took out his knife and began cutting away the duct tape binding her mouth, hands, and feet. He ripped off the tape covering her mouth, and some hair with it, and Nina cried out in pain.

"Start moving," said Baer, yanking her to her feet. "That is if you don't want to get frostbit."

Nina swayed, barely keeping her balance, and staggered around. Unevenly she made her way over to the shoreline. In the middle of the lake, a plane was on fire, and she stared at the flames and dark smoke, trying to comprehend what she was seeing. She looked to Baer for some explanation.

"We crashed," he said. "Put these on."

He handed her a jacket, vest, and thermal pants. Numbly Nina obeyed. She was already wearing warm clothing Baer had provided her, but was glad for the extra layering. The garments made her feel as if she were in the midst of a growth spurt; the sleeves and pant legs were too short, but the clothing was thick enough to easily fit over what she was wearing.

Her mouth was dry; her head felt disembodied. She licked her lips and tried to find words. "What happened?" she asked.

"The plane's engine cut out," said Baer, "and the pilot had to do a crash landing. He didn't make it."

The meaning took a few seconds to register. "He's dead?" she asked.

Baer nodded.

"Where is he?"

Baer tilted his head toward the burning plane. "He's getting a Viking funeral."

Nina stepped back from the shoreline as if trying to remove herself from the presence of death. She was getting over her physical shock, but what she saw around her was in no way reassuring. There was no sign of anything human. Around them was a kind of landscape she had never experienced; it looked like a frozen hell.

She hugged herself. "Where are we?"

"About thirty miles away from the drop spot where they're supposed to be leaving the ransom money."

"How—how do they know where to leave the money?"

"I gave them GPS coordinates. A bush plane is supposed to make the drop three days from now. They do as instructed, you'll soon be a free woman."

Nina tried to take all the information in. It was difficult processing what Baer was telling her. Her mind kept drifting, and she didn't like not having control over her thoughts. It was why she'd never really liked drugs or alcohol. But something was nagging at her, something that clamored to be heard over her stupor and all the aches of her body, something that made her feel sicker than she was, even if she didn't understand it yet. She tried desperately to concentrate on the elusive notion of her freedom, tried to anchor her thoughts to that.

"How are we going to make it to that drop spot if it's thirty miles away?"

"We'll have to hoof it a ways. Then we'll ride a raft. Then we'll do some more walking. A dog team'll take us the rest of the way."

Nina tried to concentrate on what he was saying. She raised her hands to her temples, forgetting for a moment her missing ring finger. The movement made her remember, the pain bringing tears to her eyes.

"Shit," she said. "Shit, shit."

The throbbing lifted her lethargy and gave her an adrenaline rush. She turned angrily on Baer and hissed, "You drugged me and put me in a fucking body bag. What the hell is wrong with you?"

Without flinching, without even looking bothered, Baer said, "I had to take whatever precautions were necessary to get you here unnoticed."

"Here?" She gestured around them. "There's no goddamn *here.*"

He said nothing, just stared at her with his hard eyes. She tried to match his stare, but finally turned away. As much as she hated to admit it, she couldn't look at him for more than a second or two without getting scared.

Instead, she studied her bandaged hand and took notice of the blank space where her ring finger used to be. Suddenly all she felt was regret: "They won't be able to reattach my finger."

"Not if you don't do as I tell you. And not if we don't get moving soon."

At her skeptical look, he said, "Don't worry. Like I told you, your finger is on ice. It will keep for a week."

Nina didn't know if that was true or not, only knew that she wanted it to be true.

Baer handed her something that looked like tree bark. "Jerky," he said. "You'll need energy for the walk."

She handed it back. "I already told you, I'm a vegetarian."

"I hope you like eating ice."

He turned away from her and finished up his salvage work. He'd taken everything he could out of the plane. She watched as, using his knife, he gutted wiring and some hard plastic and was able to construct a makeshift sled from the seat and seat covers. Atop the sled he secured a yellow bag stamped "Emergency," a big bag of beans, a few cans, and other odds and ends.

Nina kept turning her head to look around. Never in her life had she been in such a remote spot. There were no roads, no towers, no telephone lines. There was nothing. The silence added to her sense of overwhelming isolation. To her own ears, her ragged breathing was overloud. It sounded as if she were hyperventilating. Maybe she was.

She watched Baer doing his salvaging. No, what he was doing looked more like cannibalizing. *This is my chance to get away*, she thought. But where was away?

"If you're going to make a run for it," said Baer, not looking at her, "I'd head that way."

He pointed to a direction, but Nina couldn't even be sure if it was north, south, east, or west. She'd never really had to pay attention to directions before.

"Where are we?" she asked.

He shrugged. "I couldn't give you a name. This place might or might not have one. You could make a circle fifty miles around from where we now are, and you wouldn't find a single person living within that circle."

"How do I know you're telling the truth?"

"One way to find out," he said, and motioned toward the landscape. "Of course, I'm betting hypothermia will kill you within a day. That is if you don't drown, or if a griz or a pack of wolves don't find you."

Nina didn't want to be scared, but she was.

Baer started pawing through the emergency bag. "Looks like you're in luck," he said. "Our pilot had himself a sweet tooth. He packed himself a stash of big Hershey bars. You want one?"

Nina was already salivating. She went over to him and extended her right hand, holding it out like a beggar might. Baer gave her the chocolate. She used her teeth to tear into the wrapping. It was a Hershey Bar with almonds, and as she bit into it, she thought she'd never tasted anything so good. In moments the chocolate was gone. Nina began licking clean the little bits of chocolate slivers that stuck to her glove. Learning the social graces had been a part of her growing up; her etiquette teachers would no doubt be aghast to see her now. That thought didn't stop her from taking a final lick.

"You better drink up," said Baer.

He handed her a canteen, but instead of doing as he said, Nina sniffed the liquid, seeing if she smelled anything other than water.

He watched her, amused. "It's not drugged," he said.

Nina took a tentative sip, didn't detect anything out of the ordinary, and took another gulp.

"Keep drinking," he said. "You're probably already dehydrated and don't even know it. Our next water break won't be for a while. By the time we stop, it will be colder, and we'll probably have to start a fire to melt ice."

It wouldn't make sense for him to drug her now, thought Nina. He would have to carry her. She tilted the canteen back and thirstily drank.

"There are a few reflector blankets in the emergency bag, some water purifiers, waterproof lighters. He gave us everything we need to survive, including a nice .45 with extra ammo. We're going to set out at an easy pace. I don't want you sweating. If that happens, you better tell me."

"Why?"

"You don't want to get your clothing wet in this country. Your body's already working hard to stay warm, and if your clothing gets wet, it will have to work twice as hard. The wind's going to start kicking up later, and when it does, we're going to be hit by windchill. That's when sweat becomes icicles, and the cold becomes deadly. And that's why you don't sweat."

She nodded.

"It's out there," he said, lips stretched in an unsettling grin. "Can you feel it stalking? Hypothermia is the ultimate predator in these parts. It's the wolf pack that's always on your heels. It's the grizzly who's always waiting in the shadows."

Nina shivered; she wasn't sure whether it was from the cold or his *description* of the cold.

Baer went to get his makeshift sled. He started pulling it behind him, and as he moved, he began reciting the same poem he'd been uttering the first time she'd laid eyes on him:

"There are strange things done in the midnight sun
By the men who moil for gold;
The Arctic trails have their secret tales
That would make your blood run cold;
The Northern Lights have seen queer sights,
But the queerest they ever did see
Was that night on the marge of Lake Lebarge
I cremated Sam McGee."

Nina wondered how long Baer had planned her abduction. Only a handful of people had known about her Fairbanks trip, and there certainly hadn't been any media waiting for her. How was it that Baer had arranged ransom drops, transport, and waiting dogsleds?

He must have known that abducting some rich Alaskan would have been much less problematic. Why had he picked her? Nina's engagement to Terrence Donnelly made her high-profile and a greater risk. Of course, that hadn't stopped the Lindbergh baby kidnappers. Still, by now the Alaskan press, as well as the authorities, would be asking what had happened to her. Terrence would be making her disappearance a state and federal priority.

Things will work out, she told herself. *He'll get his ransom money, and then I'll be free of this nightmare. He will pay for his crime. His ransom money will do him no good.* She would testify against him. She would show the jury where he'd cut off her finger. She would describe her ordeal, and justice would be meted out. Just the thought of her hand made it throb with pain.

Before being abducted Nina hadn't believed in capital punishment—had even argued with Terrence over his position supporting it. She hadn't thought the government should be in the business of murder.

Now she wasn't so sure. An eye for an eye didn't sound so unreasonable anymore, or at least a finger for a finger. The thought of revenge warmed her when nothing else could.

Ahead of her, Baer kept walking. He never turned around.

He was humming now, or maybe just reciting his rhyme, oblivious to the elements. *No, not oblivious*, she thought. He actually seemed to like the cold. It didn't matter to him that it was freezing and that the wind was now gusting.

She had no choice but to hurry after him.

The thin layer of snow had iced up, and with every step, it cracked under her feet. The sun was setting, but there was still enough light to illuminate the bleak landscape.

"What time is it?" she asked.

"You think I carry a watch?" he asked.

When she didn't answer, he said, "It's around six thirty. That's when the sun sets during the fall equinox. It wasn't that many weeks ago when the sun didn't set until midnight. Now the days are getting shorter. Like my father used to say, 'The curtains are closing.'"

Once again Nina began to shiver.

CHAPTER FIVE

Kenny Ryan didn't liked being pulled off a fishing boat, didn't like cops, and didn't like having to cooperate with them. Seated in Hamilton's cruiser, he was making all of that abundantly clear. Hamilton worked him with a stick and then a carrot. Even though they were a two-hour drive away from his jurisdiction in Seward, that wasn't something he'd bothered to tell Kenny.

"Maybe I should lawyer up," Kenny said once again. He'd been dangling that threat from the moment Hamilton had picked him up on the docks.

"If I had something to hide," Hamilton said, "that's what I would do."

"Who says I got anything to hide?"

Kenny had dirty blond hair in need of a premium shampoo. His teeth were yellow and his fingertips brown from chain-smoking. He was skinny and couldn't keep still, was always shaking his knee or tapping his fingers. Hamilton figured him for a meth user.

Even though it was snowing outside, the driver's window of the police cruiser was wide open. Between Kenny's smoking and body odor, the car felt claustrophobic. Hamilton kept the heater running. With the promise of freedom just an open car door away, he figured Kenny might be more inclined to talk.

"You pawned the jewelry, Kenny. It's your ID that's attached to the items. Maybe you knew the jewelry was hot when you bought it, maybe you didn't. Frankly, Scarlett, I don't give a damn. My interest is in the seller, not you."

"If I help you out, what's it worth to me?"

"A lot of goodwill, Kenny. It always helps to have a friend with a badge."

"Shit. Give me cold cash any day over goodwill."

"Help me, give me something to work with, and I'll get you some money from our discretionary fund."

"What kind of money are you talking?"

"A hundred bucks."

He snorted. "That's not worth my time."

"I can also make sure the handling-of-stolen-goods charge that's hanging over your head gets waived."

"You know that's bullshit."

Hamilton shrugged. "How do I know you're not the one who stole the jewelry in the first place?"

Kenny shook his head in disgust. "Yeah, like I would have used my real name pawning the stuff if I knew it was hot." He hesitated a moment, probably considering whether he really could be in trouble, then finally said, "Gizzard was with me. He'll confirm my story."

"Gizzard?"

"Real name's Gifford."

"Address and phone number?"

Reluctantly Kenny gave them to him.

"How do you know Gifford?"

"Giz and me work charters and fishing boats. We string bait, throw chum, untangle lines, shit like that."

"And what is Gifford going to tell me about the jewelry you pawned?"

Kenny looked like he was swallowing something distasteful. He lit another cigarette, inhaled, and made sure Hamilton got a major dose of secondhand smoke.

"That we got it from this guy."

"Where and when did this happen?"

"Five days ago. Bar in Anchorage, a place called Taps. We got to talking with this guy. So he buys us a round, and then he goes another round, and then he pops for a third round. Giz and I both noticed that whenever he went digging for money, some real sparkly jewelry popped out of his pocket."

He took a deep pull on his cigarette; then he emptied his lungs in the cruiser, probably knowing Hamilton didn't smoke. "Anyway, I knew this guy wanted something, but while the drinks were flowing, I wasn't about to hurry him along."

"Describe him," said Hamilton.

"Big guy. Six foot, two hundred pounds. Maybe thirty, but could be younger or older. He had this outdoorsy kind of face with a thick, black beard. That's what Giz called him later: Blackbeard."

"He give you a name?"

"None I'd remember."

"Mention his line of work?"

Kenny shook his head.

"Any marks or tattoos on him, anything about him distinguishing?"

Another shake of Kenny's head, but then he reconsidered: "He was wearing this vest, or half coat, that was the real thing, you know, a tanned hide of some animal and not an L.L. Bean kind of thing. That, and his long hair and beard, gave him an old-time trapper kind of look."

"What did he want from you?"

Kenny took another draw on his cigarette. "Downers. Preferably roofies."

Rohypnol, thought Hamilton. One of the date-rape drugs of choice. "What did he want them for?"

Kenny smirked, offering a mean curl of his lips. "Only one thing roofies is for."

"You get him the drugs?"

"I made a call. Gizzard was the one who went and did the pickup."

"I'll need the name of the dealer."

Kenny balked for a moment and then must have decided he'd already made his deal with the devil. "I think his real name is Decker, but everybody calls him Scratch and Sniff. The Anchorage cops would know him."

"How did you end up with the jewelry?"

"Seller's market," said Kenny. "I said the pills would cost him three bills. He said he wanted to barter some jewelry of his ex-girlfriend's that was worth a few grand. I didn't tell him that I'd already gotten an eyeful of the jewelry. He gets me to take a look at the stuff, and I act like I'm doing him a big favor and offer an even swap for the pills. Blackbeard gets all offended at that, but I tell him I'm broke. He wasn't any too happy about it, but finally agreed to the deal."

"How long did it take Gizzard to get the pills?"

"He was back in less than an hour."

"So while you were drinking with Blackbeard, what did the two of you talk about?"

"He wasn't exactly the talkative sort. He made me sort of nervous the way he kept looking around. And he only nursed one drink the whole time." Kenny offered the last sentence as if the man was guilty of a criminal offense.

"So he was on the alert?"

Kenny nodded and then remembered something. "Damnedest thing," Kenny said. "Out of the blue, Blackbeard tells me they got a rat problem in the bar, and he seems sort of annoyed by it, as if he found a rat turd in his drink. Then he pulls a piece of meat out of his pocket—a little piece of jerky or something—and he tosses it into the corner. All the while I just keep shooting the shit. Giz hasn't come back yet and I don't want this guy taking off, so I've got it going in cruise control, and I figure it's all mellow and everything, when suddenly he pulls out this knife and tosses it all in one motion, lightning quick, but at the same time real casual-like, like it's something he does every day. The knife goes maybe ten yards on the fly and skewers this rat dead center. See, the jerky he'd tossed earlier had drawn out the rat. I'm kind of wondering if I'm seeing straight, 'cuz he's not looking over at the rat and he's not talking about what he's done, but a minute later, when the rat's stopped twitching, he gets up and retrieves his knife. He wipes the blade once or twice on the carpet, then slips the knife behind his belt loop and never says a goddamn word. Gizzard got back not long after that, and we did our transaction, and then he took off."

"You ever see him before or since?"

Kenny shook his head.

* * *

Greg Martin was waiting for Hamilton in his Seward office. The sergeant wasn't surprised to see him. As a courtesy he'd called Martin and left a message that some of his wife's jewelry had turned up in an Anchorage pawnshop. Martin had probably already talked to the Anchorage cops or with AST. He'd likely come to Seward as a last resort. Martin knew Hamilton was still working his wife's disappearance. Everyone else had put it on the back burner.

The two men eyed each other warily. There were still hard feelings between them. Hamilton had never been fully convinced of Martin's innocence in his wife's disappearance. The guy certainly wasn't as squeaky-clean as he'd tried to come across.

Martin wasn't any more enamored of him, he knew. The guy had blasted Hamilton to the press, categorizing him as "Barney Fife." Of course, he hadn't been any more charitable to the Alaska State Troopers, calling them "Keystone Cops." When asked for a comment, Hamilton had replied, "Apparently what Mr. Martin knows about police work comes from old movies and television shows."

"May I sit?" asked Martin, his words more a challenge than a request.

Hamilton gestured to a chair. He hadn't seen Greg Martin in almost two years, but he'd kept tabs on him. Martin had aged; his boyish looks were transitioning to a more adult appearance. Now he was beginning to look his age. At thirty-two, he even had a few gray hairs.

Welcome to my world, thought the forty-eight-year-old cop.

"Thank you for calling me about Elese's jewelry turning up."

Hamilton shrugged. "I told you I would keep you up-to-date with the case if there was any news. I make a point of keeping my word, even though you seemed to have some very public doubts about that."

"Tell me you'd be practicing your best etiquette if your wife was stolen away. Am I still your prime suspect?"

"You're still a person of interest."

"So nothing's changed, right?"

"It looks like your circumstances have changed. Those are some nice threads you're wearing. Around here I rarely see Italian designer shoes."

Instead of hiding the shoes, Martin raised them up for his inspection. "So, what you're really saying is that I've benefited financially from my wife's disappearance?"

"If the Bruno Maglis fit."

Martin laughed. "Would you rather I was wearing sackcloth and ashes?"

"You aggressively pursued a payout of your wife's insurance policy. I heard you threatened to sue them for bad faith to get the money."

"They were looking for any excuse not to pay. And I needed the money after you and your ilk tarred my reputation. No one was very keen on hiring the geologist who was involved with the disappearance of his wife. It's taken me all this time to rebuild my career. And now I'm going to use that insurance money to help find my wife's killer."

Hamilton raised his brows. "How are you so sure she's dead?"

"It's no coincidence that her jewelry has now turned up. The timing tells me it's something more."

"The timing of what?"

"This," said Martin. He waved the copy of the *Anchorage Times* he'd been holding and tapped the banner headline. The typeface was big enough that Hamilton didn't even have to squint to read it. DONNELLY'S FIANCÉE MISSING!

"You're thinking there's a connection between Donnelly's fiancée and Elese's disappearance?"

"My wife's jewelry turns up at the same time Nina Granville goes missing."

"There are a lot of people who think Nina Granville went missing on her own accord."

"Elese went missing in September," Martin said, "and three years later, this woman disappears in September as well. I don't think the timing is a coincidence. The abductor is counting on winter to cover his tracks."

"The abductions happened in different cities," said Hamilton. "Your wife got taken in Seward, and this Granville woman went missing in Fairbanks. As for your wife's jewelry, it turned up in Anchorage."

Martin pointed to the picture of Granville on the front page. "Look at this picture. Nina Granville and my wife could be sisters. They could almost be twins."

"Newspaper pictures always look alike."

Martin shook his head. "I looked up some other pictures of Nina Granville on the Internet. She's a few years older than Elese, but they have the same dark hair, the same blue eyes, the same figure, and they're virtually the same height and weight."

Hamilton reached for the newspaper and looked at the picture of Nina Granville. She was a beautiful woman, no doubt about that. And there was no doubt she looked like Elese Martin—but that wasn't something he said aloud.

"You talked to the suspect who pawned Elese's jewelry, didn't you?"

Hamilton scratched his chin and wondered who Martin's source was. Someone in AST had probably passed on some information just to get rid of him. "I still have an interest in the case," he said.

Elese Martin had gone missing on his watch in his town. AST had taken over the investigation, but Hamilton had never been able to let it go. It stung his pride being painted as a country bumpkin with a badge. He was a good cop.

"What did he say about the jewelry?" said Martin.

"He traded the jewelry to a large, bearded man for pills."

"What kind of pills?"

"Date-rape kind," said Hamilton, "Rohypnol."

Martin sat up straighter. "I'll bet he used those pills on Donnelly's fiancée."

"You're getting ahead of yourself."

"Everything fits: the timing, his trading the jewelry for the pills, the way Elese and Nina Granville look alike."

"That all might just be a coincidence," said Hamilton.

"You don't believe that."

"I try not to jump to conclusions, either," Hamilton said, and then pointedly added, "It's my job to be skeptical."

"Four days ago he got his pills," Martin insisted, "three days ago Elese's jewelry was pawned, and yesterday Nina Granville turned up missing."

"You didn't mention one piece of jewelry," Hamilton said, "and that's Granville's engagement ring. You wear a ring worth a quarter of a million dollars, and you better believe it's going to attract some attention, usually the wrong kind. That might explain her disappearance."

Martin shook his head. "When Elese was abducted, there was speculation that she was taken for her valuables, but since her jewelry just turned up now, I guess we both know that's proved to be bullshit. I don't think this woman was taken for her ring, either."

"The guy who pawned Elese's jewelry said our suspect had a dark beard. He called him 'Blackbeard.'"

"Blackbeard," said Martin, nodding his approval. "Right now Blackbeard is trying to do his Cheshire cat thing. He thinks all he's left behind is his smile. We can't let him get away with it again."

CHAPTER SIX

Nina was used to pushing through pain. In high school she'd discovered distance running and had kept up a running regimen ever since. Endurance was her greatest strength. She was more the tortoise than the hare, able to press on for mile after mile. She tried to run in at least half a dozen marathons every year. The solitary bumper sticker on her car read *26.2*. Other marathoners knew what that signified: the distance of a marathon was 26.2 miles. Quitting wasn't something Nina did, but now she was being pushed to her limit.

They had walked most of the night; Baer said they needed to be at the river at first light. He kept reminding her that if she was to have her finger successfully reattached, they needed to hurry. That had been carrot enough for Nina. But now that she was looking at the raft, she found herself balking. This wasn't a Zodiac, but a platform of spindly trees that had been spliced together.

"You can't be serious," she said.

"It will save us more than ten miles of walking."

"So will a grave."

"She floats like a dream. I built her with a lot of care."

Nina looked disdainfully at his creation and then at the river. Ice was forming at the water's edge, and she could guess how cold the river had to be. "I'm no Huck Finn."

"You'll get on the fucking barge, Cleopatra, whether you like it or not."

His voice dared her to challenge him; unspoken were the consequences of her refusal.

Nina stepped aboard the raft.

* * *

From the shore the current had appeared gentle, but once Nina boarded the raft, her perspective changed. The current was moving much faster than she expected—or liked. Because the craft wasn't watertight, frigid water oozed up through all the cracks. She'd covered her feet and body with the plastic bags Baer had insisted on, but the spray still found a way to get through.

Baer worked to keep them close to the shore. He had a long wooden branch that was in constant motion, whether as a rudder or a pole or an oar. Their passage was mostly calm, punctuated by mad dashes and frothing water. Nina's tiredness staved off her panic more than anything else. She didn't scream when they almost flipped over, even knowing that falling into the cold water could very well mean her death. Overcome by shock and exhaustion, it was all she could do to hold on.

Her senses were already overloaded when Baer began singing "O Sole Mio."

This can't be happening, Nina thought.

They were on a rickety raft fighting the current of an Alaskan river, and Baer was acting like a Venetian gondolier. He stared at her and sang:

"O sole mio
sta 'nfronte a te!

O sole
O sole mio
sta 'nfronte a te!
sta 'nfronte a te!"

Nina knew the tune, but not the words. To hear them here, though, under these conditions was more than surreal. In fact, Nina was sure it was the most bizarre thing she had ever experienced. She wasn't sure whether to laugh or cry. Was she traveling the River Styx with Charon at the helm? Or was this a Marx Brothers film taking place on the canals of Venice?

Baer finished his song. "Hold on," he warned, dipping his pole deep into the water.

He fought the current, pushing and poling, until he brought the raft skidding and clawing atop a gravel bank. Wet and shivering, Nina jumped ashore.

Baer secured the raft and untied the cargo. The bags had somehow survived their journey. He opened up the emergency bag, took out one of the tarps, and spread it on the ground. Then he surprised Nina with some dry socks, gloves, and a sweater.

"Nothing will kill you faster than cold hands and feet," he said. "Get off your wet things while I make a fire."

She removed her socks, gloves, and coat, replacing them with the dry items. It took Baer less than five minutes to build a roaring fire. Next to it he constructed a lean-to from branches and laid out their wet articles of clothing. Nina almost cried tears of happiness when he presented her with a PowerBar. Between the food and fire, she soon nodded off.

* * *

Nina didn't know how long she slept, only that it didn't feel like long enough.

"If you want to get back to the Hamptons," said Baer, "we need to get moving."

Nina stood slowly, trying to hide how unsteady she felt. Since being abducted and drugged, she'd suffered enforced marches, the elements, and dehydration. All of that had left her exhausted. Baer led the way, seemingly effortlessly, pulling behind him his makeshift sled and all their possessions. Nina trudged along after him, following his trail.

The space between them gradually lengthened. Nina's entire body hurt. She was sure she was black and blue all over from being tossed around the cargo hold. Now she knew what it felt like to be tumble-dried.

Each step was more difficult than the last. When she ran marathons, she'd developed tricks for continuing when she didn't think she could. She would imagine some carrot. Maybe it was the idea of a smoothie or mocha iced coffee that she promised herself at the end of the race. Sometimes the idea of a bubble bath was enough, or the mental promise of sitting down to a hot fudge sundae or eating a tub of buttered popcorn.

But her mind and body were both failing her now. She didn't know what lay at the end of this workout, and she was afraid to find out. The promise of reattaching her finger wasn't enough. Her tank was empty, and nothing she could think of could keep her going. She felt like a windup doll running down.

"I can't go on."

Nina wasn't sure if she said the words aloud or just thought them. Only when Baer turned toward her was she sure that she'd spoken.

"It's only another six miles or so," he said.

"Can't," Nina said, coming to a complete stop.

She began sinking into the boggy ground. If she didn't move, if she didn't pull herself out of the muck, maybe the swamplike tundra would just swallow her. The death march would be over.

Even the elements turned against her; it began to sleet. Nina didn't have the strength to bundle up or the inertia to put one of the plastic bags over her head. She was at the mercy of whatever the sky threw at her.

"You need to drink," said Baer. "You need to eat. Your body is shutting down."

He was probably right, but she didn't care. She made no move to drink from her bottle, just continued to stand there, swaying with the wind. As the cold wind blew at her, she wondered if she should let it topple her over to the ground. She'd read somewhere that freezing to death was one of the more pleasant ways to die. Supposedly you just went to sleep and never woke up. She hoped that was true.

"Here," said Baer, thrusting his bottle at her.

She looked at the bottle, but was slow to react, or at least too slow for Baer's liking. He slapped her, and she staggered backward. Nina's face burned, and she could feel the imprint of his gloved hand on her face.

He extended the bottle again, and she took it and started drinking.

"More," said Baer.

Nina methodically drank until she finished all the water, and all that remained was ice.

He took the bottle back and said, "We need to get moving. If we don't move, we'll die."

"I can't," she said. "I need—time."

He could hit her, but it wouldn't make her move. And if he left, she wouldn't run after him. Even death no longer seemed like such a threat.

He studied her. Nina was sure he would hit her again or threaten her, but he did neither. She wished she could be the enigma that he was. She couldn't get a read on her captor; he was foreign to her thinking.

He must have seen something in her that convinced him that neither his blows nor his threats would get her moving. Bending down, he made space on the salvaged airplane door that he'd been using as a makeshift sled for their bags and provisions.

"Get on," he said.

Nina was too tired to know if she was happy or sad that her journey was not yet ended. She sat down, and Baer rearranged some of the items on top of her lap.

"If you don't want to lose your fingers and toes to frostbite," he said, "you better remember to keep wiggling them."

"I already lost a finger," she thought, or perhaps said aloud.

Baer began pulling the sled. Nina curled up, lowering her head between her knees. She didn't want to see. The landscape around them seemed to be endless and endlessly dispiriting. It was hostile and foreign, and it frightened her. She draped her coat around her in hopes of escaping the sleet, cold, and wind, but there seemed to be no position where the elements didn't find her.

Just when she thought nothing could get worse, Baer started reciting his favorite poem:

> "Now Sam McGee was from Tennessee, where the cotton blooms
>   and blows.
> Why he left his home in the South to roam 'round the Pole, God
>   only knows.
> He was always cold, but the land of gold seemed to hold him like
>   a spell;
> Though he'd often say in his homely way that 'he'd sooner live
>   in hell.'"

* * *

The howling awakened Nina from her cold stupor. She'd thought her skin was so frozen as to be insensate to anything, but the primordial cries sent a current up and down her body and made her sit up straight. *Wolves,* she thought. From her sled she looked around, but she saw no pack.

The howls grew louder, and Nina reacted to them, picking up a piece of the salvaged airplane prop and holding it like a spear. Over the howls she heard a wheezing sound, and then realized it was Baer's laughter.

"You never heard dogs before, *cheechako*?" he asked.

"Dogs? But I thought . . ."

When she realized what he was telling her, tears started dropping from Nina's eyes. The dogs meant one thing: her freedom. When they'd set out from the downed plane, Baer had said there would be a dog team waiting for them. They'd made it to the dogs. Everything was going to be all right. She and Baer would ride the dog team to the drop spot, and after he got his money, she would be released.

"Thank God," she finally managed to say. "Thank God."

"It's time you got out of the sled and got your blood flowing," Baer said. "It's another half mile to the dogs."

Nina exited the sled on wobbly legs. She no longer cared how cold she was or how every part of her body hurt. Her nightmare would soon be over, and all of this would be behind her.

She followed Baer into a narrow canyon. It wasn't an easy walk—ice and snow had formed over the trail—but as they wended deeper inside, the way gradually widened. Wind rushed down through the pass, and with it brought the joyous canine chorus. Nina wondered if she had ever heard such excited howling and barking, and the welcoming calls made her feel a little giddy.

"The dogs sound so happy," she said.

"You'd be happy, too, if you knew dinner was on the way and you hadn't eaten in a week."

Nina wasn't sure if she'd heard correctly. Her thoughts were jumbled, and she was still having trouble focusing. It wasn't the drugs anymore—those had to be mostly out of her system by now—but the cold and the circumstances made thinking more difficult.

"The dogs haven't eaten in a week? That's terrible! Why would you starve them like that?"

"There aren't exactly any kennels around here."

"That's no answer," she said, speaking over the desperate howls.

"I wish I had your self-righteousness, but I guess that only comes when you've had a lifetime of privilege. Before I left, the dogs got about twenty pounds of meat each. They ate until they couldn't eat anymore. They had their feast, and now they've had a bit of famine. In the animal world, that's the way it is for carnivores. It's pretty much always been that way for humans, too. But then you're not a carnivore, are you? You're a vegetarian."

To Nina's ear he made it sound like a dirty thing.

"You could have left them dry food."

"I wonder why I didn't think of that. Or I could have left them cake. Next time I'll let them eat cake."

Nina had to bite her tongue. It wouldn't do to engage this psychopath.

"Let's pick up the pace, Marie," he said.

Although Nina tried to keep up with him, it was all she could do to keep Baer in sight. From up ahead he yelled something back to her, but his voice was lost in the chorus of dogs.

"What?" cried Nina.

"Follow my path exactly!" he yelled.

At first she couldn't understand why he wanted her to do that, but that was before she began encountering objects on the trail meant to discourage two- and four-legged trespassers. Any misstep could have landed her on boards out of which poked large nails, what her father had described as "fifty penny nails"—but those seemed to be the lesser hazards. There were waiting steel traps that looked wicked even in the dim moonlight. Falling the wrong way meant potentially losing a limb.

Up ahead she was surprised to see lights being activated by their motions. The lights illuminated the front of a cabin and the outline of a shed. Stacked high along the front of the cabin were piles of cut logs waiting to be used as firewood. Baer was already busily removing plywood boards that barred the entrance to the cabin. The plywood had a porcupine defense: sharp wood screws riddled the board, pointed deterrents to anything seeking entry. The pointed spikes brought to Nina's mind the image of an iron maiden, and she shuddered at that thought.

Baer used a long screwdriver to remove the screws holding up the plywood blockade. He cursed a screw that was giving him trouble, and his invective seemed to scare it into submission. After removing the plywood, he lifted up what looked like a spiked unwelcome mat and propped it against the side of the cabin. Baer reached for the door handle and opened it. Unlike doors Nina was used to, it opened out, not in.

"Hurry it up," he shouted, motioning her to get inside, "before I go deaf."

The dogs were loudly clamoring for dinner.

Nina stepped inside the cabin, and Baer closed the door behind her. Outside she could hear him working on clearing away other nail blockades. Finally the dogs grew quiet; their long-awaited dinner must have arrived.

The quiet made it easier for Nina to think. She tried to ignore the distasteful smells in the cabin, breathing through her mouth so as to not be overwhelmed by the odors. It smelled as if something had died while burrowed deep within the walls. Hopefully they wouldn't have to stay here more than the one night. In the morning they would set out for the spot where Baer's money had been dropped. The sooner he got the cash, the sooner she would be released.

The cabin only had one window, and little of the late afternoon light penetrated inside, leaving the interior shrouded. The space wasn't large—probably not even four hundred square feet. She remembered that Thoreau's cabin in the woods near Walden Lake had only been 150 square feet. Her professor at Smith had said Thoreau had just enough space for a bed, a desk, and three chairs. That was the extent of his furnishings. For Thoreau it had been enough.

Baer's cabin was at least twice the size of Thoreau's, but it still felt small and crowded. Nina was already feeling claustrophobic.

The door opened, and Nina moved back, edging toward a wall. Baer walked to a rough-hewn table in the kitchen supported by a leveled stump. There he lit a match and applied it to the wick of an oil lamp. After adjusting the flow of the fuel, the small cabin was better illuminated.

"Home, sweet home," he said.

A woodstove sat in one corner, but not the kind Norman Rockwell would have drawn. It wasn't made of cast iron as much as it was cast-offs. The sink, if it could be called that, was a big plastic bucket that had once housed detergent. Resting on a shelf above the bucket, a five-gallon rectangular water container fed tubes down into PVC piping that served as a sink faucet.

The kitchen took up about a third of the cabin. The combination living room and bedroom were closest to the kitchen. Instead of a traditional mattress and box spring, a homespun futon with fur blankets and skins covered a wooden support. Next to the bed was a worktable, and lining the cabin wall were apparently the tools of Baer's trade—at a glance, Nina could see snowshoes, traps and snares, stakes, cables, coil springs, knives, brushes, shears, and frames. On another wall hung dozens of hides of all shapes and sizes in the process of being prepared.

Nina had never been inside an abattoir, but she suspected it would have a stench much like that which pervaded the cabin. As a girl she'd read lots of fantasy novels. It would be easy to imagine this place as a troll hole.

The toilet—if it could be called that—also contributed to the stench. The toilet bowl was a five-gallon plastic bucket that hung down in a slot cut out from a homemade chair. Covering that bucket was a toilet seat attached with bungee cords. Everything was out in the open; privacy wasn't a consideration. There was a container that held wood shavings and sawdust. Nina felt as if she'd stepped back into time. She was sure even Ma and Pa Kettle would have had better plumbing than this.

Her look of revulsion appeared to amuse Baer. "There's an outhouse just down the path," he said, "but in the middle of winter, this indoor toilet is somewhat of a godsend. When it's thirty below, this is usually the preferred alternative."

Nina didn't comment. She saw no need to discuss toilets, but Baer continued with his potty talk.

"Toilet paper is another luxury you probably take for granted," he said.

"I doubt whether most people consider toilet paper a luxury."

"The Inuit used snow to wipe themselves," he said. "Most of the year I do as they did. In this climate that makes a lot of sense."

"What makes more sense is proper plumbing. There have been more deaths from untreated sewage than there have been from all the world's wars."

"Is that so?" said Baer. "I guess you know your shit."

Nina ignored his comment and his mocking smile. She shouldn't have said anything. It was better to not engage him. She finished looking around the cabin—not that there was much to see. The area was functional. Everything had its purpose—or multi-purposes. But she had trouble understanding the reason for the enclosed space that abutted two of the cabin walls. The caged structure looked almost like a cell. The pen was constructed of heavy wire mesh and rebar. Maybe it was a holding area for minks and other furred animals. There were no furs in Nina's wardrobe, and there never would be. Maybe that's why she was getting this bad feeling in her stomach.

She could feel Baer's eyes on her, but tried not to acknowledge them. "When will we leave?" she asked.

"Leave?" he said, and scratched his beard as if trying to fathom her question. "I guess you don't know your shit after all."

"What do you mean?"

But at a primal level, Nina was afraid she did know what he meant. Her heart hammered in her chest. She could feel a flush coming over her skin. Every warning sign in her body was activated, every defense mechanism primed.

"You think I don't know how fast Dudley Do-Right would come down on me if I tried to collect ransom money? Besides, what good is money out here?"

"But . . . what about my finger?" Nina asked.

Beneath her terror she knew the answer.

"I threw it out in a field right after I removed it," he said. "I'm guessing a raven probably found it. Or it's being chewed on by some vermin."

She gasped, the hollowness in her stomach making it hard for her to speak. "Why did you lie to me?"

"First rule of trapping: entice the animal into the trap. You played along with me because it suited your wishful thinking. That's why humans are easier to trap than animals. They don't listen to their instincts."

"If you're not holding me for ransom, why have you done this?"

Nina tried to contain the shrillness of her words and hide her desperation, but even she could hear the panic in her voice.

"How have you liked our honeymoon so far?" he asked.

No. This wasn't happening. This was the worst-case scenario she'd been afraid to think about. She needed to keep him talking. She had to play for time, for any advantage. "My idea of a honeymoon doesn't involve abduction, drugging, and mutilation."

"You're right," he said. "It hasn't been a proper honeymoon. We haven't even consummated our marriage yet."

Talk wasn't going to help. Nina backed up, looking around for a weapon.

Baer reached for his belt and loosened it.

CHAPTER SEVEN

Nina awoke with a blinding headache. She gingerly explored her head and found a lump that ran along the left side of her temple. A layer of dried blood extended from her cheek to her chin.

Her nose throbbed. It was swollen and painful to the touch. Baer had backhanded her, smashing her nose. The beating was bad enough; his talking had made it excruciating.

"Women are like foxes," he said. "All you have to do is hit Mr. Fox hard across the bridge of his nose, and he'll stiffen up and fall. That smack to his nose knocks him unconscious. It works like a charm, and it's a useful thing to know. If you hit him just right, you don't damage the goods. Then all you do is break his neck or strangle him. Do it that way and the fox dies without a mark on him."

Nina had resisted his attack with every fiber of her being. With her teeth and nails, she'd lashed out at his eyes; with her feet and knees, she had kicked him. But her struggles had only seemed to excite him that much more. At first Baer just deflected her blows, but when she refused to yield, he began beating her. And then he had told his fox story, hit her on the nose, and knocked her senseless.

With trembling fingers she reached inside her pants. Her insulated pants were loose, uncinched. She felt under her thermal underwear and discovered the stickiness on the inside of her thighs.

She'd been raped. The realization made her stomach heave, and vomit spilled out of her holding pen onto the floor. She threw up until her stomach was empty, but that wasn't enough. She retched over and over, dry heaves, until the tangled knots in her stomach made her feel as if she were on fire.

Her body shivered violently. Rape was something she had never imagined could happen to her. She hugged herself and tried to still her shivering, but she seemed to have no control over herself. Her skin itched all over, and she started scratching. She was dirty, so dirty. She wondered if all the water in all the oceans could ever make her feel clean.

Something moved across her leg, reminding her of Baer's clawlike touch on her skin, and she found herself screaming. Immediately she regretted having cried out. Although it was dark inside the small cabin, there was enough light for her to see Baer's form rise from under furred blankets. She felt the burn of his eyes on her and turned from them.

"What is it?" he said.

Nina fought off hysterical laughter. He had raped her, and he was asking, "What is it?" There were no words for what it was. If she screamed and howled for hours unto days, that might begin to speak to what it was.

She realized he was still waiting for her answer. She wanted to spit. She wished there were some way to adequately show her hatred and defiance. It didn't seem right that Nina should ever again speak to this subhuman. But at the same time, she feared the consequences of her silence. He'd shown what an animal he was. *No, not an animal*, she thought. *No animal would be that brutal.*

"Something crawled over me," Nina said.

Baer nodded. From the corner of her eye, she saw him raise his chin. He was more animal than human the way he listened and then sniffed the air. In the silence she could hear faint sounds coming from within her pen: clicks and small squeaks. In the gloom she saw his lips pull back; it was like watching a jackal smile.

"Shrew," he said. "You can hear it, but even more, you can smell it. A shrew has a musky smell all its own. I hadn't gotten around to cleaning out a mouse nest in your pen, but I'm sure there's no longer a need. That shrew probably made a meal of them days ago and has come around again hoping to find some seconds."

Baer rose from his pallet, naked.

"Thing about a shrew is that it's always hungry. Every day it has to eat its body weight in food, or it dies. Imagine that kind of pressure. It's a part of what makes them what they are. Failure is death."

Nina turned her head. She drew her knees to her chest.

"If there's any source of food, shrews will sniff it out. What they can't see, they make up for in smell. They're pretty much blind as bats. And like bats they got a sonar kind of thing going for them. It helps them find food. That's why you hear that clicking going on."

Baer made his way into the kitchen.

"It's their hunger that makes shrews vulnerable. That's what you use against them, that and their sense of smell—and their nastiness. That's how you get rid of a shrew problem."

She listened to his clattering. She wanted to scream to drown out his voice and the noises of whatever it was he was gathering.

"Ounce for ounce there's no more bloodthirsty creature on the planet. Two or three times I've stumbled on shrews fighting out in the wild. You couldn't pay to see a fight any more ferocious. They jump and twist and bite and shriek and roll around. And what makes it even more interesting is that they often fight to the death. Neither is willing to give or get quarter. They open up cuts all over one another, and there's no resting. You'd think the fights would be short, as fast and furious as they are, but I've seen them last a quarter hour or more. In the end there can only be one victor, and if you've got the stomach for it, you see what the fight was all about. The loser gets eaten."

Nina shuddered. The excitement in his voice—his apparent blood-lust—sickened her. She tried to hide her distaste, tried to hide any expression at all. She wanted to be invisible to him.

Baer approached her cage. He paused to pick up two more items along the way: a key to unlock the handcuffs that secured her holding pen, and a pail full of sawdust. He casually spread the sawdust over her vomit, then unlocked the handcuffs. Nina moved as far away from the opening as possible, but the cage was too small, and she found herself trembling. She was furious at her own weakness, but that still didn't stop her from shaking.

"It's time to *tame some shrews.*"

She was sure he was looking at her when he said that. Even though her head was averted, she felt his eyes on her. Then she heard him reaching inside her cage, and she cowered. Two days ago she would have said with certainty that she was incapable of cowering at anyone or anything.

"It's the simplest of traps," he said. "All you need is a wobbly stick, a bucket, and a pungent piece of meat. Every shrew in and around this cabin—every shrew within a quarter mile of here—is now getting a nose full of that meat. Mark my words: the dinner bell is clanging nice and loud. Mm, mm, mm." He made a smacking sound with his lips.

"For this shrew party, I attached a piece of jerky to the middle of the wobbly stick, and put some caribou meat down in the bucket. Now all we have to do is sit back and watch the tightrope act."

Nina had no intention of watching anything. She kept her head averted from Baer and his bucket. For a minute or two, there was silence. Then she heard him whistling the tune of "The Man on the Flying Trapeze." It was as grating to listen to as his poem. But she would have listened to his poem all night rather than the sounds she was now hearing after something dropped into the bucket.

"They never get as far as the jerky," Baer said. "Shrews aren't very good at logrolling. The wobbly stick gets them every time."

From inside the bucket, Nina could hear the sounds of the shrew tearing into the meat. It ate undisturbed for several minutes, but then Baer began whistling his tune again. Not long afterward, a second shrew fell into the bucket. Within moments it sounded as if war had broken out. Nina would have covered her ears but for fear of that drawing attention to her. She was forced to listen to this fight to the death. And when it was finally over, she had to endure the worst sounds of all: the crunching of bones as the victor began making a meal of the victim.

"In the light of the morning, there will only be one shrew left alive," said Baer, "and lots of little bones. All we have to do is wait a little while for the next one to come along."

Baer stayed around for two more battles, but finally even he grew tired of the carnage. He locked her cage with the handcuffs and then retreated to his pallet. It wasn't long before Nina heard him snoring. Only then did she feel secure enough to let out her pent-up air. Her underarms were soaked. His being near to her was torture.

Nina started at the sound of another shrew dropping into the bucket. Then the horrifying fighting started anew.

CHAPTER EIGHT

All eyes were on Terrence Donnelly as he approached a bank of microphones. The press conference was taking place right at the airport. As Donnelly looked over the gathering, the crush of media quieted down.

The gravity of the situation could be read on the congressman's face. Usually he was the picture of confidence, but now he was clearly hurting. And he was also clearly human.

The congressman looked out to the room. "The woman I love is missing. If I could move heaven and earth to find her, I would. But what one man can't do, one state can. I am calling on all of Alaska to help me find my fiancée."

Donnelly blinked away tears, and then in a husky voice offered a $2 million reward for information leading to the safe return of Nina Granville.

* * *

Deputy Chief of Staff Cody Wood was Donnelly's point man with the Alaska State Troopers, as well as the overall investigation. Since

Nina Granville had first been reported missing, Sarge had maintained constant communication with the authorities. He'd given the Alaska State Troopers a head's-up that the congressman would be offering a reward. AST hadn't liked that idea, claiming they didn't have enough personnel to handle the expected deluge of leads, but Donnelly wasn't going to be deterred. Sarge had told AST that he could bring in private contractors to assist them, but the local authorities had liked that idea even less. They didn't want "mercenaries" on their turf. The higher-ups at AST had also balked at the idea of the Feds taking over the case, although they were already working with the FBI field office in Anchorage.

So far there were no leads, despite media speculation to the contrary. Donnelly hoped the reward money would change that.

* * *

The congressman's media relations director, Marilyn Grant, scheduled several press events. Donnelly was making sure his fiancée's disappearance got maximum airplay. The Chena River was their second stop. Nina Granville had last been seen in the proximity of the river in downtown Fairbanks. Donnelly positioned himself with the river behind him and asked anyone who might have seen anything to come forward. Several hundred people had gathered for the press conference. His bigger audience would be watching on television.

After finishing with his spot, the congressman's inner circle conferred inside of a Yukon SUV. In addition to Donnelly, Marilyn, and Sarge was Chief of Staff Tom Howard.

"I'm afraid we have a potential situation," said Sarge, "that might or might not rear its head during the time we're here."

"Let's assume Murphy's Law is in play," said Howard. Those on staff referred to him as "Doubting Thomas."

"There's a story that hasn't yet broken," Sarge said, "that suggests Nina is a runaway bride."

"That's bullshit," said Donnelly.

"Of course, it is," said Marilyn, "but it's not surprising. What's the basis of the story?"

Terrence was the third Donnelly whom Marilyn had worked for. In appearance she looked like a kindly grandmother; in reality she was as tough as nails.

"Nina made some entries into her tablet," Sarge said. "They were harmless, but I can see how they might be open to misinterpretation. I had AST get me a printout."

He handed the page to Donnelly. The congressman studied the paper and then said, "So what?"

Marilyn and Doubting Thomas quickly scanned the sheet. Entered on it were the words:

Learn to surf.

Go on one of those cross-country skiing excursions where you ski from lodge to lodge, stopping for a getaway in each.

Take scuba diving lessons. Get good enough to look for hidden treasure.

Work to save an endangered species (preferably something cute— is that silly?—yes, but still find something that's cute)

Have kids? I think so, but have only two, and don't start popping them out until I'm thirty-five.

Tango in Argentina.

Participate in an archaeological dig.

Do something that matters.

"How is anybody getting a runaway bride out of what's here?" asked Donnelly.

"You're not mentioned," Sarge said. "Neither is the wedding or the honeymoon. And what she wrote could be interpreted as dissatisfaction with the course of her life. The list could be read as her wanting to go off the reservation so that she could pursue her list of activities."

Donnelly was shaking his head. He wasn't buying it. "How do we even know when Nina wrote this? It could be a long-ago wish list."

"AST was able to determine it was written during her flight to Alaska."

"We can explain it in terms of your honeymoon," said Marilyn, "and future vacations the two of you were planning."

"I don't remember our discussing any of those things."

"Maybe she was hoping to talk you into doing some of those activities with her," said Howard.

Hearing such an explanation from Doubting Thomas didn't sound right to anyone.

"Nina wanted to go somewhere warm and exotic," said Donnelly.

"Still," said Marilyn, "the two of you hadn't yet settled on a destination."

"This by itself is nothing," insisted Donnelly.

Sarge shifted in his seat. His discomfort communicated itself to Donnelly, who said, "You got anything else?"

"I'm sure it's nothing," Sarge said, "but you know how the media is."

"Spare me the soft soap."

"During Nina's flight from Seattle to Fairbanks, she sat next to Mark Cunningham, an executive for ExxonMobil. According to Cunningham, Nina told him she was visiting Fairbanks for pleasure, and not for business."

"Nina was probably just protecting her privacy," said Donnelly.

"Cunningham also said Nina told him she was meeting up with an old college friend and that the two of them would be doing some extended sightseeing. Although she didn't specify the sex of her college friend, Cunningham got the impression that she was meeting up with a male friend, and wouldn't be surprised if it was an old beau."

"Old beau shit," said Donnelly. "Do I need to point out that Nina went to Smith? We're talking about a women-only college."

The congressman shook his head. "This is just the kind of thing we don't need. It's static. It's a distraction. If it surfaces, we have to hit it head-on and discount it. We need to keep everyone's eyes on the prize, and that's Nina. Someone took her. Someone else must have seen something."

He opened his mouth, but then shut it tight. Everyone in the vehicle pretended not to notice his trembling lips.

CHAPTER NINE

It had been the longest night in Nina Granville's life. Even if she hadn't been forced to listen to shrews fighting to the death, she wouldn't have slept. The one surviving shrew was trapped in a bucket, but that wasn't what was unnerving her. The monster who had raped her was only fifteen feet away. All night she'd been thinking about escape and revenge, but was still short a plan for either.

She watched as Baer stretched out his arms and then pushed aside his fur blankets. Nina turned her head from him and pretended to sleep, although she doubted she was fooling him. He was more animal than human, using his senses in ways that reminded her of Caesar, the Granville family's German shepherd. But Caesar was domesticated. Baer was not.

Soundlessly he walked to the door. It was still dark outside, and Nina guessed that dawn was at least an hour away. There was a part of her that wondered if dawn would ever arrive again.

"It snowed," he said, sounding pleased.

The words made it clear he knew she was awake, just as he knew she was listening to him now. "But it will only last for two days at most, so I'm going to have to get the team moving. I need to retrieve whatever provisions are salvageable that survived the drop out of the plane."

Nina wondered if he planned to take her with him. Would it be worse going with him or staying behind?

She listened as he used the toilet, making no effort at propriety. Civilization was an encumbrance to him. Nina pretended not to feel her own pressing bladder. She would not engage him; she would not beg.

"If things go right," he said, "I'll be back within three days."

Baer didn't seem to notice her lack of response, or he didn't care. After a while she heard the sound of sizzling meat, and then smelled it. Since she'd adopted a vegetarian diet, the aroma of cooking meat had lost its appeal for Nina. There were even times when she felt sickened by the odor of sizzling flesh. But not now. The scent of the meat was making her salivate.

Baer seemed to divine her hunger and its cause.

"It's the fat," he said. "When you live in the north, you crave it more than anything else. In the middle of winter, it's what keeps you alive. More than starches, more than carbohydrates, you want the fat. That's where you get your energy. In January we'll be thankful for all the pemmican I've stored away. I used the recipe of the native peoples, half rendered fat and half dried meat."

Nina tried to tell herself it sounded disgusting, but at the moment it didn't. Usually she kept GORP around to snack on—good old raisins and peanuts. And while she wouldn't have turned down a handful of GORP, the thought of it didn't have the appeal of the aroma coming her way.

Baer brought her a hunk of the meat in a pan different from the one he'd cooked in. Nina supposed the battered cookware served as platters and plates, and the canteen he was holding was the water glass.

"Room service," he said.

She didn't move as he unlocked her cage and placed the pan inside the enclosure. Her eyes remained closed, and she tried not to react as he reached inside her pen and removed the shrew bucket with its wobbly stick.

"Just like I told you," he said. "One living shrew and a lot of bones."

She heard the click of a hasp being opened and the rasp of a knife being pulled from its sheath. She tried not to flinch at the angry cry of a shrew being speared, and its last scratching.

"Stinks in life and stinks in death," said Baer. He walked over to the cabin door and stepped outside to dispose of the shrew.

Nina made for the open door of her pen. Her legs were through the opening, but her body didn't follow. Baer walked back inside. Their eyes met, and Nina made a quick retreat back inside of her cage. Baer continued to stare at her. His scrutiny unnerved Nina, and she turned from his gaze. In his right hand, he held his large knife. He must have wiped the shrew's blood off in the snow; only an icy, red residue remained. He cleaned the carbon steel, wiping it on the sleeve of his coat in a stropping motion that Nina couldn't help but find threatening.

"Were you planning on going somewhere?" asked Baer.

"I-I wanted to stretch my legs."

Nina had never been a good liar, and Baer seemed to find her explanation amusing. "So, you wanted to stretch your legs?"

She didn't answer.

He walked toward her pen, and Nina tried to get as far away from the opening—and him—as possible.

"Here's your honey pot," Baer said, replacing the bucket. "Now you got all the comforts of home."

He hadn't yet put away his knife. Nina stared at the sharp blade. It scared her, but looking at him was even scarier. "Before I go," he said, "I'll need a bon voyage. You catch my French?"

"No," said Nina.

"Oh, I think you *parlez-vous* just fine."

"No," she said again.

"I guess you like it rough."

She looked up into his dead eyes. "I guess you must like the idea of dying by lethal injection."

"That's not my idea of death do us part. All you have to do is honor and obey me, and we'll get along fine. I don't give a rat's ass about the love part. And I hate to step on your fantasy, but I've been to this rodeo a few times before, and I'm the one that's walked away from Mrs. Baer, the first and second. Besides, there's no capital punishment in Alaska. How's that for enlightenment?"

She spoke quickly and fiercely, trying to get through to him. "You have no idea how many people are looking for me right now. My fiancé is Terrence Donnelly, Congressman Terrence Donnelly. Terrence and his family have enormous influence. I'm sure he's brought all sorts of resources into play. When you're caught, you don't want to make matters any worse for you than they already are."

"I'm not too concerned, Mrs. Baer."

"I am not Mrs. Baer. I never will be Mrs. Baer. Do you think you can hit me over the head with a club like some kind of caveman and call me your wife? Women aren't property."

"I guess I'm old school. Ever hear the term 'wilderness bride'? That's what you are now, Mrs. Baer. Women used to come willingly, or not so willingly, out to the wilderness."

He closed the space between them. There was no place for her to escape.

"You can make it easy on yourself, or you can make it hard. Out here there's only one law, and that's the law of survival. That's the start and finish of everything. So the question to you is: Do you want to survive?"

"If the cost is submitting to you, then I would sooner die."

"Your choice," he said, and came at her.

Nina tried to claw his eyes, but he grabbed her left hand, crushing her fingers. She screamed, almost blacking out from the pain. That's where he'd maimed her, where he'd cut away her ring finger.

Baer pressed his knife against Nina's throat, but she didn't yield. She bucked and kicked and slapped, but he used his weight to pin her body down, and then he slowly cut off her air supply until she lost consciousness.

CHAPTER TEN

Nina was still seeing stars when she awoke. It was like awakening with the flu. Her thoughts were hazy, her temples throbbed, and her throat burned. It had probably been fewer than two minutes since Baer applied the sleeper hold on her, but that had been more than enough time for him to violate her. The stickiness she felt between her legs told her that much.

Her fog gave her an excuse to not think. She could hear Baer moving around the cabin, preparing for his trip. In her fugue it was like background noise, a television playing in another room. She couldn't be sure if he talked to her or not. There came a time when Nina realized he was gone. His absence took some of the weight off her chest, but at the same time she realized how alone she was.

Living in Manhattan there were always sounds of people on the move. Nina had even invested in a white-noise setup so as to drown out the racket and give her some peace. She'd picked the sound of rain falling. What she'd never considered while living in New York City was the comfort there was in numbers. In a city of more than eight million people, privacy was usually the rarest of commodities. She was used to the encroachment of people; this seclusion scared her.

At first she didn't even know she was crying. Unbidden, the tears streamed down her face. She was acting like Louise, her best friend from Smith. As much as she loved Louise, she tired of her waterworks. She'd cried over everything and anything—the boyfriend who forgot her birthday, the A? on an exam. That wasn't Nina's way. She wasn't stoic and didn't think she lacked sentiment, but she rarely cried and never like this. The tears were nonstop, and she cried without accompanying sounds. She felt broken.

The black dog came on her suddenly. That's what Winston Churchill had called his bouts of depression. Until now she'd never really understood what that meant. She'd never fallen into that hole, that bottomless pit. But now the black dog had opened its maw, and it felt as if it was consuming her.

For half a day she didn't move. The tears stopped and started on their own, and she made no effort to wipe them away. Her spirit was too weighted down; it was as if the switch to her soul had been turned off. She tried to be angry, but she felt too tired to even hate Baer.

Once or twice Nina tried to reach out to God, but her prayers felt futile. There was only the unrelenting blackness that no light could penetrate. She couldn't escape, just as she couldn't escape her cage. The darkness and pain made her yearn for escape, and for the first time in her life she thought of killing herself.

The notion grew in her mind, but she was slow to act upon it—not because of moral qualms or the finality of suicide—but because it was so difficult fighting her inertia to go ahead with it. It was all she could do to consider how she would go about killing herself.

Hanging wouldn't work. The cage was too small for that. And if there was poison in the cabin, it was out of reach. Cutting her wrists seemed the only viable method available, but even that wouldn't be easy. She had no knife, no blade of any sort. She wondered if she could use her teeth to tear into her flesh, but there had to be a better way.

She needed to find a loose screw, or nail, or wire somewhere in her holding pen. There had to be something she could use. But the black dog held her immobilized. As much as Nina wanted to escape her pain, she couldn't muster the will to do it.

It had only been a few weeks earlier when Father Mario had discussed suicide in the Rite of Christian Initiation for Adults class that she and Terrence were enrolled in. Everyone referred to the instruction as marriage classes. Nina was taking them so that she might convert to Catholicism. The Donnelly family hadn't insisted she become a Roman Catholic, but it was clearly something they wanted her to do. Maybe it was lucky she wasn't officially a Catholic yet. The Methodist church she'd grown up in didn't categorize suicide as a sin.

She'd always thought pills would be the way to go, but that wasn't an option. And starving herself would take too long and hurt too much. She wanted to die before the beast returned, before he had a chance to attack her again.

The cabin began to grow incrementally darker. Baer had raped her in the darkness before dawn. The better part of a day had passed, and Nina had barely moved. Night would soon arrive. If she was to search for a way to die, she needed to start looking now.

She sat up and waited for her dizziness to pass. It was almost enough to make her give up and collapse once more into the bedding. Her inertia had relegated her pain into the background, but now it reasserted itself. For a few moments it felt like Baer was beating her again.

She took a deep breath and began her exploration. Baer seemed to have put more time into the building of her cage than he had the cabin. Many of his materials seemed to have come from a salvaged dog kennel. Thick wood reinforced by metal framing, rebar, and mesh wiring extended around three sides. Her jail was roughly four feet high, four feet wide, and six feet long. Baer had reinforced the cell with a second layer of mesh-welded wiring. Nina tried pushing and pulling on the metal pickets, but felt no give in them. She checked for rust pockets or worn metal, but the posts and rails were solidly constructed and evidenced little wear.

The fencing was bolted down into the wooden flooring. Baer used the top of the cage as a storage ledge. The wooden walls of the cabin had been similarly reinforced by rebar and wiring. Baer hadn't skimped on the use of bolts, screws, and nails. There was no escaping his jail, or at least no escaping it while alive.

She needed something sharp. Somewhere in the cage there had to be something that could do the job.

Nina gathered her fur blankets and placed them in one corner of her cell; atop them she put the canteen, chamber pot, and pan of food Baer had left her. In the waning light she began probing the spaces with her fingers. The spaces were too small for them to penetrate. She looked for a weak spot, an area where she might be able to strip the wiring away, but only skinned her fingers in the attempt.

There had to be a chink in the armor. Her uncle had built a custom log cabin on a lake and had talked about the extensive chinking it had needed to keep out the elements. Nina started tapping at the logs, hoping to hear a hollow sound. There had to be some knots or holes or cracks. Maybe she could pull free a length of wood and make a sharpened stake or a daggerlike sliver.

She thought of Dracula. You needed a silver stake to kill a vampire. And then she thought of Baer. Killing him wouldn't require a silver stake, or at least she didn't think it would.

"I could make a stake," she whispered, "and hide it, and the next time he comes at me, I could drive it into his heart."

The idea gave her hope. Maybe there was a way other than killing herself. She continued to tap and pull and claw. She thumped another section of log. The sound was different, as was the feel. Maybe it was the chink in the armor she was looking for. There was some kind of cavity under the wood.

A section of the log gave way, but Nina's excitement faded when she saw what was there. She hadn't exposed a weak spot or the makings of a stake. Just an old caulking tube.

She pushed the tube aside, hoping to find something in the logs she might exploit, but the space was just a natural indentation where the wood was inverted. She continued her search, but something nagged at her, a thought pesky enough to find its way through the dark shroud that enveloped her. Why had the tube been hidden?

Nina picked up the caulking tube and saw it had no bottom. She brought it up close to her eyes. The tube wasn't empty, but rather filled with rolled-up papers. She carefully tried to slide everything out. It was a snug fit, but with a few twists, she was able to free everything. At first glance she was disappointed. The tube was full of trash, or at least that's what it looked like. A bunch of oddments had been stuffed inside: thin cardboard, remnants from sacks, large labels taken from the backs of cans. The entire hodgepodge had been bound together. And then Nina realized that what she was holding were actually paper substitutes gathered from a multitude of sources. The way everything had been put together almost made it look like an art project.

Nina turned some of the curled pages, squinting in the waning light. Writing covered the scraps, too small to make out. She flipped a few more pages. The document was full of drawings, maps, and pages with more writing. She turned the cardboard front cover and was just able to make out the words on the white sacklike paper that made up the booklet's opening page.

"Dear Sister," Nina read.

She brought the manuscript to within three inches of her eyes. What was that second line? Impatiently she tried to decipher what was there. The encroaching darkness made it difficult, and it must have taken her the better part of a minute to decipher the letters and then make words out of them.

Do not kill yourself. You are not alone.

An onslaught of tears fell from her eyes, but at their root wasn't despair but joy. Whether or not the message was meant for her, it felt like it was. The message in this unique bottle had saved her.

With great care she rolled up the document and placed it back inside the tube. Tomorrow at first light, she would read all that was there.

Nina put her cage back in order. Even that small activity left her exhausted. If she was to survive, she had to eat and drink. She reached for the pan with the meat, jerky, and starch. Baer had left her an enormous cut of meat, what her father would have called a Flintstone portion.

She began tearing chunks free and chewing away ravenously. Nina had been a vegetarian for the last six years. But now she was a carnivore.

CHAPTER ELEVEN

"What did you hear?"

Greg Martin didn't even bother to identify himself over the phone. Not that he needed to. Ever since his wife's jewelry had turned up, he'd been pestering Hamilton in person and by phone.

The cop was tempted to say, "Nothing," and then hang up. But that wasn't his way. He was naturally patient and a good listener. Maybe that came from being the oldest of four kids. Maybe it came from being the father of two kids.

"I already told you if anything meaningful turned up, I'd call you. And since I didn't call you, what's that tell you?"

"Was there any footage of Blackbeard?"

"That's a negative. That bar where he had his meet-up and arranged for the roofies has no surveillance cameras."

"What about nearby businesses?"

"It's off by itself."

"Have you talked to the state troopers about the suspected tie-in between Nina Granville's disappearance and my wife's?"

"Lots of people are convinced Nina Granville is nothing more than a runaway bride."

"There was a time when a lot of people were saying the same thing about my wife."

Hamilton thought about his own wife. They'd been married a quarter century. Carrie was his partner. She worked full-time as a dental hygienist and did the lion's share of raising their kids. If Carrie had turned up missing, he probably would have been a lot more obnoxious than Martin had ever been.

"Yes, I've been in contact with the troopers. They've assured me that they're treating Granville's disappearance as a possible abduction, and part of their investigation will be to see if there is any connection between her case and your wife's."

"That sounds like lip service."

"It's not. But AST is stretched thin."

"How many years you think I've been hearing that line?"

AST had 1,300 officers working all of Alaska. In the Lower 48, there were dozens of *cities* that employed more officers.

"Whether you like it or not, the state troopers are officially handling your wife's case and Nina Granville's. They'd have the latest information, not me."

"You're the only cop who seems willing to entertain the idea that both women might have been abducted by the same man."

"If you're trying to flatter me, it's not working. In my book you're still a suspect."

"I can live with that. But if I got away with murder and if all I wanted to do was collect on my wife's life insurance, then why am I doing everything I can to find out what happened to her?"

Hamilton decided to put his full skeptic on display. "It's possible you want to be involved in the investigation to take preemptive action against whatever evidence we've uncovered that might implicate you."

"And so I'm using Nina Granville as a huge red herring by tying her into my wife's disappearance?"

"I don't have the answers as to what you're doing or why you're doing it."

"No, you don't. But your presuming my guilt isn't helping either of us."

Hamilton didn't answer other than to say, "Is there anything else I can help you with, Mr. Martin?"

"Do you know that a private plane went missing a day after Nina Granville went missing?"

"Where did you hear that?"

"I'm a member of the Alaska Airmen's Association, and they sent out an e-mail. They were contacted by the Alaska Air National Guard Rescue."

"I wish a private plane going missing was unusual, but it's not."

On average there were more than five plane crashes in Alaska every year, far more than anywhere in the Lower 48.

"So you don't think it's possible that Nina Granville was abducted and then flown somewhere? Or that the same thing could have happened to Elese?"

Hamilton took a moment to answer. There were certainly precedents in Alaska for killers being pilots. "You think a pilot did the abducting?"

"I don't know," said Martin. "Both the Alaska Crash Database, which monitors all missing planes in Alaska, and the NTSB, don't like giving out much in the way of details to a civilian. I imagine they'd be more amenable to talking to a cop."

"Maybe I'll make a call."

"It's also possible the pilot might not have known what he was carrying."

"That sounds far-fetched."

"I'm a private pilot now," Martin said, "and I'm telling you, if the payload was packed the right way, the pilot could unwittingly have transported human cargo."

"I'll take your word on that."

"This pilot could have been collateral damage. The abductor might have decided to do away with him because he feared he might make some connection with the Nina Granville disappearance."

"You're assuming a lot."

"Isn't that what you're supposed to do when supposed coincidences keep turning up?"

"Like I said, I'll make a call."

"How about letting me come along if you do an investigation?"

"Civilians can't be involved in an investigation."

"Since the pilot lived in the Anchorage area, I assume you'll be having this talk outside of Seward. That means you're outside your jurisdiction, right? Doesn't that make you a civilian?"

"I'm still a cop."

"But if what you're doing is unofficial, there would be nothing to prevent me from coming with you, right?"

"Nothing but me."

"I told you about the missing aircraft."

Hamilton thought about it. "If anything pans out, I'll call you."

* * *

Hamilton still wasn't sure if he should have invited Martin to the interview. As far as he was concerned, it was probably just another wild-goose chase. But it would give him more opportunity to question Martin.

The stop-and-go traffic on Glenn Highway made Hamilton impatient. Their destination was Eagle River, a neighborhood north of Anchorage. The drive wasn't helped by the gray fog and rain. Ahead of them a Ford F-150 honked its horn. The truck's bumper sticker read: WE DON'T GIVE A DAMN HOW YOU DO IT OUTSIDE.

"Most outsiders would never imagine traffic jams in Alaska," Martin said.

It wasn't surprising that the guy had spent enough time in Alaska to pick up the local lingo. When an Alaskan referenced "outside," or the "south," it translated as anything outside the state, but usually referred to the continental United States.

"Still," Martin continued, "this is nothing compared to Seattle. At rush hour the whole city becomes a parking lot."

"What prompted you to become a private pilot?"

Hamilton kept his eyes on the road, but he saw Martin glance over. "Are you interviewing me?"

"Old habits die hard. I'm Javert, remember? Wasn't that what you told the press?"

Hamilton had learned that this Javert was a made-up book character who was rigid, unable to deviate, and fanatical in his apparent delusion—a fictional cop who spent most of his career trying to arrest a good man.

"You remember every insult ever thrown your way?"

"Most of them. So, why did you get your pilot's license?"

"I did it for my job, mostly."

"A trooper I know said that earlier this summer you were flying around the state. It sounded like you were conducting your own investigation."

"I went to a few places and asked a few questions."

"What did you find out?"

"Less than I would have liked."

"I know the feeling."

"You still haven't asked me the question you're dancing around," said Martin.

"Which is?"

"If I'm sure my wife is now dead, then why am I still obsessed with finding out what happened to her?"

"And why are you?"

"Because now more than ever, I want to nail the bastard that took her from me. But I also have this selfish desire to say 'fuck you' to everyone who thought I was involved with Elese's disappearance."

"Am I at the top of your 'fuck you' list?"

"You're up there."

"So you think of yourself as Dr. Richard Kimble?"

"*The Fugitive*—great movie. There's more than a passing resemblance." Martin stretched out his arms as much as he could in the enclosed space. Maybe he was fitting himself for a cross. "But Kimble was arrested and convicted of his wife's murder. I wasn't even arrested, just convicted by the court of public opinion. That stigma still follows me."

When Hamilton didn't respond, Martin said, "No comment?"

"Not one you'd like to hear."

"Go ahead."

"To me it sounds like you have a guilty conscience."

"I do. My wife was stolen away from me, and I didn't do anything about it. That's why I'm trying to do something now, even though it's too late for her."

Martin turned his head to gaze out the window. "I suppose you think that shows even more of a guilty conscience?"

"I don't know."

Both men fell silent as traffic inched forward. After a while Hamilton said, "Robert C. Hansen used to operate in these parts."

"Who was he?"

"Hansen was called the Butcher Baker," said Hamilton. He pulled onto the exit ramp. "He died recently. A lot of people celebrated when they heard that news. I was one of them."

"He was a murderer?"

"I'm pretty sure he was Alaska's most prolific murderer. We know of seventeen of his victims, but he's suspected of a lot more than that.

He had his private pilot's license and flew a number of his victims to his hunting shack on the Knik River."

"How far is that from here?"

"It's only about forty miles north. They found ten or eleven of his victims there. That's where he had his infamous 'Meat Shack.' That's where he raped and murdered. But what was the most horrific were Hansen's cat-and-mouse games with his victims. Deep in the woods he stripped them of their clothes and then gave them a head start. Hansen was an experienced hunter, and they didn't stand a chance. He tracked the women down and killed them. I can't imagine how terrified they must have felt."

* * *

Danni Houston met the two men at the door of her condo, her eyes anxiously moving from one to the other. When Hamilton offered his name and showed his wallet-badge, Danni was visibly relieved.

"I was hoping you were the one I talked to," she said, "but when the two of you showed up all serious-like, I felt like one of those military wives, sure that bad news had just arrived on the doorstep."

She motioned for Hamilton and Martin to come inside, talking the entire time. "I've been jumping every time the phone rings. It's like I want to answer it, but I don't want to answer it, and I'm not sure what to do. I want to hear about Tommy, but only if I know it's good news.

"Take a seat, both of you. Can I get you something to drink? There's coffee ready, and Diet Cokes in the fridge."

Both men declined her offer, and Danni reluctantly sat down on the edge of a chair—perhaps to allow her feet contact with the ground, or perhaps as an indicator of her anxiousness, or a combination of both. Danni was no more than five feet tall, even though her spiked blonde hair added several inches to her frame. She was heavy but curvy, what Hamilton's dad would have appreciatively described as "pleasantly plump."

"I'm afraid we don't have any updated information on Mr. Carter's whereabouts," said Hamilton. "As you know, he remains missing. That's why we're here. It's our understanding that you were one of the last people he talked with before his flight."

"I tried to tell him to call it off," Danni said. "Anyone could see it wasn't a good day to be flying, but Tommy tried making a joke of the whole thing. He said he'd flown on plenty of small dog warning days."

Hamilton nodded. Meteorologists in Alaska sometimes referred to windy days as "small dog warning days." As in, tie down your small dogs if you don't want them blowing away.

"When he flew out, I had this feeling something was wrong. I was in the shop all day—I'm a hairdresser—and that feeling kept growing stronger and stronger. I remember talking about it with some of my clients. That's how I met Tommy, you know. Our salon has these windows that look out on the street, and Tommy said he saw me working and figured the best way to meet me was to come in for a haircut."

Hamilton smiled and nodded again. His calm seemed to have relaxed Danni. She was now sitting comfortably in her chair and no longer looked ready to bolt.

"First time I met Tommy," she said, "he started in on the jokes. I remember he asked me what Alaskan women had in common with a bottle of beer, and when I said I didn't know, he said, 'They're empty from the neck up.' And so I told him I wasn't an Alaskan woman, but was born and raised in Boise. That was my mistake. From that moment on, he called me his 'sweet potato,' 'small fry,' or 'hot patootie.' You ever hear the Meat Loaf song 'Hot Patootie'? That became our song."

"It's a good song," said Hamilton with a smile. "It was in that crazy movie with the drag queen mad scientist, wasn't it?"

"*The Rocky Horror Picture Show*," said Danni.

"That's the one."

From the corner of his eye, Hamilton could see Martin turn and look at him with surprise. He hadn't expected him to know either the song or the movie. Like most people, he had trouble imagining a cop as a human being.

"So, how long have you lived in Alaska?" Hamilton asked.

"Just over a year," she said. "I arrived the July before last. I didn't intend to stay, but everything seemed to click. There were so many men around here, I sort of felt like a supermodel. Of course, that was before I learned what every woman in the state knows: the odds are good, but the goods are odd."

"I resemble that remark," said Hamilton with another smile.

"How long have you and Mr. Carter been going out?" Martin asked. Hamilton was surprised his patience had lasted as long as it had.

"He first sat in my chair about eight months ago," she said. "He came every two weeks for a trim and said he'd never been so well groomed his entire life. The third time I was cutting his hair, he asked me out. Tommy said he'd rather spend money wining and dining me than spend it on his hair."

"Take us back to the morning of Tom's flight," Hamilton said. "Did he say anything about his destination or his client?"

Danni sighed and gave a little shake of her head. "My mama always used to say I had a brain like a sieve. I've never been good at remembering things."

"From what I understood when we talked," said Hamilton, "Tom worked part-time for a private air charter, and he also had his own side jobs."

Danni nodded. "He has some regular runs for Arctic Charter, or as Tomcat calls them, Shark Chowder, but he's only a part-time employee there. Tommy has his own side business. That was how he was able to afford his plane."

"And this last flight was booked through his business, right?"

She nodded slowly. "I think that's one of the reasons he didn't want to cancel. He makes a lot more money doing his private charters. He also knew his client was expecting him, and there was no way to contact him."

"And why was that?"

"His client didn't have a phone, and I guess he was traveling. Tommy had to fly to a meet-up spot they'd prearranged."

"Do you know where that was?"

Danni shook her head. "I do know Tommy had to get up really early. It was pitch-black outside. He said it was going to be a long day for him. That's why he told me he had to be gone before the butt-crack of dawn."

She smiled. "That's how Tommy talks."

"If Tom went to a meet-up spot," said Hamilton, "I assume that means his client wasn't in Anchorage."

"That's right. I'm pretty sure he was flying to a meet-up spot on some lake north of here."

Her face pinched up as she tried to remember more. "A lake near Stalk Meaner. I don't know where that is, but Tommy has nicknames for just about everything and everywhere."

"What do you mean by that?"

"It's like he calls Anchorage Rainchorage, and Fairbanks Square Banks, and Wasilla Meth-silla, and Homer Homeroid."

Hamilton repeated the nickname. "Stalk Meaner?"

Danni nodded her head.

He racked his brain trying to make a connection with Stalk Meaner. "I'm guessing he meant Talkeetna," he said.

"Maybe," said Danni, shrugging. "I've heard the name, but I don't even know where that is."

"As the crow flies, it's fewer than a hundred miles from here. There are a lot of planes that fly in and out from there. It's a popular takeoff spot for glacier flying and flightseeing of Mt. McKinley and Denali National Park."

Martin spoke up again. "Let's assume that was the pickup spot. You have any idea of where their destination was?"

She shook her head and then reluctantly smiled. "I know it's not going to help you, and I know I should be mad at Tommy, but if you'll excuse his French, he said they were flying into Bumfuck, Egypt. That's Tommy for you. He's full of expressions."

"But we can assume they were going somewhere into the bush?" said Hamilton.

"I think so," she said. "Not that Tommy usually calls it the bush. He calls it BFE, or flying into the vagitation, or going into the pubes. Tommy likes his racy talk, but he's all bark. Once I got to know him, I learned his he-man bluster was an act."

"What about this passenger?" asked Martin. "It seems he must have flown with him on multiple occasions. Did Tom tell you his name or say anything about this man's business?"

She shook her head. "I'm not even sure which one of Tommy's passengers this was."

"Let's assume this particular client lives in the bush," said Hamilton. "Do you remember Tom talking about clients who live there?"

Danni made a face. "I know he had runs flying Natives to their villages. And he had some arrangements with hunting and fishing guides. A lot of those guides are pilots themselves, but Tommy flew charters so they could stay working on the ground. There were also teachers he flew, along with government workers and pipeline employees."

She stopped talking, and a thoughtful expression came over her face. "He did talk about one fellow, though. He called him Grizzly Adams."

"Grizzly Adams?" said Hamilton.

Danni nodded. "He's this trapper who lives somewhere in the bush. Tommy said he was a real character."

"In what way?"

"Tommy said he was a survivalist who thought the world was going to hell in a handbasket, and that civilization was on the brink of destruction. I guess that's why he was living somewhere in Bumfuck, Egypt."

CHAPTER TWELVE

At first light, Nina dug out the caulking tube. She listened for any sounds and forced herself to be patient and make sure Baer wasn't anywhere nearby. He'd said he would be gone for days, but Nina knew better than to trust anything he said.

She'd slept little, but still felt better than she had since arriving at the cabin. The black dog continued to weigh her down, but her world was no longer completely dark. All night she'd pondered the words that had seemed almost divinely meant for her. Over and over Nina had repeated them. Even now she whispered, "Dear Sister, Do not kill yourself. You are not alone." It was almost like the words were some magical incantation. They were Nina's spell against the darkness.

With trembling fingers she pulled the packet from the tube. She was nervous. Could she have imagined that message as a form of self-preservation? The timing seemed too coincidental. It was like a suicidal person walking a deserted beach and finding a lifesaving message in a bottle. Things like that didn't happen.

Or maybe she'd find the simpler answer was that the note was simply meant for someone else.

Nina prepared herself for disappointment and opened up the booklet. But then she saw the words. They were just as she'd remembered them. She hadn't imagined them, and she wasn't crazy.

Dear Sister, Do not kill yourself! You are not alone.

Nina reached out and touched the writing, feeling it with her fingertips as if she were reading Braille. The words were written in large, reassuring letters. They welcomed her to turn the page and keep reading.

She did that, turning over the rough-hewn cover, which appeared to have been constructed from a cereal box. The handwriting on the second piece of paper was much smaller and utilized all of the available space. The salvaged paper, she saw, had come from a large bag of flour that had been turned inside out. As Nina thumbed through the booklet, she could see that a number of the journal's pages had come from that same flour bag. The other pages of the booklet consisted of oversize labels that had been carefully removed from their packaging.

My name is Elese Martin, and since you are reading this, it is likely I am dead. I don't want you to suffer my fate. I want you to live.

Right now you're wondering how I knew you were ready to take your life. When the monster took me and when I realized help wasn't coming, I also searched every inch of this cage looking for something sharp to kill myself. Like you, I didn't find anything. I am glad of that now.

This book must be our secret. Don't give the monster any reason to suspect its existence. He is suspicious enough, and hypervigilant. Luckily, our cage is too small for him to enter. He conducts his searches by pulling out the covers and whatever he can reach. Hide the tube in the base of the pen.

When the monster stole me on my honeymoon, I went from the loving arms of my husband, Greg, to being raped by a man I hated. That is what the monster does. He rapes and defiles. The monster says that I am the "second" Mrs. Baer. He says his first so-called wife drowned, but I don't believe that. I think she chose death as her escape.

Reasoning does not work with the monster. Do not waste your breath. These are your only two options: kill him or escape. Or better yet, kill him and then escape. Harden your heart. That is the only way.

The monster has kept me confined for over two years, which is how I know his routines. From the middle of September until approximately the end of February, he lives in this cabin. He moves to his second cabin when the hunting and trapping plays out here, making it his home in March and April. That winter cabin is smaller and even more primitive than this one. He stays there until the breakup, which is when the icy rivers give way to running water. That is when the monster travels to what he likes to call his "summer retreat." It is his fanciful term for a prison he has made out of a long-abandoned military post used during the Cold War. My last two summers were spent in a bunker I think of as an underground dungeon. For weeks at a time, he went off to work summer jobs, leaving me locked up belowground. No one heard my screams.

That is why you must plan your escape now. Leaving from here is your best chance. The monster thinks this spot's remoteness, and the daunting winter, make escape impossible. You can take advantage of that. In the smaller cabin and in the Cold War bunker, there are fewer opportunities to get away.

In the pages that follow, I will provide you with information and maps, and whatever I can tell you about this area. Know thy enemy. And remember that you are not alone. I am with you.

I hate the idea of my family and friends not knowing what happened to me. And I hate the idea that I could not say my good-byes. When you escape, you must be my voice.

Love, Elese.

Nina ran her finger along Elese's signature. She knew it was just her imagination, but the signature seemed to be giving off heat.

It almost felt as if Elese was there with her. As if her secret sister knew her.

Nina turned the page. At its top was the heading RULES OF SURVIVAL.

In precise but tiny handwriting, Elese enumerated those rules:

Your First Rule is to survive. Do whatever it takes. There will be countless reasons to give up and die. None of those matter. You must endure.

The Second Rule is to prepare for your escape. Every day you must learn whatever you can, even if it doesn't seem important. And every day you must be planning. You don't know what it will take to get away. Assume it will take everything.

The Third Rule is to study your enemy. You have to learn what he already knows. You will have to know what he is likely to do. Do not let your hatred blind you. Study his every movement as if your life depends on it. It likely will.

The Fourth Rule is to be unafraid. Fear leads to doubts. Fear leads to inaction. If you believe in yourself, your old life will remain within your grasp.

The Fifth Rule is be ready to act. The right time might be at any time. When planning your escape, do not assume there will be a perfect time or perfect opportunity. An imperfect opportunity might be your best and only chance to act.

The Sixth Rule is to prepare for war. And in order to prepare for war, you must know your own weaknesses, as well as the weaknesses of the enemy. If you are deficient in one area, do your best to improve. Learn how to compensate for your shortcomings, and prepare to exploit his. If the monster is overconfident, take advantage of his hubris. Prepare for war. And in war, if you know what the enemy will do, then plan accordingly.

The Seventh Rule is to respect the land. Do not curse the bitter cold; that's wasted energy. In this environment there are a thousand ways to die. It is up to you to find the thousand and one ways to survive.

The Eighth Rule is that when you get the chance, you must kill the monster. Visualize his death. Consider the many ways in which his death could be achieved. Do not rule anything out as being wrong or something you could not do. When Baer abducted you, he stole your life. If you are to reclaim that life, you must end his.

Nina was only two pages into Elese's book, but her heart was racing, and her hands were damp.

She was thinking about preparing for war.

She was thinking about surviving.

Her eyes ran up and down the page, scanning the eight rules. It almost felt like Moses had come down from the mountaintop with his stone tablets. There was a difference, though. Part of his message was *Thou shalt not kill.*

Nina preferred Elese's message: *Kill the monster.*

She turned to the next page.

CHAPTER THIRTEEN

"It's October."

"Thanks for the news flash, but I have a desk calendar."

"You should have consulted it. You told me you would get back to me in October."

Hamilton was usually able to swallow his anger, but he'd had enough of Greg Martin's attitude. "Today is October first. I didn't tell you I would get in touch with you on the first fucking day of October. I said that after I looked into a few things, I'd get back to you. That was four days ago."

Instead of backing off, Martin said, "We got a real lead. It's the first real lead we've had in three years."

"We're not even sure it's a lead. It could be a coincidence."

"Carter is still missing, isn't he? What did his friends say?"

Danni Houston had provided him with the names of Tomcat's three best friends. He had contacted them to see if he could learn anything more about Grizzly Adams.

Hamilton took a deep breath. He shouldn't have let Martin get under his skin. A few months ago his doctor had put him on ACE inhibitors for hypertension. He hated that he was taking blood-pressure medicine. It made him feel like an old man.

"One friend said Tomcat liked to talk about sex and sports a lot more than he did about his work. And I'm still playing phone tag with another friend. But I did get a few things out of a guy named Canardy, who Tomcat nicknamed Canary."

He tapped his pen against the desk. "According to Canary, on a few occasions Tomcat talked about a big, bearded mountain man who lived in the middle of nowhere and made his living trapping and hunting."

"That's our link to Blackbeard."

"That's not a link. Four out of five men in Alaska have beards."

"That sounds like a made-up statistic."

"It's the statistic of someone who has lived here all his life."

Maybe that was the problem, thought Hamilton. He'd lived in Alaska all his life. Carrie had been brought up in Oregon. Early in their marriage, the two of them had talked about settling somewhere else, but Hamilton had found one reason or another to stay in Alaska. His fifteen-year-old daughter, Dorothy—whom he still thought of as Dot—had already announced her intention of going to college in California.

"What else did this Canary say?"

"He seemed to recall Tomcat calling Grizzly a nut job, and said he was waiting around for World War III. According to Canary, Grizzly told Tomcat the world was 'a red cunt hair' away from being destroyed during the Cold War, and that it was even less of an RCH now."

"I always wondered how that phrase came into being."

"I think we can safely rule out Shakespeare and the Bible."

"Have you looked into the Talkeetna connection?"

"It's a *potential* Talkeetna connection, and no, I haven't had time. I did try to get AST to check on that, but the troopers said they were too busy with their own leads to take a look at it anytime soon. With the reward money that Donnelly is offering, they have more so-called leads than they know what to do with."

"We're onto something. I know it."

"I don't know about that. But I'm still looking."

Hamilton had never stopped working the Elese Martin case. His pride wouldn't let him. Just because he was pretty much a one-man band in Seward didn't mean he hadn't tried to do everything right. He supposed he had a chip on his shoulder, the cop out in the boonies who wanted to believe he was good enough for the big leagues and hadn't blown the case.

"Since you're not getting anywhere with the troopers, maybe you should try and get an appointment with Terrence Donnelly."

"What's the advantage in that?"

"Donnelly has lots of juice. If you can get his point man on board with what we're working on, maybe he can get us the resources we need."

We and us, thought Hamilton. Since when had they become a team? He thought about giving Martin a reality check. They weren't a team. But Hamilton decided not to pull his chain up short.

"I'll add it to the list," the cop said.

"I'm thinking about getting a haircut three days from now. You okay with my stopping by your office afterward?"

It took Hamilton a moment to figure out what he was being told. Martin was going to sit in Danni Houston's chair and ask her questions while she did his hair.

"Long way to come for a haircut."

"Maybe I'll be able to see better afterward."

"It's supposed to be a free country."

"I'll see you Thursday. Put me down on that desk calendar of yours."

"Done," said Hamilton, and hung up.

The cop ran his hand through his hair and realized he could use a haircut himself.

CHAPTER FOURTEEN

Nina turned the page and found herself staring at a familiar-looking eagle at the top of the page. Just above Elese's drawing of an eagle were the capitalized words: YOUR PASSPORT. In one of the eagle's talons was an olive branch, and in the other were arrows.

She flipped through a few more pages and saw that Elese had drawn maps of the surrounding area, complete with field notes.

The day before, Nina had been ready to commit suicide. That had seemed like her only way out. But now she was looking at her passport to the outside world.

Maps usually daunted her—she'd never had a good directional sense. Her father always liked to tease her and say she was directionally challenged. If the sun wasn't rising in the east or setting in the west, Nina usually had no idea of the direction.

But Elese's personality showed itself even in her mapmaking. It wasn't only that she was a talented artist, which she was. With a few strokes of her pen, she gave faces to mountains and substance to rivers. But what Nina appreciated most were the glimpses of her secret sister's humanity. Like a cartographer of old, Elese had indicated the great unknown with the words *Here there be dragons*. And while the purpose of her mileage key was to estimate distances, Nina also had the sense that she wanted her to know that the outside world was within her reach. In the midst of figures, Elese even offered a snapshot into her own heart.

Hunting Shack	13 miles (+/- ~ 2 miles)
Winter Cabin	25 miles (+/- ~ 3 miles)
Manley Hot Springs	50 miles (+/- ~ 10 miles)
Tanana	80 miles (+/- ~ 10 miles)
Summer Bunker	110 miles (+/- ~ 12 miles)
Fairbanks	200 miles (+/- ~ 25 miles)
San Francisco	3,000 miles (+/- ~ 300 miles)
Heaven	(*See* San Francisco)

Beneath the mileage chart, Elese had drawn a side mirror with the caution: *Objects in mirror are closer than they appear (or not!)*. Underneath her drawing she had explained:

I have never been to Manley Hot Springs or Tanana, and had to guesstimate their route and distance on the map. Baer rarely referenced either. He doesn't like to give out any information that might be useful to your escape, or survival, and he will avoid answering questions that might empower you. It will be up to you to listen and fill in the blanks.

It is to his advantage if you are completely dependent on him. If you are reliant on his knowledge and skills, you are not a threat. I often think to the lesson my snow blindness taught me. I didn't immediately make the connection between my getting headaches and having eyestrain and not wearing anything to shade my eyes. It only became clear to me on a day I went snow-blind. The glare burned my retinas. I had to do my own self-diagnosis while stumbling around. It was my mistake for not noticing that Baer always wears hats and sunglasses even on overcast winter days.

The monster is watchful of everything you do. You must be even more watchful of him. Learn from him even if he would prefer you did not.

I would never have known about his hunting shack had we not been caught in a terrible storm while working the far reaches of his trapline. I am not sure if even Baer could have made it back to this cabin under those whiteout conditions, and certainly the shack was much closer to where we were. Baer called it his "any port in a storm," which is what it is. The structure is more of a lean-to than anything and was barely large enough to accommodate us and the dogs, but it served its purpose.

Even though the monster seems uniquely suited to this inhospitable place, he is still cautious. The hunting shack was his insurance policy, as was the older-looking revolver he brought out late at night to clean. He either thought I was asleep or wouldn't notice he had a firearm I had never seen before. Baer is not rash. He is methodical and likes to hold his cards close to his chest. He plays for the advantage and the upper hand. That's why he stashed away a spare gun.

It is also why Baer is vague about directions. He wants you to believe that escape is impossible and that civilization's nearest outpost is unreachable. He won't tell you directions; that's why I've drawn these maps. And he doesn't reveal many of nature's secrets, but I will. Don't thank me, though. My favorite teacher of all time was my seventh-grade science teacher, Miss Bryant. I used to hang on her every word, and she taught me these things:

1. Moss usually grows on the north side of trees.

2. Water generally moves north to south.

3. Clouds and weather conditions typically move from west to east.

4. The stars can provide you with directions. All you need to do is identify the North Star in the sky. It's part of the Little Dipper's handle. Both the Big Dipper and Cassiopeia point to the North Star. Once you locate the North Star, all you have to do is draw a line to the earth. That's true north.

Miss Bryant did not steer me wrong. She won't disappoint you, either.

Your best chance for escape is to get to the Tanana River and follow it east. That will get you to Manley. Once there, you are free!

Although I have not been to Manley, my travels to the winter cabin and "summer retreat" (Baer's words, not mine) familiarized me with much of your route. The Tanana River will be completely iced over in winter. I have only been there after the spring breakup, but I imagine the easiest and straightest way to Manley would be to walk along the ice.

Sometimes even in this remote wilderness, the outside world rears its head. Bush planes are infrequent, but on occasion they fly overhead. You can't expect a pilot to see what he's not looking for, especially in a terrain where it is so hard to stand out. Creating a successful distress signal might be a means for you to escape the monster.

Before we married, my then-boyfriend Greg took me camping and taught me the "rule of three." One of anything is easy to overlook; three of anything stands out. A pilot will take notice of three man-made structures, be it fires, flags, or piles of rocks, whereas he is likely to overlook a solitary signal. The more you can make objects stand out, the better your chance for rescue. Rocks are more likely to be noticed if they're formed into a pattern like a triangle. And when you fashion your distress signals, pick the best possible places to position them. You don't want your markers to be lost in shadows or a forest. If you're trying to catch the eye of a bush pilot, you'll need to try and imagine his perspective. Anything with color is good. You need to make something that stands out from the environment.

And X marks the spot isn't something only found on treasure maps. Greg told me an X signal means that you require medical assistance or help. If you can, make an X using a pile of stones. And make those stones even more visible by using flags or markers.

Of course, if you can kill the monster, your escape becomes easier. You can succeed where I failed. He might seem more animal than human, with the nose of a bloodhound, the eyes of a hawk, and the ears of an elephant, but he still bleeds. He is used to long hunts. If you flee from him while he is still alive, you must find some advantage over him that gives you a chance to successfully escape.

Nina finished reading. Elese had devoted six pages to the Passport section of her book. Nina looked at the entries on the maps. It would be essential to memorize all the landmarks. According to Elese, there were spots in which she would be able to see Denali, allowing her to use the huge mountain as a reference point.

There was so much she needed to learn, thought Nina. All the maps and information felt overwhelming. Escaping from hell seemed all but impossible.

But at that moment Nina noticed something on one of the maps that looked a little off. She brought her eyes closer to see. What was it? Was that a bespectacled figure looking out from behind a tree? It was.

The man peering out of the wilderness looked familiar. And then Nina realized what she was seeing. The cap, glasses, and striped shirt gave him away. Elese had drawn a picture of Waldo.

Nina started laughing. She had found Waldo.

She was in a cell in hell, but still she was laughing even when she had thought she would never laugh again.

CHAPTER FIFTEEN

At the sound of barking dogs, Nina broke into a sweat. Baer had been gone for four days. There was a part of her that had been afraid he wouldn't return—the food he'd left, even the jerky, was long gone, her canteen didn't have much water in it, and her chamber pot was full and needed emptying—but she'd been more afraid at the prospect of his return than of her starving.

Outside she could hear him tending to the dogs. She wiped the perspiration off her face. She didn't want Baer to know how much he scared her. His return made her remember what had happened to Elese. She had written of her plight toward the end of her book. The opening pages had been all about the business of surviving and escaping, but the last few pages had been more personal.

> By now you're wondering why it's taken me so long to attempt my escape. It wasn't only that I needed to learn the lay of the land. Until recently I had the responsibility of my baby.
>
> When I first realized I was pregnant, I didn't think I would be able to love the baby growing in me, but I was wrong. At the time

I thought the only good thing about being pregnant was that the monster stopped raping me. He was afraid he might do harm to his precious child growing inside of me. I expected to hate my baby, but the moment I saw him, I fell totally, completely in love. Baer named him Daniel, but when he wasn't around, I spoke aloud my baby's secret name. He was Denali, which means Mighty One. But mighty as he was and as loved as he was, my baby was called to heaven. When he was six months old, Denali became sick. His skin broke out. I'm not sure if it was a virus that caused his rash, or whether he might have had measles or mumps. When my baby began to burn up, I applied cold compresses and tried to make him drink, but he became worse. I begged Baer to take us to where we could get medical help. On my knees I implored him, but the monster refused.

I was holding Denali when he died. Hours after he was dead, I still held him close. I didn't trust the monster to give my baby a proper burial, and he had to wrench him out of my arms. Baer said he cremated my baby and offered his ashes to the wind, but I don't know if he did. One day I would like Denali remembered with a service. If I do not survive to see to that, I would be most grateful if you saw to it.

He will try to entrap you as he did me, Sister. In his grand delusion the monster sees himself as a patriarch, whose descendants will replenish the planet after its apocalypse. He knows that if you conceive, escape will be that much more difficult. A few times he has spoken of his own mother abandoning her "responsibilities," and he's darkly alluded that she paid the price for that.

After Denali died, I fell into a black hole. I was ready to die. But my captivity has taught me perseverance if nothing else. Had Denali been alive, I might not have chanced escape. My first responsibility was to him. But now it's up to me to gain my freedom one way or the other.

I wish I cared more about whether I live or die. When my boy was alive, I feared for his life more than I did my own, but now it is time for me to leave this place.

The cabin door suddenly flew open. The monster looked at her. "Still alive?" he asked.

* * *

From inside her pen, Nina watched Baer bringing inside all that he'd been able to successfully salvage. Among his finds was the large dog-food vault, which had survived the fall. There were also some bags of beans and rice that had landed more or less intact. Several plastic jars of peanut butter also came out unbroken, a sight that made Nina salivate.

"We might actually have enough food so we're not reenacting the Donner Party this winter," Baer said, "although I wish we had more meat hanging in the wanigan."

Nina didn't respond.

His gaze took in her pen and the pan, which now only had remnants of bone. "I guess you're not a vegetarian anymore. That firm resolve of yours held out for all of what? Did you even make it one day?"

Rule Number One, Nina thought. *Survive.*

"It's good you're not one of those people who die for their principles. Those people don't last here. To survive a winter here, your heart needs to freeze into stone. It's a cold you'll carry to the end of your days."

That thought got him reciting a familiar verse:

"And there sat Sam, looking cool and calm, in the heart of the furnace roar;
And he wore a smile you could see a mile, and he said: 'Please close
      that door.
It's fine in here, but I greatly fear you'll let in the cold and storm—
Since I left Plumtree, down in Tennessee, it's the first time I've been warm.'"

If her heart froze into stone, Nina thought, it might make matters easier. While Baer recited his poem, she thought about Rule Number Eight: *When you get a chance, kill the monster.*

CHAPTER SIXTEEN

While Baer was away, Nina hadn't spent all her time studying Elese's notes. She'd taken the largest bone from the slab of meat he'd left her and had been sharpening it. After rubbing it against the wiring and rebar, it had been honed to a point. It wasn't until she was crafting her weapon that Nina realized Baer had given her the means to kill herself all along.

I never really did want to kill myself.

But killing a monster was another matter entirely.

Nina pretended not to notice Baer's approach to her holding pen. Palmed in her hand was the sharpened piece of bone. She visualized striking him in the eye or the neck, and then striking again and again. *I can't hesitate*, she told herself. *I have to be as brutal as he is.*

As he unlocked her cage, Nina tensed, ready to swing her weapon, but instead of coming after her, Baer simply turned around and walked back to the kitchen. Nina took several deep, steadying breaths. She'd been sure he was going to attack her.

Baer was in the process of making some kind of flour mixture. Between pounding the dough on the counter, he spoke to her: "Empty your honey pot. Any bones go into the food wastebasket."

He pounded more, not bothering to look at her. "I haul everything that doesn't burn to a spot well away from here, especially any food or bones. Those are magnets for animals."

Nina hid her sharpened bone among the furs and then crawled out of her pen. For the first time in days, she was able to stand up. At first her back was tight and resisted straightening out. She did a few quick stretches. *If I don't want to lose strength and flexibility,* she thought, *I'll need to do isometric exercises when I'm confined.* Baer already had a physical advantage over her; it was up to her to not be some cooped-up chicken awaiting slaughter.

At the portable toilet she hesitated a moment, unsure of the routine.

"Dump it in there for now," Baer said, "and rub out your honey pot with sawdust. When you prove yourself, you'll be allowed the privilege of going outside and using the outhouse."

"Where do I wash my hands?"

"There's a bucket in the kitchen, and I'm boiling some more water now. To make sure the drinking water is safe, it has to boil at least three minutes."

As much as Nina didn't want to engage with Baer, she knew Elese was right about her needing to learn all she could.

"Safe from what?" she asked.

"Beaver fever, among other things. You get beaver fever from a parasite that contaminates the water. If you get the fever, it could lay you up for two weeks. Out here that could be a death sentence. So you boil the water or snow."

Nina finished with her chamber pot and then stood there hesitantly. As much as she didn't want to return to her prison, she felt safer inside her pen than standing in the open anywhere near the monster.

He looked up from his dough and eyed Nina's pan and the bone remains inside it. Nina averted her eyes, afraid he might somehow be able to divine what she was hiding in her pen.

"All food remains go in that container," he said, signaling with his head to a plastic storage bin in the corner. "And your honey pot goes back in your *quarters*."

He said the last word as if he were British royalty, and his lip curled up in amusement. Then he added with his mock accent: "Is that where you will want room service delivered, madam?"

"I can carry my own food," Nina said.

Especially if it meant keeping some distance between them.

She carefully dumped the contents of the pan into the bin, eyeing Baer the entire time.

Without turning to look at her, he said, "I have to use up the shortening I salvaged before it goes bad. Biscuits and flatbread will start coming out in about twenty minutes."

Nina could feel her stomach tighten as her hunger asserted itself.

"And then I'll use the hot oven to cook up some sea biscuits."

"What are sea biscuits?"

"Hardtack," said Baer.

"Hardtack like Columbus and his crew ate?" she said.

"Sea biscuits, or edible rocks, as sailors used to call them, were around long before Columbus."

"And that's what you eat?"

"That's what *we'll* eat when food stocks get low. Last April that's about all there was to eat. The dogs survived on it. But even they had trouble chewing up old hardtack, and we're talking about the same dogs that have no trouble snapping caribou bones."

"Why would anyone choose to live this life?" she asked.

"You'll see why," said Baer, "and sooner rather than later. When the shit hits the fan, and believe me it will before very long, the civilized world will go up in smoke. The war games are coming, and those will be the final games for most. Only a few will survive. One day you'll have an appreciation for hardtack, even more than Claude and his pan chocolate."

Nina tried to hide her surprise. She didn't remember mentioning Claude and his pastries to the monster. It must have been something she'd said while drugged. Baer missed very little. She needed to be as vigilant as he was, and more.

"If you want to soften up the hardtack, you can soak it. That way you won't lose your fillings when you eat it."

He gave her a sly look. "But you don't have any fillings, do you? You have thirty-two perfect teeth."

Nina didn't like him knowing that she had no fillings; she didn't like him knowing anything about her.

Baer went back to his work. The top of the makeshift stove was crowded with pots. Steam rose from a vat of boiling water. Next to it were two large pots with lids. Baer carefully lifted the lids and dropped in tins filled with dough.

"You like my dual ovens?" he asked.

Nina didn't respond, but he didn't seem to notice. "The stovetop needs to be nice and hot to get the oven effect," he said.

Her New York apartment had come with a designer kitchen, but Nina rarely cooked. Her Wolf stove and range were both immaculate. That's because cooking eggs and boiling water for pasta was the extent of her culinary repertoire. She couldn't remember whether she'd ever used her convection oven. You would have thought in the three years she'd lived in the same apartment that she would have cooked a frozen pizza, but it was always easier just calling for takeout. Maybe that explained the glistening state of her Sub-Zero refrigerator; it was usually empty save for yogurt and sparkling water. As for entertaining friends, in addition to all her favorite take-out places, she had two caterers on her speed dial.

She watched as Baer mixed flour, water, and salt into a paste. He reached for an old wine bottle that had apparently seen long use as a rolling pin, and rolled out the dough, measuring its thickness by the top of his index finger's fingernail. When he seemed satisfied with the shape and consistency, he pulled out his knife and began cutting the dough into several dozen squares. Next he poked holes into the squares. He used a salvaged plastic dispensing tube, whose point was about the same thickness as a knitting needle. Each biscuit ended up with at least a dozen holes.

When Baer finished with his first batch, he turned to Nina and asked, "You ready to get your hands dirty?"

She tried to hide the unsteadiness in her voice. "I'd rather get my hands clean. It's a wonder I don't have an infection already."

The condemning note came through in her voice, but Baer ignored it. "That wasn't going to happen. I made sure I doused my knife, and your wound, with alcohol and antibacterial soap."

And you cut off my finger while doing it, Nina thought.

He reached up to a shelf and pulled down a small pot. Using it as a ladle, he scooped out some of the water that was already boiling on the stovetop and dumped it into a bucket.

"There's your hot water. And on the shelf over the table is a jar of spruce pitch salve. That's the bush answer to just about everything and anything. It's an antibacterial cleanser, cleaner, and solvent. Dab some of that on your wound if you're worried about germs."

He returned to his hardtack assembly. Even though he appeared to be ignoring her, Nina was wary of potential traps. She made a careful approach to the bucket, skirting the back of the kitchen, before retreating with the bucket and salve in hand.

There was only one actual chair in the cabin, a compilation of cut birch put together to form a tripod. Nina didn't expect much in the way of support or comfort, but was pleasantly surprised the chair wasn't rickety. The wooden seat even had a cushion of fur. As much as she hated to admit it, Baer was one of those people who could manage to build just about anything with only chicken wire and chewing gum. He understood how things worked and seemed to have an innate sense of how to put things together and take them apart.

She carefully removed the dressing on her hand. The bandage hadn't been changed since Baer cut off her finger. Nina tried not to wince; if he was watching her, she didn't want to look weak. No matter what she saw, no matter how awful her hand looked, she wouldn't react and give him the satisfaction of seeing her flinch or look repulsed.

The last of the bloody dressing came off. The wound had no smell—a good thing. An ugly red scab had formed over the remains of her ring finger. Baer had made his cut at the middle joint, leaving about a quarter of her finger.

He left me a stub, thought Nina.

She lifted her hand up, staring at it critically. Enough of the finger remained to house a ring, even her oversize engagement ring. But she knew she'd never put a ring on that finger. That would be like celebrating her amputation. And it would be no more effective than putting lipstick on a pig.

When she was a teenager, Nina had been approached by the first of many model scouts. But modeling held absolutely no interest for her. They tried to entice her with the prospect of big money and exotic shoots, but she wasn't swayed. When one scout pushed too hard, Nina said, "I'm not giving up pizza to be a model."

"You can have your pizza and eat it, too," the scout had told her. "What about being a hand model? You've got the long, tapered fingers; narrow hands; and perfect fingernails we're looking for. And the best thing about being a hand model is that you can eat anything you want."

Nina had heard of people using their hands to make a living, but had never heard of them using their hands that way. She thanked the scout, but she had no interest in being a hand model, either.

Now even that isn't an option, Nina thought.

She dipped her left hand into the water and gingerly started rubbing, being careful to leave the scab intact. The warmth of the water felt luxurious. Nina splashed some of the water on her face and then rubbed her cheeks and forehead. She closed her eyes and could almost imagine herself in a warm, sudsy bathtub.

The aroma of baking biscuits filled the air. No perfume had ever smelled so enticing, and despite her best intentions, Nina found herself drooling like some dog. As much as she told herself that she wanted nothing from the monster, Nina wanted biscuits.

When Baer announced, "Biscuits are out," Nina let a few minutes pass before going to get some. She wasn't going to let him know how desperate she was. Nina stole into the kitchen while Baer was busily making hardtack. She grabbed four of the biscuits and then scurried out. In the living room, she sat with her back to Baer and ate. The biscuits were warm and delicious. Nina was usually a slow eater, but she bolted the food down. In New York she would have eaten the biscuits with butter and honey, but at that moment, she doubted any condiment could have made them taste any better.

When she returned to the kitchen for seconds, Baer said, "Back already?"

Nina's only response was to grab four more biscuits. The second batch went down almost as fast as the first. Once more she ate with her back to Baer, and Nina remembered how their family dog had eaten with his back turned whenever he got into something he shouldn't have. But she wasn't eating on the sly like Caesar had; it just felt that way. The cabin was too small for there to be any privacy.

I've been here less than a week, thought Nina, *and I already have cabin fever.*

There were no books to read, other than Elese's secreted journal. There was no television or radio, no audio or CD player, no tablet or computer. There weren't even playing cards or games. Most of the cabin's contents wouldn't have looked out of place three centuries ago—or in the time of cavemen.

Nina knew she should be following Elese's advice and learning whatever she could, but right now all she wanted to do was digest her meal as far away from Baer as possible.

As she cleaned up the bowl of water and replaced the salve, she looked at her maimed finger. The idea that her ring finger would never again be whole bothered her more than she would have thought. She had the sense that not only had her finger been cut away, but part of her spirit as well.

Before returning to her cell, she looked carefully around for anything she might use as a weapon. The traps had sharp edges, but getting one into her holding pen wasn't a possibility. There were no knives out in the open, and Baer's bowie-size knife always stayed with him. From what she could determine, he even slept with it.

While Baer continued making his hardtack, Nina crawled inside her pen. If only she could lock the door behind her. Nina covered herself in the fur blankets and then felt around for her piece of sharpened bone and clenched it tight.

Sleep was slow to come, but that wasn't surprising with her rapist lurking nearby. Finally she did fall asleep, but not before visualizing several scenarios in which she plunged the sharp bone deep into Baer's eye. It was a strange way to ease into slumber, but at least it allowed her to still her underlying rage long enough to fall asleep.

She awoke sometime later in a panic. It's a nightmare, she told herself, but a nightmare would have been far preferable to what it really was. The nightmare was just starting. Muscled arms had pulled her from her cell and now pinioned her shoulders. As dazed as she was, Nina tried to find her bone.

"Looking for something?" Baer hissed. "Next time you scheme to stick me with a bone shank, I'll cut you with your own weapon and make you squeal. You'll scream even louder than you're screaming now."

Only then did Nina realize she was screaming, but she couldn't stop.

CHAPTER SEVENTEEN

Greg Martin stood at the doorway of Sergeant Hamilton's office, awaiting permission to enter.

"Nice haircut," said Hamilton, and gestured for Martin to take a seat.

Martin took off his sleet-drenched coat and hung it on the coatrack outside of the office. "The calendar says it's October fourth," he said. "Doesn't that mean we're barely into fall?"

"Alaska only has two seasons," said Hamilton. "Winter and construction." He pointed to a coffeepot. "The joe is hot. It's shitty, but hot."

Martin poured himself a mug, took a sip, and winced. "You're right on both counts," he said, and took a seat.

"So, was it worth traveling more than two thousand miles to get a haircut?"

"It was if it helps catch Elese's killer."

"Does that mean you got something?"

"I think our Grizzly lives somewhere in the vicinity of Manley Hot Springs."

"And how did you come to that conclusion?"

"It was something Danni remembered."

"Tomcat told her he was flying there?"

Martin shook his head. "You know how he had his nicknames for just about every city?"

The cop nodded.

"Well, while Danni was doing my hair, I was asking her about the last morning she spent with Tom. I think it was easier for her to do her talking and remembering in the salon. It was clear she was more relaxed there than when we saw her. The only bad thing was that she wasn't able to just blurt everything out because of the other people there. But even that might have worked to my advantage because she started leaning in and whispering in my ear. I kind of felt like her confessor.

"I learned she and Tom made love very early that morning. According to Danni, that put a bounce in his step, and he went around loudly singing a dirty song. I asked her what song, and she told me it was the theme to *Two and a Half Men*. Being familiar with that show, I said I didn't remember any dirty lyrics, and Danni said, 'Well, you know Tommy.' Then she whispered his song in my ears. I think it stuck in her mind because of his choreography."

"The floor is yours," said Hamilton. "Feel free to demonstrate the song and dance."

"I'll pass. But what Tom was singing was, 'Men men men men, Manly Cock Springs men!' Only he apparently cupped himself with his hand when he sang the manly cock springs part."

"And you interpreted that to be Manley Hot Springs?"

Martin looked a little deflated by his tepid response. "Why else would he say 'Manly Cock Springs'?"

"Because men are stupid, and he just got laid, and he probably liked going around waving his hard-on to a song with the word 'manly.'"

"I think you're missing the context. Danni was telling him he should stay put and cancel the flight, and Tomcat was thinking about where he had to fly. That explains his coming up with those lyrics."

Hamilton wasn't convinced. "Or it could explain him extolling his erection."

"Remember what Danni told us about Tomcat giving every place a nickname? Like Fairbanks was Square Banks and Homer was Homeroid, and how we interpreted Talkeetna to be Stalk Meaner? Judging from his wordplay, what could Manley Hot Springs be other than Manly Cock Springs?"

"I don't think I want to conjecture."

"I wouldn't have even known that name if I hadn't been studying maps of the Alaskan interior. Danni didn't even know there was such a place as Manley Hot Springs."

"It's usually just called Manley," said Hamilton.

"You know the place?"

He shrugged. "There's not much to know. I've been there once. I'm guessing a hundred people live there, which makes it one of the major metropolises in the interior. For a long time, it was where the most easterly road in Alaska ended, but now they've begun expanding the road to go another forty miles east to Tanana."

"What kind of hot springs are there?" asked Martin.

"The nonexistent kind. During my visit the locals told me the closest I could come to soaking in a hot spring was paying for a cement bath in this greenhouse in town that was fed by a spring."

"I guess tourists wouldn't be curious to visit a place called Cement Bath."

"You're right about that."

"Tell me about the surrounding area."

"It's pretty much complete wilderness."

"The kind of place a mountain man would like to call home?"

"If you were looking for isolation, you could sure do worse."

"I'm betting that's where he's holed up."

"Even if you're right, you have no idea of how big an area you're talking about. Finding him would likely take a coordinated aerial search."

"I'm ready to fly there when you are."

"I'm talking about a search where you'd need multiple aircraft, or maybe bringing in the air force, and even that might not be enough."

"So, how are we going to make this happen?"

We, thought Hamilton again. The cop still wasn't comfortable with that royal *we*. It had almost been easier when the two men were adversaries.

"*I* need to build a better case than what's currently there, which is what *I* am trying to do."

"What are you working on?"

Hamilton debated whether to answer. If Martin hadn't flown to Anchorage and then driven to Seward, he probably wouldn't have told him anything. But he'd come a long way for his haircut.

What the hell, he thought.

Hamilton raised himself out of his seat and walked to a wall where there was a mounted map of Alaska. He pointed to Talkeetna, which was north of Anchorage.

"I kept wondering if we could be right about Tomcat flying Grizzly out of Stalk Meaner, aka Talkeetna. On the face of it, that just didn't seem to make sense. It's not like Talkeetna is convenient to anything."

His finger settled on a spot in the southern Kenai Peninsula. "But I came to realize maybe that was the point. When Grizzly snatched your wife in Seward, he would have needed to get out of town fast to avoid roadblocks or having his vehicle searched. He probably counted on a two- or three-hour head start, and knew the more distance he put behind him, the better would be his chances of not getting caught."

Hamilton traced a route north with his finger. "As it turns out, Talkeetna is about a five-hour drive from Seward. It was a spot far enough away from where the main search was taking place to avoid any police scrutiny."

He moved his finger up the map, stopping on the city of Fairbanks, and then began tracing a route south. "Talkeetna is also a five-hour drive from Fairbanks, but in the opposite direction. With both abductions

Grizzly's idea would have been to grab the victim and get out of town before anyone noticed.

"Talkeetna would have been a perfect spot for Grizzly to take off from, especially if he was using an unwitting pilot. He even found a way to bypass the Talkeetna airport and any unwanted scrutiny. Three rivers merge in Talkeetna, and there are lakes all around, so floatplanes are a common sight. And if you're looking for privacy, that's the place. Remote camping spots abound, with no one looking over your shoulder. I think it tells you something about the mind-set of Talkeetna that their long-standing honorary mayor is a cat named Stubbs. It's a live-and-let-live community.

"But there was one sticking point to my theory of Talkeetna being where Tomcat and Grizzly met and where they took off from. How was Grizzly able to transport his victims? He either had help from a third party, or he had to be driving some kind of vehicle.

"On a hunch I decided to check on any stolen vehicles found abandoned in Talkeetna. As it turned out, my timing was good. Just yesterday a cargo van was found tucked away among trees on the outskirts of Talkeetna. No one knows how long it's been there, but we do know it was reported stolen in Fairbanks on the day after Nina Granville went missing. That prompted me to do some more digging. I went back and checked on every stolen vehicle dumped in the Talkeetna area in the last five years. As it turned out, there have only been six vehicles abandoned there. And lo and behold, one of those vehicles was found four days after your wife went missing, and five days after it was reported stolen in Anchorage."

"That ties everything together," said Martin. "That puts Grizzly and Tomcat together in Talkeetna."

"I'll be trying to convince AST of that."

"How far is Talkeetna to Manley?"

Hamilton pointed out the two spots on the map. "They're not close," he said. "From the looks of it, I'd say they're about one hundred and thirty miles apart, but that might have been Grizzly's intent from the first. We know how he likes to be far away from any likely search area."

"How far could Tomcat's plane fly without refueling?"

"He was flying a Cessna 185, which has a range of about eight hundred miles, but Carter's plane was equipped with an auxiliary fuel tank that had another twenty-three usable gallons. That means he could have flown close to a thousand miles without refueling. Since the flight from Anchorage to Talkeetna isn't even a hundred miles, he would have had plenty of juice to fly just about anywhere.

"Now, I'm no mathematical whiz, and I don't have a compass and pencil handy to figure out the radius of a circle, but I'm thinking the plane could have flown around four hundred nautical miles in any direction."

With his finger he demonstrated his imaginary circle and then said, "See many villages or towns in that area? This whole space is almost totally uninhabited."

"So what's stopping the troopers from searching in the Manley area?"

"They're not going to devote those kinds of resources on the basis of Tomcat's ditty. We need more."

Hamilton took a seat at his desk and then began rummaging through his in-box until he found what he was looking for. He handed the paper to Martin and said, "These are now being circulated."

A drawing of a heavily bearded man with long, dark hair and hard eyes stared out from the page.

"Yeah, I know," said Hamilton, reading Martin's unenthusiastic expression. "It's generic, but you never know. I talked to the head of Village Public Safety Officer Program, which is the branch of AST that sends troopers deep into the bush. I was promised that everyone associated with the program would get a copy of the drawing, along with a BOLO."

"Someone will have seen something. No one can just disappear."

"I wish I had your optimism," said Hamilton. "But how is it that three women were imprisoned in Cleveland for ten years, with neighboring houses all around, and no one was aware of them being there? And think about what happened to Jaycee Dugard. She was held captive for eighteen years in California, and no one noticed. And let's not forget how Elizabeth Smart was a captive in plain sight.

"Not one of those women was imprisoned in some remote location. They were imprisoned right on Main Street, USA, or close to it, but no one was aware of them.

"If our Grizzly is living off the grid or holed-up in some remote cabin, I wouldn't count on prying eyes or on people asking questions or some witness coming forward."

"So, how do we get someone to come forward?"

"I was thinking of putting alerts out on bush radio," said Hamilton, "and on Trapline Chatter. I'll offer up a description of Grizzly and say that he's wanted for questioning in the disappearance of Tom Carter."

"Why not mention Nina Granville as well?"

Hamilton shook his head. "That would muddy the waters. I want credible leads, not guesswork generated in the hopes of winning the lottery."

"Excuse my ignorance, but what's Trapline Chatter?"

"It's a radio program that broadcasts from North Pole, Alaska. For some of the villages and those in the bush, it's their primary outlet to the outside world. The news is almost like an old-fashioned party line, with everyone getting the skinny about births and marriages and birthday greetings, along with news specific to the bush."

"I better enter it as one of my presets."

"You do that."

"Maybe Grizzly himself will be listening and we'll flush him out. He can't remain the invisible man forever."

CHAPTER EIGHTEEN

"The water's coming! Dig! Dig! Dig!"

Luke furiously scooped out sand to widen their moat. Their sand castle was being threatened by the tide.

The two of them had spent the last hour building their fortress and beautifying it with all the shells they'd collected that morning. Nina joined her brother in trying to save their castle. She flung the sand aside using her pink shovel. Luke was down on his knees moving sand between his legs like a dog.

"Let's pack it up for the day, kids."

"Nooooo," Nina whined, trying to stave off both her father and the tide.

Her mother knew bribery trumped reason: "Let's go for lobster rolls," she said.

Luke stopped his digging. "I want an Italian sandwich," he said.

"We can get both."

Nina slowed her shoveling, but she wasn't quite ready to give up. Or maybe she just wanted her mom to sweeten the bribe.

"Can we get some steamers, too?" she asked. She loved steamed clams dripping with butter and garlic.

"I don't see why not," her mother said. "We're on vacation."

In a place that was far away but much too close, she heard a loud grunt, and then felt a weight roll off of her. Nina tried to hold on to Ogunquit Beach. She didn't want to leave, but she felt the Maine sun disappearing. She tried to hold its rays between her fingers, but it was like trying to hold onto seawater or granules of sand. Everything around her was dissolving.

Nina opened one eye. She was a long way from Kansas and from Maine and from Ogunquit Beach.

"When are you going to learn?" That's what the monster had said while choking her until she passed out. She wondered if one of these times she wouldn't awaken.

If she'd been able to answer him, she would have told him, "Never." As she started coughing, she was glad there was no mirror in the cabin. Her neck had to be black and blue all over.

Elese had written about her own experiences in surviving the monster's attacks and had advised Nina to disappear. It was something she was still working on.

Unless you're pregnant, the monster will continue to force himself onto you. I fought him for months, but that only seemed to encourage him. While passive resistance doesn't stop him, it diminishes his pleasure. He feeds on your terror and rage, so I have learned to withhold that by disappearing.

You probably are confused. How could I possibly disappear? It took me time to learn my disappearing act. At first I worked on disengaging. I pretended he wasn't there. But it wasn't enough to pretend. I had to find a way to vanish. I had to leave behind my body so that I gave the monster my shell and nothing more.

I disappeared, traveling through time. I didn't travel back far, but then I didn't have to. At first I tried to return to Greg, but that wasn't enough of an anchor to keep me grounded. Denali was and is.

That is where I go time and again. To Denali. I hold him and look into his eyes. He's my sanctuary, and we are together again.

I know you have a place like that, a place you can go where there are no monsters.

Nina was still getting used to finding her sanctuary. It meant a journey to the past and the happy memories of the vacations she'd spent with her family at Ogunquit Beach.

Across the room Baer was washing up. Nina didn't have that luxury. She crawled back into her cell, took a rag, and wiped away his ejaculate.

Please, God, she prayed, *don't let me ever be pregnant by this monster.*

Her mother had said it took almost two years of trying before Nina was conceived. Nina hoped her reproductive system would be just as picky as her mother's.

Please, God, she added again.

She thought about disappearing to her childhood vacations at Ogunquit Beach. *Why do I return to my family's love,* Nina wondered, *and not the love of my fiancé?* The answer was one she would have preferred to not think about, but in this cold place, it was yet another cold truth.

* * *

Later she watched Baer getting ready to go out. He held not only a rifle, but a fishing pole. If not for Elese's words, Nina would have gladly slept the day away, but she knew that kind of escape wouldn't help her. If she hoped to escape this hellhole, she needed to familiarize herself with the surrounding area.

"I want to go fishing."

Baer turned toward her. Nina could see his surprise: Usually she refused to speak.

"Do you even know how to fish?"

She and Luke had gone fishing with their father in some of Maine's lakes. Nina had never liked putting the night crawlers on the hook;

her father had always done that for her. Mostly she'd caught bluegills, but she remembered landing one bass. Of course, her father had also removed the hook from the fish's mouth.

Nina nodded.

"You're not crate-trained yet."

She fought off the urge to scream, "I am not a fucking dog!" An outburst wouldn't get her what she wanted.

"With me there we'll catch twice the fish."

Baer seemed to consider that. Nina turned her eyes from his, afraid of revealing what she was thinking.

"I never told you the story about the newlyweds, did I?" said Baer.

Nina shook her head.

"A couple got married after a whirlwind courtship," he said. "On their honeymoon the two of them went out horseback riding. They hadn't gone very far before the woman's horse had a misstep and almost threw her from her saddle. Seeing that, the husband jumped to the ground and walked up to his wife's horse. Staring into its eyes he said, 'That's one!' And then he remounted, and the two of them continued their ride.

"A little while later, they approached a stream, and his wife's horse came to a sudden stop, forcing her to grab the pommel to avoid being thrown. And so her husband did the same thing again. He jumped down from his saddle, went eyeball-to-eyeball with her horse, and with a shake of his finger he said, 'That's two!'

"After he remounted, the couple began riding again. Everything went fine for a while, but then something spooked the woman's horse, and it started bucking, tossing her to the ground. So her husband dismounts and again approaches her horse. 'That's three!' he yelled. Then he pulled out a gun, shot the horse in the head, and it fell over dead.

"The wife is horrified at what's happened. She screams at her husband, 'You murderer, you horrid beast, how could you do such a terrible thing?'

"And he looks at her and says, 'That's one.'"

It's a joke, thought Nina. She hadn't known Baer was capable of telling a joke. But it wasn't a joke as much as it was a threat.

"Do you understand the moral of that story?"

With a voice she hoped was steady, Nina said, "I somehow missed it."

"Bad behavior has consequences. You want to go fishing with me? I'm not sure if you're ready for such an outing. It could be you have ulterior motives. Let's say you try to act on those motives and I catch you trying to do something you shouldn't. What you need to understand is that there are consequences for your behavior. And don't expect a warning shot from me. You won't hear me say, 'That's one.'"

"What consequences?"

"It depends on the crime. If you choose to not listen to me, you might lose an ear. Maybe I'll tell you to go one way, and you'll decide to try and run off in the opposite direction. That might cost you a toe. And what if you attempt to sneak off? I'd have to track you down. I'd have to use my eyes. And because of that, you might have to forfeit one of yours."

His threats hung in the air.

"That's one," he said with a smile. And then, losing his smile, he asked, "Do you still want to go fishing?"

* * *

Nina carried both rods, along with the tackle box. Baer had a shotgun over his shoulder, along with his holstered handgun. They took one of the dogs with them. She had expected the sled dogs would look like huskies or malamutes, but the dog was smaller than either of those breeds. Baer called it an "Indian dog," whatever that was. The dog was a medium-size black-and-white male; his coat was thick, but not wolflike. He was friendly and responded enthusiastically to Nina's petting. Behind them the other dogs howled their disappointment from the fifty-five-gallon metal containers that served as their doghouses.

"You're keeping him from his job," said Baer, not approving of the affection she was doling out to the dog.

He made a clicking sound, and the dog left Nina's side and ran ahead.

"What job is that?" asked Nina.

"He's our bear alarm. It's that time of year for bears to be fattening up for winter, and I prefer they don't do that at my expense."

Nina found herself looking around. She was a city girl and knew about two-legged predators, but this was different. In this place there were things that could kill her, that could make a meal out of her. The cold she felt wasn't only from the frigid air, and she involuntarily shivered.

Still, it was good to be out of the cabin. How long had she been imprisoned? She did a mental count. *It had been at least a dozen nights,* she thought. She'd arrived during a cold snap, and then it had thawed. Since then the days had been getting colder. Frost had developed overnight, and in the early morning the thermometer hadn't gone up much, if any. It felt as if it were in the low thirties, although you wouldn't know it by Baer. He wore only a flannel shirt and looked comfortable.

Nina tried to mentally map their route, but within minutes she was hopelessly lost. It was all she could do to keep up with Baer. He moved with an assuredness that seemed to belie the terrain. The landscape couldn't seem to make up its mind, quickly changing from rocky to boggy to frozen. They passed through a variety of microclimates, going through fog and mist into sun. There were ferns and sedge; stands of spruce and hardwood; and then bottomlands with willow, alders, and aspen. In some spots you could not see the forest for the trees. All of this, and more, was within a mile of their cabin.

Baer came to a stop at a riverbed. Although there was some ice along the banks, most of the river was clear. The far bank wasn't more than a dozen yards away, with the water level ranging from a few inches to several feet.

"In a week or so, this stream will ice up," said Baer, "and it will likely stay that way until May."

May was more than seven months away. It was already cold enough, to Nina's thinking; she couldn't imagine that long of a deep freeze.

While Baer scanned the water, Nina tried inconspicuously to regain her breath. As a runner she prided herself on her conditioning, but it had taken fewer than two weeks in a cage to make her soft. Half an hour of walking had drained her. The physical toll of her captivity was apparent; she wondered about the mental toll.

I can't let him exhaust my spirit, she thought. *I have to stay strong.* Her lips mouthed the words, "Rule number eight." But in her head she could hear Baer saying, "That's one."

"You going to show me how to fish?"

Nina heard the taunt in his voice and saw it in his upturned lip. "I don't even know what we're fishing for," she said.

"That shouldn't stop a master fisherman like you. We're going for grayling. They're like trout, but less picky. They'll take flies, spinners, spoons, or jigs."

"I'll watch you first." *I'll watch your every move*, she thought.

Baer walked over to a nearby willow and placed his shotgun in its crook. The handgun and holster stayed with him, worn low on his hip, his gun ready to grab. There was something about his swagger that reminded Nina of the gunslinger in every western movie.

After opening the tackle box, Baer pulled out what looked like a small white tassel. "White and black jigs usually work best this time of year. All you need to do is thread the jig onto a hook."

In the time it took him to explain, he'd already threaded his jig.

"You want to work with the current," he said. "Graylings like to hole up in pools. Sometimes there are five or six all in the same area."

He pointed to an area twenty yards downstream. "My guess is they're waiting in that calm area that's just before the bend."

Baer cast his line, and it was taken up by the current. "Let it run a bit before you start reeling. You don't want to reel too fast. Just bring it back nice and easy."

He stopped talking; the tight line did his telling. The pole bent slightly; Baer already had a fish on the line. With assured and measured movements, he brought his fish to shore. Then, with his large hand he cradled the belly of the fish to control its thrashing. Using the flat end of his large knife, he smashed the grayling's head. It stopped struggling. With the same knife, he gutted the fish, then threw its entrails into the water. Then he gathered some moss and laid the fish atop it.

"When we catch more fish, we'll string them up and tie them down in the shallows," he said. "You can fish this spot while I head downstream."

Without a backward glance, he took his rod and walked away. Nina divided her attention between where Baer was going and the threading of the jig. When the hook caught on her index finger, she shouldn't have been surprised. She sucked the wound and watched as Baer settled on a spot and began casting.

Was this her opportunity? Baer was fast, but Nina knew she could get to the shotgun before he could. She'd never fired a shotgun, had never fired a gun of any sort, but she could pull a trigger. She knew next to nothing about guns, but she recalled they all had safeties. Had Baer put the safety on? And if he had, where was it located? She wished she'd thought about that during their walk. She should have been more watchful. She should have observed where the gun's safety was. Made casual inquiries about what kind of shotgun it was.

She seemed to remember that some shotguns were designed for big game, and some were used to hunt birds. If only she knew the range of this particular shotgun. Baer was carrying a handgun. Who would be able to shoot the farthest? And how many shells was the shotgun holding? His gun had a magazine. It would certainly have more rounds.

She was tempted to look at the shotgun, but she didn't. If Baer turned around, she wanted it to appear that all her attention was on the jig. But it was odd, wasn't it, that Baer wasn't keeping tabs on her? Of course, he already had another fish on his line, and that seemed to be commanding all of his attention. But it wasn't like him to not take notice of everything she was doing. Even more out of character was his leaving a weapon behind. During her time as captive, he'd made sure she had no access to anything that might be used as a weapon. And he seemed to have preternatural senses about any threat. Baer had known about her sharpened bone. He seemed to know everything she was thinking and even anticipated what her hatred might spur her into doing. Leaving his shotgun behind made no sense. Unless . . .

It's a test.

His back had been to her when he'd walked over to the willow. She remembered him suddenly turning his head, as if seeing or hearing something, and she'd followed his gaze. It was then that she'd heard an unfamiliar sound. Now she guessed that sound was a shotgun shell being unchambered.

He wanted her to go for the shotgun.

That's two, she thought.

He was giving her just enough rope to hang herself.

Nina cast the line, pleased when it actually landed near to where she'd hoped. The shotgun would stay where it was until Baer retrieved it. That was the right move, Nina was sure. But there was a part of her that wondered if her nerves had failed her, and if her inaction was because she was afraid.

Know your enemy, she thought. That's what Elese had written. Nina exhaled pent-up air and suddenly felt reassured. She was getting to know her enemy, and she was certain that Baer wouldn't be so careless as to leave a loaded gun behind.

She reeled in her line and then tried a second cast. As Baer had shown her, she let the current take the jig. After it played out, she began cranking the reel. That's when Nina noticed the pull. There was a fish on the other end of the line.

The exhilaration of the moment was something she hadn't expected. It felt like an electric charge that extended from the line to the rod to her arms. She began reeling and pulling, then forced herself to slow down. It was important she land the fish. She could see it now in the clear water. Colors flashed: hues of pink, blue, and gold. But instead of smoothly bringing the fish to shore, she panicked as the grayling fought back, and she made the mistake of jerking hard on the line. Luckily for her, the yank cleared the fish out of the water, but that wasn't the same as landing it. When the grayling hit the shore, the hook came free from its mouth, and it began thrashing up and down; each flip and flop brought it closer to the water.

Nina fell to her knees and tried grabbing the fish. One moment she had it, but the next it wriggled free.

"No!" she cried.

The grayling was almost to the water. She grabbed a fist-size river rock and pounced on the fish. Before it could make its escape, she brought the stone down on its head, stunning it. The grayling's thrashing slowed, but it still wasn't dead. Nina raised the stone, then brought it down again, this time with killing force.

As she caught her breath, Nina's eyes stayed on the fish. In death its colors were fading. While alive, its speckled belly had looked as if gold dust had been sprinkled over it, but now that orelike sunshine was turning gray. Dead fish eyes looked at her. Nina wasn't sure what she felt.

"Good fish."

Baer's voice came from directly behind her and made Nina start. Not for the first time, she wondered how a big man could move so stealthily. He picked up the fish, made quick work of it with his knife, and then laid it down on the moss. There were four fish in total; Baer had caught two more in that short time.

She watched him as he made his way downstream. He picked up his rod and started fishing again. It was a signal for Nina to do the same. She got to her feet, and only then noticed the mud and blood on her hands. She bent down at the bank and rinsed her hands in the cold water, fighting the urge to pull them out before they were completely clean. Her fingers felt like icicles. She wrung her hands and then blew on them.

Until I escape, Nina thought, *cold hands are just one more thing to endure.*

She picked up the rod and cast her line.

CHAPTER NINETEEN

Nina watched Baer make what he called a "log cabin" for the cooking of their fish. At a spot off the river that was partially sheltered from the wind, he gathered the makings for the fire. Using the pointed end of a rock, he cleared a small depression in the ground. In the hollowed space, he laid down his tinder, which consisted of a layer of moss, bark from a birch, and resin and needles he'd cut from a spruce. Atop the tinder he placed a handful of small, dry sticks.

The logs were next. He'd found a snag and been able to snap off the dead branches. He quickly trimmed the branches with his knife until there were eight pieces of wood roughly the same size.

From his pocket Baer pulled out a black strip of cloth that wasn't even half the size of his thumb. "What's that?" Nina asked.

"Char cloth," he said. "Otherwise known as surefire."

Nina didn't know what a char cloth was, but saw how it worked. Baer struck a piece of flint, and the shower of sparks set the char cloth to smoking. He leaned over and gently blew on the smoldering cloth. With each breath the flame sprouted up higher and higher. Baer added more kindling, and then quickly constructed his log cabin. He put down the foundation of two logs, positioning them right next to the tinder and kindling, and built up from there. There were four stories to Baer's log cabin. From above it looked as if he'd built an elaborate structure for playing tic-tac-toe.

It had been a long time since Nina had eaten from a campfire. She and Luke had thought that few things were more fun than cooking hot dogs over a fire. Nina remembered how they used wire hangers to skewer their franks. The fish was being cooked in much the same way. Baer had speared half a dozen of the graylings with green sticks, laying them out atop the log cabin. Nina was glad for the fire, basking in its warmth.

"Not much fat to a grayling," said Baer. "They cook up quick."

The dog had settled next to Nina. "What's his name?" she asked.

Baer looked puzzled for a moment before saying, "Three."

"What kind of a name is that?"

"It's not a name, it's a number. Each dog has a number. He's Three."

"Why don't you give him a real name?"

"It's as good a name as any, and better than some. This one musher got quite a reputation for giving his dogs some colorful names. You knew when his team was coming down the trail by the laughter of the spectators. Everyone would crack up when they'd hear him yelling, 'Come on, Fuck. Hurry it up, Shit. Faster, Cock. Let's go, Cunt. Pick up the pace, Piss.'"

Nina didn't hide her disdain. "What a shame I missed that."

"Makes Three sound good in comparison, don't it?"

Instead of responding, Nina asked, "Do you even know my name?"

"You're Mrs. Baer the third," he said. "But since you don't seem fond of that, I guess I could call both you and the dog Three."

The dog, hearing its name, looked up.

"Or you can call me by my given name, which is Nina."

"Nina?" he repeated. "It sounds like you already have a number for a name. Doesn't that mean nine?"

She shook her head. "It's a shortened version of a much longer name. But it's also a Native American name. Nina means 'strong.'"

"Strong, huh? I hear Indians used to come up with names based on things that were going on around them. That's why you hear names like Owl Calling and Running Deer. At least that's what my friend Broken Rubber told me."

"What about your own name?" asked Nina. "Is Baer your last name? I can't imagine a mother giving her child the first name of Baer."

Baer's smirk disappeared. He shrugged and didn't answer.

"What's your mother's first name?"

When Baer answered, it wasn't his words, but his tone, that threatened. "Why would you ask about my mother?"

Elese had written that Baer was prickly about the subject of his mother. Nina wondered if she could find a way to use that to her advantage.

"Aren't men supposed to be what their mothers made them?"

"My mother is long dead."

"What killed her?"

"Curiosity," he said.

His threat hung in the air, and neither of them said anything else until Baer announced, "Fish is done."

Unmindful of the heat, he pulled three of the skewers from the makeshift rack. Nina grabbed some leaves and tried to use them like oven mitts. She took hold of one of the remaining skewers, holding on to both sides of the stick as if she were holding a piece of corn between two cob holders. The skin of the fish had flaked away, leaving firm, white flesh.

The fish rapidly cooled, and Nina started pulling the meat from the bones. Two years ago she'd eliminated seafood from her vegetarian diet, but there had been a time when she enjoyed ordering trout *meunière*. Even without the butter, white wine, lemon juice, parsley, and salt and pepper, the grayling was still tasty.

Most of the fish they'd caught weighed in at around two pounds. Nina had thought she wouldn't be able to even finish one, but it wasn't long before she started in on her second. The dog—Nina refused to call him Three, although she hadn't yet come up with another name—had remained at her side, and Nina rewarded him with pieces of the fish.

"Catch," said Baer, tossing the dog the remains of his fish.

Everything disappeared, including the head, bones, and tail.

Nina's breath caught. "The bones," she said.

"What about them?"

"They could pierce his intestines."

Baer threw the remains of his second fish, and like the first, it was inhaled. "Better tell him that. Of course, if he could speak, he'd say you were crazy. My dogs have always eaten up the whole fish, bones and all, and they're just fine. They're not fussy. That's how they're able to survive and thrive. They love entrails and offal; they devour smoked chum and frozen eels. Give 'em a bird carcass, and they'll do everything but thank Jesus."

He took the remaining fish from the fire and started eating. "Dogs gorge because they never know when they'll eat next. In this climate you can learn from them. Eat when you can, and eat as much as you can."

"I'm full."

"There's a lake that's only a ten-minute walk away. We'll catch another dozen fish for the other dogs while we try for a duck dinner."

"Is your rifle for duck?"

"You mean my shotgun? But that's not what you really want to know, is it? What you're really curious about is whether this shotgun could take down a two-legged sort."

Nina said nothing, which only seemed to amuse Baer. "I'd have thought in finishing school, they would have taught you how to be more subtle in asking how you go about killing someone."

"I never went to finishing school."

"You're not a debutante? I kind of feel I've been cheated. You're not as advertised. And here I thought I'd hooked up with a high-society girl, Mrs. Baer."

"Sorry to disappoint you. And I am not Mrs. Baer. I'm engaged to be married to another man."

"Oh, that's right. Some kind of big muckety-muck. How's that working for you?"

"It will work out. You'll see. At this moment I know he's doing everything he can to have me found. It wouldn't surprise me if law enforcement was getting closer and closer to rescuing me."

"Why not angels?" asked Baer.

"What do you mean?"

"I mean if you're going to practice wishful thinking, you might as well go all-in."

"I don't think you understand just how powerful an enemy you've made."

"I don't think you understand I don't give a shit. If you want to think the cavalry is coming, go ahead. Why, is that their bugles I'm hearing now?"

She'd had enough of his goading and turned away.

"Most people can't stand the thought that they're in it all alone," he said. "It's too scary a prospect for them. Almost everyone wants to think there's someone, or something, out there ready to help. But you're just deluding yourself, *Nina*, if you think someone is coming to rescue you."

It was the first time he'd used her name, but Nina was no longer sure if that was a good thing.

* * *

"Stay here with Three," said Baer. "I don't want either of you spooking the waterfowl."

"Down," Baer commanded, and Three sank to the earth. "You stay."

Nina had the feeling he meant the commands for both of them, but she continued to stand while Baer silently stole off. The monster was taking a roundabout route to the lake, which was only several hundred yards off. He kept low to the ground and seemed to be able to cover space in such a way that there were few discernible movements. It didn't take him long before he was lost from sight.

The day had grown colder, and Nina was feeling the chill. She was underdressed for the elements, and the fire was already reduced to embers. As much as she liked the idea of fleeing, she knew she needed to better prepare for her escape. Her survival would depend on that and more.

"He's right that I shouldn't count on others," she told the dog. "Elese said the same thing. I need to be able to survive on my own. And that includes being able to deal with the cold."

She'd already memorized much of what her secret sister had written. She closed her eyes, doing her best to visualize Elese's words.

Of course, it's not enough knowing directions, and which way you should be heading. You must plan for unimaginable cold. Watch how Baer prepares for extreme weather. Take stock of what he puts in his pack. In addition to his knife and gun, he always carries several fire starters, tinder, a poncho, trash bags, and a reflective tarp. When you attempt your escape, you'll need to pack those items as well. They take up very little space, and yet not having them would certainly mean your death. The poncho can be utilized for any number of things—as a raincoat, as an overhead covering, or as a ground cover.

In cold weather you must keep your body off the ground. The more layers you can put between you and the frigid earth, the better your chances for survival. That's one reason for Baer's plastic trash bags. He fills them with leaves, twigs, moss, and anything that might act as insulation.

Before you attempt your escape, you'll need to know how to make a shelter and utilize materials that can offer a break from the wind. That might mean you have to build a lean-to or a snow cave. In those circumstances a reflective tarp not only works as a shield from the wind, but more importantly it reflects heat back to you. You'll want to position it parallel to your fire in order to get as much of its warmth as possible.

Nina opened her eyes. The world around her was just as hostile, but she felt a little more confident. The dog had curled up at her feet, and she leaned down to stroke its nape.

"There are people looking for me," Nina said. "I know it. But like my mom always says, 'The Lord helps those who help themselves.'"

A loud cracking sound split the air. Nina's first thought was thunder, but that was before she heard a rapid succession of the same sounds, one right after the other. Exploding echoes reverberated around the lake, causing an exodus of birds into the air. She watched them flapping their wings in all directions.

"Let's go," she said to the dog.

He whimpered, unsure whether to follow her or to remain where he was as Baer had instructed him. "Come on," she said sharply.

The dog followed her.

* * *

Half a dozen birds were laid out, and Baer was busy working on them. At their approach he stopped his work and scowled.

"Bad dog," he said, his voice low and mean.

The animal cringed and tried to hide behind Nina.

"I told you to stay," Baer said, and started toward the dog.

"I told him to come," said Nina.

"Then you can blame yourself for his beating."

Baer raised his hand and struck the dog, causing it to yelp. He raised his hand a second time, but Nina stepped between man and dog.

"Hit me instead," she said. "He only did what I told him."

Nina closed her eyes as Baer's hand descended. She tried not to flinch like the dog had. But instead of hitting her, he struck the dog again. She wanted to comfort the howling animal, but was afraid that would only make Baer hit him again.

"I need to count on my dogs doing what I tell them," he said. "It could be the difference between life and death. They are not pets. They are not playmates. They serve a purpose. They must respond to my commands. I can't have them wandering off when I need them."

"I won't interfere again," Nina said.

"You had better not, because the next time I'll kill him."

She nodded, and hated herself for her placating posture.

"Since you interrupted my field dressing," he said, "you can help me."

She followed him over to the laid-out birds. One of them had already been butchered, with its parts put away into a plastic bag.

"I got lucky," he said. "I snuck up on a bunch of birds in the shallows. There are hunters who don't think it's sporting to shoot sitting birds. I say if the birds are stupid enough to be flocking together, take advantage of them. Not that it's usually that easy. I was able to get behind a natural blind of skunk cabbage. My old man used to say, 'If you can see the eye, the bird will die.' He was right."

Baer lifted up a bird Nina recognized as a Canadian goose. "To dress this goose, you really don't even need a knife, but it does make it easier to remove the wings."

He sliced away the wings, and Nina fought off queasiness in her stomach. Surprisingly, there was little blood.

"There's a bone in the middle of its breast." Baer demonstrated while he talked. "You feel for that. Once you find it, then it's mostly a matter of peeling away. Pull the skin off the breast area and peel down to the legs. Then you want to take the legs off the bird. You can pull them off or cut them off."

He demonstrated with two cuts of his knife.

"That gets you a thigh and a leg. All that remains is pulling the feathers off, and then you either cut or snap away the feet."

He did his plucking in seconds, and then his cutting. In not much longer than it would take to remove the packaging that came with store poultry, half the bird was already dressed.

"Now you find its backbone," he said, pointing it out. "After that it's simply a matter of pulling the skin back and making a few cuts. Then you remove the bird's neck and pull some feathers."

Nina had always imagined plucking feathers to be an arduous process, but Baer pulled them away from the skin with what looked like minimal effort.

"You want to clean out the cavity. That means pulling out the heart and liver. We'll keep them separate from the rest of the meat. For the sake of space, I'm going to cut out the breastbone and then pull away the meat."

She watched him finish dressing the bird. In a little more than three minutes, it was dismembered and the meat bagged.

"Your turn," he said. "Would you like a mallard or another goose?"

Neither, she wanted to say. During her years of being a vegetarian, she hadn't eaten meat, let alone been involved in its butchering. Her stomach roiled at the thought of having to hold a still-warm animal.

"Goose," Nina said, hoping she might remember some of what he'd just shown her.

"Smart choice," he said. "It's more work plucking out the pinfeathers of a duck."

He wiped his knife clean with moss and then handed it to her hilt-first. Their eyes met, and she read his dare. She was now holding a weapon. Would she try and turn it on him? As tempting as that thought was, Nina knew she had little chance to hurt him. He was on the alert, ready for her to attack.

Her eyes turned to the goose.

"Cut the wings off at the joints," he said. "Because we're doing a quick field dress, we won't be collecting the down. Normally I keep the feathers. I've seen how you like to wrap yourself up in that duck-and-goose-down comforter. Few blankets are warmer. Without that kind of insulation, it would be hard to survive the winter."

She was grateful the knife was sharp. The blade easily sheared away the goose's wings. She did as Baer told her, working as fast as she could, ignoring her bloody hands. It was easier not to think about the way Baer looked at her like she was an animal waiting to be butchered. With a few cuts here and there, anything could become skin and bones.

Like her finger, thought Nina. He had enjoyed describing his expert removal of it. Baer liked his butchery.

"Not bad for a first effort," he said, and extended an open plastic bag her way. "Toss it in."

She did as he asked.

"Knife," said Baer, and she numbly extended it with the blade pointing at him.

He reached under her hand and, with his fingers on the hilt, took the knife from her. "While I make quick work of the rest of the birds, you can be fishing. Look for a clear area to cast. You want to set yourself up where it's open and your line won't get snagged."

* * *

A cold mist hung over the lake. It wasn't quite raining, but the air was thick with condensation. If it had been any wetter, you could have wrung water out of the air. Nina stopped at a puddle to wash her bloody hands. The water was just at the point of freezing over, and it stung her hands. She rinsed them clean and finished the drying by rubbing her clothes. Her fingers were red and puffy, and no matter how much she blew on them, they refused to warm up.

At the first promising spot, she stopped and cast her line. The earlier exhilaration she'd gotten from fishing had vanished. She worked the line slowly. After half a dozen casts, she moved on to another spot, but had no better luck there.

Third time's a charm, she thought, and began walking along the lake frontage. Nina hadn't gone far before being confronted by the sight of huge paw prints. She came to a stop in midstep, and for a moment her leg hovered inches above the ground. A current ran up and down her spine. Only a bear could leave paw prints so large. She found herself unable to move. She'd never considered the expression *frozen in my tracks* as anything other than a cliché, but that was before finding herself in just such a situation.

Baer was fishing maybe two hundred yards from where she stood. He had the shotgun and handgun. Nina studied the area around her. She had no idea whether or not the prints were recent. She took a few deep breaths and began backing away. She made sure she was going in the opposite direction of where the bear's tracks had been heading.

What if the bear were watching her now? What if it was sizing her up as a meal? Before her arrival in Alaska, Nina had always felt so in control. She'd had command over her life, or at least that's the way it had seemed. Now it was all she could do to survive another day. In this place, in these circumstances, she wasn't even at the top of the food chain. That was a scary thought. She was out of her element, and vulnerable in an environment where missteps meant death.

Nina continued walking backward along the river. Baer and the dog were closer now. As far as she was concerned, they'd already caught and killed enough creatures for a day, but Baer was following the ant's advice and not the grasshopper's. He was preparing for winter.

The sooner they caught enough fish, she knew, the sooner they'd leave. She faced the river and cast a line, and immediately felt a bite on the end. Her luck seemed to have changed. She began reeling her line in. When she finally landed the fish, she felt more relief than excitement.

Fishing wasn't the same when you had to worry that you might be part of another creature's menu. She scanned the area around her for a weapon. She was pretty sure a rock wouldn't stop a charging bear, but that wasn't the purpose for it she had in mind. In the American Museum of Natural History in New York, she'd seen stone tomahawks on display. That's the kind of rock she wanted, a weapon that could bludgeon as well as cut. Finally, close to the riverbank, she spotted the perfect stone. It was as big as her hand, with a wicked-looking edge. By itself, the rock was an effective weapon. If she could find a way to secure it to a branch, she would have her tomahawk.

She made sure Baer wasn't looking her way when she picked up the rock. It was heavy, weighing several pounds. She slid the stone into her pocket; the coat was bulky enough to hide her contraband.

Then she went back to her fishing. The cold sliced into her hands and made it difficult for her to hold onto the rod. Baer was still within shouting distance, but had kept moving away from her along the shoreline. She'd seen him pull in a number of fish; she hoped they were almost done.

Nina cast her line, and after only a moment felt a tug. She tried to reel in her catch, but her frozen fingers only seemed to work in fits and starts, and the motion was much jerkier than she would have liked. Somehow, though, she managed to bring the fish to shore. She grabbed a river rock and brought it down on the grayling's head. She still wasn't comfortable with the killing, but had grown better at it, and was glad when the flopping stopped. She huddled over her catch, blowing on her fingers. It was getting cold enough that she could now see her breath. A shadow slid over the fish. Her head twisted back. That's when she saw the knife.

Nina's scream didn't quite emerge from her throat; it was choked off when she realized the knife wasn't meant for her.

Baer picked up the fish she'd caught, quickly gutted them, and then added them to his string.

"There are bear tracks that way," said Nina, pointing in the direction from which she'd come. "They're less than a quarter of a mile away."

He gave her a dismissive look and said, "There are bear tracks a lot closer than that."

"You saw them?"

"How could anyone have missed them?"

"Why didn't you warn me?"

"You want a warning? Here it is. There's always something out there. And you especially need to watch out for vegetarians. Every year moose hurt and kill a lot more people than bears."

She didn't know if he was telling the truth or mocking her, or maybe doing both. He slung the fish and poles over his shoulder, handed her the bag with the dressed birds, and began walking away from the lake.

Nina hurried to keep up with him. On the way back, she tried to memorize the route, but her untrained eyes were unable to pick out any of the landmarks that Elese had taken pains to point out. Everything looked the same. She offered up a mental apology to Elese: *I'm trying.*

As they walked, Nina could feel the weight of the stone in her coat pocket. With nighttime approaching and no idea where they were, it probably wasn't the right moment to think about braining Baer. But what if there was never a better time?

She tried to choreograph in her mind how she might pull off the attack. There would only be the one chance. She considered the best place in which to strike him. It was too bad she couldn't consult with him. Baer excelled in killing.

Maybe she could make it a trial run, Nina thought. She could practice taking him out. She quickened her pace, trying to close the gap between them, but he somehow managed to stay a few steps ahead. Finally she moved in right behind him, but the bell lap had already been called. Barking dogs alerted her that they were nearing the cabin.

The cabin made Nina feel equal parts dread and relief. For the moment she didn't have to face up to murder. Hunger had been gnawing at her for hours; it would be good to eat, and good to get out of the cold. But she knew she wasn't returning to a shelter. She was coming back to her prison.

"Do you need to stop at the library?" Baer asked.

"Library?" she said.

"The reading room," he said. "The necessary, the backhouse."

At Nina's look of incomprehension, he said, "The shitter is down this path."

She looked where he was pointing and could just make out the small dingy structure of an outhouse.

While she hesitated, Baer said, "Go or not. I'm feeding the dogs."

He left with the fish, and Nina decided to use the outhouse. The closer she got to the structure, the more she thought it looked like an upright coffin. But it wasn't a coffin you'd want to be buried in. There were cracks and holes in its walls, and she knew it would be drafty and inhospitable. She opened the door. There wasn't much more to the room than a circular cutout in the shelving. Next to the hole was a pile of old magazines, although Nina couldn't imagine a worse place to read.

Of course, it was possible the magazines had another use; she'd heard that in the aftermath of the depression, the Sears/Roebuck catalog had been a mainstay in farm outhouses. Nina supposed she should be grateful that there were a few rolls of real toilet paper in this outhouse. It was too bad that there wasn't any disinfectant or soap, and no running water.

The dogs must have been busy eating, for they didn't bark at her as she walked up the path toward the cabin. Baer stood waiting at the front door. Nina stopped short of where he was, keeping her distance.

"What's in your right coat pocket?" he asked.

"Nothing," she said, and then patted outside her pocket and feigned surprise. She reached inside the pocket, removed the stone, and did a pretend double take.

How had he known? Her coat was bulky and should have easily concealed the rock.

"The bear," Nina said, coming up with a story without any hesitation. "As soon as I saw its tracks, I picked up this stone. It was the best weapon I could find."

She'd never been a good liar, but she knew it was important for Baer to believe her, or at least to not be certain that she was lying. The consequences for his disbelief, she was sure, would be severe.

"I was too scared to scream," she said. "Those paw prints were five times the size of my own hand. I almost ran to you, but I was once told you never run in the presence of a bear. I heard doing that can trigger a bear into attacking you. So I backed up slowly."

"And you thought that rock would protect you?"

"It was the only weapon available to me. I figured if a bear charged, I could at least throw the rock and hope that might distract it. And if that didn't work, I was going to play dead. Isn't that what you're supposed to do if a bear attacks you?"

Instead of answering her, he said, "And how is it that the rock just happened to remain in your pocket?"

Nina shrugged her shoulders. "I forgot about it."

"Really? How much do you think it weighs?"

Nina hefted it. "Not very much," she said.

"I'm guessing it's about three pounds."

"It doesn't seem that heavy."

"That's not what your body was saying. On the walk back, you were leaning to your right. That seemed a little curious to me. Hunters have to notice those little things. Anything out of place tells a story."

"If I was leaning to my right, I'd guess it was because the bag with the bird meat was slung over my right shoulder."

Nina had put the bag down while removing the rock from her pocket, but now reached down and lifted it up, demonstrating its heaviness.

"There's probably fifteen pounds of meat in here. Is it any surprise I was listing to one side, with all that meat slung over my shoulder?"

She tried to leave no room for doubt in her explanation or in her body language.

"A boulder wouldn't stop a charging bear," he said.

She looked at her stone and shrugged. "At the time it seemed a lot better than nothing."

"Had you thrown your stone at a bear, it would only have provoked it."

"I'll have to remember that."

"On the other hand, I imagine that stone would be a very effective weapon against an unsuspecting human. Look at its wicked edge. If you brought that rock down hard enough, I imagine it would cleave a skull."

Nina said nothing.

"And with a stone even smaller than that, Goliath was brought down, wasn't he?"

"That's what the Bible says."

"So if that's what the Good Book tells me, why shouldn't I be in fear for my life?"

Nina tossed the stone aside. "I simply forgot the stone was in my pocket. Next time I see bear tracks, I'll move closer to you."

"*Next time*," he said, "if I suspect you of smuggling a weapon, I'll strip-search you before I let you into the cabin. And if that prospect doesn't daunt you, imagine the weather being thirty or forty below. Just think how fast you'll experience hypothermia. On a scale of things to fear, frostbite should be about as scary to you as a grizzly. You've already lost one finger. You don't want to lose more, do you?"

Nina shook her head.

Baer stepped aside and she scurried into the cabin.

CHAPTER TWENTY

For four months of the year, Seward was cruise central. Huge ships came into port bringing thousands and thousands of tourists. It was hard for the locals to not feel they were on display just like the wildlife. They were "quaint." But it was those tourist dollars that kept Seward going.

Hamilton slapped the folder down on his desk. He was nuts even thinking about taking Carrie on a cruise. Still, he'd been promising her a nice trip ever since they got married, but money was tight, their kids needed them, their jobs needed them—it was always something.

If they were going to do it, this was the time to do it. Every year her doctor prescribed antidepressants for her seasonal affective disorder. Carrie had even gotten this bright light that mimicked daylight. Still, every year, the ever-shorter days made Carrie blue.

His desk phone rang, and Hamilton picked up. The voice on the other end of the line said, "It's been a month since Nina Granville disappeared."

He didn't like Greg Martin's prompts, but by now he was almost used to them. "Wasn't it Einstein who said time was relative?"

"Apparently Einstein missed his calling as a cop."

"You calling about theoretical physics?"

"I'm calling about the Nina Granville case."

"Why are you calling me?"

"Because the detective's not in. He's never in."

"Maybe he's working the lead I passed on to him yesterday."

"What lead?"

"Those flyers that were circulated got a potential bingo by a resident of Tanana."

"That's near to Manley, right?"

"They're about forty miles apart. Unfortunately, the ID is secondhand."

"What do you mean?"

"A villager in Tanana saw the poster. According to him, his second cousin was acquainted with Tomcat. He said that on one or two occasions, Tomcat flew this cousin to Tanana. He claimed this same cousin had a conversation with Tomcat about this mountain-man client of his who lived in the wilderness somewhere southeast of Tanana."

"How do we talk to this second cousin?"

"We wait for the troopers to find him, or we wait for him to turn up. He's an Athabascan, like most Tanana villagers, and apparently he likes to come and go. His cousin says he worked on a fishing boat this summer, but no one knows where he is now. My contact said he'd call me when his cousin shows up."

"You got to be kidding."

"I'm hoping AST will decide to track him down."

"Let me guess: they didn't promise anything."

Hamilton didn't say anything.

"Would it help if I flew us to Tanana for a face-to-face interview with your caller?" asked Martin.

Hamilton considered the offer for a moment. "I don't think we'd learn anything more in person. I get the feeling my contact is more comfortable talking by satellite phone. He might not even be inclined to open his door to a cop."

"Why?"

"In May of 2014, two Alaska State Troopers were shot dead in Tanana while investigating a supposed dispute over a couch. It's a close-knit community of only a few hundred people, so everyone knows everyone. Some of the villagers might not like the idea of a local cozying up to a cop."

"You given any more thought to contacting Donnelly's guy?"

"I don't like doing an end run around the troopers," said Hamilton, but then added, "I did get his name and number, though."

"You going to call?"

"I suppose it couldn't hurt."

"I'd like to be in on the meeting."

"He's probably not going to want to talk to a civilian. He might not even want to talk to me."

"Tell him my wife was abducted just like Nina Granville was. Tell him I have some unique insights into this case."

"If he agrees to talk to me, I'll see if I can get you an invite."

"Thanks," said Martin, and then added, "One more thing. Any idea when I'm going to get my wife's jewelry back?"

"Call Anchorage PD. As far as I know, it's in their possession, unless it was passed on to AST."

"Keep me in the loop."

As if Martin was giving him much choice in that matter, thought Hamilton, but he wasn't given the opportunity of saying that or anything else. Martin had already hung up.

The cop looked up the number for Sergeant Cody Wood, Donnelly's man in Alaska, but before dialing his number, he began wondering about something else.

Hamilton put aside Wood's number and decided there was someone else he needed to call first. And then he'd stop by Once in a Blue Moose and see if they had any nice roses or flowers for his wife.

CHAPTER TWENTY-ONE

The fire in the cooking stove generated just enough heat to be felt throughout the cabin, making the room not quite an icebox. Nina was glad to be able to remove a few layers of clothing and enjoy the relative warmth. Baer didn't ask her to help with dinner, and she was content to let him cook up the goose and duck meat. She watched as he threw a handful of fat into a large frying pan and then seasoned the bird with salt and pepper. In lieu of rice or potatoes, he tossed some of his hardtack into the pan. The hard biscuits began to soften as they soaked up the juices and fat.

The aroma from the game birds made Nina all the hungrier. It hadn't been that long ago that such a smell would have repulsed her. Food had never seemed important to her before, but then she'd never had to doubt where her next meal was coming from. In New York she'd always stocked her work desk with protein bars, which served as lunch when she was too busy to eat. But the idea of food had changed for her. It was no longer a vehicle to see Terrence or her friends. It was life.

Of late, Nina had noticed that her senses seemed to be heightened. Her primordial instincts seemed to be kicking in, which would explain her being able to see, smell, and hear as she never had before. At the moment, though, she wished her hearing weren't so acute. Baer was doing his singsong chant again, reciting that strange poem he was so fixated on. It was like a horror movie. You would promise yourself not to watch the scary scene, but then find yourself unable to turn away. The poem drew her in that way.

> *The Northern Lights have seen queer sights,*
> *But the queerest they ever did see*
> *Was that night on the marge of Lake Lebarge*
> *I cremated Sam McGee."*

"What poem is that?" she asked.

Baer didn't answer for several seconds. Nina knew if she hadn't interrupted him, he would have recited the poem in its entirety. It was almost as if he fell into a trance during its telling.

"It's 'The Cremation of Sam McGee,'" he finally said.

"Who wrote it?"

"Robert Service," he said. "I suppose he wasn't a poet you studied at Harvard."

Nina didn't correct him to say that she'd gone to Smith. Nor did she tell Baer that he was probably right about her college not having taught the poetry of this Robert Service. Her alma mater had its standards, and doggerel wouldn't count as poetry worthy of study.

"I've never heard of him."

"Harvard failed you."

Terrence had gone to Harvard. She was willing to bet her fiancé had never heard of Robert Service or his poem, either. Baer was looking at her, awaiting her response. Nina regretted having engaged him in conversation and said nothing.

"The poem speaks to the north. You think I give a shit about a Grecian urn?"

Nina was surprised that Baer was even able to make that reference. It wouldn't do for her to underestimate him. He presented himself as lacking in book smarts, but he wasn't ignorant. No, he was cunning and all too observant. It would be at her peril if she forgot that about her enemy.

"The poem is about one man's death," said Baer, "and another man's making good on a vow. Didn't Shakespeare write about those kinds of things?"

"But this Sam McGee dies," said Nina, "and then he's cremated, and in the middle of his ostensibly being burned to ashes, he requests the door be closed so as to keep the cold out."

"You ever cremate anyone?"

Nina's head recoiled in surprise: "Of course not."

"It's not as easy as you'd think."

"You've cremated someone?"

"Three people," he said.

"Or three and a third," he added enigmatically.

"How did that come about?"

"They died."

"Who died?"

"Why are you so *fired* up to know?"

Baer seemed proud of his pun, or maybe he was just using it to try to deflect her questions.

"I don't think most people in this world have cremated one person," she said, "let alone three and a third."

Baer added some fuel to the stove fire and took his time before replying. "The first person was my mother," he said.

"Your mother?"

"Father wasn't pleased when she skipped out without telling him."

"He killed her?"

"She took a bad fall, he said."

"How terrible that must have been for you."

"It was her choice to take off. It was her choice to abandon her own flesh and blood."

Those sounded like his father's words, thought Nina. "How old were you?"

"Eight, I suppose."

"I am sorry."

"I wasn't the one who was cremated."

Nina wasn't so sure.

"It's not easy to build a pyre that does the job," he said. "I helped my father pile up wood waist-high, but that still wasn't enough. For a body to burn to ashes, you need a blazing heat that lasts for hours. The fuel ran out before she did, but it was so hot we couldn't approach anywhere near to where her body was, so we had to toss the logs from ten, twelve feet away. It's not a pleasant sound when a log strikes charred flesh and bone. It's like the hollow cracking of a rotted branch, but worse."

"What about the other cremations?"

He took his time before answering. "The first Mrs. Baer and the second Mrs. Baer both burned at the stake, even though neither was a witch."

"How did they die?"

"The first Mrs. Baer drowned, or it seemed that way. She fell into the river and didn't care enough to pull herself out. And the second Mrs. Baer . . ."

He thought about it for a few moments before making his pronouncement. "I guess she died of a broken heart more than anything else."

"What was it that broke her heart?"

"Dwelling in the past," he said. "That's something I don't do."

Baer glared at her, and she retreated from his look. *I'm sorry, Sister,* thought Nina. There had been a part of her holding out hope that Elese had somehow survived. It was silly, of course, but she hadn't wanted to accept the reality of Elese's death. She didn't know how Elese had died, but it was true enough that she had died of a broken heart. With Denali's death the light had gone out of her life. Without her son to look after, she'd been willing to risk everything to escape.

I'm sorry you didn't make it, thought Nina in silent prayer.

Baer was humming the tune he used with his poem. It was almost a cadence. Even without words it was easy to recognize.

"Is your Sam McGee poem set in Alaska?" Nina asked.

Baer stopped his humming and shook his head. "Service wrote about Canada, but the far north is the far north. Lake Labarge is not more than seven hundred miles from here."

"You've been there?"

"Once," he said. "It's off the Yukon River near Whitehorse. I visited in July, but the water was still colder than a witch's tit. They say it never warms up."

"Then why would anyone live there, or here, for that matter? The only reason Sam McGee came to the far north was to try and strike it rich. But he hated the cold here. Like him I'd rather be in Plum Orchard, Tennessee, or just about anywhere else."

"It's *Plumtree*, Tennessee," he said. "And I guess you're shit out of luck."

* * *

They ate dinner without exchanging any words. Nina wondered if she'd made a mistake being honest with him. Silence would probably have been the better way to go. She should have just endured his reciting that awful poem. He'd gone back to it while doing the dishes. His words had driven Nina into her cage, where she'd unsuccessfully covered her ears.

"Till I came to the marge of Lake Labarge, and a derelict there lay;
It was jammed in the ice, but I saw in a trice it was called the
  Alice May.
And I looked at it, and I thought a bit, and I looked at my frozen
  chum;
Then 'Here,' said I, with a sudden cry, 'is my cre-ma-tor-eum.'"

Nina wondered what a "marge" was. She thought it could mean the shore or the outskirts, but couldn't be sure from the context of the poem. And had a boat named the *Alice May* really sunk in the lake?

He continued his reciting. It was almost like he was saying a prayer, with the words not as important as his utterances of faith.

She fell asleep to his droning.

* * *

Nina slept through the night and awakened in the morning to the sounds of Baer moving around the cabin. For once she hadn't had to face up to one of his hated nocturnal visits. Resisting his advances would have meant suffering another beating or strangling. Even if there was no choice in the matter, she hadn't yet reached the point where she could let herself be tacitly complicit in his raping her. It was false pride, she knew, and didn't do her any good. What was even worse was that he seemed to enjoy her struggles.

Whatever spared her rape was a good thing. Baer seemed to be in a hurry. In the semidarkness she watched him making circular loops out of wire. Each of the loops was nine or ten inches in diameter. It almost looked as if he was making hangman's nooses.

"Are those snares you're making?" asked Nina.

He nodded. "In case you can't feel it, there was a cold snap last night. All the streams and shallows iced up. I need to visit a few beaver lodges this morning."

"You're going to set traps?"

"Snare poles," he said. "You put them under the ice along the beaver run."

"Will I be coming along?"

He shook his head. "I got a later start than I would have liked. That's what happens when you eat too much. I slept like the dead."

Nina wasn't sure if she liked the idea of being left behind or not. As much as Baer's absence appealed to her, the only way she could better plan her escape was by familiarizing herself with the surrounding landscape. And observing Baer's survival skills in action could only help her getting away.

"Why not let me tag along?" Nina asked.

"Because you'll slow me up," he said.

"Will you at least let me out of my cage to go to the bathroom?" she asked.

Baer thought about it for a moment, shrugged, and then unlocked the door to her holding pen. Nina kept her eyes on him as she scrambled out of the cell. She'd slept under several fur and down-filled blankets, and without their warmth she began to shiver. Still, she was glad to be free of her cage.

When Nina stepped outside the cabin, the cold made her turn around and return for a blanket. She wrapped herself up in a handmade down comforter and then faced the chill air for the second time, following the path to the outhouse. There was enough light that she could see the way, but not enough to see very far around her. Gusting wind rattled trees and made Nina jump, fearing potential predators.

"Welcome to my morning pee," whispered Nina. "As if the possibility of freezing to death isn't worrisome enough, I also have to be wary of some wild animal sneaking up on me."

Nina stomped along as loudly as she could, hoping her noises might scare off any animal within listening range. With the light of day, she could see the outhouse more clearly, but that didn't make it any more appealing. Outhouses, Nina was sure, were a male invention. Comfort was not part of the construction equation. As she sat down, she noticed there was some give to the plywoodlike shelving.

"And now I have another fear," said Nina. "Death by crapper."

She propped herself up with both of her hands so that she was elevated over the hole. It might have been a silly reassurance, and Nina knew it had to look ridiculous, but positioning herself that way lessened her fear of falling in. Of course, making like a gymnast working the pommel horse was no way to take a pee.

At least I don't have to worry about my dismount, she thought.

It was already freezing, and it was early fall. She didn't want to think about the polar winter that was coming. Nina wondered if any backside had ever frozen to an outhouse. That might even be worse than a tongue to the flagpole. She didn't think about it for long because the wind, finding its way through the structure's many cracks, chilled her exposed flesh. She finished up as quickly as her bladder would allow and hurried back to the cabin.

Baer was ready to leave. He'd constructed a sling over his shoulder to carry all of his snares. There was a fur draped around his waist that was a combination holster and construction belt. In addition to his gun, he carried an ax, a knife, and wire-cutter pliers. Today he'd chosen a rifle over a shotgun.

"Hurry it up," he said, gesturing with his head to her holding pen. "There's some duck in there for you."

"If you don't lock me up, I could do some cleaning."

"You can clean up after I get back. Now get inside."

Nina crawled into her cell, and he locked the door behind her.

"Are you taking the dogs?" she asked.

"One of them."

"How about leaving the others in the cabin with me?"

"That wouldn't be very smart."

"And why is that?"

"There are two kinds of bear. The one kind runs off when it hears dogs barking. And the other kind doesn't hear barking as much as it hears the sound of a dinner bell."

Nina thought of the dogs chained up to their metal-drum houses. "That's happened before?" she asked.

"Why else would I tell you that rooming with dogs is a bad idea?"

As Baer walked out of the cabin, Nina found herself with yet something else to worry about.

She waited until she was sure Baer was far away from the cabin before digging out the secreted journal. Better to be safe than sorry—her mother had always gone around saying that. Nina thought of her family. Usually she went home for Thanksgiving. Her parents and brother were probably wondering if she was alive. It seemed almost unreal that she was so far away from them and there was no way for her to get word to them. She felt like a prisoner of war denied communication with the outside world.

I am still alive, she thought. *I am still fighting. I haven't given up.*

She retrieved Elese's book. Her secret sister had been imprisoned for much longer than she had. Both of them had been raped and abused by the same man, and although Elese had suffered unimaginable loss, she had still reached out to Nina.

Today Nina found comfort in the last few pages, personalized with drawings and stories. Elese had remembered Denali in a series of etchings. One drawing showed Denali's wide, innocent eyes staring out at the world. In another he sucked at his mother's breast. And there was a picture of him atop a bearskin rug.

These are all that remain of her son, thought Nina. *This is all that is left of him.*

Elese had also drawn an ink etching of her husband with the identification of "Greg." He was closely eyeing what appeared to be a rock. She'd added an entry that read, *It grieves me to think I have left Greg in limbo. I was his anchor, he told me. How adrift he must be!*

One of Elese's more unusual entries she'd titled "Scaring a Monster."

I'm not sure if Baer's distrust and hatred of women has to do with his mother or his upbringing, but it makes him the monster he is. There is a part of him that is afraid of women, even though I'm sure he would say that is ridiculous. He likes to call women "witches" (and worse). I get this sense he fears women and their "dark" magic.

During our honeymoon at sea, the anthropologist on our cruise ship gave a lecture where she said that the Native women used to sing and whistle to the northern lights so as to entice them to come closer.

The first time I saw the aurora borealis, I did just that. I whistled and sang and danced. The monster did not like that. It made him uneasy. I think I somehow tapped into that old sisterhood, and my voice seemed to become a chorus.

He tried to hide how uncomfortable I made him feel. He said I was acting as if I'd lost my mind, and he tried to speak over my singing and whistling. Then he pretended that he'd had enough of my "nonsense" and went inside.

Who says you can't scare a monster?

The bottom half of the page was taken up with a drawing. Even without color and with only the inking of her pen, Elese's picture reminded Nina of Van Gogh's *Starry Night*. It was the swirls and the stars, she decided. Elese's version of the northern lights pulsated even on paper that had once served as the label of a large can. One of Nina's favorite things about the picture was the absence of the monster. He wasn't even there in dark spirit.

Elese had banished him. That was the strength of sisters, thought Nina. A bond someone like Baer could not understand. It was men like him who had conducted witch hunts for centuries. They were afraid of women.

Nina turned to the third page from the end. She always hated coming to the end of Elese's booklet. It was all she had of her.

In this cold and difficult land, I think it is important that you find your totem. It could be an eagle or wolf or bear. Maybe it will be a fox, mink, marten, or wolverine. The smallness and stealth of a mouse or vole might appeal to you. Perhaps you look to the sky and feel one with the raven or bald eagle. Or your spirit soars when you hear a chickadee cheerfully cry out, "Chick-a-dee-dee-dee," even in the cold of winter. Or you see yourself swimming like a silvery salmon, or seal, toothed walrus, or whale. When your totem shows itself, you will be drawn to it.

Beneath those words was the drawing of a large, muscular hare.

My totem is the Arctic Hare. The first time I saw one running, I felt my spirit take flight. An Arctic Hare doesn't run so much as it bounds. It pushes off like a kangaroo and sails through the air. Every time I see one racing, it takes my breath away. Of course, usually you don't see them. You walk right by them, especially in the winter when the hares turn white and blend in with the snow and only their ears show a little black.

I think if I am to get away from the monster, I will need that near invisibility of my totem. And I will need the hare's speed.

And if this proves to be my last will and testament, then I will to you my spirit, Sister.

Nina wondered if she would find her totem. She did not have to wonder about Elese's spirit. It was hers to carry, and to carry her, now.

CHAPTER TWENTY-TWO

The meeting had come together much faster than Hamilton would have thought possible. Of course, it meant his taking a day off work to get from Seward to Fairbanks. It was a good thing his wife Carrie tolerated his obsession. Carrie referred to Elese as "the other woman." Whenever Carrie caught him daydreaming, she knew he was thinking about the case.

It wasn't a trip the cop would have liked at the best of times, and traveling to Fairbanks in November was *not* the best of times, but that's where Donnelly's man, Cody Wood, was heading up the Nina Granville task force. The first part of the trip, the drive to Anchorage, had been fine. Hamilton was used to putting miles on his cruiser. But flying was another matter. He hated flying. He'd taken a turboprop out of the Ted Stevens Anchorage Airport and white-knuckled it to Fairbanks. The name of the airport always struck Hamilton as being ironic. Ted Stevens had been a longtime Alaska senator. In 2010, Stevens had died in an airplane crash. And more than thirty years before that, his first wife, Ann, had also died during a plane crash. There seemed something strange about naming an airport after someone who'd died flying.

The shuttle dropped Hamilton off in front of the Chena River Lodge. Wood had set up his headquarters in a hotel not far from where Nina Granville had stayed in Fairbanks. The cop wasn't surprised to see Greg Martin waiting for him as he stepped out of the van.

"I thought I'd have to go up to the meeting without you," said Martin.

Hamilton didn't bother to point out that he was ten minutes early. He had no doubt that Martin had probably been waiting for hours.

"Lead the way," said Hamilton.

* * *

Wood personally greeted them at the door. He hadn't lost his military posture, standing ramrod straight as he shook their hands. He was six feet tall, trim and fit, and appeared to be in his late thirties. Hamilton found himself unconsciously sucking in his gut and standing a little straighter in the other man's presence, but when he realized what he was doing, he thought, *To hell with that*, and reverted back to his usual slouch.

"Thank you for coming," Wood said, as if the meeting had been his idea.

He showed them into the outer room of his suite. It looked like a low-tech Pentagon war room with flip charts, whiteboards, and maps. The three men took seats at a table that must have been commandeered from a banquet room; Wood took a position at the head of the table. Nina Granville's disappearance could be documented by the flyers, pictures, and print matter on the table. The flyers featured her attractive face. At the bottom, displayed in prominent letters and colored in what looked like US currency green, was the promise of REWARD.

"I hope we can dispense with any formalities," said Wood. "Most people call me Sarge because of the dozen years I spent in the army."

Hamilton took his cue and said, "Evan," and Martin said, "Greg."

"As you know I work for Congressman Donnelly as his deputy chief of staff. I started in his office while the government was paying for my education in DC. As they say, politics makes for strange bedfellows."

Hamilton wondered how many times Sarge had used that line. The man did not strike him as being naturally urbane. He came across as tightly wound, even in this informal setting.

"Now before we go any further," Sarge said, "I need to tell you something that was brought to my attention only this morning. Given this information it's possible we wouldn't even be having this meeting, so I apologize if that's the case."

He moved around some paperwork on the table until he found what he wanted. Then he pushed the blown-up photo toward the two men. The picture showed a shapely, tapered hand, but that only seemed to be the backdrop for a huge, sparkling diamond.

"That's a blowup of Ms. Granville's hand," he said. "As you can see, it shows her engagement ring."

Sarge made eye contact with each man. "What I am about to tell you needs to be kept confidential. Any leaking of this information could negatively impact the ongoing investigation."

"Understood," said Hamilton.

Martin shrugged and added, "Mum's the word."

"Nina Granville's engagement ring turned up this morning," Sarge said. "Or at least part of it did."

"Part of it?" asked Hamilton.

"The diamond has been cut. The piece we have is approximately one carat. Whoever is trying to dispose of the diamond must have realized it could be easily identified in its present form. But there were enough identifying markers even with the one carat for it to be flagged."

"Where did this carat turn up?" asked Hamilton.

"In New York City," he said. "Right now we're trying to track down how it made its way from Alaska to New York and who might have had possession of it during that time."

"Have any arrests been made?" said Hamilton.

"I am not at liberty to give out any details of the investigation. Because of next Tuesday's elections, I had already planned to fly back east today, but this development has changed matters. It's likely that after today, Congressman Donnelly's temporary offices here in Alaska will be shut down."

Hamilton said aloud what he was thinking: "You think she's dead?"

Sarge measured his words and said, "We have made no such conclusion. We do recognize that my presence here, however, is no longer necessary. AST will continue to handle the investigation, and I will be in daily contact with them."

"This diamond turning up doesn't mean she's dead," said Martin.

Hamilton raised a brow at that. Why, then, when his wife's jewelry had turned up in Anchorage, had he assumed she was dead?

"I will continue to hope Ms. Granville is alive," said Sarge, "but the emergence of part of her ring is a game changer."

"Why is that?" asked Martin.

"Because that's what the detectives working the case believe. They think they now have the motive behind her disappearance. When I originally came to Alaska, most people were convinced that Nina Granville had disappeared of her own volition. She was the so-called runaway bride. Of course, there were plenty of other theories as well, including . . ."

Sarge took a moment to raise his hand and then began enumerating the theories starting with his thumb.

"One, Ms. Granville is the latest victim of the 'Donnelly Curse.' As I am sure you are aware, many think that same curse was responsible for two Donnelly assassinations and several familial heartache stories, as well as other unfortunate and untimely deaths the Donnelly family has suffered.

"Two, Ms. Granville is a political prisoner, who was taken by enemies of the Donnelly family.

"Three, Ms. Granville was abducted for ransom.

"Four, Ms. Granville was taken by some stranger for unknown purposes.

"And five, Ms. Granville was a victim of a robbery."

Sarge had run out of fingers on his hand, but not theories. "There are also those who believe her disappearance was a result of an alien abduction, and I've heard from people who suspect the involvement of the Illuminati, the Bilderbergers, or the New World Order.

"I admit that I am not an imaginative man. Because of that I usually look for the simplest explanation to any problem. From the first, I said that Ms. Granville was not a runaway bride, and when no ransom demands were made, it became clear she wasn't taken for ransom or as some kind of international bargaining chip. That left what I thought was the most obvious cause for her disappearance. In fact, the moment I heard Ms. Granville was missing, the first thing that came to my mind was her engagement ring. If you wear a ring like that, you become a target. That was one of the reasons I advised her not to go to Alaska without a security detail."

Sarge turned his attention to the photo of the engagement ring; Hamilton and Martin did the same.

"No one wearing that ring could keep a low profile. The stone is huge and flawless and catches the eye. It's described as museum quality, and for good reason. It should be in a museum."

They could all see how the diamond setting extended almost to the Granville woman's knuckle on her ring finger.

"I am not a betting man," said Sarge, "but if I was, I would say the wrong person took notice of that ring. I doubt whether the robbery was planned. And knowing Ms. Granville, I am sure she didn't quietly hand over her ring to the robber. In a situation like that, matters can quickly go south."

"That's assuming a lot," said Martin. "The police weren't even able to determine if there was a crime scene."

"There was sleet and pouring rain. If there was any blood, it was likely washed away."

"You said when you heard Nina Granville was missing, the first thing that came to your mind was her engagement ring," said Martin. "The first thing that came to my mind was my wife."

"The troopers have briefed me on your theories."

"I'd like to brief you on them," said Martin.

"I'm listening."

"My wife was taken in the latter part of September. Nina Granville was also taken in September. A pilot named Tomcat Carter, and his aircraft, are missing. Tomcat was picking up his passenger, a mysterious man we know by the name of Grizzly Adams, at a lake in Talkeetna. This Grizzly Adams bears a resemblance to the man called Blackbeard who sold my wife's jewelry. There were two stolen vehicles found abandoned in Talkeetna within days of when both my wife and Nina Granville went missing. As for where this Grizzly Adams might be, judging from what the pilot said to his girlfriend, his destination was somewhere in the vicinity of Manley Hot Springs. The likelihood of this was further corroborated by a source in Tanana who called Sergeant Hamilton. Supposedly last year our missing pilot had a conversation with one of his passengers about this trapper/survivalist who lived out that way."

Sarge pursed his lips. "You think this trapper is Grizzly? And this missing pilot flew Grizzly and his human cargo into the bush?"

"That's what I think," said Martin.

* * *

"I'm actually encouraged," said Martin. "Do you think Sergeant Wood is going to follow through?"

He and Hamilton sat down to coffee in the airport lounge before their flights.

"I'll be checking to make sure he does."

"If he gets the air force involved like he said, that could be huge. It sounded like he'd already had talks with that brigadier general at Eileson."

Eileson was the air force base southeast of Fairbanks. "Never forget the power of purse strings," said Hamilton, "and that Donnelly is on the House Committee of Armed Services."

"I never gave any thought to the possibility of using drones. High tech might get Grizzly where nothing else would."

Hamilton nodded. Sarge had said he would try to get the general to set up a drone surveillance program over the area where they suspected Grizzly of being holed up. If Sarge was right, the remoteness of the land and the cold might actually help them in their search. The drones, equipped with thermal imaging and infrared cameras, would likely have fewer false positives flying over a landscape barren of humanity.

"It went better than I expected," Hamilton agreed, "especially in light of that diamond showing up."

"I don't know why everyone would assume Donnelly's fiancée was dead just because of that diamond."

"Didn't you make that assumption when Elese's jewelry turned up?"

"That's different. Elese was gone for three years."

"But how is it you seemed so certain?"

Martin avoided his eyes. He shrugged and said, "I just was." Hamilton waited silently. Martin made a strangled sound that was part sigh, part exasperation. "Are you ever going to stop beating that dead horse?"

"I don't like it when people lie to me."

"You're right. I didn't tell you the full goddamn story of my life right off the bat. And why did I omit certain things? Because you were doing everything possible to paint me as the prime suspect. I was desperate. I needed you to stop fixating on me and find Elese. That's why I fudged the truth. I did it for Elese."

"You make lying sound noble."

"It must be nice being perfect."

"You didn't tell me about your first wife. You never volunteered that you'd been arrested."

"When are we going to get beyond this déjà fucking vu?"

"Among her other complaints, Candy said you stole her jewelry, and provided a list of the pieces that were missing. You denied that. But lo and behold, some of that jewelry turned up in an Anchorage pawn shop. Would you like to explain that?"

Martin's jaw clenched. "When I married Candy, I had no idea what love was. I was young and dumb, and I mistook lust for love. I'd never heard of borderline personality disorder, but I sure know about it now because Candy is a textbook case. And when I told my borderline wife I wanted to have our marriage annulled, she made my life a living hell."

"See, I'm interested in the time line," Hamilton said. "Candy said you scared her into the annulment. And at the time you made those threats, you were already with Elese, weren't you?"

Martin snorted. "You know what bothered Candy more than anything? She saw how happy I was. She could see how I'd changed. Before Elese I had no idea what love was. It hit me like lightning."

"So Candy knew about Elese?"

"She did and she didn't. I think it had to be apparent I was head over heels in love. But I never talked about it with her, or even with my friends. I didn't want to jinx it. I kept our relationship quiet. Our honeymoon could have almost qualified as an elopement."

"Did you steal the jewelry from your ex-wife?"

"Do you want to arrest me? Is that it?"

"I'd like to hear the truth."

"Yes, I stole the jewelry. But it was jewelry I gave her—jewelry my mother gave me before she died. Mom wanted me to give her jewelry to the woman I loved."

"What would you have done if Candy hadn't agreed to the annulment?"

"She had no reason not to. She got everything she wanted."

"You still haven't answered the question."

Martin remained stubbornly silent.

Finally Hamilton said, "Anything else you want to clarify?"

"Yeah," said Martin. "You seem to think it's suspicious that I now believe Elese is dead, and you want to know why that is."

Hamilton nodded. For the longest time Martin had held out hope that his wife was alive.

"You want an explanation? Here it is. Nine or ten months ago, Elese came to me. I suppose you'd say she came to me in a dream, but that's not how it felt at the time. She was happy and smiling and at peace. And she told me that she had left her body, but that wasn't reason for me to grieve."

Martin's voice wobbled. "I knew it really was Elese. That was just like her. She was looking in on her stray. I was that stray. Did I ever tell you about the time it was pouring rain, and she got soaked trying to help this poor, lost dog? She had the biggest heart of any person I've ever known."

Angrily he dug at a watering eye with his knuckle. "You going to arrest me?" he asked.

"No," said Hamilton.

"Then go to hell."

Martin stood up, threw ten dollars down on the table, and walked away.

CHAPTER TWENTY-THREE

"How did you survive this place for as long as you did?" said Nina.

In her solitude Nina had taken to talking to Elese. She knew crazy people often talked to themselves and hoped she wasn't now among their number, but it wouldn't have surprised her if she was.

"I've read your words over and over. I'm sure I would be dead if you hadn't written. But how did you manage to come off sounding so measured and reasonable? On days like today, I feel crappy through and through, and I'm so damned angry. You are the Zen master, and I'm the unenlightened shit.

"I usually don't curse, you know. My mother is a rather proper woman, and she frowns on it. She always told me it wasn't ladylike. But Mom was never put in a freezer and raped repeatedly.

"You were. All the god-awful things that have happened to me happened to you. I wish you'd written more about your anger. I would have listened. Misery loves company. Maybe you didn't have the time to write any more than you did, or maybe you didn't see the purpose of it.

"Every day it's getting colder. I never imagined this kind of cold. And there's no getting warm. But I don't have to tell you that. You survived for years.

"I think it's mid-November. If I'm right, I've been imprisoned not quite two months. I'm trying to put into practice everything you told me. But deep down there's this part of me that's angry with you. I know that's not fair, especially with all that you did. Most people in prison might carve their name on a wall. Or because they're angry, they might write 'fuck you.' But you wrote a book. How was that even possible? And you managed to do it even under the watchful eyes of our monster jailer. As if all that wasn't a miracle enough, you even figured a way to smuggle the book to me. So why am I so pissed off?

"You're dead, that's why.

"The monster won. And if you couldn't beat him, then how in the hell do you expect me to come out on top? You wrote the survival manual. Why didn't you survive? You provided me with maps by which to escape. Why didn't you get away?

"You wrote me a book of hope, Pollyanna, but since you failed, what hope do I have?"

Nina was breathing hard. Her hands were balled into fists. A minute passed before her fists unclenched and her breathing became normal.

"I'm sorry, Sister," said Nina. "I blamed the messenger. And I know the messenger was only trying to help me."

It was time to do her exercises, Nina decided. She needed to be in the best possible shape if she hoped to get away. And besides, her only chance of getting warm was through exercise.

Nina started kicking the walls of her pen. She used the leverage of the small holding cell to try to inflict damage. One day, she hoped, its walls would come tumbling down. But after a long workout, it became apparent that today wouldn't be that day.

Being cooped up wasn't easy. She'd become used to Baer's letting her join him on his outings. If he wasn't hunting or trapping, he was collecting wood or cutting out chunks of ice to make water. The more she went out, the more Nina familiarized herself with the area. After the first couple of trips, she'd been able to identify a number of Elese's landmarks.

"Maybe he's punishing me today," she said. "He's commented on how I'm always asking questions, and it seems like he's always observing me whenever I'm trying to get my bearings. He might have decided to put the brakes on my learning. Or maybe it was something else. Maybe he didn't want me around because he had his own agenda and didn't want me seeing or hearing what he was doing. And he did seem very protective of his pack this morning."

It was unlikely that Nina would have been aware of Baer's behavior had not Elese written about it. She pulled away the covers and dug out the caulking tube housing Elese's words. After turning a few pages, she found the pertinent passage.

> Baer likes to be the magician, knowing the tricks but never revealing them. I wonder, though, if he might have a shortwave radio. Some of his rants refer to events of which I'm not aware and that seem current. And on a few occasions, I've seen some kind of electronic device wrapped up in his pack. The best look I had was during the blizzard that drove us to his hunting shack. He left his pack open, and even through Bubble Wrap, I saw the glint of something that could have been a radio or oversize phone. Since that time I have done my best to see what might be in that pack, but he has been careful to keep it hidden.

"The monster likes his secrets, doesn't he? You might be right about his having a radio. Last night he was having one of his apocalyptic rants and started talking about a killer strain of Middle East respiratory syndrome spreading like wildfire through the slums of Egypt. It was worse than SARS, he said. How would he have known that?"

Nina turned a page. Cold War history seemed to have colored Baer's views of the world. Elese had also written about that.

For the last two summers, I've been imprisoned at an abandoned military base, a relic from the Cold War, west of Fairbanks. The prison certainly suits Baer's paranoia. He sees the world poised on a precipice, with nuclear destruction just one push of the button away. In the midst of our fallout shelter, he makes his survivalist views seem commonsensical.

The entire base was bulldozed except for the fallout shelter. The years have not been kind to the bunker. Pipes are gutted, and there is mold and mildew. The thick, concrete walls, meant to be impregnable even to Russian radiation, are crumbling in places. The bunker is where the soldiers would have gone underground in the event of nuclear war. There are signs of old water storage tanks. Baer says the soldiers had enough food and water to last them a full year, along with a special recirculating air system designed to protect them from fallout.

When I'm in that dark bunker, it feels like the world has come to an end. Summer is when Baer fishes and trades his furs—he's gone for weeks at a time. I know what it feels like to be entombed. He leaves me with jerky and water, chained to a short, hateful leash. When he returns I'm never sure how I feel. Glad that my death sentence has been lifted. Bitterly disappointed that he is still alive.

"I know that feeling, Sister," said Nina. "I know that feeling."

CHAPTER TWENTY-FOUR

Nina picked at the food Baer had left in a pan and tried not to dwell on her queasiness. Her stomach hadn't felt right all day. Although she wasn't sure of the date, even without a calendar, she knew her period was overdue.

"There are all kinds of reasons why Aunt Flo might be late," she said.

All day she'd been carrying on a one-sided conversation with Elese and saw no reason to stop now.

When she ran cross-country, at least half the girls on the team weren't menstruating. A lot of that was attributable to low body fat. She'd lost weight here. The change in diet could have thrown her body off-kilter. And that wasn't even accounting for all the stress.

Was it any wonder her body was rebelling? She'd been drugged and beaten. And how many times had her air supply been cut off? Almost every day her body had been subjected to physical trauma. That kind of shock had to be playing havoc with her system. I can't be pregnant, she told herself.

Don't let me be pregnant, she prayed.

Her body hurt, and all day it had felt like she might have the flu, but that didn't mean she was pregnant. Baer had beaten her the day before and the day before that. She'd resisted him, and he'd hurt her. It wasn't surprising that she was feeling the way she did.

"Besides," she said to Elese, "I've had a lot of pregnant women tell me they never felt better. They didn't feel sick."

Of course, Nina's mother hadn't been lucky like that. Her mom had said she was sick as a dog during her two pregnancies. She claimed that her morning sickness extended from the moment of conception to the time of delivery—morning, noon, and night. Nina found that difficult to believe, but her mother wasn't usually prone to exaggeration.

"I'm having sympathetic symptoms, that's all," Nina said. "Earlier today I was reading about you and Denali. That's probably why I'm thinking about this."

But that didn't explain the food she hadn't been able to eat. She'd been ravenous during her captivity, but not today.

The sound of barking dogs startled her. She knew by now that this wasn't their alarm signal; this was their happy barking. The monster was nearing the cabin.

Tightness squeezed her chest and throat. She found it hard to breathe.

Please be tired, she prayed. *Please just eat and go to bed.*

She waited for the door to open. He seemed in no hurry. Nina wanted to believe that was a good thing, but what it felt like was a horror movie. Any moment now and the monster would jump out.

Finally the door opened, and with it came a cold draft. Nina began shivering. When Baer stepped inside, his eyes immediately locked on hers.

"I've been thinking about this," he said.

"No," said Nina.

He started toward her cage, disrobing as he walked. He unlocked her cage.

"No," Nina said again, balling her hands into fists.

"You must like it rough."

When he pulled the door open, he was already erect. Nina caught his musky scent. His hairy chest was like a pelt and stank of the dried sweat of a day's exertions. Just as his garments were stripped away, so was any veneer of civilization. It was an animal that reached for her.

His touch was enough. Nina threw up. There wasn't much in her stomach, but she relieved herself of all that was there. And then she began dry-retching.

Nothing else would stop the monster.

"I'm pregnant," rasped Nina. "Damn you to hell forever."

Baer took a step back from her cage. His tumescence was rapidly deflating.

"Are you happy?" screamed Nina. "Are you fucking happy?"

"I am," said Baer.

CHAPTER TWENTY-FIVE

On the third ring Martin answered with, "Yeah?" His voice was decidedly unwelcoming. Since their dispute at the airport, neither man had contacted the other.

"Since I promised to keep you in the loop on your wife's case," said Hamilton, "I thought I'd pass on some news to you."

"I'm listening."

"Guess who returned home to Tanana for Thanksgiving?"

Martin's voice thawed a little. "I didn't know Alaska's Native people celebrated Thanksgiving."

"They do it their own way. They're probably more likely to serve ptarmigan instead of turkey and salmon pâté in place of yams. And for dessert there's no pumpkin pie. It's usually salmonberries with Crisco."

"Crisco?"

"That's what I've been told."

"That sounds about as traditional as the Thanksgiving I just had."

"What did you eat?"

"Kung pao chicken. And when I cracked open my cookie, my fortune said, 'The fortune you seek is in another cookie.'"

"Really?"

"I put the fortune in my wallet as proof for the doubters."

Hamilton ignored the jibe. "I would have asked for another cookie."

"I've gotten used to living with uncertainty."

"I talked to our guy. His name's Jack, and he confirmed that he did fly with Tomcat, and that they did have a conversation about this survivalist client of his. In fact, what prompted their talk was that they happened to be flying in the vicinity of where Tomcat always dropped off his mountain man."

"Did you get a general location?"

"I got better than that. I now have what I think is an exact location. Tomcat did a little detour to show Jack, Grizzly's lake."

"What's its real name?"

"It's not on any map as far as I can tell. And Jack didn't know its name. But after talking with him, I'm pretty sure he was able to pinpoint its location."

"I'd like that information as well."

"What are you going to do with it?"

"I'm going to try to find the likeliest route that Tomcat would have flown from Talkeetna to that location, and then I'm going to fly that route."

"What kind of pilot are you?"

"I haven't crashed yet."

Hamilton said, "You're going to need a spotter."

"Are you volunteering?"

The cop sighed. "I must be crazy."

* * *

Because all the waterways were already frozen, the two men flew out of the Talkeetna Airport in a single-engine plane with tundra tires.

Hamilton was grateful that Talkeetna had an asphalt runway. In the interior of Alaska, you were lucky to get a gravel runway.

Neither man spoke for the first few minutes they were airborne. Hamilton didn't want to distract Martin from his piloting, so he pretended to look out at the scenery. It was only when his fingers started hurting that the cop realized he was holding on to his armrest with a death grip.

Speaking over the engine noise, Martin said, "So, did you tell Major King Kong about Jack's turning up?"

Hamilton wasn't sure if he'd heard correctly. "Major who?"

"Major King Kong," said Martin. "He's a character in my favorite film of all time: *Dr. Strangelove.*"

"That's an oldie."

"Nineteen sixty-four."

"And remind me: Who was this Major Kong?"

"He's the Slim Pickens character who rides the nuke down, screaming, 'Yahoo.'"

Hamilton nodded, remembering. Slim Pickens had been riding the ultimate bucking bronco. "Forgive me for being slow, but I'm still not getting who this Major Kong is who I was supposed to have told about Jack's turning up."

"I was giving Donnelly's aide-de-camp a promotion. He didn't come across like a sergeant."

Sergeant Hamilton wasn't sure if that was a dig against him or not. "What's a sergeant supposed to be like?"

"Less slick, less official."

I resemble that remark, thought the cop. "He is working for a politician," said Hamilton, and then after a few seconds, added, "No, I did not tell Major Kong that I'd heard from Jack."

A conspiratorial look passed between them. "Any reason for that omission?" asked Martin.

The cop shrugged. "Since our meeting I've called Sarge—Major—twice. The conversations were hurried. It felt like he was holding a stopwatch and timing our talk."

"What did you learn?"

"They still haven't been able to determine how that piece of the diamond got from Alaska to New York."

"So much for the major's theory that the case was all but solved."

"To his credit, Sarge did follow through with the general at Eielson. I talked to the general's adjutant, and he confirmed that they've been sending out their 'birds,' otherwise known as drones. He also made a point of saying AST would be contacted if they came up with anything, and that it would be best if I got my updates through them."

"That sounds like what I've been hearing for years."

The cop looked out the window and was surprised for a moment at how high they were. Their conversation had almost made him forget they were in a plane.

"Funny you mentioned *Dr. Strangelove*," said Hamilton. "That movie was all about the Cold War. From what Tomcat told people, our Grizzly was kind of fixated on the Cold War."

"He's not the only one," said Martin. He did a bad Sarah Palin imitation: "I can see Russia from here."

"Yeah, and I see Paris, I see France." He didn't finish the rhyme. "Back in the early sixties, Alaska was ground zero for the Cold War. Everyone was afraid the Russians would come marching over the Bering Strait. That's why a bunch of DEW stations—Distant Early Warning—were built throughout the Arctic, along with White Alice communication sites all over Alaska."

"Alice Who?"

"More like Alice WACS."

"Alice what?"

"I don't think we'll be competition for Abbott and Costello. Alice was an acronym for Alaska Integrated Communications and Electronics."

"And what was WACS short for?"

"White Alice Communications System. That's why the communication sites were referred to as White Alice. Because of the Arctic snow. I think they're all abandoned now, but there were a few sites in the interior. One of them is east of Manley."

"So, Alice had nothing to do with *Alice in Wonderland*?"

"Not a thing, as far as I know," said Hamilton.

"Maybe the song 'White Rabbit' was inspired by White Alice."

"I don't know that song," said Hamilton.

"You're kidding? It's a classic. Grace Slick and the Jefferson Airplane sang it in the sixties. I was sure it had to be in your wheelhouse."

"How old do you think I am? I spent my college years with Nirvana, not Al Jolson."

"You still should know it. A classic is a classic."

Martin began singing the song.

"Even with your singing," said the cop, "that's sounding familiar."

* * *

They flew for a while not saying anything. Finally it was Martin who broke the silence. "Keep your eyes peeled," he said. "I charted the weather on the day of the flight. The conditions were bad. I know I wouldn't have gone up in that kind of weather."

"A plane crash would explain a lot of things. It would also debunk our conspiracy theory." Hamilton studied the wilderness beneath them. "This would be a shitty place to crash."

He glanced over at Martin. "Not that there's a good place."

"Don't worry. I'm not getting any ideas."

Martin's head moved from right to left, his eyes scanning. "I've never been in this part of the state. I still can't get used to not seeing any sign of civilization. No roads, no towers, no power lines, no houses. No anything."

"The nearest road—the only road—is north of here. Only in Alaska would they call a gravel road a highway."

"There's a highway somewhere around here?"

"Most of it is unpaved. The Elliot Highway is the most westerly road in Alaska. It goes from Fairbanks to Manley, and now they're working on extending it to Tanana."

"Maybe Manley will become a real hub."

"Yeah, it will go from one hundred residents to two hundred." Hamilton paused and then added, "Believe it or not, there was a time when Manley Hot Springs was synonymous with mass murder."

"You're kidding?"

Hamilton shook his head. "I was just a kid when it happened. I think I was a senior in high school, so that would be back in 1984. This drifter named Michael Silka killed his neighbor in Fairbanks, and then he ended up fleeing to Manley. His idea was that he would be a survivalist, a mountain man, but just a few days after he arrived in Manley, his rampage started. He killed six villagers and tried to escape John Law by traveling along the Tanana River. Alaska State Troopers went after him with helicopters and found him on a tributary to the Tanana. He fired at them—killed at least one cop and wounded one or two others before the bastard was shot down."

Hamilton shook his head again. "I think I remember all that so vividly because it was a more innocent time back then, or at least it felt that way. Alaska wasn't used to mass murders. The world wasn't used to mass murders. Sounds silly, but to me it felt like the Silka shootings opened Pandora's box in this state. He tainted Alaska forever." He looked over at Martin. "You ever wonder if evil leaves behind a trail?"

"What do you mean, like some kind of ghost?"

"No, not like that. I'm thinking that it kind of poisons everything around it, and the evil seeps into the landscape, unseen but felt."

"You mean like an evil toxic dump?"

"Something like that," Hamilton said, nodding. "I'm not talking a Stephen King novel. But I've been in places where bad things have happened and I've felt this darkness, and I kind of wonder if it calls to its own."

"You think Grizzly was attracted to this area because of that?"

"I think it was more a case of his wanting to be far from any probing eyes."

"If he's alive," said Martin, "and he's the one who took Elese, I want to be the one who kills him."

Hamilton tapped his ears. "That engine is sure loud. I'm afraid I didn't hear what you just said."

Martin nodded and said no more, understanding the hint.

"The Mafia likes to say revenge is a dish best served cold," mused Hamilton. "If that's the case, this place surely fits the bill."

* * *

As frigid as it was inside the plane's cabin, Hamilton knew it was a lot colder outside. Although he'd lived in Alaska all his life, what struck him was how devoid of people this landscape was. The wilderness was both exhilarating and threatening.

Hamilton continued with his spotting, looking out the windows and scanning the area around them with binoculars. Like most people he was used to seeing man-made environments. That thumbprint was noticeably absent. Only snow and ice covered the ground.

He lowered the binoculars when the single-engine plane began bobbing on the wind currents. Up until then the flight had been remarkably smooth, but once the turbulence began, he suspected his face looked green.

"Did I ever tell you I'm not too keen on flying?"

"Not in so many words," said Martin, "but your clenched palms, sweaty face, and terrorized looks kind of clued me to your condition."

"And you thought you would soothe my nerves by flying just above the tree line with the wind shaking the plane?"

"I did it for you; I was afraid you'd complain about not being able to see."

"What's the last thing that goes through a bug's head when it hits a windshield?"

"What?"

"Its ass."

Martin took the plane up.

"In search of Bumfuck, Egypt," Hamilton said. "That sounds like a bad reality TV show. I wonder how Tomcat came up with that one."

"I thought cops knew all the off-color slang."

"I thought we did, too."

"Having spent a few years in the Land of Lincoln, I can tell you about B. F. Egypt. If you go to South Illinois, you'll find towns with names like Cairo, Thebes, and Karnak. The area is known as Little Egypt. Before the interstates were put in, traveling from Chicago to South Illinois wasn't an easy proposition. If you were traveling from the Windy City, those little Podunk towns seemed like they were deep in the sticks."

"If BFE means the middle of nowhere, I'd say we've arrived."

"No argument here."

Martin exhaled a vapor trail. The heater was going, but the plane was still freezing. "It's colder than a Siberian well-digger's ass," he said. "Anyone would be crazy to live here this time of the year."

Hamilton rubbed his hands in agreement. "It's so cold, if you lived here you'd have a tough time even having warm memories."

Below them, he thought, it looked like a pen-and-ink etching, everything black and white and stark. He didn't say it, though. People were never comfortable with poetic cops.

He raised his watch for a look. "It's noon in Alaska. You know what that means?"

"What?"

"Happy hour."

If you went by the disappearing sun, it would be hard to argue. Martin nodded but didn't smile. "Before too long we'll have to turn back," he said. "These days are just too damn short."

"December in Seward means you get about five hours of daylight between sunrise and sunset. And here the days are even shorter."

Both men grew silent, weighed down by the approaching darkness. They flew in silence for another quarter of an hour.

"We're not very far from Grizzly's lake," said Martin, "but I think it's time to wave a white flag."

"No argument here. I was beginning to get tunnel vision anyway."

"You're not done with your looking. We'll be flying a little bit of a different route back, so you'll need to keep staring out your window."

"Great," said Hamilton.

He rubbed his eyes while the plane turned around, and once more took up his rubbernecking. They were about fifteen minutes into their return journey when he saw it. He sat up straight and pointed to a spot off to his right. "What the hell is that?"

Martin craned his neck to look through the window at where Hamilton was pointing. On the ground below them, it looked like red paint had been scattered around the icy landscape.

"Could it be blood?" asked Martin.

"Blood wouldn't be that color," said Hamilton. "It usually looks more like rust than whatever that is we're seeing."

Martin angled the plane lower for them to get a better look. "What about a wolf kill that got scattered around? Maybe they were feasting just as it began hailing or sleeting. That would have iced everything up. And it would explain why everything is splattered all about."

"That's no wolf kill. And what we're seeing isn't blood."

"Then what is it?"

"If I had to guess, I'd say we're looking at tomato sauce."

"Tomato sauce?"

"Maybe spaghetti sauce."

"That's quite a spill of tomato sauce."

"Not if a couple of those Costco seven-pound cans exploded all over the ground."

"You really think that's what we're seeing?"

Hamilton nodded. "You toss one of those cans out of an airplane, and I wouldn't be surprised if it ruptured and splattered everywhere. And that's just the kind of provision a mountain man would be packing. They stock up on big bags of beans, rice, and pasta. All you need to do is add some wild game and tomato sauce, and you got yourself something almost edible."

"But why would anyone throw seven-pound cans of tomato sauce out of an airplane?"

"You're the pilot. You tell me."

Martin thought about it for a moment and said, "If it wasn't a prank or an experiment, there's only one good reason. They needed to lose weight in order to gain altitude."

They'd flown past the red landscape; Martin began the slow process of turning the plane around to get a better look at what was below. To Hamilton it felt as if they were doing a strafing run. They flew close to the ground—too close for his comfort.

"Okay," he announced, "it sure as hell looks like tomato sauce. Now stop scaring the hell out of me and get the plane up in the air."

"How about I find a place to land, and we get a sample of what we're looking at?"

"That sample is going to have to wait. I don't want to be a statistic. Let's get out of here while there's still light."

Martin sighed and then nodded reluctantly. "So close," he said.

"The spaghetti sauce isn't going anywhere."

"When are you available to return so that we can search the area?"

"I'm tied up most of this week."

"There's nothing you can do?"

"I'll try."

"We're close, I know it. The plane Grizzly hired likely iced up, and they had to throw out provisions."

"You like jumping to conclusions."

"It's him," said Martin.

Instead of commenting further, Hamilton asked, "You hungry?"

Martin nodded and said, "I'm starved."

"I don't know about you," said Hamilton, "but I got this sudden hankering for Italian."

CHAPTER TWENTY-SIX

Nina was praying more than she ever had. She prayed for help and guidance, but most of all, she kept praying for a miscarriage. She wished she had the kind of faith to fear no evil while walking through the valley of the shadow of death. But she was scared of plenty of things, starting with Baer.

No time for a pity party. She had to find a way through that valley of death. She was pregnant and felt like shit, there was a psychopath who had to be dealt with, and the world around her was scary and frozen.

Tough and be tougher.

I am a runner, Nina thought, *and runners don't give up on a race.* Marathoners find a way to get to the finish line. It doesn't matter if they're in last place. They still finish. And that's what she had to do.

* * *

Baer stood outside her pen, waiting for her to stop retching. Nina knew that he wasn't looking out for her as much as he was the cause of her indigestion. When she finished spitting up, he handed her a bowl of broth. In the mornings it was all she was able to keep down. He'd placed some hardtack in the bowl. The broth had softened the hard biscuit, and Nina took a few bites of it.

"I'm not sure about you going out with me today," he said.

Ever since learning she was pregnant, Nina had made a point of working outdoors with Baer. Yesterday she'd shoveled dog shit and chipped away dog piss. Baer had done the heavy lifting, carting everything away to compost, but Nina hadn't used her pregnancy as an excuse to avoid work. Now, more than ever, she felt the need to act. There was no way she wanted to give birth in the wild, far from medical help. She had to find a way to get away well before then.

"I'm sure," she said.

"I'll be checking the traplines today. There's not enough snow on the ground for me to harness the team, so that means walking more than a dozen miles today, most of it over hilly terrain."

"That sounds better than being cooped up here."

"You look like you're ready to throw up."

"I can hold it down."

He frowned. "I'm not sure if working the traplines is something a pregnant woman should be doing."

"Do you want me to have a healthy child? It will need to be healthy to survive nuclear fallout. Even a fever can be fatal to a baby if it doesn't develop a strong immune system."

She knew she was playing not only on Baer's end-of-world fears but also on Daniel's death. She could likely tell him anything about prenatal care and he would accept it as gospel. The advent of her pregnancy had changed their relationship. That was something Nina was trying to use to her advantage.

When he didn't immediately answer, she said, "There have been all sorts of studies showing that a mother's exercising makes the fetus stronger. The worst thing you can do to a developing baby is to keep me penned up."

She spoke with such conviction that she almost believed what she was saying, even though she had no conception of whether it was true or not.

"Okay," Baer said.

* * *

It's conditioning, thought Nina, pushing to keep up with Baer. *I'm preparing for the race of my life.*

But she'd never had to do conditioning with her stomach flip-flopping and her hormones at war. Still, she wasn't carrying all the extra weight that Baer was. In his pack basket were traps, stakes, a small shovel, an ax, snares, scents, lures, and bait. That was in addition to water, food, and an emergency tarp. Nina wouldn't have been surprised if he were carrying fifty pounds of equipment and supplies.

They were both wearing snowshoes, which made their walking easier. Nina assumed her snowshoes had once belonged to Elese. They were constructed of lightweight high-tech material. Because she weighed so much less than Baer, walking on snow was actually easier for her. Nina couldn't afford to be carrying much in the way of extra weight when she tried to escape. That meant she'd have to make the attempt before she was five months into term. After that time her body would betray her with too much extra weight.

"Something's in the snare," said Baer.

Be dead, prayed Nina. The last animal, a muskrat, hadn't been. The animal had been caught in what Baer called a floating raft set. He'd dispensed the muskrat with a shovel, all the while extolling the virtues of its meat, fat, and fur. It was all Nina could do to not throw up.

"It's a marten," he said, sounding pleased.

Nina was glad to see that the cat-size animal looked to be as stiff as a board. She watched as Baer removed the wire from the marten's neck.

"It looks like a mink," she said.

"Same weasel family," said Baer, "and same fierceness, but bigger. This one struggled so hard it strangled itself. Sometimes they're so desperate to get away they wrench hard enough to break their necks."

Nina wondered if those marten purposely killed themselves. What would she do to escape the line?

Baer ran his hand along the dark fur and said, "Beautiful pelt. Of course, when it ends up in a stole or coat, it's not called a marten anymore. I guess that doesn't sound expensive enough. It becomes a sable."

He tossed the stiff animal into a burlap sack he was carrying in the pack basket and began setting another snare.

Nina turned away from him and tried to hide her gagging, but of course he noticed. "With all the shit that's happening in the world," he said, "you should be thankful. Having a baby out here away from the wars will likely save its life."

Hearing his garbage was almost enough to make Nina puke again. "Are you serious?"

He nodded. "Terrorists are gathering weapons of mass destruction. And let's not forget the nuclear threat posed by Russia, China, and Pakistan. People don't realize there are about fifty wars going on right now. And any one of those could be the tinderbox that sets off the whole world. People think America is secure. They don't realize when the time comes how fast the Lower Forty-Eight will be toast. Of course, so will the rest of the world. The only spots on the globe where anyone will have a chance of survival are places like this."

"And after that apocalypse, it's your job to repopulate the world?"

He either didn't hear her sarcasm or chose to not respond to it. "There is nothing more important than family."

His words sounded long-rehearsed.

"There are women who might like this kind of . . . adventure," Nina said. "Why not go find a pioneer woman who wants this kind of lifestyle?"

"I couldn't afford to spend my life looking."

"But you might have found a woman who loved you."

"Believing in romantic love is the worst mistake a man can make. Or a woman. What easier way is there to deceive someone? The notion of love only leads to regrets and disappointment and worse."

Once again, to Nina's ears it sounded like he was repeating what someone else had said, or remembering what someone else had done.

"Did your father love your mother?"

Baer's face showed his dislike of her question. "She betrayed him. And she betrayed me."

"How did she do that?"

"She left like a thief in the night. You don't leave your family."

The words sounded wrong. Baer wasn't one to say things like "thief in the night." But his bitter father might have. He might have said those words over and over to his young son.

"I heard her," said Baer.

"What did you hear?"

"I heard her when she was leaving. I think what alerted me was that she was trying to be overly quiet. She was about to go out the door when she saw me. I saw her surprise—and fear. She whispered for me to go back to sleep. And she begged me not to tell."

"But you did?"

His only answer was a shrug.

"Losing a mother at any age is difficult," Nina said.

"She made a bad choice. She paid for that choice."

"Do you understand how those abandonment issues have followed you?"

"'Abandonment issues,'" said Baer, his tone clearly disdainful. "When I was in Fairbanks, I saw a T-shirt that caught my eye. It said, 'If You Love Something, Set It Free.' And right below that it said, 'And If It Doesn't Return, Hunt It Down and Kill It.'"

Nina wondered whether he'd hunted down and killed Elese.

"If you're done puking," he said, "let's get moving."

* * *

After fifteen minutes of hard walking, Baer came to a stop and began setting up some snares.

"Stay off the game trail," he warned Nina, gesturing her over to the side.

It took her a few moments to make out what he was referring to. The trail was distinguished by a flattened area that had overgrowth on either side. It was in that space where Baer was positioning his snares.

Nina looked a little more closely and could make out some paw prints. There was also some scat visible along the trail. She'd heard Baer comment more than once, "Shit and spoor will tell you all you need and more."

She watched him repositioning sticks and brush and realized he was putting up obstacles to try to get the animals to take the path he wanted.

"You're trying to direct the game," she said.

"No shit, Sherlock. I did the same thing with you."

"The only thing I remember is tripping."

"Like any animal, you chose the path of least resistance. I let the animal think it's making a choice, but all the while I'm pulling the strings. I funneled you along and used debris to narrow the path, making you go where I wanted. With some of my traps, I use guide sticks. That's what I did with you, but I had to use what was on hand, so I set you up with construction material and trash."

"I was preoccupied. I was concentrating on something else."

"That's how you get your prey. The animal you're going after might be on the scent of something. Or maybe it wants to get back to its den and is traveling along a path it's been on a hundred times before. The only difficulty with getting you was that when you work with snares, you usually try to get the animal to put its head through the loop. They get snared, and the garrote does the rest. I couldn't do that with you.

And I couldn't use a spring trap. So I had to work it so that you would put your foot into a snare. I made you step over a perceived obstruction right into my snare."

By the sound of his voice, Baer was remembering his handiwork proudly. It made her both angry and embarrassed. He'd played her like a rat in a maze.

"Most animals aren't as easy to take as you were," he said.

Inside of her gloves, Nina clenched her fists. Baer was using his hands for a different purpose. He made loops from the wire, measuring them with four of his fingers. Then he walked over to a nearby stand of trees, found a snag, and started stripping off its branches.

"If we want to catch us a brace of bunnies," said Baer, "we got to be smarter than our prey. Dead sticks are better than green ones. You don't want the rabbit eating. You want him going into the snare."

Baer speared the stick in the ground and then positioned the snare, using two small sticks to prop it up. He slid the sliding noose with apparent pleasure, and Nina found herself grinding her teeth. The bruises around her neck had almost faded away, but she hadn't forgotten. She would never forget his brutality. Her being pregnant had stopped his attacks. As far as Nina was concerned, that was its only benefit.

He began positioning sticks and branches to the sides of the snare. "If everything goes right, our bunny will walk right into the hangman's noose. I've made the snare short enough that our rabbit can't bite the wire."

He tested the noose. "Usually our Playboy Bunny panics, and she strangles nice and quick."

She heard the insinuation in his voice and responded to it by walking away. She'd traveled the route of Baer's traplines enough times now to know the general direction in which they ran.

"Hope you don't get caught in a spruce trap," he said. "That's not a good way to die."

Nina kept walking, but Baer caught up with her a few minutes later. "Aren't you quick as a bunny?" he said.

"What's a spruce trap?" she asked.

"It's also called a tree well," he said. "Why do you think I'm always telling you to stay clear of trees and their overhangs?"

"I don't know why. You've never bothered to explain it to me."

"Spruce traps are pockets that form near a tree, but you usually can't see them because they're hidden by a layer of snow. That's why it's always good to stay clear of trees, and when you can't, you should be tap, tap, tapping around them like a blind man. I've heard tree wells kill more winter backpackers than anything else. They fall in the well and suffocate. They learn their lesson too late."

Baer sounded amused. Nina hoped she could use his smugness against him. They started out again, and when they came to a streambed, Baer began setting his spring traps. Nina had come to realize that he used different-size traps for the different prey he was going for. Marten seemed to be his preferred prey. Before setting his traps, Baer studied tracks and trails. In addition to securing them to the ground, he also set up leaning poles, placing the traps on platforms above the ground. In one spot he used a hollow log and positioned the trap just outside the wooden opening.

"Curiosity killed the cat," he said, "and the marten."

But at that moment Nina wasn't listening to him. In the distance she could hear a baby crying. She didn't think about the potential of being rescued by other people. The only thing that mattered to her was that here in the wild was a child in need.

"It's a baby!" she cried.

Baer started laughing.

"Listen!" Nina said, not understanding his amusement. "Can't you hear? It's a crying baby!"

"It's a horny male porcupine," said Baer.

Disbelieving, Nina said, "What?"

"That's his mating call."

Nina waited to hear the cry again. After half a minute, the silence was broken by the wail. Now that she was listening critically, she could tell it wasn't a baby after all.

"You know how porcupines mate?" Baer asked.

She didn't answer.

"Very carefully," he said.

* * *

Baer seemed confident about the prospects of the day's last site. "Sometimes trappers have to be like farmers," he said. "You prepare your crop."

"And how did you do that?"

"I picked a likely spot where I put down a lot of husks, chaff, and sawdust, and whenever I came by, I amended the bed with seeds, crumbs, berries, and cabin trash. What you'll see is almost like a compost pit that's about twelve feet around and maybe three inches deep. It didn't take long before all sorts of vermin set up home in my compost pile. The voles are everywhere. And that's brought a host of predators. Yesterday I saw tracks of mink, marten, fox, and lynx. They've all been coming around to feed on the voles and mice. I'm counting on a good end of the day."

Nina saved her breath and nodded. As a distance runner, she'd trained in altitude, but in this wilderness she was struggling to keep up. She wasn't sure if it was the terrain, the conditions, or her pregnancy. Even with her snowshoes the ground seemed to pull at her and make every step a challenge, but she wasn't going to concede to Baer that she needed a break.

She heard some strange groaning, and for a moment thought it was Baer who was struggling, but the sounds weren't coming from him. This time she didn't react as quickly as when she'd heard the porcupine.

She listened to more unearthly groaning, and then what sounded like whistling.

Baer saw her looking around and trying to search out an explanation. "The water is talking," he said. "It becomes noisy this time of year. It knows it's giving up the ghost."

"What do you mean?"

"The creeping cold is applying the brakes. It's making it difficult for the water to breathe. The ponds and lakes have mostly iced up. What you hear is the last of the running water. It's offering up its gurgled, dying complaints."

Nina was surprised that Baer almost sounded poetic.

"Our honey hole is just ahead," he said.

He increased his pace, anxious to see what was waiting for them. Nina had to jog just to stay close to him. Then he slowed up.

"Shit," he said.

Nina tried to see what he was seeing. There was nothing. And then she spotted the big paw prints.

By then Baer had reached the empty first trap. "Shit!" he screamed, and kicked the trap. The second trap was empty, as was the third, fourth, and fifth. All the traps had been sprung.

"That she-bitch is dead," he said, spitting on the ground. "When I catch up to her, I'll make sure she dies a slow, painful death. And afterward I'll cut off her head and put it on a pike."

Nina knew better than to ask questions. She watched as Baer went around kicking traps and mouthing oaths. She'd seen him angry before, but this was the first time she'd seen him lose his control.

"Fucking she-bitch," he said over and over, as if that should explain everything.

Nina studied the ground. They weren't bear prints, but they were large, like a dog on steroids. But even to her untrained eye, she could see that something looked wrong with some of the paw prints. The impression looked incomplete, as if half the paw was missing.

"That's right," said Baer, answering Nina's unspoken question. "She-bitch is missing half of her left paw. Last year I had her in one of my traps. And she made the choice to gnaw away a good part of her foot to get free. I didn't think she'd survive with only half her front paw. It's tough enough surviving with four good legs out here. But the she-bitch made it."

His laugh was bitter. "And she's not one to forgive and forget. Twice last year the she-bitch sprung all my traps. And she always likes to leave me a calling card."

The pile of shit sitting in the middle of the clearing wasn't the only thing the wolf had left. There were yellow trails all around the sprung traps.

"Don't eat the yellow snow," Baer said, pretending insouciance.

Nina knew it was an act. She knew he was still raging. She kept her eyes averted from him, but not because of his glowering. She was afraid of him seeing how happy she was.

"The she-bitch signed her death warrant," he said. "Tomorrow I'm going to hunt her down."

Nina thought of Elese. Her secret sister had advised her to find her totem.

I am a wolf, Nina thought.

CHAPTER TWENTY-SEVEN

Morning sickness came on hard, and Nina woke up vomiting into a pan Baer had left in her pen.

Children had always been a "someday" proposition. It scared her to think that there was now an unwanted ETA.

Even though it wasn't yet dawn, Baer had gotten up when Nina began retching. He threw on his clothes and prepared his pack.

"You'll be staying here today," he said.

As sick as she was feeling, Nina wanted out of her cage. She came away with more knowledge from every outing, and that gave her confidence that she might be able to escape.

"Why?" she asked. "Being cooped up isn't good for me or the baby."

"One day won't hurt either one of you. I'm taking the team and going after the she-bitch. We'll be covering a lot of territory."

Nina felt her stomach lurch, but it wasn't morning sickness. She was afraid for the wolf. The animal had escaped from Baer's trap. It was a survivor. And not only that, the wolf continued to defy him. Maybe she could find a way to sabotage the hunt.

"I know about covering territory," she said. "I'm a runner. I'll keep up."

"Yesterday was an easy outing, and you weren't able to keep up. Today will be twice as hard."

"I'll be up for it. I'm just getting back into shape after being locked up too long in your jail."

He shook his head. "Tomorrow you can walk until you drop, but today the she-bitch gets all my attention."

Nina didn't like his name for the wolf. *I'll give her a worthy name,* she thought.

Baer walked over to her cage and began unlocking it. "You got five minutes to do your business while I string up the team," he said.

* * *

It was possible the wolf would be dead by the end of the day. Spending time coming up with a name could be just a waste of time. But despite that, Nina felt compelled.

"I wonder if children are still raised on the story 'Little Red Riding Hood,'" she said to Elese. "I remember how scary the big, bad wolf was. And that's how I thought of wolves until I saw this old movie called *Never Cry Wolf.* I believed wolves were scary and mean and vicious. But that movie changed my whole perception of wolves."

Talking gave Nina something else to think about other than her roiling stomach. Baer had left her a plate of jerky and dried berries. Right now she couldn't even look at the food without feeling ill.

"I keep thinking about how the wolf chewed away part of her foot in order to get free," she said.

She took off her glove and looked at her own maimed finger.

"I'm going to start looking at my hand differently. I was ashamed of seeing my maimed finger, but not anymore. It's a symbol. The monster's traps maimed us both. But the wolf hasn't stopped fighting him, and I'm not going to, either."

The wolf had escaped Baer's metal jaws in the only way she could.

"How about 'Freedom'?" said Nina. She let the silence build for a few moments, as if listening to an answer from Elese. Then she nodded her head and said, "Yes, politicians have cheapened that word."

Nina wondered if she was including her own fiancé in that assessment. During her short time being part of Terrence's world, she'd already attended enough political events to make her cynical.

"What about 'She Who Can't Be Trapped'?"

Nina waited a moment and then sighed. "Yes, that is long," she said.

She tried out another name: "'The Great Houdini,'" she announced, and then made a face. After a moment's thought, she came up with, "'The Great Howldini.'"

No and no, Nina thought. But then she found herself smiling.

"'Lady Liberty,'" she said, and thought about that for a moment. "That's close, but it's too symbolic and it's too human."

And then Nina clapped her hands. "'*La Loba*,'" she announced. "Yes, that's it."

* * *

Nina spent most of the morning studying Elese's maps and survival tips. In some ways it was putting the cart before the horse, but she had to be ready to act if any chance presented itself. She studied her sister's words as if cramming for finals.

Or The Final, thought Nina.

She came up with mnemonic connections to help her remember. For moss and north, she thought of the abbreviation of Minnesota, *MN*; to remember water generally moving from north to south, Nina took the first letter of each word and made the word *WaNeS*; clouds moving west to east had her thinking *CaWEd*.

When she was finally satisfied that she'd studied everything to the point of having memorized it, she turned to the penultimate page of

Elese's journal. Her sister had titled this next to last entry "The Great Escape." Nina wished she could be sure Elese had been writing about getting away, but in rereading this entry, she'd found something ominous in her words. Had she been writing about dying?

For the longest time, I have been planning my escape. In order to be free of the monster, I believed it would either be necessary to kill him or to make sure I had enough of a head start that he couldn't catch me.

I spent countless hours mulling over what you are likely thinking about right now. Could I find a way to lock the monster in the cabin? Could I burn the cabin down with him inside? Could I do an outhouse run at night and use the darkness to escape? Could I somehow trap him? Was there a way I could engineer an escape and then use myself as the bait to ensnare him?

There were always so many scenarios and so many things to think about. And of course, I was afraid of failure, knowing how severe his punishment would be. Getting away was only the beginning, and possibly the easiest, of my difficulties. How do you survive for long enough to get back to civilization? There are no street signs out here; there are no roads. There are rivers to surmount and mountains to cross. There is the threat of wild animals, and the even bigger threat of the cold. Break a bone, and you die. Fall in the wrong spot, and you never get up.

Everything changed when Denali died, though, because I no longer had to be scared for him. And I no longer had to be scared for me.

Part of me died. Or all of me died. I can't be sure which is closer to what I now am. Some days I feel alive; other days I am a ghost.

What will I be escaping to? My boy is dead. And Greg seems more of a dream now than anything else. Maybe he always was a dream. That's how it feels. And it's been so long. For his sake I hope he has moved on.

Can a ghost escape? I suppose I will try. It will certainly be easier now. Since Denali's death the monster no longer locks me up. He lets me come and go. The opportunity to get away has never been easier. But I wonder when I am out there if I'll have the will to go on. I am certain of one thing, though: when I leave I won't let the monster bring me back alive.

Sometimes I am convinced that I am already in the underworld.

When I was a girl, I loved reading about the myths. There were these goddesses I thought were so incredible, like Diana and Aphrodite and the Fates and the Muses. But even the gods and goddesses had problems. It wasn't like their lives were perfect. Even the gods could be star-crossed.

One myth that has always stayed with me is the story of Orpheus and Eurydice. It bothered me as a girl. And it bothers me even more now. Like Eurydice I was taken by a monster at my wedding. Eurydice died when she was bitten by a serpent. The venom that struck me down came from a thousand different bites and was slower-acting.

Orpheus, the son of Apollo and Calliope, couldn't accept Eurydice's death. He traveled to the underworld and used his music to convince Hades to let him deliver Eurydice from death, but with the proviso that he could not look back until both he and his bride were free from the underworld. In the end Orpheus blinked. He looked back and lost his love.

Too often that is what I do these days. I look back. I remember Denali and can't help but think that I do not want to live in a world where he does not exist.

Nina wiped away her tears and then rolled the booklet up and hid it away. It was already getting dark outside. Every day was shorter. Every day finding light became more elusive.

Her stomach rumbled. Half the day she felt sick, and half the day she felt hungry. She tore into the jerky and finished all of it. Afterward she wrapped the furs and comforters all around her and fell asleep.

She awoke with a start in what felt like the middle of the night. It was as dark inside the cabin as it was outside; Nina held up a gloved hand and could barely see it. Nearby she could hear dogs yelping. Their howls made her shiver. They were crying out their hurt and fear, sounds she only heard when Baer beat them.

Nina listened while Baer chained up the dogs. She pretended to be asleep even after he stormed inside and started banging around pots. His breath came out in aggrieved huffs and puffs, like an old locomotive train starting up. He got a fire going in the woodstove and then used his big knife like an ax, cutting into a side of meat. Nina's ears told her all this. She didn't need to look to know Baer's routine. After a long day on the trail, he was preparing to make sure the dogs were fed and hydrated. Each would be getting its own big bucket of meat soup.

Baer tromped out of the cabin with the food. The dogs were too important a resource for him to mistreat them for very long. Nina wished that was also true of her.

With Baer outside, Nina didn't have to hide her emotions. The covers shook as she laughed quietly. Baer would only be this angry for one reason. *La Loba* was alive.

And so am I, Nina thought. *And so am I.*

CHAPTER TWENTY-EIGHT

"Bears have the right idea," said Martin. "Sleep away the winter."

"Let me guess," said Hamilton. "You'll be eating Chinese food on Christmas."

The year was passing far too quickly. Christmas was only three weeks away.

"Chinese takeout," said Martin, "with the TV tuned to that channel with the log burning. That's what I did last Christmas."

"You sound like you're an old man. What are you, thirty-one?"

"I just turned thirty-three."

"Do you think Elese would approve of you spending Christmas eating moo goo gai pan?"

"As long as it doesn't have MSG in it, she'd probably be okay."

Hamilton saw a small smile come to Martin's face. He continued, "Mu shu pork with plenty of plum sauce was always her favorite."

Then Hamilton noticed the other man's smile turning into a frown. "We never had a Christmas together."

Hamilton nodded to show he'd heard and went back to looking out the window.

"I'm assuming you didn't share our find with our friends at AST and Major Kong," said Martin.

"And what makes you assume that?"

"You're up here flying with me."

"I let the fates decide if I'd tell them about our spaghetti-sauce find," said Hamilton. "All they had to do was call me with an update. Since I never heard from either the troopers or Sergeant Wood, I decided not to share, at least not until we confirmed our find and searched the surrounding area."

"Did Donnelly's reward have anything to do with you keeping your mouth shut?"

"You think greed is the great motivator?"

"It inspired a lot of people to look for Nina Granville."

"Sorry to disappoint you. I assume I don't qualify for the reward. Law enforcement is typically excluded."

"But you're doing this on your own time."

"You don't need to remind me. My wife does a good enough job of that."

"You should get some reward for all the unpaid time you've put in on these cases. Or at least a reward for the time you spent on the case when you weren't investigating me."

Martin's words came with a smile, but Hamilton heard their undertones.

"Your wife's disappearance got its hooks into me."

It was Martin's turn to nod to show he'd heard. A minute later he asked, "So, what would you do with a million dollars?"

"You mean right after I quarterback my team to a Super Bowl victory?"

"Even cops are allowed a pipe dream."

Hamilton shrugged and shook his head. "I guess I'd put a lot of it into college funds. My oldest kid is already sixteen. You want sticker shock? Look at the prices of colleges these days. And I've been promising Carrie ever since we got married that we'd go on some nice trip, maybe finally get to Europe. We never really had a honeymoon."

"I wish I could say the same thing."

Hamilton wondered if his gallows humor was a defense mechanism or a sign that he was healing.

He raised his binoculars and once again began scanning the terrain around them. Martin had calculated various courses based on what he would have done if he'd been piloting a plane in trouble. If Tomcat's plane had gone down, that would explain a lot of things. Of course, collecting Grizzly's skeleton wouldn't be as satisfying as bringing him in, but if Nina Granville's skeleton was also identified at the crash site, they could connect the dots to Elese Martin and put two cases to rest.

Snow began falling. Earlier there had been rain. They'd also flown through clear skies.

"Isn't this the kind of weather that got Tomcat into trouble?" Hamilton asked.

"His was a lot worse. This is just a little bit shitty. You'll know a lot shitty when we encounter it."

"You're not the most reassuring pilot I've ever flown with."

"And I'm sure I'm not the most experienced pilot, either."

"There you go again."

When the snow started falling harder, Hamilton asked, "Are we there yet?" When his kids were young, they'd driven him crazy asking that.

Martin checked the GPS reading. "Almost. Keep looking for a crash site."

"I'll keep praying I don't end up as *part* of a crash site."

Five minutes later Martin pointed his index finger toward the ground. "You want tomato sauce with that?" he asked.

"Glad to see that son of a bitch is still there. I've been wondering if we both might have seen the same mirage."

"We're lucky the tomato sauce was absorbed into the ice. Otherwise the rain would have washed it away."

Martin nosed the plane down. They were flying with tundra tires, and he needed to find a suitable landing spot where there weren't large snowdrifts. Most bush pilots were already flying with skis, but he'd explained that he hadn't trained with them. He took his measure of a few likely spots. Hamilton had some misgivings as to how he was doing his measuring.

"Running into a tree isn't my idea of a good landing," he said. "How about getting this crate above the tree line?"

Martin nodded, and the plane gained some altitude. Then they circled the area again.

"It's not only the landing I need to think about," said Martin. "There's also the subsequent takeoff."

"I like the sound of landing, but I like the sound of takeoff even more."

Martin made his choice, and the plane began its descent toward a landing area about a half mile away from the tomato sauce. Hamilton closed his eyes, unable to watch. He was glad his job came with a life insurance policy. The payout might be enough to cover the expense of college for his kids as well as his funeral.

* * *

"Smooth as could be," said Martin.

"Was that after the fourth bounce or the fifth?"

The landing might not have been perfect, but at least they were down safely. "Let's get moving before we freeze to death," Hamilton said.

Martin consulted his handheld GPS, and the two men began walking. They'd gone no more than a hundred yards when they saw what looked like a flag flapping in the wind. As they drew closer, they saw their flag was actually a mesh bag impaled on a snag. Hamilton pulled the bag down and displayed the find.

"Long-grain enriched rice," said Martin.

"I kind of doubt this was the setting for a wedding."

"Fifty pounds," said Martin, still reading.

Hamilton went down on his haunches, his eyes moving around the area.

"What are you looking for?"

"Traces of rice," he said. "I can't see much, but the wind could have scattered it, or voles, mice, and birds might have found it. Not to mention my eyes aren't what they used to be."

He ran his glove over the mixture of snow and ice and nodded. "Some of the grains are mixed in with the snow and ice, making it all but invisible."

He straightened, then folded the remnants of the mesh bag and put it in an evidence bag he'd brought along.

"The plane must have been in a bad way for them to have been throwing everything out," said Martin. "That's desperation time."

The two men continued forward; neither spoke. Hamilton hoped they wouldn't stumble over any plane wreckage, or worse, bodies. Finally they came to the red-hued ice. He didn't say what he was thinking: the whole area looked like one big blood splatter. He'd worked a few horrific crime scenes that looked similar to this.

He kneeled down and pulled out a penknife. He chopped free a red icicle, stuck it in his mouth, and began sucking. His face didn't give away anything.

"Well?" said Martin.

"You say to-mate-o, I say to-ma-toe."

Martin didn't look amused.

"It could use some garlic and basil," said Hamilton, "but it's definitely tomato sauce."

"So what the hell do we do now?"

CHAPTER TWENTY-NINE

The sun had set a few hours earlier, but the dusk colors lingered in the sky. Nina stood in front of the cabin's only window. It seemed pathetically small and made the cabin seem that much smaller. There was only the one window to prevent heat loss, but she longed for more natural light. As the days had shortened, she'd begun to feel like a spindly plant desperately reaching for light.

Baer was working at his furs; there was no escaping the sights and smells of his handiwork in the small space. Nina hated the whole process. So much death went into his work. He was always busy stretching and scraping and tanning his kills. Nina especially hated the braining, which involved Baer's taking the animal's brain and essentially making a soup out of it that he rubbed into the hide. The stink was more than she could stand; luckily her morning sickness was more manageable now. Baer had given up asking her to help process the furs. Whenever Nina got too near his work and those rancid brains, she started retching.

The monster thought that was a sign of her being weak. He mockingly called her a "delicate flower." One day he would learn she wasn't.

Nina hoped that day would be soon. Was she already entering the second trimester? She tried to count the days of her captivity. The calendar date she came up with surprised her.

"Is today Christmas?"

Baer looked up from his work. "Why? Santa Claus might not live too far from here, but I don't think he'll be making any deliveries tonight."

"So, it is Christmas?"

"I don't follow the days on the calendar too closely. I'm more of a clock-watcher."

She could hear the amusement in the monster's voice but didn't respond to it, hoping he wouldn't say more. But he was already on his soapbox.

"Of course, I don't watch the same clock that others do. They run around doing their nine-to-five being dupes to their timepieces. The clock I'm watching is the Doomsday Clock. You ever hear of it?"

Nina shook her head. It was her fault for having gotten him started.

"The Doomsday Clock is operated by a group of scientists. And before you assume they're crackpots, that couldn't be further from the truth. They're all Nobel laureates. Imagine the ultimate brain trust. And where do you think all these geniuses have pegged mankind on the Doomsday Clock?"

"I don't know," Nina said.

"According to them, it's five minutes to midnight. They just reaffirmed that time. Of course, it went unnoticed by the masses. People around the world are too blind to realize it's almost midnight. And you know what happens at midnight? Game over. It's the end of the line for almost all of humanity. We'll have a good view of the end of the world from here."

"I think it is Christmas," said Nina, "which isn't a day on which I want to hear about the end of the world."

Baer made a disgusted noise, but she didn't care. What were her parents and brother doing? Nina had spent Labor Day with her family and told them she wouldn't be joining them for Christmas this year. She'd agreed to be with the Donnelly family in Greenwich.

Are they thinking about me tonight? Are they still looking for me? Does anyone believe I'm still alive?

"I love being in New York at this time of year," she said, speaking more to herself than to Baer. "When you walk the streets of New York, you hear Christmas music playing out of department-store loudspeakers. And on every corner there's a Santa Claus ringing a bell. The city is awash in colors. There's red, green, and silver everywhere. The window displays are like pieces of art. Every year I go to Macy's just to see what they have on display. It's always something different and something unique."

Nina had always thought she hated the commercialism of Christmas. In New York the department stores started actively pushing the holidays in October. More than two months of Christmas hype made it easy to burn out on the season. But now she was nostalgic for all of that.

"I've seen pictures of New York City," said Baer. "It looks like an ant colony. I can't imagine anything worse."

Nina stared out the small window. She didn't expect to see anything. There was just darkness beyond the double-pane glass. That's all there ever was at night.

"Oh!" she said, an exclamation more than a word. "Oh!" she repeated.

The magnificent colors could not be contained by the small window and swept into the cabin. Unmindful of how cold it was, Nina ran to the door and opened it.

And there she saw the sky dancing, and the land awash in the Northern Lights. She found herself extending her hands to the shimmering waves of green, purple, and orange, and the hues of red and blue. The entire horizon was awash in wavy light.

Nina walked down the path, wanting to be closer to the light, wanting a vantage point where the vista wasn't obscured by the silhouettes of trees. She found an open area. The sky was afire. The lights were alive, undulating and throbbing. In her head she heard music; the tune was as unknown to her as what she was seeing. Wild magic filled the air. If leprechauns, brownies, and elves had appeared in front of her and danced like dervishes, Nina wouldn't have been at all surprised.

I would join them in their dance, she thought.

"The aurora borealis," said a voice from behind her.

Baer tried to contain the uncontainable with a name.

Nina moved away from him. Her eyes were on the sky. She saw what Elese had seen and tried to show with her drawing. Nina had always thought Van Gogh's *Starry Night* was merely impressionistic exaggeration. Now she would forever think of it as an understatement.

"You're looking at electronically charged gaseous particles," Baer said.

"The science can wait," Nina said.

Her dismissiveness didn't sit well with Baer. "I thought Harvard girls liked to know the science. Or do you want the explanation offered up by savages? They thought the lights were spirits."

"They *are* spirits," she said.

"You want a light show? Nuclear bombs will produce the greatest light show in history. From here we'll see the nuclear display of color and winds after every big city in the world gets nuked."

His talk was killing the magic and making the music in her head grow fainter. Nina wasn't going to let that happen. She began to whistle, dance, and sing. She raised both of her hands to the pulsating lights, opening up her palms and spreading her arms as if imploring the lights to come closer to her embrace. She didn't know what tune Elese had whistled; it didn't matter. She called to the lights.

"What the hell are you doing?" said Baer.

Nina implored the lights to come closer. She wanted to dance with them. They would be her partner.

"You're acting crazy."

Baer moved away from her, unsettled. Nina thought of her secret sister.

"The lights hear me," she said. "They're coming closer now."

"You're fucking nuts," he said, and then turned around and retreated into the cabin.

Nina heard the door slam, and she was left alone with the streaming lights.

CHAPTER THIRTY

Without a calendar Nina couldn't be sure if it was New Year's Day. It didn't matter, she supposed. She only had one resolution: to get away.

It was scary cold outside, and she dressed carefully. They were going to work the trapline on the kind of inclement day when no one should be venturing outside. She covered herself from head to toe, but in the midst of her layering, she felt it again.

There was something going on in her stomach other than nausea. It was almost like butterflies were fluttering around her gut. The tingling sensation hadn't felt quite like a pinch, nor had it been indigestion or gas. Every so often she'd felt this little popping, almost like a carbonated bubbling. But now it was more pronounced.

She knew what it was. The baby was kicking.

But it was too soon, wasn't it? Nina wished she could talk to a doctor or consult some manual. Was this normal? In the movies that first kick was always a joyful time. She'd had friends tear up talking about feeling that first kick. The only thing she was feeling was terror.

Her stomach fluttered again. Denial wasn't going to help. The baby was giving her a wake-up call. Every kick told her it was time to escape.

She wasn't ready yet. She was still working on putting together her survival pack. She had found some of the necessary items. They were hidden away, and she prayed that Baer wouldn't find any of her stash. But she still felt grossly ill prepared.

Physically she was fit. Since her imprisonment her body had changed, and not because of the pregnancy. She'd become leaner and more muscular, had regained much of her old running form. She'd fought through blisters, muscle aches, and hardening herself to the elements. Every day was a rigorous workout. She was getting in shape for a purpose. Vanity wasn't driving her; desperation was.

During their walkabouts Nina had learned to reconcile the lay of the land with Elese's maps. Still, it scared her to think that the success or failure of her escape would likely hinge on her being able to successfully navigate the wilderness. She would have to rely on her pathfinding and Elese's cartography.

At least dying was no longer a foregone conclusion. She wasn't going out on a suicide mission. She'd become proficient in trapping, could make a fire under adverse conditions, could read tracks and field dress game. Through Elese's instructions and watching Baer, Nina knew how to make an emergency shelter. She'd made wickiups and snow caves, and had sat out storms in them. And even though Baer had never let her use his rifle, she'd studied him firing it. Given any opportunity, she would be ready to shoot.

But three months of preparation still wasn't enough. She wondered whether a lifetime would be enough.

"Last chance for you to bow out," Baer said, checking his emergency pack. That was his routine every day. Baer was methodical in his preparations. He was even more cautious than the animals he hunted. "It's so cold we're going to have to put booties on the dogs' footpads."

Nina nodded. On two previous occasions, they'd put what looked like miniature mukluks around the paws of the dogs. Without those coverings the cold and icy conditions would have torn their pads.

She took a step outside. Despite being dressed for winter, for a moment she felt like she'd jumped into cold water. Her mouth involuntarily opened, and her intake of breath almost felt like brain freeze. The cold came at her with its long knives; a thousand cuts penetrated her fur armor.

The only solution was to move. Nina followed Baer over to the doghouses. To help deflect the cold, the metal drums had been stuffed full of insulation and elevated half a foot off the ground, with a padded pallet beneath them. The opening into each barrel was just big enough for the dogs to squeeze in and out, which shielded them from the wind. Once inside their barrels, they curled up into a ball, and you could just make out their eyes.

The dogs were slower than usual in exiting from their houses. Although they wagged their tails and appeared to be in good spirits, Nina thought their enthusiasm was muted. Given a choice, she was sure, they'd stay put for the day.

Baer bent down and began putting booties around the dogs' paws and unchaining them. He'd just finished with the third dog when he straightened up and scanned the sky.

"Hear that?" he asked.

Nina strained to hear. No matter how many layers of clothing Baer wore, his hearing was animal-acute. Nina heard a faint buzzing sound that might have been a mosquito, but she knew that Alaska's unofficial state bird could not survive the winter.

"It's some kind of aircraft," Baer said. "It's a long ways off, but of late there's been a lot more air traffic than usual."

Nina kept her head lowered. She didn't want him to see the excitement in her eyes.

"It could be they're looking for our dearly departed pilot," he said. "It's possible his plane was discovered in that lake, even though by this time it must be buried under four feet of ice. I wouldn't have thought they'd be able to find it."

Baer turned his black gaze on her.

"I wouldn't get your spirits up about the possibility of anyone spotting you," he said. "Even the best eyes in the sky would have trouble seeing us. You see, I picked out this spot not only because there are no people around, but because it's a mite inhospitable. No one would think to settle here because it's too hilly and there are too many trees to be able to use a snow machine. But it's those same trees and hills that make us almost invisible."

He bent down to put a boot on the next dog. "And even if they did find the crashed plane, they'd never guess how far away we are from it. Where we're sitting is far from their search zone. And if they get closer, that only means one thing: time to vamoose."

Or time to escape, thought Nina.

* * *

"Gee!" yelled Baer, and the dogs turned to the right.

Nina stepped on and off the sled as conditions dictated. She and Baer rode when there was a straightaway, but most of the time they walked, or at least that's how it felt. The wind whipped at them; even through her layers of clothes, Nina felt its lash. It was a cold that burned. Baer, as usual, acted impervious to the elements. To the accompaniment of wind, he took up his favorite dirge:

> *"Now Sam McGee was from Tennessee, where the cotton blooms*
> *and blows.*
> *Why he left his home in the South to roam 'round the Pole, God*
> *only knows.*
> *He was always cold, but the land of gold seemed to hold him like*
> *a spell;*
> *Though he'd often say in his homely way that 'he'd sooner live in hell.'"*

"Don't you know a holiday song or poem?" Nina shouted, trying to be heard over the wind and doing her best to derail his rendition.

"Yes, I do," he said. "Apparently you haven't been listening as closely as you should." And he started in on the third verse.

"On a Christmas Day we were mushing our way over the Dawson trail.
Talk of your cold! through the parka's fold it stabbed like a driven nail.
If our eyes we'd close, then the lashes froze till sometimes we couldn't see;
It wasn't much fun, but the only one to whimper was Sam McGee."

Nina tightened the covering of her head to try to keep from hearing.

* * *

Baer's mood worsened as the day went on. His traps and snares had come up empty, and he didn't even have his she-bitch to blame. The trapline was roughly in the form of a cloverleaf that bridged two bodies of water. Usually they were able to travel along half the cloverleaf one day, and the other half the next.

"This goddamn cold spell caused a goddamn cold spell on our trapline," he grumbled.

It was difficult to make out his words; his facial hair had iced up, and his nasal drip had resulted in long icicles that resembled a walrus's tusks. Baer slapped at his face, but the ice resisted his blow.

Nina thought of one of Elese's last entries in her book. It was easy to imagine Baer as being something less than human and being something more than human.

"I hate being skunked," he said, making it sound as if the animals hadn't come to his traps just to spite him. And then he added, "Lately the pickings have been getting all too slim around here."

Nina didn't like the sound of that, especially with his earlier threat to "vamoose." Was he already considering a move to the winter game camp? Elese had warned her how much harder it would be to escape from there.

"It's just one bad day," she said. "The animals had the good sense not to venture out when it was so cold."

"But the sun will come out tomorrow, right? Isn't that what Annie says?"

What Baer knew, and didn't know, always surprised Nina. She would never have imagined he knew who Little Orphan Annie was.

"I hope so," said Nina.

"Let's get the hell out of here."

CHAPTER THIRTY-ONE

The next morning Nina awakened to an already dressed Baer.

"I'm going out solo this morning," he said. "You have five minutes to powder your nose."

"Are you taking the dogs?"

"They've got the day off just like you."

"Are you hunting?"

"Yeah, I'm hunting down information. You have four minutes now."

Nina wrapped herself in a parka. It was clear no more answers would be forthcoming. Baer enjoyed his secrets.

She hurried down the path to the outhouse. These days her favorite fantasy involved a luxurious bathroom. She dreamed of a hot bath, but right now she'd even settle for toilet paper. The outhouse TP had run out a month ago.

Nina knew not to delay. By complying with Baer's demands, she'd gotten more time outside her pen. Baer was standing at the door when she returned. He wasn't carrying any snares or traps. Whatever he was going to do didn't involve trapping. She moved by him and went to the pen. Inside she could see he'd placed a plate of food with some grayish-looking meat that appeared to be more frozen than not.

She crawled inside her cell, and he locked it behind her. Baer checked the door to make sure it was secure, and then went out the cabin door and off to his business, whatever that was.

Nina burrowed under the furs and comforters. As weighty as they were, these days there never seemed to be enough. It felt as cold inside as it did outside. But she had to plan for when she wouldn't have a roof over her head or as many furs covering her body.

She spent the morning doing a mental inventory of what provisions she had and what she would need. Lately she'd been spending extra time outside tending to the dogs. Keeping their metal-drum houses cleaned was more work than anyone would have guessed. And she usually brought them their heated-up meat broth at least twice a day to make sure they were getting enough water. She also checked on them at night after her trip to the outhouse. Her visits weren't only social time. She wanted Baer to become used to her spending a few minutes with the dogs.

But she hadn't spent all her time with the dogs or doing chores. She'd also been readying for her getaway. Putting together an escape pack put her in danger. At any moment Baer might notice something was missing. He missed very little. And although Nina had chosen discards, including tarps, plastic bags, some rope, and an old pot, she was still afraid of being found out. She didn't even want to think of what he might do if he discovered what she was up to.

While there was still light, Nina decided to study from Elese's book. By now the maps were burned into her mind. But forgetting anything could mean death.

"I think you've prepared me as best you can, Sister," she said.

Elese's booklet had been pulled out and put away so many times that its cardboard backing was fraying. Nina's intent was to pore over the maps, but instead she found herself turning to the book's last page.

"I wish you had written a different ending to your book. I guess I wanted the fairy tale ending." She ran a finger over the page. "Did you know this would be your final entry? Or did an opportunity to escape arise and not give you the chance to write anymore? It seems too abrupt to me, but I suppose any last page would have been. It means the end of hearing of your voice. Your good-bye came too soon for me."

Elese had titled her last entry. At the top of the page, she had underlined the words *The Winter Bear.*

On the day before we put into dock in Seward, Greg and I went to a lecture given by the cruise ship's anthropologist. She spoke about Alaskan legends and told us about a beast the native people feared more than any other: the Winter Bear.

According to legends, this Winter Bear refuses to hibernate. He wanders the frozen landscapes, ever hungry, ever in search of food. But his appetite isn't what makes this creature so scary. The truly frightening thing about the Winter Bear is its pelt. At the advent of winter, this beast seeks out flowing water, and when it emerges from its swim, it becomes transformed into a creature of ice. Hoarfrost covers the bear in a coating like plate armor.

No arrow can penetrate the Winter Bear's icy shield; even bullets are no match for it. The Winter Bear knows this. It walks through villages with impunity, taking what it wants and leaving behind a trail of death. Few who have seen the Winter Bear have survived.

I remember during the anthropologist's talk, I began to shiver. Greg did not know the cause of my chill, but he put his arm around me. I pretended to be comforted, but I was unable to put the story out of my mind, even when the anthropologist began talking of other legends. And that last night before I was taken, I had a terrible nightmare. The Winter Bear with his icy sheen came to me like a haunting ghost. I could see all too clearly that its icy transformation had made the creature something no longer flesh and blood.

The next day Baer abducted me. That is an accurate description of what happened, but it's so incomplete. The monster murdered what was. He took my old life from me and stole me away to hell.

In the time since, I have wondered if my hearing the story of the Winter Bear was a portent. Is Baer my Winter Bear? Am I one of those victims who saw the Winter Bear and did not survive?

The Baer who stole me away wanders the cold. He is ever hungry. And like the Winter Bear, I am afraid he is not quite human.

I must find a way to kill the Winter Baer. I must find a way to shatter his icy armor.

Nina felt the stub of her ring finger. All she had to do was rub it, and her hate was ignited. So that's what she did.

"You *have* found a way to shatter his armor," she said, "and that's through me. I will kill the Winter Baer."

CHAPTER THIRTY-TWO

"They think they've found the plane," said Hamilton.

"*Think?*"

"Sergeant Wood got the Pentagon to release a few of their latest toys, including special salvage drones. One of them picked up what was described as a 'metal signature.' That's where AST got involved. They sent out a plane and got visual confirmation of a downed bird."

"So you're saying they confirmed it was Tomcat's plane?"

"I wish I was saying that. The downed plane is buried under four to five feet of solid ice."

"When are they going to dig it out?"

"That's not going to happen, at least anytime soon."

"Why not? It's only ice."

"That was my reaction. Apparently both of us don't have any idea of how much work that kind of salvage operation would entail."

Martin wasn't accepting that. "They cut down a lot of wood, and then they start a big fire atop the ice. It can't be that hard."

"I'm just the messenger. AST and NTSB are both willing to wait. The way they see it, more than three months have passed since the crash. The best-case scenario is that there were crash survivors, but since no one has come forward, that seems unlikely."

"Donnelly is accepting that?"

"He's making sure every inch within a twenty-five-mile radius gets combed over."

"I wish I had the data they did. Any chance I can get it?"

"So far it's been what's ours is theirs and what's theirs is theirs. What data do you want?"

"I want to know the exact location of the plane. I could enter that information and make a topographic map."

"What good would that do you?"

"I'm not sure. Geologists love their maps."

"I'm sure I can get you the exact location of where the plane is," said Hamilton.

"I appreciate it."

"You should know I'm still holding back one piece of information from their investigation."

"And what's that?"

"I haven't told them what Jack told me. They don't know about Grizzly's drop-off spot."

"So they know where the plane is, and we know where Tomcat wanted to go."

"That's about the size of it."

"Care to guess how far the two lakes are from each other?"

"I'm thinking it's about twenty miles."

"Are you up for another outing?"

"Afraid you'll have to go without me. I'm tied up for the next few days."

Hamilton wasn't lying about his commitments. But the truth was he'd had more than enough of flying. He didn't want to tempt the fates. Unfortunately for him, Martin did.

"It's going to take me that long to get ready anyway. I have my own work. I'll also need to study some maps and route our course."

Hamilton sighed and said, "Wonderful."

CHAPTER THIRTY-THREE

After a long day of working the traplines, there was little to show for their efforts. Baer had said next to nothing during their disappointing outing. Nina found his silence scarier than his raging, as she had no idea what he was thinking. As they neared the cabin, the dogs began moving with renewed vigor. The end of the day was in sight.

Baer broke his long silence. "While I start dinner," he told her, "you put the dogs away and get them settled in."

She was glad for any time away from Baer. She led the dogs to their houses and unhitched them from their harnesses. Nina had given each a private name instead of a number, something Baer didn't know, and while attaching them to their individual ten-foot steel chains, she affectionately whispered their names. Moondoggy, Oscar, Bandit, and Romeo happily entered their insulated homes.

There were two unoccupied metal drums. In past years Baer had run larger strings of dogs. The extra drums were now being used as storage, housing the dogsled and equipment. Into them Nina stowed the sled, harnesses, gang lines, ropes, holsters, snow hooks, and bags.

A rising moon offered her just enough illumination to be able to see. The eyes of the dogs reflected back at her; eight circles of greenish glowing followed her movements. The dogs knew it was dinnertime. The intensity of their eyes seemed to increase as she walked over to the meat shack that Baer referred to as the wanigan. She removed the spiked doormats from in front of the wanigan and opened the latched door.

The cupboard wasn't bare; half a dozen slabs of smoked meat still hung from the ceiling, along with racks of jerked meat, but the larder was significantly reduced. With all the open space, it now looked as if there'd been a fire sale on meat. It surprised Nina how much food two humans and four dogs had gone through over the last three months. Nina thought it likely that she'd eaten even more than Baer. Even though she'd been sick half the time, the other half of the time she'd been ravenous, eating everything and anything.

The chum salmon, which had been a fall staple for the dogs, were all gone. Now they were getting varieties of meats at which Nina could only guess—among them beaver, muskrat, and rabbit. Baer had used an ax to precut some smaller cuts of meat for the dogs. They gnawed on the meat for hours; it always sounded as if they were chewing bones, which wasn't surprising, as the meat was frozen solid and every bit as hard as a bone.

As usual Nina slipped the dogs a little more meat than Baer would have.

"Soup!" yelled Baer, and Nina hurried up the path to the cabin, where she retrieved the still-steaming twelve-quart stockpot.

What Baer called soup was a mixture of mush, offal, meat, and water. Getting liquid to the dogs was as important as getting them food. Part of the difficulty of sledding on such cold days was making sure the dogs—and humans—were properly hydrated.

She poured the sludge into each of the dogs' bowls, and they started lapping it up. Everything would be gone before the cold had a chance to freeze the liquid.

With the dogs now cared for, she carried the empty stockpot back to the cabin. The pot was old and had been mended countless times. As she opened the cabin door, Baer suddenly appeared in front of her. He extended an arm, stopping her passage, acting like a human tollbooth.

"Strip," he said.

"What?" She hoped she'd misheard.

"Strip," he repeated.

"Why? I swear I'm not carrying a rock or any weapon."

"Then take off your clothes and let me see."

"Why don't you frisk me? That might save me from freezing to death."

He shook his head. "You're up to something. I know it. I can feel it. And you need to understand the consequences of your actions."

Nina tried to hide the wave of relief she was feeling. He suspected something was wrong, but he had nothing tangible, or so it seemed. Still, Nina knew better than to just yield to his demands. She was sure that would make him even more suspicious.

"You're paranoid. And I shouldn't have to pay the price of your paranoia."

"The sooner you strip down to nothing, the faster you'll be able to come inside and warm up."

Nina tried playing the baby card, as she had on other occasions. Making him defensive might keep Baer from scrutinizing her any closer than he already was.

"What if the baby gets a chill?"

"Then this will teach you not to put the baby in danger in the future. I know you're up to something. I can see it in your eyes."

"This is crazy."

"I'm waiting."

"Goddamn you to hell."

He smiled and then offered up a line from his favorite poem: "Then 'Here,' said I, with a sudden cry, 'is my cre-ma-tor-eum.'"

"You're a bastard."

With unfeigned reluctance, Nina removed her clothing. Each layer's subtraction brought the weight of invasive cold, and it became harder and harder for her to breathe. But Baer wasn't satisfied until she was naked. Even her boots had to come off. She was forced to stand there completely naked while he rummaged through her clothing. In a matter of seconds, her exposed flesh turned bright red, as though she'd been burned.

Baer stared at her hard nipples. In a husky voice, he said, "You could cut diamonds with those things."

Through chattering teeth Nina managed to say, "I'd—rather—cut off—your—balls."

Baer laughed and stepped aside. Nina almost fell into the cabin. Her hands felt like blocks of ice and were so devoid of feeling, she had trouble opening and closing her fingers merely to pick up her clothing. She dragged her coats and pants over to the stove and stood just inches from it, desperate for its warmth. Even after five minutes had passed, she was still trembling uncontrollably.

"You need some food in you," said Baer. "That will stop your shivering."

"I'm—shivering—because you're—an asshole."

"You're beginning to look better. I guess your temper is warming you up."

While he prepared tea and broth, Nina made him work around her. She only gave up her spot at the stove when she began feeling dizzy and knew she needed to get off her feet. The next thing she remembered was hearing a voice and thinking someone was shouting from a distance. She opened her eyes and shook her head. Baer was standing in front of her holding a steaming mug. Nina had no idea how long she'd been asleep; the aroma of cooking meat told her it had been a while.

She took the hot mug; it warmed her hands and soon warmed her insides. When she'd first come to the cabin, there had been two full containers of bouillon, one beef and the other chicken. Only a teaspoon or two of the chicken bouillon remained. As she slurped the salty liquid, she could feel her equilibrium returning. It was the nourishment she needed, or maybe it was what her baby needed.

A few minutes later, she got the bloody meat she was craving. Baer had cooked up a caribou roast, along with what must have been the last of the Eskimo potatoes. Nina gorged on the meat.

While she sucked at the marrow, Baer worked on his furs. She pretended to not observe his tying together pelts. It was clear Baer was making preparations for the winter move. How much time did that leave her? Did she have a week? Did she even have a day?

If she was to attempt her escape, it had to be soon. No, not soon. Now.

But I'm not ready yet, she thought. Her heart was racing, and she felt faint. Imagining the moment was different from daring it. There were only three outcomes: a successful escape, recapture, or death. The monster had already threatened to cut away some of her toes should she ever try to escape.

In high school Nina had played Emily Webb in Thornton Wilder's *Our Town.* Her family had helped her rehearse the lines. Even now Nina could remember Emily's final farewell to Grover's Corners and her family.

Was she that ghost already?

A dozen years had passed since her performance. *"It goes so fast,"* she thought, remembering Emily's words. *"Oh, earth, you're too wonderful for anybody to realize you. Do any human beings ever realize life while they live it?"*

Until now what Nina had remembered most about the play was how her family and friends were in the audience, and how loudly they cheered when she came out for her curtain call. She'd posed with roses instead of smelling them. She'd smiled for the cameras instead of insisting her family join one another in a group hug. Instead of celebrating a play, she should have celebrated life.

I never understood the play until now, Nina thought.

She remembered Emily's lament, Emily who had wanted one more look at her precious world before being taken back to her grave.

It was time to say good-bye to Grover's Corners, thought Nina, and take on the challenge of finding a way to survive.

She gathered her warmest clothing and wrapped herself in layers while Baer continued doing his packing. All of her extra socks went under her vest.

Nina took her plate to the kitchen and began cleaning up. She pretended to snack on the leftover food while stuffing hardtack under her clothing. Her heart was pounding so hard that she was afraid if Baer said anything she wouldn't be able to hear it.

She finished up with the dishes and then walked to the door as she had dozens of times before. Nina usually visited the outhouse before being locked into her holding pen for the night. She reached for the door handle and then held the door tightly so that the wind wouldn't pull it from her hands. She was holding her breath, not daring to look in Baer's direction save from the corner of her eye. He didn't even bother to look up from his work. When she shut the door behind her, she had to lean against it for a long moment while gathering her breath. She swallowed down several mouthfuls of cold air, readying herself for the race.

The primitive solar lights registered her presence with a feeble flicker. Nina had rehearsed what to do scores of times, choreographing each step in her mind. She knew that every moment counted. Her window of opportunity was ten minutes at most.

She had left her snowshoes outside the door and quickly put them on. There was just enough moonlight to illuminate the pathway to the doghouses. Nina called out a muted greeting, alerting the dogs to her presence and staving off their barking. After their long day, they exhibited no desire to run out to greet her, but instead remained curled up in their houses.

Nina stepped inside the wanigan. In the corner of the meat shack, hanging from a hook, was one of Baer's old backpacks. It was empty, but wouldn't be for long. Nina hurried around the wanigan, reclaiming items she'd hidden. Beneath an old fishnet, she retrieved a broken fish spear with a three-pronged head. Then she dragged a makeshift bench to the middle of the floor. It was rickety but supported her weight. A big beam ran the length of the ceiling; hanging down from it were chains and hooks that supported cuts of meat. The beam worked as a shelf of sorts; two weeks before, that's where Nina had found Baer's secreted ulu knife.

She'd known about the knife but not its location. On several occasions she'd spotted Baer using the knife to cut meat in the kitchen. When she'd asked him about its funny design, Baer had said it was a tool historically used by Alaskan Natives. The knife looked something like an ax blade. It had a wooden handle, which you rocked up and down when cutting things. Baer said he'd made the tool himself, shaping a slate blade. It was clear he preferred his bowie knife for most tasks; it was also clear he'd hidden the ulu knife, which was why Nina had made a point of looking for it whenever an opportunity presented itself. She quickly filled the pack with other items from around the wanigan.

Into the backpack went an old pot, tinder, char cloth, flint, and matches. There hadn't been a spare emergency tarp, but she'd found heavy plastic, which she thought could work as a substitute. One of her best finds had been the reflector blanket taken from the airplane. An old caribou hide would have to serve as her sleeping bag, along with plastic bags that she'd fill for insulation. Along with the ulu knife and spearhead, she packed rope and some snares. She filled the rest of the pack with jerky, taking much of what remained.

Nina stopped outside. Just off the pathway was a bowling ball–size rock. She suspected it had been unearthed when the cabin was built. Nina carried the stone along with her.

Her presence was beginning to make the dogs restless. Nina bought their silence with some of the jerky. As they happily began their gnawing, she took the ulu knife and cut all the lines, ropes, and harnesses that went with the dog sled. After that she wrapped the rock in plastic so as to muffle its sound and began hammering at the sled. Each blow made her cringe, but it didn't take her long to bend the runners, smash the footboards, and crush the brakes. For the time being, the wind was her ally. It whistled and whipped and masked the hammering.

When she finished she was sure even Baer couldn't jury-rig the sled without a day's work.

She went back inside the wanigan. In addition to its being their meat locker, it was also the storage locker for spare traps. Nina bypassed the biggest of the long spring traps, a bear trap that must have weighed close to fifty pounds, choosing instead the wolf trap. The bear trap was too big for her to safely operate, and she feared losing an arm while trying to depress the springs.

She hurried down the path. She didn't have the time to set the trap with Baer's methodical manner. He liked to dig out a spot and then anchor the trap with one or two stakes. Sometimes he used wax paper to prevent the trap from freezing up. He was also careful about making sure the pan was free of snow. His final touch was to camouflage the area surrounding the trap with twigs and ground cover.

Even with the moonlight, the trail was obscured, shadowed over by trees. Nina picked one of those deep shadows that extended to the middle of the path and placed the trap on the ground. She hoped it would pass for one of the many rocks and roots along the path.

Her time working the trapline had only reinforced her hatred of traps. They were nasty things, toothed and mean. At least she didn't have to bait this trap. It was a blind set, put in a spot Baer might be likely to step in.

Do your job, she prayed. *Catch a monster. Have my enemy step on you. Snap shut and shatter his foot. Amen.*

Maybe it wasn't an appropriate prayer, but Nina didn't care.

With trembling hands she spread apart the waiting jaws. The teeth of the wolf trap were around ten inches apart. *That should be large enough*, Nina thought. Baer and his boots should fit within that space.

Nina finished and carefully backed away from the trap.

She made sure her backpack was secure and then, by the stingy light of the moon, set off down the path. In her hand was a staff Nina often took on their outings. She took a few steadying breaths, but they didn't stop the pounding of her heart. It felt like a drum solo was going on in her chest. She wondered if the monster would be able to hear her telltale heart.

It felt as if hours had passed since she'd stepped out of the cabin, even though she doubted more than ten minutes had gone by. She walked at a deliberate and steady pace. This race wasn't going to be won by the swift, and she had to avoid overheating. Perspiration was her enemy. A chill could kill her.

She looked back. The cabin was no longer in sight. What would Baer do when he realized she'd fled? Would he come right after her, or would he wait until daylight to begin his tracking?

What she knew of Baer—what she hoped—was that he would wait until morning. At night it would be much harder to track her, and even Baer would have to worry about where he was walking. There were plenty of places you could break your ankle or leg or neck. You could fall over a cliff or into a crevasse. The danger of falling into a tree well would be all too real.

"Nina!"

She almost jumped. His shout was loud enough to be heard over the wind. It sounded as if he was close by. Nina stood still.

"You don't want to do this!" he yelled. "You'll die out there. And you'll kill the baby."

Nina exhaled pent-up air. He hadn't snuck up on her. He was shouting from the cabin. But was he already trying to close the distance between them? Was he sneaking down the path?

"Do you have a death wish? Do you want to murder the baby?"

That was his real concern. The all-important baby. Nina opened her mouth to reply, but then snapped it shut. She couldn't let him know where she was.

That's when she heard the snap of metal and the sweet music of Baer's screaming.

His screaming didn't last long. She could feel him taking the measure of his situation. She could hear the pained intake of his breaths. *He is in agony*, she thought, and she was glad. She opened her mouth to taunt him, but then thought better of that. Someone had once told her the most dangerous animal in the world was a wounded grizzly bear.

The trap had done its job. Now she could put distance between them. Heartened, Nina set out into the night.

CHAPTER THIRTY-FOUR

"What do you think, Sister?"

Nina waited a few moments to speak again, listening for an answer.

"I heard the snap of the trap. And I heard him scream. I want to believe he cried out in pain. That's what it sounded like. But everything he does is designed to deceive. Did he really step in that trap, or is he trying to get me to step in his trap?"

Nina looked back to reassure herself that the monster wasn't sneaking up on her.

"He's flesh and blood. He's not the bogeyman. He can bleed and die. And I can make my escape and survive just like *La Loba* did."

Nina took a moment to listen, made sure she didn't hear any pursuit, and then continued walking and talking.

"Last month I was working the trapline with Baer when I had this feeling I was being watched. Before my captivity I'm sure I wouldn't have sensed that, but my senses are more attuned now, and I've even come to rely on my little voice. It's not intuition, or at least not exactly. It's an awareness I never had before.

"There was this energy working its way up the back of my neck, and so I turned, and that's when I saw the wolf looking at me. Its coat was completely white. We stared at each other for a moment or two. It was such a short time, but it was so intense it felt as if we stared at each other for hours. And then the wolf silently disappeared into the woods.

"I was visited by my guardian spirit. I did not tell Baer what I saw, but I'm certain that it was *La Loba*. She and you are what kept me going."

Despite her predicament Nina found herself smiling. "I thought back to how she left a pile of shit right next to a trap she'd sprung. How the monster raged, but he could do nothing." The memory made her laugh. "I'll never forget her act of defiance. Or your act of defiance. It's nice to have two guardian spirits. In my mind I can still see my ghost wolf. *La Loba Fantasma.*"

Her laughter and the memory felt good. They warmed her. They inspired her. For a moment Nina was able to forget how spooky it was walking through the wilderness in the mostly dark night. The light from the moon was such that she couldn't see very far ahead of her or behind her. It helped that the wind had died down. When she'd set out, there had been gusting that threatened to knock her off her feet. Now it was a steady ten- or twelve-mile-an-hour wind.

She tried keeping to a steady pace. This was a marathon. Consistency was the key. In another hour she would build a fire and hydrate. In the meantime she had to come to a decision.

"The question is, Sister, should I be listening to my little voice, or should I listen to my ears? If Baer's hurt, that means I should reconsider my escape plan. If he's laid up or slowed down, I need to rethink the course I planned. I could take the more direct route to Manley Hot Springs, which might mean as much as two fewer days of walking. I wouldn't need to have everything work out just right. It would only be a matter of surviving the marathon and getting to Manley."

Nina turned around and tried to see through the moonlight. There was no sign of pursuit. Baer wasn't there.

"That's what I want to do. But you know what my little voice tells me? It says stay with the original plan. It says he's coming after me. It says he wants me to believe he's hurt, because then I'll be easy prey for him. He prides himself on his use of tactics. It would be just like him to pretend that he was hurt. Nothing would please him more than his sneaking up on me unaware."

Nina's pace slowed, the impasse weighing on her steps.

"You gave me your rules, Sister. And your eighth and final rule was to kill the monster. After what the monster has done to us, you'd think I wouldn't have any qualms about taking his life, but some part of me still hopes I won't have to. Before all this happened, I never could have imagined myself a killer. It's hard getting my mind around that."

Nina took another step forward, and this time she picked up her pace. "But I guess I'll just have to. I'm going to stay the original course."

* * *

Nina drank the hot water and chewed a piece of jerky while she fed the fire. She was sitting on a caribou hide on the lee side of a knoll. The water wasn't hot enough to warm her, but it did make the cold a little less pervasive. She removed her gloves and brought her fingers close to the fire, working and flexing them until they didn't feel like icicles.

She guessed that daybreak was at least three hours away. In two hours she'd stop again to drink, warm up, and take a short nap. She'd make a bigger fire to warm her feet and would put on fresh socks. If she was to survive the Ice Age, she had to stave off gangrene, trench foot, hypothermia, and frostbite.

Nina drank more of the hot water. "I'm tired, Elese," she said. "And I'm having trouble thinking. I'm hoping it's just exhaustion, but it could be an early sign of hypothermia, with the cold short-circuiting my brain."

At least she knew where she was. She'd traveled this way to get to the trapline maybe fifty times. But in a few hours, she'd be in unknown territory. "That's where you're really going to have to guide me, you know. I'll have you, your clouds, the weather and stars, and your moss to guide me. It almost sounds like a scavenger hunt, doesn't it? Did I ever tell you about the scavenger hunt my mother organized for my fourteenth birthday?

"I wonder what Mom would think of this scavenger hunt. The stakes are a little higher, I'm afraid. And if I don't find one specific item, I'm dead." Nina finished her drink and got to her feet. She felt more alert now. There was no need to put out the fire or try to hide it. If Baer was coming after her, he'd find it. After cinching up her backpack, she started walking.

* * *

Hours later after her third stumble, Nina decided it was time to stop for a break. Although it was still dark outside, the horizon was lightening. Dawn probably wasn't much more than an hour off. After choosing a spot that was partially sheltered from the wind, she set about making a campsite. She found some boughs for insulation and set them out on the ground. Then she laid down the tarp, caribou hide, and reflective blanket.

Nina took the granite ulu with her to gather materials for a fire. After cutting away bark for tinder, she used the ulu's heft to bring down some small branches. In a few short minutes, she had a blazing fire, and then she went and gathered more wood.

With a grateful sigh, she settled in front of the fire. Its welcoming warmth allowed her to take off her boots. There was no feeling in her toes, and Nina began vigorously massaging her feet. The heat and the rubbing brought back enough sensitivity to allow her to wiggle her toes. Still, Nina knew any victory over the cold was only temporary. She put on fresh socks and then restoked the fire.

She wouldn't be able to go on much farther without some rest. She settled down for her nap. Her wake-up call would be the fire's dying out. She didn't want to sleep more than an hour anyway, and when the fire was down to coals, the bitter cold would get her up.

But it wasn't the cold that woke her. It was a nightmare. She awoke screaming, but waking didn't bring her relief. Nina scanned the surrounding area. There was no sign of the monster, but that didn't mean he wasn't there.

Dawn was showing itself, such as it was. The sun was pale, lifeless, and anemic. It felt like a mirage, an illusion of what she wanted.

Nina did a few halfhearted stretches and tried to get some feeling in her digits. She stoked the fire and then went and gathered more fuel. When the fire was sufficiently burning, she filled her small pot with ice and dense snow and placed it atop the coals.

Drinking enough water and taking in calories was critical to her survival. She broke off a piece of jerky and began working on it with her teeth, but it was like chewing on petrified wood. The hardtack would be even worse. Instead of breaking her teeth over her food, Nina dropped two pieces of jerky into the water, along with one of the hardtack biscuits. The hardtack dropped like a rock to the bottom of her pot.

It took the water a few minutes to boil. Nina drank directly from the pot, sipping jerky broth and pretending she was eating bacon with a biscuit. For once she didn't have morning sickness. She didn't know whether that was a good thing or not.

"Is he out there already, Sister?" asked Nina. "I'm thinking he carefully planned for this hunt and set out before dawn. I'm hoping that my walking most of the night gave me a four-hour lead. So, what am I waiting for?"

She sighed, exhaling a vapor trail. Yes, she was tired, but that wasn't it. She was afraid. From here on she would be going into the unknown.

It seemed the right time for gallows humor. "Lions and tigers and bears, oh my!" she said.

"And Baer," she added.

He was enough reason for her to not linger. She packed up and started walking; the snow crunched under her snowshoes. At least it would be hard for him to sneak up on her.

The extreme cold had made the snow exceedingly dry, and whenever the wind kicked up, it swirled the powdery snow and ice crystals into the air, making it difficult for her to see. At the moment there wasn't much wind, but that could change at any moment.

Fog obscured the day's light. Nina hoped it would burn away, but seeing as it was well below zero, she wondered if there was enough sun to burn away anything other than hope. The haze was such that she could barely make out Mt. McKinley. If it hadn't been the highest peak in North America, it wouldn't have even been visible.

"There it is," she said. "You referenced McKinley on some of your maps. You thought it was hundreds of miles to the southeast. But I have a different goal. If your accounting is right and your map drawing is accurate, my goal is fewer than ten miles off. Now I've got to try to get there while it's still light. That's a lot of walking in these conditions.

"I can't tell you how many times I've studied your maps. I know the Tanana River is to the north and the Katishna River is to the east. And you referenced such spots as the Muddy River, Moose Creek, Lake Minchumina, and Geskakmina Lake, even though you never visited those places. All you had was Baer's accounts of them.

"But you did spend time at today's destination. And from what you drew, the way seems straightforward. All I have to do is travel west to Moosejaw Lake, and then a mile beyond that is Panhandle Pond, and from there I need to follow Sourdough Creek north. Easy-peasy, right?" she said, trying to convince herself.

Nina looked around and shuddered, from the cold or from the desolation around her.

"I've been running my whole life," she said. "I wonder if that's some kind of metaphor."

She laughed. "Quite a strange time to be getting philosophical, isn't it? I'm walking across an icy desert with a monster closing in on me, and I'm being introspective." She adjusted the backpack on her shoulders. "If I survive, I wonder how Terrence will react when he sees me. His family wasn't convinced I was Donnelly material before, so what will they say now? I'm sure they'll say I should put everything behind me and not look back. But what would be the point of my having lived through all of this to not remember it?"

She thought about that for a moment. "I remember the old me, and I wonder about that person. I *have* changed. I am not the person I was anymore. And I think that's a good thing. That person I used to be had just about everything she could want, except the awareness to know it."

Nina found herself laughing, probably more out of tiredness than anything else. It wasn't as if she'd been visited by her own version of the ghost of Jacob Marley. But her abduction had certainly given her time to think.

"When I became engaged to Terrence, all those magazines wrote about my so-called storybook life. No one saw this chapter coming. Woman proposes and God disposes. Woman plans and God laughs. I guess God must have thought I was in need of humbling. But I'm being silly, Sister. The same thing happened to you. Neither one of us did anything wrong."

Nina stopped talking. It hurt to talk. The air was so cold it even hurt to breathe.

* * *

Weather conditions worsened during the day, making it harder not only for Nina to walk, but to see. The wind had picked up, pushing around the ice crystals and snow. A creeping fog made visibility that much worse. It had gotten to the point where taking a step was a guessing game, and Nina felt like a toddler trying to learn how to walk.

Not being able to see the ground in front of her threw her off-balance. Luckily for her, the whiteout conditions were intermittent. She could see one minute, but not the next.

But what if the whiteout conditions worsened to the point where she couldn't see at all?

As she kept walking, Nina remembered the various pieces of advice offered by her high school and college running coaches. Each had their favorite sayings, and Nina heard their voices in her ear.

Push through the pain.

Oh, I am pushing. But pain is pushing back.

You can always give more.

I am trying. I am trying.

Pain is temporary.

But when will it stop? Every step hurts.

One step at a time.

Why is it that drunks were told the same thing?

A winner runs through it.

Yes, especially when second place is death. The only question is whose?

Nina looked behind her. She saw nothing to indicate Baer was coming after her, but that little voice said he was catching up.

A lump constricted her throat. For the past hour, it had been growing. It was the kind of lump you felt when you cried. It was the kind of lump you felt when you were afraid.

"I'm scared, Sister," she said. "Am I lost? Shouldn't I have come to one of your landmarks by now? With this fog and ice, I can't even be sure I'm not walking in circles."

She wondered if Elese had seen that movie about the young man who died in Alaska's wilderness. *Into the Wild.* Ever since Jack London had started writing, it seemed that every Alaska story had to have *Wild* in its title. It was a sad movie. If she didn't make it, would there be a sad movie about her and Elese?

"It's hard not to think about death," she said. "Somehow I'm afraid I missed Moosejaw Lake. On your map it looked like a large body of water. Could I be that disoriented? Should I turn around? But if I do that, won't I be walking right into Baer's hands?"

The growing lump in her throat felt like some huge goiter. It pressed on her throat and made swallowing difficult.

"I was so focused on plan A, I never thought about plan B."

Nina forced herself to stay the path. This was a marathon. You ran the race. You found a way to finish. She tried to concentrate on running clichés, and not her doubts. *Runners don't get rained out; they get rained on.* Tom Hanks had said there was no crying in baseball. Her coach had said, "There are no time-outs in running." Her favorite running quote had been on a T-shirt she'd worn: *My sport is your sport's punishment.*

It was then, through the white haze, that she caught a glimpse of what looked like a frozen lake. A moment later the body of water disappeared from view, and Nina wondered if she'd been seeing things. But then her lake reappeared, and the lump in her throat shrank enough for her to be able to swallow again. She'd found Moosejaw Lake, or at least hoped she had. It wasn't as if there were any signs identifying the spot, and neither was there any jaw of a moose to be seen. But she felt certain this was where the X had been marked on her secret sister's map.

"Thank you," she whispered to Elese, and to the universe, and then began looking around to find the best spot to make camp. She settled on a stand of frosted spruce that offered partial shelter. First she made sure there were no spruce traps waiting under the tree. Then she took some of the spruce boughs and placed them under her. It took Nina longer to make a fire than usual. The near-whiteout conditions made her stop and start. It was almost like an enforced game of peekaboo, with her seeing one minute and not seeing the next.

When she had a roaring fire going, Nina felt better than she had since fleeing Baer's cabin. She stretched her fingers and toes toward the flames; any closer and her flesh might have sizzled. There was something hypnotic about the fire, and Nina realized she was speaking to the flames:

"Talk of your cold! through the parka's fold it stabbed like a driven nail.

"If our eyes we'd close, then the lashes . . ."

When she realized she was reciting from "The Cremation of Sam McGee," she almost started to cry. *Brainwashed*, she thought hysterically. *I've been brainwashed.*

The fire hissed, objecting to the snow crystals heaved at it by the wind.

She drank as much water as she could, forced herself to eat more jerky, and warmed her limbs to the point where they weren't completely frozen. Still, there wasn't a part of her body that didn't hurt.

"I could make camp here," she said after a while. "If the monster wasn't out there, I would say that was the safe thing to do. As much as I don't want to leave this fire, I think I should stick with our plan. Even if the spring trap did wound him, that wouldn't stop him, nor would this weather. He's coming."

She blinked a few times. *Even my eyes hurt*, she thought. Maybe life was imitating art, and her lashes were freezing like in those lines from Baer's goddamn poem. But that wasn't it.

The swirling ice crystals were irritating her eyes. Trying to see through the whiteout conditions had certainly caused some eyestrain. Her face was covered, but she didn't have on the sunglasses Baer always wore. Could she be on the verge of becoming snow-blind?

Taking a stick, Nina sifted through the coals and ashes of the fire until she had a pile of soot. She'd seen athletes using eye black to reduce glare and decided to do the same. She rubbed the ashes all around her eyes. She had no mirror, but was sure she had to look like a raccoon.

Groaning, she got to her feet. Baer was coming. As long as there was light, she had to keep moving.

* * *

The lump in her throat had returned. Once again Nina was afraid she was lost.

"Am I going the right way, Sister? If Panhandle Pond was where it was supposed to be, I think I am. But the pond didn't look like it was in the shape of a panhandle. Maybe it never was, though. Maybe it was named after a panhandler.

"Of course, winter masks what everything is supposed to look like. That's what I told myself. But if I continued from there, this should be Sourdough Creek."

She turned in a circle. This creek looked more like a river. Was everything just bigger in Alaska? On Elese's map the creek appeared to run directly north. But as far as Nina could gauge, this creek seemed to meander in a more easterly route.

"You said Baer's hunting shack was within sight of Sourdough Creek. But I could have walked right by it in the fog, with these goddamn whiteout conditions. Or I could have missed it while detouring around trees and snowbanks.

"And now the sun will soon be setting. This isn't Sourdough Creek. It's Shit Creek. And I'm up it without a paddle."

Nina kept walking, her eyes searching for Baer's elusive hunting shack. Elese had said it was a small, primitive structure. Maybe the wind had blown it down.

"It's there," said Nina, wanting to believe. "You wrote that it was his port in a storm, his insurance policy. You said it was closer to get to it from the trapline than to try and return to the cabin. That means it should be here."

But what if it wasn't here? Could she create a shelter to survive the cold night? Soon it would be dark, and it would stay that way for the next sixteen hours. She needed to find a good spot to make the best possible shelter. Before too long she'd be walking blindly.

Through the lump in her throat and the dying light and the wind-driven ice flakes, Nina strained to see. Her eyes hurt now more than they had all day.

Sometimes no matter how hard you look, what you want to see just isn't there. It was like that when her cat disappeared. Callie was a sweet calico that chose Nina to be her favorite person in the world. All through middle school Callie had curled up and gone to bed with Nina.

And then her beloved cat had simply disappeared. She and Luke had put up posters, gone to the animal shelters, and organized search parties around their neighborhood.

For months Nina had kept looking for her cat. There were a few times when she was sure she heard her or glimpsed her from the corner of her eye. But Callie never came home. It was likely that some predator, probably a coyote, had struck.

How she had looked for that cat! Nina had wanted a miracle. That hadn't happened, or at least not really. It was only in one of her dreams that Nina reunited with Callie. "I looked everywhere for you," she told her cat.

Now she saw something. Not more than twenty-five yards away, she could just make out Baer's hunting shack. All of these years later, it felt as if she had finally found her beloved Callie.

* * *

The emergency provisions were scant, but to Nina they seemed heaven-sent. There was some pasta and a few pounds of black beans and lentils. For seasoning there was salt. All of the food was sealed in plastic bags, stored in a vermin-proof plastic container, and put away in a crate.

But Nina hadn't traveled to the hunting shack in the hopes of finding food. She was there for something else, something that wasn't immediately visible.

"You saw it, Sister," Nina said. "You wrote about it. You saw him cleaning it. It's still here, isn't it? It has to be here. It's my only chance to even the odds."

Elese had described the gun and this hunting shack as Baer's insurance.

"But he wouldn't leave it out in the open, even in this remote place, would he? He'd be afraid that in the summertime, some hunter might stumble upon this shack."

The structure was about sixty square feet. It wasn't even sparsely furnished. There were no tables, chairs, or beds. The shack was empty, save for a portable woodstove made from a thirty-gallon steel drum. The woodstove was supported by a tripod arrangement of wooden legs wrapped in wire. The opening at the top was a hole about six inches in diameter, where you would rest a pan or pot. From what Nina could determine, the fuel was placed in the bottom of the drum.

Would an unused woodstove be a good place to hide a gun? She reached her arm down the hole, but only found old ashes at the bottom of the canister. In the open area between the three legs of the wood-stove, she found a rusted can filled with sand. In the middle of the sand was a candle. That would solve one immediate problem. It was growing darker by the moment.

Nina lit the candle and began searching the small space. She remembered how the ulu knife had been hidden among the beams in the wanigan, but there were no rafters in the shack. She searched the spaces in the crude wooden floor, but found nothing. Then she started rapping on the walls. The shack had no window, and only a solitary shelf about the same size and thickness as a railroad tie. Atop the shelf were old cans and jars. Baer hadn't gotten around to hanging a rack of moose antlers; it rested next to the wall. Hanging from the rack's points were skins and a few old snares. On the ground next to the antlers sat a box of kindling and small sticks.

Nina tapped around the shelf, but couldn't find any area that sounded hollow. She held the candle up to the metal cans and jars. All had been recycled from their original purposes and were now being used as containers. She took the top off of one glass jar and found that it was filled with Baer's spruce pitch salve. Other containers housed fishing line and lures. One five-gallon plastic construction bucket that had held joint compound was acting as Baer's tool chest, as well as the repository for his oddments. Nina sifted through it, moving aside screwdrivers, old saw blades, pliers, nails, screws, bolts, nuts, wiring, and braces. The only way to get to the bottom, she decided, was to pour out its contents.

She tipped it over. One of the last items to fall out of the bucket was a plastic Ziploc bag. At first glance Nina could only see a greasy rag, but then she noticed it was wrapped around something. She opened the sealed bag, removed the rag, and found herself holding an old revolver.

Nina had never held a gun, and she took a few minutes to familiarize herself with it. She found a pin below the barrel and pulled it out. Then it was just a matter of the cylinder swinging to the left. To her disappointment, the bullet chambers were empty.

She went back to sifting through the overturned bucket and was relieved to find another sealed plastic bag holding four bullets. Were they the right ammo? She fit them into the chambers and closed the cylinder. Everything seemed to fit and click. She'd planned on testing the gun, but with only four bullets, she couldn't do that.

As far as Nina could see, the revolver had no safety. She stored the gun inside her parka and hoped she wouldn't end up shooting her foot.

Normally Nina might have been concerned about carbon monoxide poisoning from lighting a woodstove indoors, but the shack was anything but airtight. It was a wind deterrent, but not windproof. Smoke was a bigger concern; the woodstove wasn't vented to the outdoors. Nina decided to take her chances. She filled the bottom with tinder. When that started to flame, she added additional fuel. There was surprisingly little smoke.

A few minutes later, the water began boiling. It was anticipation of the food even more than the cold she was experiencing that made Nina's hands shake. The idea of having a meal of pasta and beans had her drooling. She knew her body had burned a lot of calories walking and staving off the cold, but she hadn't realized how hungry she was.

Nina boiled the beans along with the pasta. She salted the water and, using a handmade wooden spoon, snuck tastes of the liquid while everything cooked. The idea of drinking starch-infused water might have once made her gag, but now it tasted like the nectar of the gods. She kept drinking from the small pot while continually adding ice.

The end result of her cooking resembled a stew. Nina didn't pace herself. It took her less than a minute to finish everything.

Feasting on seconds sounded like a wonderful idea. Nina melted more snow and ice, and then added lentils along with a piece of jerky. While the mixture boiled, she went in search of more wood. Even though the smoke seemed minimal, she left the door to the shack open for ventilation. As quickly as she could, she gathered an armful of sticks and small branches. Then it was just a matter of adding pasta to the pot and waiting.

The second time around, she didn't eat quite as hurriedly. Nina knew she'd need the calories. Her full stomach and the shelter were conspiring to have her lie down and sleep. But she couldn't.

This was a race where she couldn't win through speed. Baer was faster and stronger than she was. At the end of the day, he was probably no more than an hour behind her. He would have made his camp by now. He would know that time was on his side. He would know the limits of her endurance.

Baer would think she was traveling without a clue as to where she was going. He didn't know about her secret ally. He would never guess she was in his hunting shack.

Nina closed her eyes and tried to ignore the irritation she was feeling. It almost felt like a grain of sand was lodged under her eyelid.

Her lips felt chapped as well. Even though her entire body had been covered, the cold had found ways to breach her armor.

She rubbed her nub of a finger, trying to spark her anger, but it wasn't enough to get her moving.

"I can't afford to fall asleep, Sister," she said, but she did.

CHAPTER THIRTY-FIVE

Nina awoke shivering. The candle had gone out, and the shack was in darkness.

"No!" she cried, panicked that she'd sabotaged her plan.

But maybe it wasn't too late. She lit the nub of a candle, put some food in her pack, and braced herself for the cold and the dark, and most of all, what awaited her.

She'd known that once the monster was on her trail, she wouldn't be able to shake him. That's why she was leaving the hunting shack. That's why she was traveling in a direction that went against her every instinct.

She was glad for the darkness. Her eyes still hurt. And she didn't want to see what she was walking into.

* * *

Nina picked her spot and made camp just before dawn. Her pupils felt as if they were sunburned. She resisted scratching at them.

She moved like a zombie, shuffling instead of walking, lurching instead of moving. Her thoughts were slow and lumbering, and she had to remind herself to complete the tasks at hand. She gathered wood and made a fire. Her eyes hurt, and she decided to cover them up by cutting off a piece of the tarp and making it into a bandana.

Blind man's bluff, she thought. *Or blind woman's.*

Nina hoped she'd set up her camp in time. Baer would have tracked her like he would any animal. He believed in stealth, and few things made him happier than delivering a kill shot to an unsuspecting creature. Baer believed a deliberate hunter was the best kind of hunter.

That's why he wouldn't have tried following her trail in the dark, or so she hoped. He knew his prey and wouldn't have felt it was necessary to continue tracking her at night. He would have assumed she had no idea where she was going or what she was doing.

"Do I know what I'm doing, Sister?"

The coldness Nina felt wasn't only from the elements.

She stayed close to the fire, only moving when absolutely necessary. The way she was hunched over, Nina knew she looked defeated. Her body shivered violently, and she thought, *Someone just walked over my grave.*

Or maybe a monster was looking at her through the scope of his rifle. She could feel a heat, first in the middle of her forehead, and then her heart. That's how Baer liked to line up his shots. He picked the best angle and kill shot.

What was it he saw?

Would he shoot her from a long distance?

No. That wasn't Baer's way. He would want to humiliate her. He would enjoy sneaking up on her. He would want her to piss her pants.

Nina had tramped around the area, had done her best to make it look like her tracks were coming and going in several directions. If he suspected she'd been to his hunting shack, he might keep his distance.

Her face and ears were covered. She wouldn't be able to see his approach or hear it. He would take note of that. He would think she was snow-blind, or so she hoped.

But even then Baer wouldn't make a direct approach. He'd circle around. He'd get downwind of her. And then he'd carefully move in, getting as close to her as he could without her knowing he was there.

Know your enemy, Elese had told her. She did.

* * *

Nina felt the telltale heat on the back of her neck. Nina was sure she was being watched.

She resisted the impulse to give in to her alarm, to remove the scarf and look around. It was one thing to imagine she was being watched, and another thing to confirm it. She needed to follow her plan, even though she knew at that moment she might very well be in Baer's crosshairs. What if he announced himself with a shot? He might think her proper punishment was to put a bullet in her foot.

The baby will stop him from doing that, Nina thought. Baer wouldn't chance hurting the baby. She prayed that was so.

How close was he? Because the scarf only loosely covered her ears, she could still hear. She didn't think even Baer could approach unheard. When she walked, the icy snow crunched under her feet. She tried not to show in her posture how carefully she was listening.

There—that might be something. But it was a far cry from the crunching noise she made while walking. Baer, though, was more animal than human. Would he stalk his prey by crawling along?

Her whole body prickled as though a rake were going up and down her spine.

She'd witnessed how Baer liked to sneak up on his prey. It wasn't only because he prided himself on getting an easy shot. It was his way of proving his superiority.

She fought the impulse to look around. He needed to believe she was a lamb ready to be led to slaughter. That was the story her body language needed to tell.

She couldn't panic, scream, or run, no matter how hard her heart was racing. She had to be ready for his attack or touch or voice. She tried to control her breathing and her nerves. It wouldn't do to hyperventilate now. The torture of just waiting was the hardest task of all. But this wasn't a fright show where a dressed-up character was going to jump out and scream, "Boo!"

Here the threat was all too real, but she couldn't let fear immobilize her. She would have to respond more appropriately to the threat.

* * *

Minutes passed. She began to believe she'd only imagined the noise. All of this time, she'd been relying upon a feeling. She hadn't definitively identified Baer with any of her five senses. What if it was only her nerves that were talking?

She couldn't linger in this spot much longer. Survival meant finding a way back to civilization.

Nina took a deep breath. The cold hurt her lungs. *I need to get moving*, she thought. But that wasn't what her inner voice was telling her. She heard another sound. Or was it the wind?

So she waited. Hiding her anxiety made the wait that much harder. She swallowed down her scream. It was like holding down vomit.

And then a voice whispered in her ear, "Miss me?"

She reacted instantly, throwing herself away from the sound of his voice. As she rolled on the ground, she pulled the scarf from her eyes.

Baer was looking at her. He appeared to be disappointed that she hadn't screamed. He must have been anticipating her terror and shock.

What he wasn't anticipating was the gun she was holding.

"I give up," said Baer, raising his arms and smiling his jackal's grin.

Nina didn't lower the gun. She centered it and pulled the trigger. Nothing.

She pulled the trigger a second time. Another click.

"I guess you never learned about old ammo," said Baer, "and cold ammo."

As he lunged at her, Nina pulled the trigger again. This time there was more than a click.

Baer stopped in midmotion, neither advancing nor retreating. For a moment Nina wondered whether she'd missed. The shooting hadn't gone as she'd planned. In her mind she'd imagined herself assuming a shooter's stance and firing under control. Instead, she'd panicked and shot wildly.

One second there was nothing. In the next, the front of Baer's jacket bloomed red. He staggered back, one uncertain step and then another. His hand reached down to his chest, and he looked at his blood-soaked glove.

"You stupid, lucky, fucking bitch," he said.

"You need to work on your dying words," said Nina.

Then she shot him a second time.

He backpedaled for several steps, but couldn't find his balance. He fell to his knees. Nina watched him look around in surprise. Then he sprawled face-forward into the snow. The tracks she'd made in the pristine white snow filled with red.

Nina felt nothing except the cold.

CHAPTER THIRTY-SIX

Nina paused in midstep at the sound of a wolf howling nearby. Or maybe she was just hearing things. Distinguishing between what was real and what wasn't was becoming increasingly difficult for her, as though she hovered between worlds.

"Is this what happened to you, Sister?" she asked. "Did the cold take away your will?" She wished she'd been able to ask Baer what had happened to Elese before he died.

Nina kept walking. By her calculations Manley Hot Springs was still at least thirty miles away. At the moment it might as well have been a million.

"I thought when I killed Baer, everything else would fall into place," she said. "What I didn't take into account was this place."

The night before, she'd made it back to the hunting shack and slept for a long time.

In the morning she'd felt she could do this. The walk to Manley seemed possible, especially with the monster being dead.

Besides, what were her options? Going back to the cabin would have only delayed the inevitable death from starvation. And she didn't want to kill the dogs in the hopes they'd provide enough meat to get her to spring and to safety.

"In running terms, I've hit the wall. My tank is empty. There aren't even any fumes. Did you lie down in the snow, Sister? Did you curl up and go to sleep?"

She trudged forward a few more steps. "I shot him in cold blood, you know. But I have no regrets. The monster will never imprison another woman. The monster is dead. Maybe my heart has already turned to ice."

She stopped walking and looked around. "Is it time?" she asked. "I keep lightening my load. It's like I want to float off." She'd rid herself of the pistol and the rifle she'd taken from Baer's body. They were too heavy to keep carrying, and she was in no condition to hunt game. All of her will was focused on putting one foot in front of the other.

"Is it true the Native people used to deal with infirmity and old age by getting on an iceberg and floating away? That's kind of what I'm doing now. Is that what you did, Sister? I think maybe I'd rather have a Viking burial, though. At least I'd have a fire."

Nina began shaking her head. "That makes me think of Sam McGee. You must have heard that poem a million times as well."

As much as she didn't want to, she was hearing the words in her head. But she was hearing something else as well.

"It's time for a fire," she said.

* * *

It took Nina longer than she would have liked to gather the firewood and set everything up. The ephemeral daylight was already in retreat. She moved as if in a stupor, and although she tried to hurry her limbs, they only seemed able to respond with Frankenstein-like movements.

"Just like you suggested, Sister," Nina said. "The rule of three."

She finished compiling her third *X*. "*X* marks the spot," she announced. And then she added, "I tried to make you proud."

Even to her own ears, Nina sounded delirious. Everything had caught up to her: her tiredness, the cold, the shock. But she was going to see this fire blaze. It was too bad she'd be the only one to see it. Since fleeing Baer's cabin, she hadn't seen or heard a single aircraft.

"Maybe God will see my fire." The fire resisted taking.

"Do you remember the story of the Little Match Girl? With each strike of the match, she saw a different vision. And with each lit match, we learned of her hopes and dreams. And then with the lighting of her last match, her soul went to heaven. Should I be remembering my hopes and dreams like she did? I've never been much for looking back. I've always tried to look ahead."

The fire finally caught. As the wood began to burn, Nina was surprised by the flames' colors. "It must be the pitch and sap in the wood," she said. "Look at those blue flames, green flames, and ruby-red flames! We've made a rainbow. Do you remember the Northern Lights? I don't think I ever saw anything as pretty."

She put part of a spruce bough atop a fire. The smoke darkened. Then she raised and lowered more greenery, sending smoke signals high into the air.

"I am here," she said. "I was here."

CHAPTER THIRTY-SEVEN

Evan Hamilton covered his mouth and yawned. How in the hell had Martin talked him into this? He'd gotten up in the middle of the night and driven to Anchorage. Then he'd had to take a predawn flight to Fairbanks. Martin had said that was the most convenient airport from which to fly out just before sunrise. Of course, sunrise was around ten thirty in the morning. Not that the emerging sun put the cop in a better mood. He and Martin were flying to Bumfuck, Egypt, on another wild-goose chase. There was no putting it off, though. If you were to believe the National Weather Service, in the next twenty-four hours, a huge storm would be descending on Fairbanks and most of Alaska's interior.

Hamilton looked out the window to the desolate winter landscape they were flying over, and he shook his head some more.

"Whenever I get in one of these small planes," he said, "I can't help but think I'm about a half inch from dying. I mean, that's how thick the fuselage is, right?"

"You feel any better flying in a large jet?"

"I do. I always think I'm about an inch from dying."

"You inspire confidence."

"I'm still trying to remember what it was you said that got me to do this."

"It was a few things, actually, starting with the monster storm that's on its way. There was also the fact that neither one of us felt like waiting around for the ice to thaw."

Tomcat's plane was still awaiting excavation from the ice. No one was offering any ETA of when that might happen.

"Not to mention that those in charge of this case only seem to want to confirm wreckage and bodies, instead of considering the possibility of survivors."

"It's all coming back to me now," said Hamilton.

"Did you know that geologists are sometimes called 'earth detectives'?"

"No, I didn't. But then I don't know the first thing about geology."

"I've been studying it long enough to know that I don't know the first thing, either. But that's what comes of working in a field that deals with millions, even billions, of years. My point about geologists being called earth detectives is that we're always trying to solve mysteries. We look at a landscape and try to determine how it came to be. We don't see only a gorge, but the millions of years a glacier took to form that gorge. If you're a farmer, you see the soil. A geologist knows that soil was born of rocks that decayed through erosion. I see the result of sedimentary rock worn by winds and rain. When a geologist goes into the field, he has to make observations, and then take what limited information he has and try to divine answers.

"I love doing field mapping. I love observing outcroppings of rocks to see what they tell me. I love interpreting the information. I look at erosion. I consider the cycles that have gone into what I'm seeing. I check the sediment layers. Sometimes it feels like I'm in a time machine. I reconstruct how rocks got where they were. A geologist doesn't have a forward-running clock, but one that runs backward. That's geological time, with all its periods, cycles, forces, and ages. And for good measure, you throw in faults and fractures, and breaks and movements. And when you're field mapping, one of the questions you need to ask yourself is: What would I expect to find here?

"That's what I did when I looked at the maps of the area where we're going. I studied those maps, and I thought about Grizzly. What do we know about him, and what should we expect?"

Hamilton didn't think he'd ever heard Martin speak at such length, but then again, he'd usually been the one asking specific questions unrelated to his profession.

"I'm not an earth detective. I'm just a cop."

"That's what's needed, or I hope it is. I took into account Grizzly's character in relation to his comings and goings and tried to translate that information onto a map."

"What's all that mean?"

"We know Grizzly's a survivalist. We know he's probably a misanthrope. We know he's a trapper. We know Tomcat said he lived in Bumfuck, Egypt. And we both talked to Jack. If he remembers correctly, and he sounds credible, we even know where Grizzly's lake is."

"And we both agreed I should give up that information," said Hamilton. "And since I did, the drones have flown over the lake and that territory. They didn't find anything."

"That's because they haven't been looking in the right area."

"That's your geological opinion?"

"It's my interpretation based on my geological background. Humans have traveled and migrated along corridors formed by geological events. Why did Grizzly choose to land at this particular lake? We know he's secretive and paranoid. So why would we assume he lives near this lake?"

"Because of all his winter provisions," said Hamilton. "He probably packed a few hundred pounds of food aboard Tomcat's plane."

"Did you know there are two rivers less than a mile from his lake?"

"You think Grizzly had a boat?"

"He wouldn't even need a boat. The Natives have been using rafts for thousands of years. He could make one on the spot from materials that are at hand, or he could have had it at the ready."

Hamilton wasn't convinced. "You're doing a lot of surmising."

"In geology you can often find minerals in abundance in one spot, but that doesn't mean you can assume that if you start digging at that spot, you'll find the mother lode. There are occasions when you have to find the location you're looking for by factoring in things like erosion, floods, and water flow."

"So you're saying he hauled all the provisions, along with a prisoner, and transported everything down the river?"

"Without any roads around here, the people have gotten used to doing their transporting by river. If you don't believe me, just go to YouTube and watch videos of trucks floating down the Yukon on wooden rafts."

"For real?"

Martin nodded. "I'm talking about rafts like Huck Finn would have made. Grizzly took his two victims in September, when the rivers weren't yet frozen. I believe his timing wasn't coincidental. He wanted to snatch his victims just before the interior changed into the Ice Age."

Hamilton had always wondered about the timing, and rubbed his chin in thought.

"Grizzly didn't want a road or need a road," said Martin. "He had the river. I've studied the maps. I know all the rivers and tributaries near his landing spot, and I've memorized their routes. We know Grizzly didn't want to be anywhere near people, so I've come up with a few likely water routes. It was like figuring out alluvial flow."

"Or figuring out which way the sewage flows," said Hamilton.

"I like your analogy better."

* * *

The flight from Fairbanks to what Martin called the "likely Grizzly radius" was a little more than a hundred miles. During the flight Martin offered up some geological insights as to what they were seeing.

Hamilton heard about tectonic plates, the convergence of faults, uplifted blocks, and how mountains were formed. Martin pointed out tectonic activity and explained how depressions were formed. There was even some geological humor thrown in, with Martin commenting on, "gneiss cleavage." It took the cop a second to understand the pun.

"Had you ever been to Alaska before your honeymoon cruise?" Hamilton asked.

Martin shook his head. "I'd always wanted to go. In fact, I think I was much more enamored than Elese was. I probably should have listened to her."

"About what?"

"About where we should go on our honeymoon. I think she would have preferred Maui, but I told her Alaska would be much more interesting. Of course, Elese knew I meant more interesting geologically speaking, unless you're interested in volcanology, that is. Before our honeymoon we went on several getaways, and she saw how I always came home with pockets full of rocks. That's what I've always done wherever I've gone."

"So you're a rock hound?"

"That's what started my interest in geology."

Hamilton noticed Martin's half smile. "Something funny?" he asked.

"Not really," said Martin. "I was just remembering being fascinated by some of the glaciers we saw on the cruise. I was out on the deck for hours this one day hoping to see this glacier calve. And Elese had to seek me out. She knew where I'd be—and knew I'd forgotten my promise to not be long."

His smile disappeared. Hamilton knew why. It was because his wife had disappeared.

* * *

Both men had known it was a long shot, even with Martin's geological deductions. They'd been flying over the "likely Grizzly radius" for some time with no results. There had been no signs of current human habitation.

They'd also been up in the air long enough for Hamilton's nervousness to be showing itself. "Isn't it about time we called it a day?" he asked.

"Are you worried about the state of our fuel or the state of the sunlight?" asked Martin.

"I'm an equal-opportunity worrier."

"We'll turn back soon," he said.

"Don't get me wrong," said Hamilton. "I think you might be on to something about extending the search out this way. But we're going to have to bring in help."

"What about the reward money?"

"You still think Nina Granville might be alive?"

"Hope springs eternal."

"I thought you were doing this to clear your name and try to exact revenge from the SOB that took your wife."

"I am. But isn't living well supposed to be the best revenge?"

"I wouldn't know."

Martin began turning the plane, aiming it in a new direction.

"Are we going home?" asked Hamilton.

"There's one more area we need to check out."

"Don't cut it too close. Remember, I got kids."

"Roger Wilco."

"I've always wondered what the hell that means."

"Roger means received. I don't know why, but I do know it's used by civilians and the military. And Wilco is an abbreviation for 'will comply.'"

"Roger Wilco," mused Hamilton. "I like that a lot better than Mayday."

* * *

"Is that a cloud, or is it smoke?"

Martin turned his head in the direction of Hamilton's finger. Even before he answered, he began changing course. "It looks like smoke."

"There's probably some hunting cabin out this way."

"That's probably it," said Martin.

Neither man chose to mention that they hadn't seen a cabin in the last hour, nor had they seen any signs of humanity.

"Wouldn't hurt to fly lower to get a good look," Martin said casually.

Hamilton also tried to sound disinterested. "You might as well."

* * *

The fire was dying out. There were no more colors and no more warmth. The burning *X* had melted the letter into the ice, but the cold was reasserting itself.

Nina sat on the snow. She didn't even have the caribou hide under her. Maybe in a few minutes she'd try to put some insulation under her and around her, but not now. For the moment she was too tired.

She wondered if the Little Match Girl had lit her last match in similar fashion. *X marks the spot*, Nina thought. Would it also mark her grave site?

She looked at the dying fire. "I'm sorry," she said. She wasn't sure if she was speaking to Elese or her unborn baby or herself.

She thought about her own life and felt a few twinges of regret. "It was a good life," she said, "but it wasn't the one I wanted, nor was it the one I should have led. I know that now."

Too soon dead and too late smart.

A far-off buzz burrowed into her thoughts. For a few moments, she didn't register what she was hearing, other than the disturbance of the quiet. As the buzz grew louder, Nina tried to focus through her jumbled thoughts. She looked up, searching for the sound. The object grew larger in the sky, and she realized she was looking at a plane.

Only when the plane was flying over her did Nina start jumping up and down. She didn't even think to wave her arms until it was passing by. Belatedly she began waving and shouting.

But the plane was already past her, its sound receding into the distance.

"No!" she screamed.

The plane didn't hear her, of course. No one hears a ghost. It had kept flying. It had missed her.

But then she heard something louder than her doubts. The buzzing returned.

* * *

For what felt like an eternity, Nina was certain her mind was playing tricks on her.

It was only when the doors opened and two men hopped out that she started walking, unsteadily, toward the plane. The taller of the two men put one of those old-time mountie-type hats on his head, and both men started running toward her.

"Are they real, Sister?" asked Nina.

Her eyes still hadn't recovered.

In the distance Nina heard the sound of a wolf howling, and then a chorus of other wolves joining in.

"Is that my pack?" she asked, looking around but not seeing the wolves.

The men, though, were becoming clearer to her. They were waving and shouting.

"I guess I'm not a ghost," Nina said. "I'm taking you with me. We're both getting out of here."

The chorus of wolves suddenly grew silent, and Elese's voice was no longer in Nina's head. The stillness made her dizzy, and she would have fallen had she not been caught by one of the men.

Nina touched his cheek. He felt real. And then she realized who was holding her.

"Oh, Greg," she said, "is it really you?"

She watched his jaw drop. "We have so much to talk about," she said.

But that conversation would have to wait. Nina fell into unconsciousness.

CHAPTER THIRTY-EIGHT

Three days later they were finally able to have that conversation. Nina had been delirious during the flight back, and upon landing was immediately handed over to a medical team that rushed her to Fairbanks Memorial Hospital. After her condition stabilized, doctors made the decision to remove two of her toes.

When Greg entered her room, the bouquet in his hand suddenly felt small. Nina's suite was filled with flowers. She could have easily supplied the arrangements for a large wedding. But her broad smile eased his uncertainty, and when he tried to apologize for his bouquet, she took it from his hands and said, "I love it."

Then she placed the bouquet atop her stomach and held it close to her. She was still hooked up to IV drips, and there were raw, red patches on her face. Dark circles lined her eyes, and her lips were severely chapped.

"I don't know if you remember when we met," he said.

"How could I forget? Even had you and Sergeant Hamilton been angels, I don't think you could have made a grander entrance."

"On the flight back, you were semiconscious, but you did seem to wake for a few moments and make us promise that we'd see to the dogs. I think you were afraid you were going to die and wanted to be sure they'd be taken care of."

"I don't remember that. But when I started being somewhat lucid again, I was glad to hear the dogs were all right."

"Do you remember when we first met you called me 'Greg'?"

"I do," she said.

"I didn't think I imagined it, but how did you know my name?"

"Elese told me. In a drawing." She told him the story of the secret journal.

Nina's tears fell freely during her telling. "Your wife's words were my light in the darkness," she said. "She was my secret sister. And she saved my life."

Greg didn't attempt words. His Adam's apple seemed to fill his throat.

"I want to know more about her," said Nina. "I want to get to know Elese beyond her book. Tell me about the first day the two of you met."

Greg managed a deep breath. "That was the same day we fell in love."

* * *

Three times the nursing staff came and told Greg he needed to leave. Three times Nina dismissed them. But finally her exhaustion began to overcome her resolve to stay awake.

"I need a favor from you," she said. "Before you agree, you need to know that you'll probably be breaking some kind of law that extends to evidence, although what I would ask you to do is something that I think is in both of our interests."

"I guess you haven't heard that I'm considered a scofflaw of sorts. Whatever I can do to help you, I will."

"Will you get Elese's journal for me? I don't want anyone else to know about it, at least for now. If . . . What Elese wrote could bring into question my account of shooting the monster, and that's not something I want to deal with. I want to put it behind me forever."

"I don't blame you."

Nina told him about the hollowed-out caulking tube and where it could be found.

Greg said, "I don't know if you've heard about the storm that's been sweeping through the state, but it's pretty much grounded all air traffic to the interior. Weather permitting, I'll fly out in the next few days and get it for you."

"You'll have to hold on to it for me," said Nina. "I'm leaving tomorrow."

"I had no idea you'd be going so soon."

"No one does. We're trying to keep it from the media."

"Good luck. There's an army downstairs."

"I've heard them. They keep yelling questions to me with a bullhorn."

"The less you say to them, the better it is for you. Or at least that's been my experience."

She nodded. "I think Terrence's team is already working on my speech. They'll have someone in media relations read it for me. I'm sure it won't mention how much I wanted Baer dead and how good it felt shooting him."

"You're making me jealous."

She was quiet for a moment. Softly she said, "I'm still awaiting word that they've recovered his body."

"You're going to have to wait until the storm lifts, and maybe longer."

"Why do you say longer?"

"If he's covered in snow, he won't be easy to find."

Nina frowned. "It might not melt for months."

"Maybe they can bring in dogs to find him."

"I know he's dead. But in my mind, he's like this vampire. I want proof positive."

"You and me both."

Nina looked at him and nodded. No one could understand as well as the two of them.

"In a few weeks, I'll be holding some kind of memorial for Elese," he said. "You're invited, of course."

Nina bit off her reply. She needed to tell him about Elese's memorial-service request, about Denali, but now wasn't the right time. Instead, she said, "Why don't you give me the number to your cell? There are some things we need to discuss, but I'm just too fuzzy at the moment to go into them. I'll call you after I get back east."

"I'm counting on it," said Martin, and gave her his business card with his private cell.

She took it and leaned back against the pillows. "Don't leave yet," she murmured. "I'm enjoying our talk too much."

But her good intentions were no match for her exhaustion. She fought off the closing of her eyelids once, and then a second time, but finally lost the battle, and he crept out of her hospital room.

CHAPTER THIRTY-NINE

Nina sat on the deck, taking in the view of North Pond. On the other side of the seventy-five-acre Donnelly family compound in Greenwich, she'd been told there was a second private body of water called South Pond. Even though the Donnelly family had lived on the estate for more than half a century, it was still referred to as Pond Manor.

It was at Pond Manor that Nina was supposed to convalesce. Even though the air was thirty degrees outside, she was seated on a cushioned chair looking out to the pond. Nina felt unaffected by the cold.

At the sound of the door opening, she turned her head to see Sergeant Wood standing there. His posture didn't seem as straight as usual, and instead of projecting a take-charge attitude, he looked awkward and ill at ease.

"Permission to approach, ma'am?"

Nina nodded.

Sarge drew closer. His previous tactic had been to intimidate through direct eye contact, but not now. He kept his eyes mostly averted.

"I wanted you to know I offered my resignation to the congressman. At this time he has refused to accept it. However, should you want me to step aside, I will do so. I take full responsibility for your situation and all that occurred."

"I don't understand why you would think you were responsible, Sergeant."

"I should have insisted that security accompany you during your trip to Alaska."

Nina smiled. "I seem to remember that you did insist, but I refused to listen to you."

"I was the individual who headed up efforts in Alaska trying to determine what happened to you, as well as being the congressman's liaison between his office and Alaskan law enforcement and the military."

"And I am told you were tireless in your efforts."

"But I was of little, if any, help in your recovery."

"All is well that ends well, right, Sergeant?"

"If you say so, ma'am," he said, but he still looked miserable.

"I'm alive, Sarge. Life is good."

"No thanks to me. When that piece from your engagement diamond turned up, I assumed you'd been robbed and were dead."

"Most people made that same assumption."

"Did your assailant ever say anything about his disposing of the ring?"

Nina shook her head.

"We assume he sold it to a fence in Alaska," said Sarge, "but that's just guesswork."

"What I don't understand is how you were able to identify my diamond from that carat that turned up."

"A bulletin was sent out to everyone in the diamond world," he said. "Because your diamond was certified, several markers were in place. One of those markers had been put in place by a laser, which essentially gave it a unique fingerprint. There was also an identification number etched on the diamond, which could only be seen with a high-magnification lens.

And finally, it had been X-rayed from all angles. All diamonds reflect and retract in a unique way, and even with just the single carat, we were able to see this. We assume your abductor's fence had the gem cut in the hopes that it wouldn't be identified. Unfortunately, we still haven't been able to track down the original seller."

"Maybe we'll get lucky when they try to unload the rest of the stone," Nina said.

"Yes, ma'am," said Sarge.

* * *

There must have been an unseen line waiting to talk to Nina. Marilyn Grant appeared within a minute of Sarge's leaving.

Marilyn sat next to her and gathered Nina's right hand into hers, looking more like a concerned grandmother than the family's long-time media-relations director. "For all you've been through, you look wonderful."

"That's because you've been keeping the press from me. Terrence says you've been besieged."

"There is a bit of a frenzy going on out there. Everyone wants your story."

"I suppose I can't put them off forever," said Nina, "just like I can't put off certain decisions."

"Don't worry about them, and don't worry about me. You need to do what's right for you. If you want my advice, though, I'd suggest you let me schedule one interview. I'll set ground rules, choose the venue, and insist upon a list of questions to be asked ahead of time. By doing that we'll satisfy the public's curiosity and be able to defuse some of the wild speculation and rumors."

"I'm out of the loop. What rumors are you referring to?"

"Nothing more than the usual political innuendoes and conspiracy theories. There's a story going around that your abduction was arranged so as to ensure the congressman's November victory. There are also some skeptics wondering how a one-hundred-and-twenty-pound woman bested a large armed man."

"Thank heavens for a momentary lapse on his part."

"And that's how we'd dispose of one wild story."

"The true story is a lot worse. I suppose there's no avoiding talking about how he maimed me, abused me, and raped me."

"I'm afraid those are unavoidable subjects, but I promise you that they will not be belabored."

"I suppose we better address the elephant in the room," said Nina.

"I suppose we better," said Marilyn, offering a sad if supportive smile. "Several of the tabloids have reported that you're pregnant. They cite sources within Fairbanks Memorial Hospital. The mainstream media is now reporting the same thing."

"Once the toothpaste comes out of the tube," Nina said, "it's impossible to get back in."

"I'm afraid so."

"And how do we handle that?"

"However you decide. I want you to know that personally and professionally, I will support any decision you make."

* * *

Terrence appeared shortly after Marilyn left. Nina wondered if his timing was coincidental, or if Terrence had let Sarge and Marilyn deal with some of the unpleasantries before he had his talk with her.

Everyone had always said how youthful Terrence looked. That was before the heavy dark circles appeared. There were also frown lines on his forehead that Nina had never seen before. She knew she was their cause.

"Brrr," Terrence said, exhaling vapor and putting a tentative hand on Nina's shoulder. "I thought the doctors told you to limit your exposure to cold, especially in light of their having to remove those toes."

"Two little piggies," Nina said with a little smile. "The doctor promised me I'd be able to run after the procedure. What were his words? 'Your ambulation shouldn't be overly impeded by the removal of the fourth and fifth phalanges.' It's a good thing a nurse leaned over to me and said, 'Your fourth toe and pinky toe.'"

"Are you in a lot of pain?"

"Some," Nina admitted, "but even when I hurt, it feels good, because I'm no longer a captive."

They heard a rattling of cups. Mrs. Leary always managed to announce herself with her cups and cutlery. She and her husband lived at and managed the interior of Pond Manor.

"Hot chocolate and freshly baked coffee cake," said Mrs. Leary. "It's what the doctor ordered."

"You can be my doctor anytime," Nina said.

Mrs. Leary smiled and served, then left the couple alone.

Nina sipped at her hot chocolate and marveled at the taste. Mrs. Leary didn't believe in serving anything that was packaged. In her drink you could actually taste chocolate, butter, and cream.

Terrence pretended to enjoy his drink as well, but Nina could tell he was preoccupied. She'd never seen his face look as gaunt, even during his toughest political moments.

"Penny for your thoughts?"

"I'm just worried about you."

"My nightmare is over, Terrence. Whatever happens from here on in won't compare to what came before. And that includes my pregnancy."

He nodded, and Nina was sure she'd guessed right about what was foremost on his mind.

"It's not a secret that can be hidden for long," she said. "The baby is growing so quickly that in another week or two, the media won't even have to speculate over my condition."

"It sounds like you've decided to keep the baby."

"I have."

"Then know this: I will love the baby as much as if it's my own."

"You're a good man, Terrence," said Nina, speaking gently and sincerely. "I think you might be the best man I've ever known . . ."

"You're about to say *but*. Don't say it."

"That's what makes this so difficult."

He started shaking his head. "Don't say it. Don't make any rash decisions. You've been through hell, and you've hardly had any time to recover. Now is the time for you to heal."

Terrence continued talking, not letting her interrupt. "Everyone is rooting for you. My staff has fielded thousands of calls. And what people want is the fairy tale we can have. After all you've been through, don't tell me we can't live happily ever after. We can. The best plastic surgeons in the country tell me your finger can be reconstructed so that it looks almost new. Let me put a new ring on that finger."

Nina shook her head. "I'm not going to have my finger reconstructed. It suits me just the way it is."

She tried not to cry, but her eyes filled with tears, and her lips quivered as she added, "And I won't be able to wear your ring, either."

"I can't accept that," he said. "I won't accept it."

"My experience changed me."

"Of course, it did. It was horrible. Everyone understands it will take time for you to heal. Give me that time before you make a decision."

"This isn't a sudden decision. When I was enslaved, I knew that if I ever got free, I wouldn't be able to go through with our marriage."

"You're being noble," he said. "You think the baby and what you went through make you a political liability. I don't care about that. I care about you."

"I wish I was being noble. I'm not. When I agreed to be your wife, you made me feel like a princess. But that's not who I am. I know that now."

What she was saying was mostly true. Nina didn't want to admit that she was afraid of what questions would be asked when Baer's body was recovered from the snow. The circumstances that had led her to kill him were justified—but she wasn't going to subject Terrence to a potential scandal.

"I am not going to abandon you," he said.

"And I'm not going to abandon you," she said, "but that doesn't mean both of us shouldn't go different ways."

Terrence shook his head. His eyes were now as filled with tears as Nina's. "What happened to you was terrible. It was unspeakable. Why can't we let time try to heal those wounds?"

"During my captivity I realized how short and precious life is. I need to do something that matters to me, Terrence."

"I won't stand in your way."

"I can't be a politician's wife and do what I want to do."

"Then I don't have to be a politician. I can resign."

Nina stood up and hugged him, squeezing him close to her. "Why would you want to do that?" she whispered. "Politics is your calling. I have my own calling now."

CHAPTER FORTY

Nina took Marilyn's advice. Two days later she and Terrence sat in front of cameras for her one and only interview. Terrence held her maimed hand. The world heard about her horrors and her courage. Nina's only regret was that she couldn't mention Elese. Her sister's journal could implicate her in Baer's murder. For now she chose to say nothing.

Everyone commented on how devastated the congressman looked while she told her story. No one suspected the real reason for his discomfiture. They'd decided that the announcement of their split-up could wait—it was the first politically strategic decision Nina was wholly on board with since their engagement.

After the interview Nina went to her parents' house. She let them spoil her. Luke came home for a long weekend, and everyone pretended it was like old times. It was the balm Nina needed; Baer's shadow receded. It wasn't *Our Town*, or not exactly. Her role as Emily had come and gone a long time ago. But Nina tried to realize life while she was living it, as hard as that might be.

Over the course of three days, she left four messages on Greg Martin's cell phone, so she wasn't surprised when he finally called back.

"And here I was wondering if you were avoiding my calls," she said.

"I've been traveling."

"Please don't tell me you already flew to the cabin."

"And why is that?"

"Because there was something I needed to talk to you about before you read Elese's book. That's why I've been calling and leaving you messages."

"I haven't started reading her book."

"I'm glad."

"You won't be. The only reason I'm not reading her book is because it's now a pile of ashes."

Nina's sharp intake of breath bespoke her shock. "What?" she said.

"I flew to the cabin," he said, "or what used to be the cabin. Someone burned it down."

"The cabin's gone?"

"All that was left were a few metal traps."

"Why would anyone burn it down?"

"I was hoping you could tell me."

Nina couldn't shake off the numbness she was feeling. Elese's book had sustained her through so much. She felt bereft that one of her last connections to Elese was now forever gone.

"I don't have a clue."

Neither one said anything for a moment; silly as it seemed, Nina felt she'd just gotten news that a close friend had died.

"So, what was it that you needed to talk to me about?" Greg asked.

She took a deep breath. "You need to know about Denali."

CHAPTER FORTY-ONE

Almost two hundred people turned out at Glide Memorial Church in downtown San Francisco to pay tribute to Elese and Denali Martin.

Nina was glad no one seemed to take notice of her presence at the service. Maybe her black veil and gloves, as well as her overcoat, had something to do with that. No one could see her face, missing finger, or emerging baby bump.

The service let out to a rousing rendition of Leonard Cohen's "Hallelujah," sung by the chorus. And that was the word on Nina's lips and those of everyone around her as they walked out of the church: Hallelujah.

There was a crowd waiting to see Greg Martin. For more than three years, he'd been a suspect in his wife's disappearance, and now he was finally free. He also looked a little bit lost. Of course, Nina couldn't be sure if she was interpreting his condition or her own.

Someone started toward her. *The media*, Nina thought. She picked up her pace and hurriedly made her way toward Ellis Street, scanning for a cab. It annoyed her that she was walking with a limp and couldn't yet break out into a run. Physical therapy was working wonders, but she still had to get used to moving without two toes. Nina liked to complain that she was walking like Dr. Zira from the *Planet of the Apes* films.

Without any taxi in sight, a footrace wouldn't work, so she came to a stop and turned around. She opened her mouth to say, "No comment," but then saw it wasn't a reporter who was following her.

The slightly breathless man stopped his pursuit. "I didn't think you heard me there. And I'm not sure whether you remember me. With this suit I barely recognize myself. But I'm . . ."

"Sergeant Hamilton," said Nina, extending her hand.

"Guilty as charged," he said. "Say, I was just about to look for a place to get some coffee and a bite to eat. Any chance I can talk you into joining me? I always feel funny sitting by myself."

"Why not?" said Nina.

* * *

After asking the advice of a few locals, they decided that John's Grill sounded like the perfect place to eat. Everyone said it was "old San Francisco." Best of all it was only three blocks from the church.

The restaurant was as old as the locals had advertised. While waiting for a booth, Nina occupied herself by reading some framed newspaper articles. The grill, she learned, had been around since 1908. While she buried herself in reading about its past, Hamilton spent his time looking at the abundant *Maltese Falcon* paraphernalia.

"They shot a scene from *The Maltese Falcon* in this restaurant," he told her. "I'm pretty sure I remember it. Humphrey Bogart as Sam Spade comes in and orders chops, a baked potato, and sliced tomatoes. Guess what I'm going to be having? My wife's going to be so jealous. She loves old Bogart films."

A hostess led them to their booth. Hamilton ordered his Sam Spade Special, while Nina had a shrimp cocktail. A basket of hot sourdough bread was delivered to them, and Nina was soon making rapturous sounds.

"That was a nice memorial service, wasn't it?" asked Hamilton.

Nina nodded. "I don't think I've ever been to a better one."

"Quite the rip-roaring choir."

"They were incredible."

"The service wasn't without its surprises, though, was it? Or I guess Elese's boy wasn't a surprise for you. You had to have been the one who told Martin about Denali, right?"

Nina smiled. "Is this an interview, Sergeant?"

Hamilton shook his head. "No, it's not that. I guess old habits die hard, though. It's sort of ironic that Martin was my prime suspect in Elese's disappearance all these years, and because of him I came into my windfall."

"What do you mean?"

"Your fiancé put out a two-million-dollar reward for your safe return, or for providing information that led to your safe return. You didn't know that?"

Nina shook her head.

"I thought you would have heard," said Hamilton. "You lucked out being found like you were, but Martin and I lucked into a financial windfall. Each of us is collecting a million dollars."

"I doubt Mr. Martin thinks he's lucky. I'm sure he would rather have Elese than the money."

The cop pursed his lips and nodded. "I'm sure you're right about that. He got the short end of the stick for a long time, and I'm sorry to say I probably had something to do with that."

"Are you going to retire now?" Nina asked.

Hamilton shook his head. "I'm an old dog who's comfortable with my routine. But this summer the wife and I are going to get away for three months. We'll be going on the trip of a lifetime, traveling to four different continents."

"That sounds incredible."

"What about you?" he asked.

Nina patted her stomach. "I was supposed to get married in June, but now I'm going to have a baby."

"You'll be starting a different adventure."

"That's the way I'm looking at it."

CHAPTER FORTY-TWO

Nina's cell phone began ringing within moments of her returning to her small room at the Chancellor Hotel in Union Square.

"You promised you'd seek me out after the service," said Greg.

"And I tried to, but when I saw how many people were surrounding you, I decided a change of plans was in order."

"What about now?"

"I'm tired," said Nina, "which means you must be exhausted."

"I am," he admitted, "but we both still need to eat."

"I actually ate. Sergeant Hamilton and I dined together."

"I thought I felt my ears burning."

"He was actually singing your praises."

"Coming into a million dollars does change one's opinions."

"I heard. Congratulations."

"The reward your fiancé offered had most of Alaska looking for you."

"The next time we talk, I'll thank him."

"The next time?"

Nina was tired of speaking cryptically. "Terrence and I are no longer engaged; that hasn't been announced yet, so please don't say anything."

"I'm sorry," he said, "and I won't."

"I appreciate it."

"Since dinner won't work, what about breakfast in the morning?"

"I can't. Tomorrow morning I'll be boarding the Coast Starlight to San Diego."

"What's in San Diego?"

"The weather," she said. "The forecast is for the seventies. Aside from that I'll find out."

"Footloose and fancy-free?"

"More like foot with two amputated toes and full of trepidation."

"Bon voyage," he said.

"Call me," said Nina.

"I will."

* * *

Nina was wheeling her solitary piece of luggage toward the welcoming red letters of Caltrain Station when her cell phone rang.

"Don't tell me you walked," said a familiar voice.

Nina looked around and saw Greg Martin waving to her from the entrance to the station.

"You told me to call," he said by way of explanation.

Nina put away her phone and started toward him. He met her halfway, and they hugged. "I can't believe you walked," he said.

"It was only a mile and a half from the hotel."

"I've got a good excuse for not having walked. I was busy getting your breakfast and your lunch." He shook the paper bags he was holding.

"That looks like a lot of food."

"I was hoping I could eat with you."

Nina thought about that. "You want to get on a train just so that we can eat together?"

"Well, I was hoping some conversation would come with the meal. And to make your decision even easier, my plan is to get off in San Jose unless you indicate you want me to keep riding the rails. Oh, and did I mention that I brought bagels, doughnuts, hot coffee, and breakfast burritos?"

Nina shrugged and said, "All aboard."

CHAPTER FORTY-THREE

Greg Martin didn't get off the train in San Jose. At the time he was laughing too hard hearing about how Elese had slipped Waldo into one of her drawings.

"She might have drawn a picture of Waldo," said Nina, "but it was also like she was inserting her own picture. And all during my time in Alaska, it was like she was there, even if I didn't see her."

It was a fourteen-hour ride to San Diego, but neither one of them seemed to notice the passage of time.

"Elese had a drawing of you as well," Nina said. "I guessed you were a geologist or someone who had something to do with rocks."

"Why is that?"

"She depicted you holding up this rock and looking at it critically—and lovingly. Elese must have taken a long time with that drawing because she captured you perfectly. That's how I immediately knew who you were. There was no question."

"I wish I had that drawing," he said. "I'd give anything for it."

They arrived at the Santa Fe Depot at one in the morning. Since he was familiar with the San Diego area, Nina was happy to let Greg see to their travel arrangements. They stayed in separate rooms in a small lodge on the North County coast, and the next morning they took advantage of the low tide to walk to breakfast.

Their breakfast had now turned into lunch. The two of them hadn't given up their balcony table overlooking the Pacific Ocean. They'd watched the surfers ply the waves for hours and had seen a pod of dolphins demonstrating how body surfing was really done. Pelicans had regularly swept by in formations, skimming the tops of breaking waves, while along the shoreline, sanderlings timed the incoming waves with their rapid footwork.

It wasn't only the sightseeing that had kept Nina and Greg at their table, though.

"What do you think?" asked Greg.

"I think it sounds too good to be true, and my father the businessman always said if something sounds too good to be true, then it invariably *is* too good to be true."

"Nothing up my sleeves," said Greg, demonstrating. "And far be it from me to contradict your father, but this isn't a business deal."

"You're right, it's not. But what is it?"

"It's what Elese would want me to do."

"So you're willing to buy a house somewhere around here, and then let me and the baby live rent-free?"

"You forgot the part about me having claim to the master bedroom. And in a weak moment, I did volunteer to take you to Lamaze classes."

"Why?"

"I'm looking to start over. So are you. Besides that, I benefited financially from finding you. Why shouldn't you reap some of those rewards?"

"I don't like making hasty decisions."

"Then don't. Think it over. It's not like I'm buying a house on a whim. My financial advisor has told me it's a no-brainer. By having a dedicated work space in the house, I can take all sorts of write-offs. So with, or without, you and the baby, I'm still going to buy a home. I always wanted to get back to California anyway."

"It's tempting," said Nina, "but I'm thinking it's wrong."

"Why?"

"I'm damaged. I know that. Like Humpty Dumpty, I don't know if I can be put back together. Will my sex drive return? Will I be able to love a man? Only time will tell. And so if you have any romantic illusions, I need to dash them right now."

"At this time the only thing I'm offering is a helping hand," he said, "not a groping one."

Being six months pregnant, Nina knew she wasn't exactly pinup material for most men. Maybe Greg didn't have any romantic designs on her.

"There's one thing I haven't told you," she said, "and that's what I plan to do in the future. It might very well be a deal-breaker for you."

"Tell me," he said.

She did.

He didn't interrupt her, but listened to her plans about getting involved in the fight against human trafficking. When Nina finished talking, he said, "That sounds—dangerous."

"I'll do my best to minimize any risks."

"Is this plan of yours why you broke it off with Donnelly?"

"It was a major reason, even though he didn't know that."

"I'll need to think if I'm okay with this," he said. "I'm not sure living with a hatchet-wielding Carrie Nation is something I want."

"At least you didn't liken me to Lizzie Borden."

"If the ax fits," he said.

"There are plenty of other women who inspired me," Nina said. "Think of Harriet Tubman, Susan B. Anthony, and Margaret Sanger.

"And most of all," she said, "think of Elese Martin."

Greg nodded.

* * *

Nina took off her shoes and socks. She was unmindful of her two missing toes, or at least didn't let them get in the way of her walking in the surf on the way back to their motel. Greg kept his Docksides on and stayed on the sand side of her.

When Nina's cell phone rang, she mentally berated herself for not having turned off the ringer. Beach walks weren't meant to be interrupted by phone calls. But when she looked at the display, she decided to take the call.

"I didn't think I would be talking with you again so soon, Ms. Granville," said Sergeant Hamilton.

"I didn't think so, either, Sergeant."

"Evan, please. And I know this news is going to make your day. We finally found his remains."

Damn raging hormones, she thought. Tears had already started falling down her cheeks. The bogeyman was really dead. Maybe now she wouldn't have to check the locks over and over before going to bed with a loaded gun under her pillow. Maybe now she wouldn't have all those nightmares that he was still pursuing her.

She tried to speak without Hamilton knowing she was crying, but knew he wasn't fooled. "Where was he found?"

"He was about a mile from where we think you shot him."

"That far?"

"It looked like he was helped along a ways."

"Wolves?"

"I'm surprised any critters could stomach him, but yes, they got themselves a meal."

"And you're sure it's him? There's no possible question as to his identity?"

"Even though the body was chewed up, the cause of death was still visible. Both bullets were recovered. There'll be ballistic tests, of course, but it's our man."

"What about doing a DNA test on him?"

"You're about as suspicious as I am, young lady. Yes, that will be done as well. It will probably be a month or two before we get the results, but I can tell you this, Nina, he's our guy, and he's really, truly, completely dead."

"Anything new on his identity?"

"He's still a John Doe."

"Did you get anything on the background information I provided?"

His voice held nothing but sympathy. "There are lots of missing women, Nina. And nothing has come in on a mountain-man father and missing wife."

"We might never know who he is."

"We know he's dead. That's what matters."

"Yes, that's what matters."

She thanked Hamilton for calling and put away the phone. When she turned to Martin, he nodded and said, "I heard."

"I can't tell you how relieved I feel," she said, wiping away a few remaining tears. "I mean, I knew he was dead, but I also needed the proof that he was really gone."

She lifted her face up to the sun. It was a cloudless day; the shadows had lifted.

"Hold up a second," said Greg.

Nina stopped walking while he took off his Docksides and socks and joined her in the surf.

"I think we need to celebrate," he said. "And we also need to get a Realtor to start looking for that house of ours."

CHAPTER FORTY-FOUR

Five weeks after their train ride, Nina and Greg moved into a 4,000-square-foot Carlsbad home that was two and a half miles from the ocean. It was perfect for Nina; she was now in the eighth month of her pregnancy, but every day she ran to the ocean. On some days she also jogged the six-mile sandy stretch of South Carlsbad State Beach.

It was because of her running that Nina first saw Marisol.

"Greg!" Nina called.

She heard a muffled answer coming from what had formerly been the master bedroom. Greg had converted the space into an area the two of them called Alcatraz, the former penitentiary known as the Rock. It was an appropriate nickname; the room housed Greg's huge rock collection.

Museum-style cabinets lined the walls. Greg's finds were separated into the categories of rocks, minerals, and fossils. There were also numerous subcategories. The museum drawers were long and wide and pulled out to allow maximum visibility. Greg's finds were mounted inside those drawers. Each had its own display card, which identified the object, the GPS coordinates of where it had been found, and the date it was collected.

Nina would never have imagined that rocks would need any kind of special care, but Greg had told her that because some sulfides tarnished, they were best kept in dark places, and that certain minerals were prone to disintegration if it was too dry. Because of that, Alcatraz was climate-controlled with special lighting.

Lighting was also put to good use in those glass display cases housing fluorescent minerals. By daylight there was nothing to distinguish the minerals, but under ultraviolet lights, they exploded in colors, offering a rainbow of reds, blues, and greens, along with pinks, whites, and oranges.

Greg was sitting at his workstation. By the looks of it, he was packing his internal-frame backpack for his next rock outing. Depending on where he was going, Greg would fill his pack with hammers, chisels, pry bars, screen sieves, loupes, brushes, a folding shovel, safety goggles, a headband magnifier, his altimeter watch, a mineral test kit, gold pans, miner's headlamp, various pocket tools for extracting quartz, and even a battery-operated diamond saw for making cuts in the rock. His pack could weigh sixty pounds or more, and that didn't include food or water.

He looked up from his packing and smiled at Nina. At his work table was lapidary equipment, which included rock tumblers, saws, and polishing machines for such finds as thunder eggs, agates, and geodes, which he sold through a website, although Greg was quick to say it was more a labor of love than a big moneymaker. Geological consulting was where he made his money. Unfortunately, most of those jobs didn't involve working with the rocks that he loved. The majority of his work was in environmental due diligence, an area he said was a "yawner."

"Marisol's story made the paper," Nina said, handing him a copy of the *Union-Tribune*.

Greg read aloud the headline: "Doctor Charged in Human Trafficking."

Then he scanned the article and said, "Here's a surprise: his attorney says he's innocent."

"Read a little further and you'll see where his CPA wife is quoted as saying Marisol is an 'ingrate.' I guess she was supposed to be grateful for being an unpaid sex slave."

It was during one of her runs that Nina had noticed the young woman staring out the window, looking at nothing. There had been something about her despair that was palpable and had reminded Nina of her time in Alaska, when she had despondently stared out of the cabin's sole window. A few days later, when Nina was sure the woman was home alone, she tried talking with her. Using a translator app on her portable phone, Nina was able to translate Tagalog. In the days that followed, she'd gradually gained the young woman's trust.

The young Filipina had confessed to Nina that she was in the United States illegally. She'd entered the country thinking she would be working as a domestic in the house of the doctor and his wife, but her employers had other ideas. For almost two years, she'd been kept as a virtual slave, abused physically and sexually. She didn't speak English and was afraid of the police. Her captors had warned her of terrible consequences should she try to alert anyone.

"I'm feeling guilty not being there to help her through every step of the process," said Nina.

"You have good reasons for staying in the background, but at least you didn't leave her high and dry. You made the call to Health and Human Services, got her a lawyer, and then put a support system in place for her."

"If at all possible, I want to keep flying under the media's radar."

"Is it the Alaska and Donnelly story you don't want to talk to them about, or are you worried that any notoriety might interfere with your plans to be this avenging angel?"

"I prefer the term 'advocate,'" said Nina. "I want to be a resource for women in need. And that means keeping my private life private.

"Marisol was being held two miles from here, Greg. This is supposed to be an affluent community where things like that don't happen. In a multimillion-dollar home a few blocks from the beach, a board-certified doctor held a woman prisoner, and no one even noticed."

"I know. It's shocking."

Nina shook her head. "What's shocking is that situations like hers are more common than anyone thinks. Human trafficking is a thirty-two-billion-dollar-a-year industry."

"You've made me aware of that. You've also made me aware that violent gangs and criminal families are running these slave rings. And that's why I think it makes a lot more sense being a human-rights lawyer with the power of the government behind you. You know what's a lot scarier than being an advocate? A lawyer."

"It would be years before I could act, and there are hundreds of thousands of women like Marisol who need help now. Besides, a lawyer is supposed to be an officer of the court."

"You make that sound like it's something bad."

"No, but it is something that's limiting."

"Then get involved with one of those groups you keep talking about."

Nina had researched The Hope Project, Polaris, and The Coalition Against Trafficking in Women. She'd also considered getting a position with the National Human Trafficking Resource Center. All of them did good work. But she wanted to do more than apply Band-Aids to gaping wounds.

Greg's tone softened. "It's just that I don't want you getting hurt. In another month's time, you're going to be a mother. Right now you should be thinking about mobiles and scrapbooks and picking out cute little baby outfits."

"I do think about those things," Nina said. "You know how I've been trying to make an Elese scrapbook for the baby?"

"I know. You've told me I'm the world's worst chronicler."

"The world's worst chronicler of anything non-rock-related."

Unfortunately Greg wasn't much of a photographer, and there was a paucity of pictures and Elese's artwork. It didn't help that Elese had come from a small family.

"Luckily you make up for my shortcomings."

In addition to making an Elese scrapbook, Nina had also decided to re-create Elese's journal. She was pretty sure she remembered all of Elese's words verbatim. She would probably have to hire someone to do justice to her drawings.

"Just like Elese made up for my shortcomings," said Nina. "She saved my life, and I'd like to think I was spared for a reason. I have to pay a debt and pay it forward. I have to do it for Elese."

"So, do you have a name for this proposed business of yours?"

"It's not a business. It will be more like a word-of-mouth service. But I'm thinking of identifying that service with a code name."

"That sounds like spycraft. Will I be hearing someone whispering from the bushes, 'The red fox roams the moors at midnight'?"

Nina laughed. "You're close," she said. "Did I ever tell you the story about *La Loba Fantasma*?"

CHAPTER FORTY-FIVE

Nina had worried that she might not be able to love her baby, but those fears vanished the moment she held Elese Carver (Elese's maiden name) Granville—called Ellie from the first—in her arms.

Her friends had told Nina that everything changed when you became a mother. And while it was true that Nina had to put another human being's needs ahead of her own, Ellie's birth didn't change her plans. If anything, her daughter made her that much more determined to help those in enforced servitude.

In the year since she and Greg had started sharing a home, the two of them had grown closer. It was clear from what Greg did and said that he was hoping they might become a couple. He didn't press her, though, which was good. Nina was still healing. Alaska had changed her. It was possible she could be a loving wife, but not yet. Nina was progressing at what she thought of as baby steps. Maybe she and Ellie would learn to walk together.

With her daughter asleep, Nina was sitting at the kitchen table going over the checklist for what she called Operation Esperanza, which was the Spanish word for *hope*.

Greg came up behind her and rubbed her neck. "How's it going, Bronson?" he asked. His hands lingered, moving back and forth along her shoulders.

Charles Bronson had starred as the character Paul Kersey in five *Death Wish* films. After a brutal attack in which his wife was killed and his daughter was raped and left in a catatonic state, Kersey took the law into his own hands and went around wreaking justice.

"Bronson went around shooting people," Nina said. "I go around making a point of *not* shooting people."

"The people you're dealing with don't have your compunction. You better remember that."

"I do."

"When are you leaving for the badlands?"

Operation Esperanza would take place about thirty-five miles southeast of El Paso, Texas. "I'll drive there on Sunday, and if all goes as planned, we'll finish up just before dawn on Monday."

"Are you sure you don't want me going with you?"

She shook her head. Greg was scheduled to fly to Denver in the morning and be gone for the next week. "If anything goes wrong, it will be better that you're working at a job. That way you could claim you didn't have any idea what I was doing."

"You think you're emancipating these women," he said. "What do you think *Los Fuegos* will think?"

"I'm more concerned about the women."

"You shouldn't be. Do you know how *Los Fuegos* got their name? They're called the Fires, or the Fiery Ones, because that's what they like setting. Their weapons of choice are big flare guns. If you don't think that sounds like a terrifying weapon, then you've never seen the result of their handiwork. Their flare guns are powerful enough to burn a hole right through a body. That's something they've proven over and over. And the equation gets a lot more horrific when they add accelerant, which they seem to enjoy doing."

"That's why I make sure that everyone involved takes precautions to maintain our anonymity. I won't be intimidated."

"Then you're the only one who won't be. Los Fuegos intimidated the Mexican government. When the authorities tried to clamp down on them, the gang made a show of arms in Laredo, Juarez, and Tijuana. From all over those cities, flares were shot into the air. There was a haze of colored smoke hanging over all those cities. They showed their presence in a pervasive and persuasive way."

"You seem to know a lot about them."

"I wish I didn't know as much as I do; then maybe I wouldn't worry as much as I am."

"I'm taking every precaution."

"I hope that's enough. These are the same people you crossed when you hijacked their sex shuttles. You can't count on their continuing to turn a blind eye to anyone or anything interfering with their business. They'll consider this an act of war. And you know how they treat their enemies."

"I know. I'm no Bronson. The plan is to get in and get out."

"Remember: Ellie and I need you."

She took his hands into hers, brought them next to her cheek, and rubbed them. Greg took that as an invitation to lean down for a kiss. Nina tilted her head, offering a cheek instead of her lips, and Greg settled for a kiss there.

* * *

In the morning Nina drove Greg to the airport. He wasn't traveling light. In addition to his suitcase and briefcase, he had his backpack.

"Part of the reason I took this job is that Colorado is a great place for rock hounds," he said. "There are a few spots I can't wait to check out, but I'm feeling guilty about taking playtime while you're doing what you're doing."

"Don't," said Nina. "I hope you find the mother lode, but if you don't, see if you can bring home an *ohbez* or two for Ellie."

Greg laughed and said, "Will do."

Every day Ellie was making more and more sounds. One of her favorite words was "ohbez." It was an exclamation she used when looking at Greg's sparkling rocks under ultraviolet lights. Nina thought she knew where the "oh" in ohbez came from. She invariably exclaimed, "Oh!" every time she looked at the minerals under the lights. It was a delight she shared with Ellie, who always made happy sounds along with her declaration of "ohbez." Nina and Greg had incorporated the word into their own vocabulary. Now, whenever anything was special or caught their eye, they said, "Ohbez."

Nina waited while Greg finished unloading his luggage from the car. Then he came around to the driver's-side window.

"Ohbez," Nina said.

It was one of those baby steps toward saying, "I love you."

"Ohbez," he agreed.

And then he kissed her. This time Nina didn't avert her lips.

* * *

It was easier for Nina to do her work while Greg was gone. She tried to think of every contingency and imagine all the worst-case scenarios.

This was the third operation she'd headed up. "Old MacDonald" had been her first challenge. Marisol's attorney had introduced Nina to several women she worked with. It didn't surprise Nina to learn that most victims of human trafficking were women, and half of them had children. The attorney's friends opened their homes to the dispossessed. From them Nina had heard rumors of Old MacDonald—his real last name was Sanchez. In his Central Valley farm in South San Joaquin, he took in women and their children and never paid them for their work. His claim was that he'd "bought" them and that they needed to pay off the debt he'd incurred in getting them. Before seeing to the freedom of the women and children, Nina first had to make arrangements for their lodging and employment. It wasn't enough to open a door and say, "You're free," especially when you didn't speak English and didn't have a green card. She'd rented a bus and, when Sanchez was away from his farm, had gathered all his economic captives.

The "Sex Shuttle" had been next. Enslaved young women were being transported throughout the west for the purposes of prostitution. With help from the inside, Nina had hijacked two of the shuttles and freed a dozen women.

Now she was working out final details for Esperanza. The women were being held at an old chicken ranch. Instead of caged chickens, there were caged women. Because the ranch was in an unincorporated area called Pequeno Rio, there were few governmental services. That was how Los Fuegos liked it. What few authorities there were had been bought off.

That was one of the reasons Nina had decided not to contact the FBI, Department of Justice, NHTRC, or Homeland Security. All of those governmental agencies dealt with human trafficking, but they were typically cumbersome and slow. There was no way they would be able to move on the ranch without Los Fuegos knowing first. That wouldn't help the women being held there.

* * *

Nina had first learned of what was occurring at the ranch after getting a message from a priest, a man who identified himself as Padre Diego. When he'd called *La Loba*'s private number, he was clearly afraid of leaving a message, not knowing with whom or what he was communicating. It must have surprised him hearing a Norteamericana say, "If you have not dialed this number in error, then leave a message. And remember: you are not alone."

The padre left his name and number. When Nina called back, she learned how the priest had obtained her very private number.

"The Sunday before last, I received the first message in the offertory plate," he said. "I knew it was written by one of the women from the ranch. The only outing the women are allowed is Sunday Mass, but even then they are closely watched. Those that come to church are each given five dollars by their guards for the offering. The note was slipped under the money. It was a prayer for the Lady of San Guadalupe to deliver her. And it asked me to contact *La Loba Fantasma* to help in this matter.

"I did not know this *La Loba Fantasma*. I wondered who or what was this ghost wolf. I thought it might be a local superstition. My people love their stories of the *chupacabra, ahuizhotl, hoga,* and *campacti.* I also wondered if *La Loba Fantasma* could be another name for *Santa Muerta.* And so I did not act at first, for I had no idea how to go about contacting a ghost.

"The following Sunday I received a second note in the offertory. And this one I did not ignore. It referenced *La Loba* and *lanzadera sexo.* I did not know what that meant, but at least it gave me something to go on. And so I made discreet inquiries. I asked a woman who I know is involved in the *Tren de la libertad*—the Underground Railroad for the dispossessed—whether she had ever heard of *La Loba Fantasma.* It took a few days, but an anonymous caller left me your phone number."

Nina's Spanish was good enough that she understood the priest's reference to the sex shuttle and *Tren de la libertad.* The priest then told her about the women at the chicken ranch.

* * *

Because Nina had wanted no one to see her face, she'd worn a special mask while overseeing the hijacking of the two sex shuttles. The wolf mask had not only hidden her features, but had bestowed upon Nina a feral quality. Her mask wasn't scary as much as it was realistic. It didn't look like a werewolf and didn't come with red eyes and huge teeth. The mask frightened because it presented the head of an unfathomable wolf.

Nina had added her own touch to the mask. She'd been inspired by the minerals that showed their secret colors under black lights. And so she'd purchased what she thought of as war paint and applied the colors to the mask. She was convinced it was those colors, more than it was any weapon, that made the drivers comply with her every command. The clip-on black light came on every third second and revealed the iridescent face of the wolf. Her orders were spoken with an eerie sibilance, or so it was remembered by those who were rescued.

Word of *La Loba Fantasma* had circulated far wider than Nina could ever have guessed, all the way to one of the girls being held at the ranch.

* * *

The remoteness of the ranch could be turned to her advantage, Nina thought, sitting at her desk. By using a cell-phone jammer, the jailers wouldn't be able to call for help. She'd already used one of those jammers while hijacking the shuttles. With each action her arsenal was getting larger.

Ellie began fussing in her playpen. When Nina's mother had visited, she'd claimed that Ellie was the spitting image of Nina when she'd been a baby. She did have her big, blue eyes. And already she was showing dark hair. Usually she had an infectious smile; supposedly Nina had been good-humored as well.

"There, there," said Nina, putting aside her work. "Mama is here. Come to Mama."

Nina was doing her best to ensure that *Mama* would be Ellie's first word.

"Ohbez," said her daughter.

Or at least her first word after *ohbez*.

"That's very close to *Mama*," said Nina. "Did you want to go see the pretty lights?"

She leaned over, lifted Ellie out of her playpen, and then the two of them went down the hall to Alcatraz. The room was in complete darkness until Nina turned on the UV lights, and then it felt like a pathway to a hidden world was revealed, with all the glowing minerals showing the way.

"Oooh," said Nina.

"Ohbez," said Ellie.

"Say, 'Mama,'" said Nina, kissing her daughter. "Mama."

"Ohbez," said Ellie.

* * *

Nina put Ellie to sleep with a bottle. Having a daughter who was now weaned made it easier for *La Loba* to operate.

Nina returned to Alcatraz to turn off the lights and noticed one of the drawers was partially open. Since the drawers were positioned on sliders that automatically closed, it meant there had to be an obstruction.

She pulled the drawer all the way open. It closed on its own, but only about three-quarters of the way. Nina searched for the blockage, but there was no obvious obstruction. Like the other drawers, this one was full of rocks. She bent down to get level with the stones and then noticed that one of the rocks, a green mineral, was sticking out. Greg liked to give background history on his stones, and she seemed to remember him saying that this type of mineral had been mined in Israel long before the birth of Christ. There was some story behind its name as well. It looked like green mallow leaves. And then Nina remembered its name: malachite.

When she checked the identification card, she felt like taking a bow. According to Greg's annotations, he'd unearthed the sample in the Bisbee, Arizona area seven years ago on March 20. The GPS coordinates for his find had also been entered on the card.

After Nina repositioned the malachite, the drawer easily closed, but something was nagging at her. She opened several other drawers and did her mental comparisons. For some reason the drawer with the malachite wasn't as deep as the other drawers, even though she wasn't sure how that was possible. In her side-by-side comparisons, she could see the drawers were the same size.

Her interest piqued, Nina held her finger and thumb apart to measure the vertical depth of the drawers. By her guesstimate, there was a little more than an inch difference in depth between the malachite drawer and the other museum drawers.

She took a hard look at the malachite drawer and then began tapping around. There was only one way to be sure of her suspicion, Nina decided. She grabbed a piece of paper and listed the order of the samples. Greg liked everything just so; it wouldn't do to have any of his rocks out of place. Satisfied that she could return everything as it was, Nina removed all the items from the drawer.

When it was emptied, there was nothing to indicate that the drawer had a false bottom other than its difference in depth. There was clearly less space for the rocks to sit in. She pulled the drawer along its runners and then lifted it out. Even without the rocks in it, the drawer was bulky and heavy. Nina lugged it over to one of the shorter cabinets and propped the drawer atop it. She studied the underside of the drawer and almost overlooked the tiny hole toward the back. It took her a minute to rummage around and find something thin enough to fit into the hole. She pulled apart a pen, inserted the nib and ink cartridge into the space, and pushed upward. A panel lifted, and Nina reached into the drawer to pull it free.

The first thing she noticed was the gold nuggets. None of them was large; most were BB size, but with the current price of gold, there were enough of them that she could understand Greg's need to build a secret compartment. In addition to the nuggets, there were also several small glass vials filled with gold dust. Wine-red semiprecious gemstones, what Nina was confident were garnets, filled one of the compartments. Some of them were loose, and others were embedded within stones. There were also a few funny-looking layered rocks, a kind she'd never seen before. The gold, garnets, and strange rocks didn't come with identification cards, but there were two stones in the drawer that did. One was identified as G. M. Epidote, and the other labeled nephrite jade. Greg hadn't been his usual thorough self with his identifications; there were no GPS coordinates and no dating of the finds.

Maybe the secret compartment was Greg's version of a junk drawer. But then most junk drawers held spare change, not four or five ounces of gold.

Nina put everything back as it was. The next time she talked to Greg, she might, or might not, reveal what she'd found. They weren't married, after all; when they'd moved in together, they'd still practically been strangers. Besides, she told herself, when it came to his rocks, Greg still acted like a kid; it was just like him to have a secret compartment.

She closed the drawer and turned off the lights, seeing for a moment an afterimage of the glittering rocks against the deep, fathomless darkness. She shivered.

Then she left the room and returned to her office. To her calling. There was still a lot of preparation to do for Operation Esperanza.

CHAPTER FORTY-SIX

Nina accepted the incoming call on her car's Bluetooth system.

"I'm calling to wish you luck," said Greg.

"As long as you don't say, 'Break a leg.'"

"Don't break a leg," he said.

"That sounds good."

"Where are you?"

"I'm not quite at El Centro."

"You still have a long drive."

"About ten hours," she said. "And then the wait."

"For the dawn's early light?"

"The plan is to go in predawn. Supposedly the ranch shuts down at three in the morning. By three thirty everyone should have cleared out. And barring insomnia, by four thirty everyone should be asleep."

"I'm sure it will all go like a charm. How's Ellie?"

"She was all smiles this morning when I dropped her off at Grandma Gail's."

Gail wasn't really her baby's grandma, but Nina had given Ellie's sometime caregiver that name.

"Maybe I was hearing things," Nina added, "but this morning I'm pretty sure she said, 'Mama.'"

"That must have been a thrill."

"It was."

"Of course, you've been lobbying her for months."

"I won't deny it."

"It will be nice to hear something other than 'ohbez.'"

"Are you working today?"

"I'm glad to say I'm not. Today's agenda is for me to be a rock star."

"Looking for anything in particular?"

"I'll settle for a modern-day Cripple Creek gold strike. Short of that, a few aquamarines would be nice."

"Good luck to you as well."

"Let's plan a joint celebration when we both get back."

A brief wave of unexpected sadness washed through her, but she needed focus now, not emotion. "I like the sound of that."

* * *

Nina crossed the Arizona border into Yuma and then continued along Interstate 8 over to Interstate 10. The desert that was Arizona showed itself. Millions lived in Phoenix, but to Nina's thinking, those people were more mirage than not. The real Arizona was the desert.

"Here we go again," she said. "Can you hear me, Sister? It's hot outside, but I'm cold. You've got my back, don't you?"

She was going to war again. She needed her sister.

"Did my heart really turn to ice?" she asked. "I remember it being that cold. Maybe that's what it took to survive. Maybe that's what it will take now."

She'd downloaded a number of songs for her drive and called up one now, Sia's "Elastic Heart." It was how she chose to think of hers.

As the desert went by, Nina cycled through her playlist, including Hozier's "Take Me to Church," Coldplay's "A Sky Full of Stars," and Kyng's "Electric Halo." She drove through Tucson listening to the Foo Fighters' "Something from Nothing" and the Pretty Reckless tune "Heaven Knows," and two and a half hours later, entered New Mexico on the storm of Katy Perry's "Dark Horse."

"Sun Tzu said the supreme art of war is to subdue the enemy without fighting. That's what I want to be able to do. But it won't happen today, will it? It's difficult to wage a war when you're uncertain how many fronts you must fight it on. But I think I know, Sister."

After a while she added, "Long drives give you a long time to think. But when the answers are ugly, what good is it to think?"

* * *

Padre Diego had supplied them with most of their intelligence. He'd never been to the brothel, but he'd heard the confessions of those who had.

The two drivers met up with Nina at the prearranged spot outside of El Paso. Even though they were only being called upon to drive, they were scared. The two women looked like what they were: suburban housewives. That wasn't a judgment; it was the world they knew. But now they were outside that comfort zone. They were volunteers in a struggle in which they believed, but now they were wondering if they were in over their heads.

With her measured tones and her apparent calm, Nina reassured them. In a situation that felt like madness, she was the voice of reason. This was a battle, and they needed to understand the objective. Nina discussed what they might expect and went over what to do if things went wrong. When she was convinced they were prepared and ready, she hugged the women and whispered, "Esperanza."

They had the GPS coordinates and directions of where they'd be going. The two drivers would park at a dirt turnout about a quarter of a mile from the ranch and await Nina's summons. Nina would park closer to the ranch.

Now it was up to Nina to go and free the captives. No one gave her a pep talk. No one told her it would be all right.

* * *

Nina had been assured by Father Diego that there were plenty of secluded spots near the ranch where she might park. She drove slowly along the dirt road, her headlights swallowed up by the darkness around her. Then she saw what she was looking for. There was an opening in the midst of the mesquite trees and chaparral on the side of the road that looked perfect. She parked the car and then examined the surrounding area. The car was well hidden amid the trees and brush. Although the ranch wasn't in sight, Nina knew it couldn't be more than an eighth of a mile away. It was twenty past three, which left her plenty of time for her preparations. There was only a sliver moon for her to work by, but that was as expected. She'd planned it that way, wanting the cloak of darkness.

At four in the morning, Nina was in position. There were two cars in the dirt parking lot. She felt their hoods, determined the engines were long cold, and then disabled the vehicles. It was likely the cars belonged to the guards. Even if she failed to incapacitate those guards, they still wouldn't be able to come after the two waiting drivers.

She shrank into the shadows of the parking lot. There were still lights on inside and outside the house, but Nina couldn't see or hear any activity. She let the minutes pass while she studied the house and surrounding area. There was no activity she could detect, no sign of a patrol, and no sounds of music. From inside the ranch, there were no flickering lights to indicate someone was watching a television.

With her wolf mask on, Nina finally emerged from the shadows and began prowling the compound. The ranch's electrical power was supplied by a generator. She disabled it, and in the silence that followed listened for any cries. No one called out; no alarms went off.

Nina turned on the cell-phone signal jammer and then put night-vision glasses over her mask. In one hand she carried a combination flashlight/stun gun. It looked and operated like an ordinary flashlight until she pressed a red button, which unleashed ten million volts. In her waist pack was a taser. There was also a bludgeon, restraints, and tools for breaking and entering.

There was only one door into the ranch house. It was there that Nina would be the most vulnerable. She'd practiced her breaking-and-entering skills inside the Carlsbad home with locksport kits. By now she was confident she could manually open any standard lockset in about a minute's time, but that was without having to worry about someone on the other side of the door blasting her with a shotgun. In this instance she'd decided speed was more important than stealth and had brought an electric pick gun to get her through the door quickly.

Soundlessly she crossed the expanse to the door. Necessity had been her teacher, and she hadn't forgotten her lessons. Before positioning the electric pick gun, Nina tried turning the door handle. Much to her surprise it turned, and she pushed the door silently open. Those in charge of the ranch apparently didn't fear a home invasion.

Using her night-vision glasses, Nina made her way forward. All she had to do was follow the snoring. One of the guards was asleep in an easy chair. Sitting on the ground next to him was a mostly empty bottle of tequila. The still-pungent odor of *mota* filled the air.

She slid by the man and went farther into the house. In the first bedroom, she found another snoring man; this one was sprawled on a bed.

Nina passed by him as well, scouting the rest of the house. She was stopped by a locked door; behind it she knew were the "coops" that held the female prisoners.

Backtracking, Nina came to the room with the sleeping man and silently closed the door to keep him from hearing. Then she went to the living room and the guard passed out in the easy chair. He didn't awaken while she tied him to the chair with a rope, nor did he come to while she put flex-cuffs around his wrists.

As she tightened the gag in his mouth, he started, but his scream was muted. The fright in his eyes bespoke what his voice couldn't. He was looking at a glowing wolf face.

She made her way to the bedroom where she silently opened the door. The second guard wasn't quite as compliant as the first, but ten million volts managed to assure his cooperation, if not his complete silence.

"Make another sound," she whispered, "and I'll light you up like a Christmas tree."

It was unclear if he understood exactly what she was saying; what wasn't unclear was the stun gun pressed into him. Nina gagged him, tied him up, and then relieved him of his gun and keys.

Nina stood outside the locked door, but didn't hear any movement from inside. When she threw open the door, she was glad to see there wasn't a third guard. The women inside awakened to her shining flashlight and her saying, "*Santuario.*"

Sanctuary.

They could not see that she was smiling. They only saw her wolf's face that glowed one second and then disappeared, only to glow again.

The women would surely have panicked and screamed if not for one among them, the woman who'd left the note in Padre Diego's offertory plate.

"*Es La Loba!*" she said.

Nina gestured for them to follow her, and the women did. Once they were outside, she made her call to both of the drivers. A short time later, *La Loba* herded four women into one car and three into the other.

"*Adios, hermanas,*" La Loba told them. "*Tener miedo no mas.*"

The ghost wolf told them to be afraid no more. And then she added, "*Usted no esta solo.*"

You are not alone.

She waved to them as the cars drove off.

* * *

The woman who had dared to write *La Loba*, a girl of fifteen named Sofia, said to the others, "Did you notice she was missing one finger? I heard she lost it while besting the devil himself."

All eyes turned to get a last look at *La Loba*, but she was already lost to sight.

* * *

Nina paralleled the road, using the night-vision glasses to make her way through the chaparral. There were prickly pear cactus and thorny mesquite to be avoided, but she was worried about other dangers. She kept low and moved from side to side. She heard the moans before she even came in sight of her car.

With the stun gun in hand, she approached cautiously. Without making a sound, keeping the brush between her and the groaning, she drew nearer. She wasn't going to be drawn into a trap—or at least another trap.

Oh, Sister, she thought.

Nina had hoped she was wrong. She'd wanted to be wrong. But hard lessons had left her with no more illusions.

Her dark clothing hid her presence. Her wolf mask was now off, but that didn't matter. It would always be there whether she was wearing it or not. She chose when and where to be heard, tossing a rock near where he was.

"Nina?" Greg said.

"Tonight my name is *La Loba*."

He wasn't listening to what she said. He was too busy pretending righteous indignation. "Did you do this? Did you set this goddamn trap? I came to *help* you."

"It's called a pig trap," she said. "I find it an appropriate name."

"What's wrong with you? I'm hurt, goddammit. I'm fucking bleeding everywhere."

"I knew you'd find the car," she said. "How is it that you came upon it so easily? It's a dark night, and I made sure it was hidden in the brush."

"You could have done a better job hiding it, all right? Now get me the fuck out of this thing."

"All week I've been pretending for your sake. It wasn't easy for me. I'm not an actor like you are. You fooled Elese into thinking you were the perfect husband. And then I bought into your act.

"In the back of my mind, I suppose I already had doubts—like why it was you had so few mementos of Elese; why you insured her supposedly because the two of you were going to have a family, and yet you've never talked about having a family.

"But in my mind everything began to crystallize with that drawer. But you knew about my discovery, didn't you?"

"No, I don't know a goddamn thing about any discovery, and I don't fucking know what you're babbling about. I do know I need help." He shook a branch in frustration and then groaned in pain. "Help!"

"The night of my discovery, I didn't sleep well. There was something unsettling about your secret compartment. I wondered what other secrets you had. And the more I wondered, the more it felt like I had vertigo. I remembered a line from a Gilbert and Sullivan play: 'Things are not as they seem, skim milk masquerades as cream.' Things were definitely not as they seemed. A man who has a secret compartment would be distrustful of everyone and everything. And I listened again to that voice in the wilderness that told me when I was being watched, and I was suddenly sure you were monitoring me."

"Listen to yourself, Nina. You hear how deluded you sound? I know how you suffered. But now I'm the one who's suffering. You have to help me! I think your trap might have hit my femoral artery. I'm bleeding like a son of a bitch!"

"Inside the house I took care of Ellie and made plans for Esperanza. I gave no indication that I suspected I was being watched. But when I wasn't in the house, I learned about home surveillance systems and how cameras could be hidden in the most innocuous spots and triggered by motion. And that from Colorado you could be watching everything going on in your house from your phone, or tablet, or computer."

Greg said, "While you were weaving your fantasies, I was working in Colorado! And I was worrying about you and your rescue missions. I could see how it was making you paranoid and crazy. I just didn't realize how far gone you were."

"I asked you how you found my car. It was a rhetorical question. This week I discovered your GPS tracker. Of course, I was looking for it; I never would have seen it otherwise. The only thing I wasn't certain of was how long it had been in place. And whether you would use it to track me down and kill me tonight. I wanted to be wrong. I didn't want to find you here."

"You're wrong! I came here to help you. I love you, Nina."

"Did you know Baer told me romantic love was the worst mistake a woman could make? He said there was no easier way to deceive someone than by pretending to be in love. I didn't know at the time he was talking about you and Elese. But now I do."

He tried shaking a branch again, but his maneuvers only hurt him.

"And I'm afraid Elese might have come to realize that as well. In her journal she wrote that you seemed to be more of a dream than anything else. But you know that, don't you? You pretended enthusiasm when I began reconstructing Elese's book, but I detected something else. I thought it was sadness on your part. But I think it was fear of being discovered. Do you remember what she wrote about you? *Maybe he always was a dream. That's how it feels.*

"Is that why you burned down the cabin? Were you afraid her words might get you caught? It was your idea to honeymoon in Alaska. Elese wrote that the two of you had never been there. That's what you told her, but it was a lie."

"You're taking everything out of context. Just give me a chance to clear everything up. I promise I will. But right now I'm hurt. I'm hurt badly," Greg pleaded.

"I surveyed the trail around here ahead of time. There was only one likely spot where you'd be waiting to ambush me. When you make a spear trap, you need the right tree and the proper angle, and you need to direct your game where you want it to go. When you pull back the tree, the stakes have to be positioned so that they come swinging at the target. I put all the pieces of the trap together in a park in Carlsbad and brought them with me. It took me less than fifteen minutes to set everything up, trip wire and all."

"We can talk about your huge, fucking mistake later! Right now I need a tourniquet. Right now you need to get me to a hospital."

Nina could hear him reaching inside his coat. She was listening to his every movement.

"Throw me your flare gun and accelerant."

"What the hell are you talking about?"

She repositioned herself, using the cover of darkness to move to another spot. "You can cut the poor Greg Martin act. You've milked your star-crossed lover role past its expiration date. Your first wife was a psychotic, and your second, sainted wife was abducted by a madman. And what would have been your third wife went afoul of Los Fuegos and suffered the terrible consequences of being doused in gas and shot with a flare gun."

"I loved Elese. I love you."

"When did you decide I had to die? Was it when I was surprised by how few of Elese's personal effects you had? Was it when I began re-creating her journal? Or was it when I made my discovery of your secret compartment?"

"I need help. Please."

"I wonder if Elese realized your deception at the end. I wonder if that was the final nail in her coffin. You feared I'd figure out your involvement over time. You feared I might put together the loose ends. And you were right to be afraid. You told Elese you'd never been to Alaska. But you had. That was where you met Baer, wasn't it?"

"There's no time to hear your conspiracy theories! I'm fucking bleeding out!"

"Yes," she agreed, "there's blood all over your hands. I should have seen that. But what you did was so unconscionable that I had trouble bringing my mind around to even imagining it. Even now it's difficult."

The sob caught in Nina's throat. She was thinking about her sister. She took a deep breath. Later she would cry, but not now.

"Your secret stash got me to thinking. I'm sure you never imagined that your stones would tell me a story, but you taught me too well. Of course, I couldn't do my research at the house. I had to pretend all was well for your cameras.

"I identified the garnets first. Wrangell garnets. Most are found along the Stikine River near a town in Southeast Alaska called Wrangell. And your epidote, which collectors call Green Monster Epidote, was probably taken on Prince of Wales Island in Alaska. And let's not forget your nephrite jade. You likely picked that up in the interior of Alaska where you were panning for gold. That's where you met Baer."

Greg's voice was high-pitched and panicked. "I saved you! And then I took you into my home! Now you need to save me!"

"You took me in so that you could watch my movements. Aren't you supposed to keep your enemies near?"

"If not for me, you'd be dead!"

"If not for you, Elese would be alive. You made her believe she was the love of your life, and all the while you saw her as nothing more than your grubstake. The insurance money allowed you access to your true passion—your gold and gems. I should have taken into account gold fever. There are all sorts of examples of what it does when it gets its grips into a man. People like you will do anything for a chance to hunt down their gems and gold. They leave their lives behind; they travel halfway around the world. You didn't want to toil as a geologist. More than anything else, you wanted to do your treasure hunting without any encumbrances."

"In the light of day, you'll see how wrong you are. But for God's sake, help me now!"

"Baer wanted a woman. So you became his pimp—worse even than these traffickers. You plotted to give him your wife. He got what he wanted, and you got what you wanted. I suppose you gave him enough money for his supplies and to charter an aircraft. All you had to do was await your payout. You even hurried that along, didn't you, when you threatened to sue the insurance company for bad faith?"

Nina laughed, but she might as well have screamed. "Bad faith," she said. "Can you imagine? Everything worked out for you and Baer until Elese died. This time Baer was on his own for finding another woman. I'm sure you weren't happy when he took me and brought all that extra scrutiny. You knew if Baer was caught, he'd likely give you up. That's why right from the first, you pestered Sergeant Hamilton. You wanted to know exactly where the case was going. Maybe you even pointed him down the right trail a time or two. Even you didn't know exactly where Baer's cabin was, but you had a general idea. When Terrence offered the reward for my return, you saw your chance for a big score and the chance to kill Baer. But I did that bit of dirty work for you."

His breathing was growing labored. "I can see how upset you are, Nina. But you have to give me a chance to prove my innocence. I'll do that if you give me some time. But if you don't help me, I'm going to die. And you'll have to live with being my murderer."

"If you want my help, throw me the flare gun and the accelerant. I won't come any closer as long as you're holding them."

He didn't immediately answer, but took a moment to consider his words. "They aren't what you think. They can be explained. I needed them as protection in case the gang came after me."

But even he couldn't make it sound as if he believed his explanation.

She caught a glint of metal and heard the skittering of the metal flare gun as it unevenly passed across the hardscrabble earth, followed by a squeeze bottle.

"Are you there?" he asked. "Are you fucking there?"

She could hear him panting. She could feel his rage.

"Nina?" he asked.

"I'm here."

He turned his head in the direction of her voice. "I made some mistakes. But lately I've tried to make up for them. Haven't I taken care of you and Ellie?"

Nina began laughing. "Oh, Greg, you're like that boy who shot both of his parents and then threw himself on the mercy of the court because he was an orphan."

"And what about you? Don't act like you don't have your own secrets. I read Elese's book, and I read between the lines of your hospital confession. You murdered Baer in cold blood, didn't you?"

"In blood so cold that it froze. Yes, I did."

"We can figure out all of our sins later. We can come to some understanding. I can make it right for you. I promise I will. But now I need your help. You don't want another death on your conscience."

"Did you ever think about Elese when she was imprisoned and tortured? I pray she died without knowing you were the Judas goat who led her to slaughter. My sister and I thought Baer was the monster. We had no idea there was another monster, one even worse than him."

"I realize what a terrible mistake I made. Give me a chance to show you and make up for it. I can do that! And you owe me. You would have died if I hadn't rescued you."

"I'm not even sure you didn't help Baer in my abduction."

"I had nothing to do with it. He mailed me your ring from Fairbanks. Can you imagine that? He sent it in an envelope with a note asking me to sell the diamond and then give him half the money. I knew he was out of control, but there was nothing I could do."

"You manipulated the investigation. You cut off a piece of that diamond to throw off the investigators and give you more time to try to collect the reward. You had to be the first on the scene to make sure Baer never revealed your conspiracy."

"That's water under the bridge. Get me out of this fucking trap!"

"You don't need my help to do that."

He attempted a tone of hurt and helplessness. "I have two wooden spikes impaled in my leg. If I try to pull free, I'll probably bleed out. You need to cut the branch off. And then with a tourniquet, we can stop the bleeding."

"Do you remember the story I told you about the wolf who chewed off part of her foot to escape Baer's trap?"

"This is no time to talk about Peter and the fucking wolf."

"Different story," she said. "But seeing as you've been crying wolf for a long time, I can see how you'd like that one better."

His tone changed, becoming more wheedling and groveling. "Help me, Nina. You believe in doing the right thing. That's why you helped these women."

"I did that for Elese. And for me."

"You're a better person than I am. Show that now. You don't want what happens today to haunt you."

"You know what I'm going to remember about today? My little girl said, 'Mama.' That's what I'll remember. And I'll remember seven women who were given a chance to get their lives back. Those will be great memories. They'll be the light that will block everything else out."

"I am sick. I get that now. I'm asking you for help. No, I am begging you."

"When the monster raped us, you raped us. And what the monster taught us, you taught us. I won't be foolish enough to forget that now."

"Please . . ."

"You betrayed your wife. You sent her to a living hell. And like it or not, you killed her. Despite all that, you would have me find a way to forgive what you did. But I can't do that. Do you remember Elese's Eighth Rule? She told me that when I got the chance, I had to kill the monster. She said it wasn't a matter of right or wrong, but something that had to be done. And so I will not betray the memory of my sister."

* * *

As Nina picked up the flare gun and bottle of lighter fluid, he was able to see her for the first time that night, and his body recoiled, suddenly afraid.

"Wolf!" he screamed. "Wolf!"

It must have been a trick of the shadows or the sliver moon or the way she approached. Maybe his blood loss caught up to him. His eyes were wide and white. She wasn't wearing the wolf mask, but he most definitely saw a wolf.

* * *

As she drove away, Nina looked in her rearview mirror. The trash fire was almost out.

Soon the sun would rise. A new day was about to dawn. Ellie was waiting for her. And so were those who would benefit from her sister's legacy. She slid her eyes from her rearview mirror and looked to the road ahead.

ACKNOWLEDGMENTS

I'm lucky that Caitlin Alexander is not the kind of editor who settles for "good enough." She constantly pushed me to write the best book possible. Her prodding sent me back to the drawing board—several times. I know how rare it is to get that kind of TLC. I am not sure if that's an abbreviation for "tender loving care" or "tough loving care." Either way I'm still thankful.

One of the most difficult things about writing this book was trying to come to terms with Alaska. The state is huge beyond belief. Maps don't do it justice. Moving characters from one place to another isn't something done easily (imagine a state that is about the size of two-thirds of the continental United States). I hope I can be forgiven with a little literary license in trying to come to terms with the state (for example, indicating there was a White Alice station in a location where I know there wasn't one).

Although I've visited Alaska, I could spend a hundred lifetimes there and still not have scratched its surface. Luckily I called upon long-time Alaskans Jim Misko and Greg Durocher to help me. In addition to being a great resource, Jim is a fine author, and I asked him to look at my manuscript with an "Alaskan eye" to try to make sure a Native wouldn't toss the book aside in disgust. As for Greg, he works with the US Geological Survey in Science Information Services in Anchorage. Greg was kind enough to answer my geology questions. When next I get to Alaska, I would love going out with Greg and the Chugach Gem and Mineral Society on one of their outings. I hope it goes without saying that any mistakes made are of my own making and shouldn't reflect on Jim or Greg or other Alaskans I pestered with questions.

As always, I appreciate the patience and understanding of my editor, Alison Dasho. A tip of my hat, also, to the rest of the hardworking crew at Thomas & Mercer. I'm grateful to be working for a publisher that does such a good job in getting my books out there.

I would also like to thank my readers. One of the great things about being a writer is hearing from you. You can reach me through my website at www.alanrussell.net or "Like" me on my Facebook page, Alan Russell Mystery Author.

ABOUT THE AUTHOR

Photo © 2012 Stathis Orphanos

Hailed as "one of the best writers in the mystery field today" by *Publishers Weekly*, Alan Russell is the bestselling author of the acclaimed novels *Burning Man, Guardians of the Night, St. Nick, Shame,* and *Multiple Wounds.* "He has a gift for dialogue," raves the *New York Times*, while the *Boston Globe* calls his work "complex and genuinely suspenseful." His books have earned him a Lefty Award for best comedic mystery, a *USA Today* Critics' Choice Award, and the Odin Award for Lifetime Achievement from the San Diego Writers/Editors Guild. A California native, Russell still resides in the Golden State with his wife and three children.

If you liked *A Cold War*, here's an excerpt from another book by Alan Russell—*Multiple Wounds*.

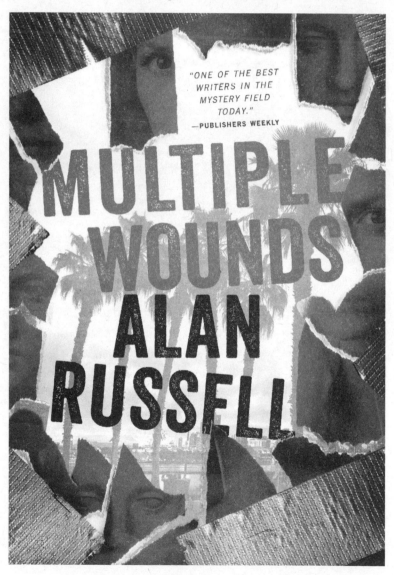

"ONE OF THE BEST WRITERS IN THE MYSTERY FIELD TODAY."
—PUBLISHERS WEEKLY

MULTIPLE WOUNDS

ALAN RUSSELL

CHAPTER
ONE

She thought of Chaos, and the original confusion, and felt as if she were a part of that tumult. Earth and sea and heaven and hell were mixed up, and everything inside of her was a whirligig. The Greek chorus was screaming in her head, all of them wanting out.

Cube state. She tried to hold on to the phrase. That's how the doctor described her states of flux. Everything was multiplied, squared, cubed, a Picasso painting.

The yellow tape stopped her: POLICE LINE DO NOT CROSS. The words repeated themselves throughout the tape, runes for rumination.

"Gordian knot," she said, talking over all the vying voices.

What was the oracle telling her? She decided the words on the tape had to be an anagram, but there were so many possibilities.

She looked at the words and deciphered a welcome among the letters. PROCEED IN. She didn't bother with the remaining letters, just slipped under the yellow banner, dragging her bag behind her. As she walked into the gallery, she thought, What if the words are a warning? They could be saying, *Sirens Plot*, or *Cronos Inside*.

Sometimes a cigar is just a smoke, Freud had said. Her analyst had once told her that.

She was at the art gallery because one of the voices had clamored louder than the others, had insisted that she change the statues' clothing, to show her respects that way. She avoided the display area, walking down the corridor toward the garden. Not for the first time she wished for blinders to help her when she was like this. She remembered watching a program on insects and being given a bee's-eye view of the world. Bees perceive scores of images and look out into a different universe than humans. In cube state, so did she.

There was a buzzing in her head and a sting in her heart as she entered the garden.

CHEEVER WAS THINKING about death. That's what homicide detectives do, but in this instance there was a merging of mortalities. The all-nighter had taken its toll on him. The echoes were getting assertive, were shouting back from the caves. You're too old for this. And you're bucking the odds. Cops who retire at fifty have the same mortality stats as butchers and bakers and candlestick makers, but those that stay on the job until they are fifty-five or older usually die within two years of leaving the force. Cheever contemplated his fifty-four years. Then he thought about Bonnie Gill. She hadn't done very well by the actuary tables herself, dying at the age of thirty-seven. That was how they had been introduced.

Bonnie Gill had been murdered in her own art gallery, Sandy Ego Expressions, a one-story structure on Tenth and J near the old Carnation Building. She had died in a garden out back, an area full of wind chimes, flowers (especially carnations), crafted pottery, and ornamental fountains that expanded on the usual motif of little boys peeing. Her throat had been slashed adjacent to an exhibition that a placard announced as *Garden of Stone*. Daylight hadn't improved Cheever's opinion of the display, but it had been worse the night before when everyone had kept being confronted by the statues. Most of the damn things were clothed. That had made it worse, especially in the semidarkness. He had kept mistaking them for human beings.

The statues weren't the kind found in public squares or the park, the men on horses and the women saints. These were statues with faces of pain and fear and anger. He had almost pulled his gun on one of them. The piece looked real enough, and threatening enough—a man holding a knife with both hands over his head. That's how Bonnie Gill had died, or close enough. She had been killed with two knife wounds—had been stabbed in the back, then had had her throat slashed.

He sought out the offensive statue with his eyes, wasn't sure whether it was the morning light or the softer stone around the knife wielder's face that gave the head such a glow. Maybe both. Cheever supposed the man with the knife was some kind of priest. That didn't seem to matter to the woman being sacrificed. Her expression was one of terror.

Cheever decided he had indulged himself too long at the crime scene. He liked to take his own impressions without the jostling of the evidence tech, and the ME, and the rest of his homicide team. He wrote down a few notes, not for himself, but for the opposing lawyers in case he ever got called to the stand. Around the department Cheever's memory was legendary. The other detectives knew he didn't need to write anything down once it was in his head. He liked to go out on a call, spot somebody he had popped ten, even twenty years back, and yell out a first name greeting. Many didn't like to be remembered. They felt uneasy, marked, like Big Brother was watching them, monitoring everything they did.

He turned and was startled to find a woman standing at the entrance to the garden. This time he was the one under observation. Shaken, it took him a moment to get his breath back, but when he did, he put his wind to good use. "What the hell are you doing in here?"

His yelling helped her. It was louder than her chorus. The cacophony submerged into the background. She closed her eyes for a moment, and when she opened them her world had changed again.

She had big eyes, he noticed. They were alert and blue and aware. She was like one of those Margaret Keane paintings where the kids' eyes take up half the picture. He had started angrily toward her, but stopped now that he saw her terrified look. He was afraid she would bolt if he breathed hard. She looked like she was ready to drop her athletic bag and run.

"I'm Detective Cheever," he said. His words didn't put her at ease.

"I'll show you identification," he said. From a distance, he offered up his brass shield. She relaxed, but just a little.

"You're trespassing," he advised her, "on a police investigation scene."

She considered his words and finally spoke: "I am the sculptor."

Cheever motioned with his head. "You did these?"

The smallest of nods claimed credit. Cheever took his time examining the artist, could tell by her body language that it was still not the right time to approach her. He figured she was in her mid-twenties. She stood around five eight and was quite thin—weighed maybe one-fifteen. The woman liked jewelry. Her ears had been pierced more than Custer's body, with at least six earrings hanging from each lobe. She went for the shiny metallic look, jewelry that could have been mistaken for fishing lures or perhaps was. Bracelets ran up her arms, and baubles and bangles had found their way to most parts of her body. She wore plenty of rings, but no apparent wedding ring. The only non-ornamental piece among her trimmings was a medical alert bracelet, but she might have been wearing it as another misplaced fashion statement. She had done a yin-yang kind of thing on her mane so that it was half black and half white. Cheever was surprised. It detracted from her natural beauty.

"What are you doing here?"

Her words came a little faster now: "Checking on my pieces."

"The *Garden of Stone*," he said, the slightest hint of sarcasm in his words.

"That wasn't the name I wanted for the exhibition."

"Oh? What name did you want?"

She mumbled her answer: "*What the Gorgon Saw.*"

"What the Gorgonzola?"

"Forget it."

Words invariably uttered when there was something that should be remembered. In his mind Cheever made sense of what she had said. What he couldn't make sense of was why she was here.

"I wouldn't worry about anyone trying to make off with your rocks," he said. "They're too heavy."

"They're not as heavy as you'd think," she said. "They're faux marble."

Cheever didn't like her answer. It sounded too goddamn superior to him. He knew lack of sleep was coloring his mood, but he still didn't like her statues. He wanted to tell her that they were pieces of crap, and not even faux pieces of crap. Her stuff disturbed. To his thinking, the best art showed a way out of the cesspool, didn't offer a wallow in it.

"You know about the murder?" he asked.

She could hear the anger in his voice even if she didn't know the source. "Yes," she said.

He closed the distance between them. "How well did you know Bonnie Gill?"

"She's represented me for several years."

Cheever let the silence build. People usually started talking about the dead, saying all kinds of things, but not this one. "That's all you have to say about her?"

She didn't immediately respond. Her expression was sad, despondent, then, to his surprise, he thought he saw a momentary smile, a glee. Her posture shifted, her face went slack, and she straightened. Her chin tilted up and her manner became imperious.

So, she thought. Cop wants a confrontation. I can play that game. "I'm not good at eulogies," she said.

They had a little stare-down. She was acting tough now. Yeah, she was a rock, he thought. Faux rock. What was that children's game? Scissors, paper, rock. It was time for paper to wrap rock. "What's your name?"

The smallest hesitation: "Holly Troy."

"Got some ID?"

"Not on me."

He flipped open his pad. "What's your address and phone number?"

Monotone, she gave him both.

"Any reason for Ms. Gill to be dead?" he asked.

"I wouldn't know," she said.

The words were offered without any feeling. Holly Troy was young to be that uncaring, he thought. Usually you have to live for a while to earn the right.

"And you don't give a damn, do you?"

Holly ignored his question. "It's going to be a bother," she said, "finding a new gallery. Not many take on statuary, or at least pieces of any size."

She was avoiding the issue of a body, playing scissors now on his paper, cutting out lines of inquiry she didn't like. It was time to rock her. Smash her scissors.

"When we discovered Bonnie Gill's body last night," he said, "she was already cool. Not cold, not in San Diego. When the dead are described as being cold that's sort of a myth. After the heart stops pumping, the body loses heat. Gradually it becomes the temperature of its surroundings. Of the air, of the ground…"

Cheever walked over to a small statue of a little girl crying. One of Holly Troy's horrors. The statue had been clothed in a yellow dress with red polka dots. The girl's mouth was open. She was scared. She was terrified. Cheever wished he could tell her everything was all right.

". . . of the stone," he said.

The anger rose in him unexpectedly. "By the time we got here she was the temperature of your fucking faux marble," he said. "But your stone doesn't bleed, lady. She did. But then you don't care, do you?"

The same question again, and another silence. Her shifting of posture was the only indicator that she had heard.

Bonnie Gill didn't fit the profile of most San Diego homicides. She didn't use or abuse, didn't have a record, was a business owner and community leader. She was an attractive woman whose death would make the taxpayers uneasy. San Diegans weren't going to like seeing Bonnie Gill's smiling, freckled face staring at them from their morning newspaper.

Cheever didn't have one of the smiling pictures. He had the other kind. The crime scene shots had been processed that morning. When Cheever had first started in homicide all the pictures had been black and white. Now they were color, the better to see with, and the better to sicken juries. To make an impact, even on the jaded.

"Two wounds," he said, holding up one of the pictures to Holly's face. She looked different now, diffident even, but Cheever didn't care. "One in the back here." Cheever slapped the spot hard, did it so she could hear the impact, and feel it. "And one here, across the throat." He pushed the second picture almost to her nose, tapped on it to show the wound, then demonstrated on his own throat with particular savagery, leaving an angry red line across his neck.

In the pictures, Bonnie looked small. Only her wounds looked large. She had red hair and looked like a fallen Raggedy Ann doll.

For some reason Cheever had lost it with this woman, something he rarely did. He prided himself on his control. It made the job possible, but something had kicked in.

"You'll have to excuse me," Cheever told her as he shoved the pictures into his coat pocket, "for mistaking you for someone who cared."